Joseph West Moore

Picturesque Washington

Pen and Pencil Sketches of Its Scenery, History, Traditions, Public and Social Life

Joseph West Moore

Picturesque Washington
Pen and Pencil Sketches of Its Scenery, History, Traditions, Public and Social Life

ISBN/EAN: 9783337405038

Printed in Europe, USA, Canada, Australia, Japan

Cover: Foto ©Andreas Hilbeck / pixelio.de

More available books at **www.hansebooks.com**

A SOUVENIR OF THE AMERICAN CAPITAL.

PICTURESQUE
WASHINGTON:

PEN AND PENCIL SKETCHES

OF ITS SCENERY, HISTORY, TRADITIONS, PUBLIC AND SOCIAL LIFE, WITH GRAPHIC
DESCRIPTIONS OF THE CAPITOL AND CONGRESS, THE WHITE
HOUSE AND THE GOVERNMENT DEPARTMENTS.

TOGETHER WITH ARTISTIC VIEWS AT MOUNT VERNON, A MAP OF THE CITY OF
WASHINGTON, AND DIAGRAMS OF THE HALLS OF CONGRESS.

BY JOSEPH WEST MOORE.

PROVIDENCE: J. A. & R. A. REID, PUBLISHERS.
1888.

GEORGE WASHINGTON.

First President.

MARTHA WASHINGTON,

Wife of the First President

PREFACE.

In the following pages the author has endeavored to narrate clearly and accurately the interesting story of the capital of the American Nation—how it has grown in the less than one hundred years of its existence from an unpromising settlement to be a bright, delightful, and prosperous city; a capital worthy of the Nation that has become in about the same length of time one of the grandest and most powerful in the world.

With the story of the development and present appearance of the city, it has been the purpose to give the fullest and most authentic particulars of all the institutions of the government within its borders, how they were established, how they are now conducted, and numerous details of national affairs, which it is believed will be of interest and importance to every American. The aim has been to present in simple, attractive form the information that readers would be most likely to desire concerning the city of Washington and the great departments of the government; to make the volume one of thorough, competent reference, as well as of pleasant reading.

Picturesque Washington is therefore offered to the public with the hope that it will prove acceptable to those who know and admire the National City, and also to those who are desirous of becoming acquainted with it and its many objects of interest.   The illustrations comprise the prominent features of the city and environs, and the government edifices.   They have been carefully executed, from special drawings, by a number of the most skillful engravers in the country.

In preparing this work the best authorities have been consulted, the writer has visited and thoroughly inspected every place described, and has also received most valuable assistance in gathering information from many high officials of the government.

More than fifty years ago an eloquent writer penned these lines : "The Nation has founded a city that bears and will transmit to posterity the name of Washington and his renown.   It is a living, intelligent monument of glory, and will reflect, as it grows in wealth and splendor, the inestimable consequences resulting to the country from his martial qualities and patriotic virtues."

Joseph West Moore.

CONTENTS.

CHAPTER V.

CHAPTER VI.

CHAPTER VII.

CHAPTER VIII.

CHAPTER IX.

CHAPTER X.

CHAPTER XVI.

CHAPTER XVII.

CHAPTER XVIII.

CHAPTER XIX.

CHAPTER XX.

ILLUSTRATIONS.

PLANS AND MAP.

THE CITY OF WASHINGTON.

CHAPTER I.

STANDING upon the lofty, green-clad hills of Virginia which
constitute the historic Arlington estate, a magnificent panorama
is unfolded as the eye sweeps northward and eastward over
the picturesque region of the District of Columbia. Two hundred feet below, the beautiful Potomac River, released from the mountain ranges that have closely restrained its silvery stream for over a
hundred miles, quickly expands into a broad sheet of placid water
and glides onward to the main, bearing many a richly freighted craft.
From the circling heights of the northern part of the District to the
river banks on the south, as far as the eye can reach, are ponderous
domes and majestic spires, countless turrets and roof-tops, emerald-
tinted parks, massive monuments, and all the evidences of a great and
prosperous city. Everywhere palatial edifices, embodying the highest architectural genius of the age, meet the gaze, and, grandly towering over all, Freedom's effigy can be seen resplendent on the huge
white dome of the Nation's Capitol. This is the city of Washington
as it appears to-day — a charming city of parks and palaces, and the
grand seat of government of "Time's noblest offspring," the United
States of America.

It is predicted that Washington is to be "the future Queen City
of the world." Its natural advantages give it a preëminence over
most American cities in picturesqueness. Its site is bordered by a
noble river and sheltered by a series of gradually sloping and thickly

wooded hills. Constructed upon an ample plan, with capacity for a
million people, the home of a liberal government whose resources
are almost unlimited, a delightful, salubrious place of residence, both
winter and summer, now thoroughly imbued with a strong desire for
advancement, for rich adornment and luxurious surroundings, and
fast gathering into its fold the excellent and desirable in science,
art, and literature — the capital of the country, if it continues its Her-
culean strides on the' path of progress for a few years longer, can
boldly challenge comparison with any other city in attractiveness
and brilliancy. The growth and development of Washington during
the past ten years have been wonderful. Nearly all the old land-
marks have disappeared, and out of a rude, unpaved, dilapidated
town has risen a stately city, with most of the resources, the pleasures, the superiority of a metropolis. Once it was called in derision
"the only child of the Nation," but now it has attained to a magnificent manhood, and is entirely worthy of the pride and admiration
of its parents.

There is a tradition that George Washington, when a mere youth,
surveying the Virginia lands of the opulent Lord Fairfax, and little
dreaming of the remarkable career fate had in store for him, predicted that some day a great city would be located on the territory
now known as the District of Columbia, as the site was so admirably
adapted for the purpose. And in later years when, serving under the
ill-fated General Braddock, he encamped with the British troops on
the hill at present occupied by the National Observatory, it is related
that he often sat at the door of his tent and gazed at the undulating
plateau on which the city now rests, noted the broad river-front and
the environing hills, and with the eye of a practical surveyor and
sagacious man, traced out the future abode of thousands. It is not
singular, therefore, that when he had reached the summit of human
greatness, and had been proclaimed the Father of his Country, he
should have exercised his authority to have the National Capital
located on the spot he had been familiar with and admired from boy-
hood.

The District of Columbia, known as the Federal Territory, as
originally laid out by the first commissioners under the direction of
President Washington, embraced one hundred square miles, so located
as to include the thrifty towns of Georgetown in Maryland, and Alexandria in Virginia, together with the confluence of the Potomac
River and its Eastern Branch, and the adjacent heights. Maryland

PENNSYLVANIA AVENUE AT VERNON ROW.

and Virginia ceded to the United States the territory required. In
1846, all that portion of the District lying on the west bank of the
Potomac was retroceded by Congress to the State of Virginia, so
that the Federal Territory at the present time comprises sixty-four
square miles, and is bounded on three sides by the State of Maryland, having Montgomery County on its north, Prince George
County on its east and south, with the Potomac River on its west.
The city of Washington occupies all the lower portion of the District. Georgetown, now known as West Washington, Tennallytown,
and Uniontown are the only other places of any importance. Washington is situated on the eastern bank of the Potomac, $116\frac{1}{2}$ miles
above the mouth of the river, and $184\frac{1}{2}$ miles from the sea. It is 14
miles in circumference, and covers a little less than 10 square miles.
From the southern part of the city, where the Potomac expands to
the width of a mile, extends backward an irregular plain having a
mean altitude of 40 feet above the river. This plain carries the city
up to the very borders of a chain of hills. The greatest length of
Washington is $4\frac{1}{2}$ miles; the greatest breadth, $3\frac{3}{4}$ miles. It stretches
along the Potomac a distance of 4 miles, and $3\frac{1}{4}$ miles along the
Anacostia, or Eastern Branch of the Potomac. The romantic beauty
of the location, the heights surrounding the city, from which extended
views of the country and the windings of the river can be obtained,

its attractive environs, all combine to render Washington one of the most picturesque cities in the country.

When Captain John Smith sailed up the Potomac in 1608, he found the country inhabited by numerous tribes of Indians, continually at war with each other, and savage and ferocious as wild beasts. The Manahoacs were known as a powerful tribe, and their favorite camping-ground was the region now occupied by the city of Washington. In the spring the tribe assembled at the Potomac to catch the luscious shad and herring as they "run" in the river, and to hold their yearly councils. Great feasts were made, and the return of the vernal season was celebrated with joyous ceremonies. The tribal councils were held very near the spot where, two centuries afterward, the people of the free United States established their council hall. The Manahoacs were constantly fighting with the Powhatans of Virginia, and their sanguinary conflicts, disease, and the introduction of spirituous liquors among them, rapidly diminished their numbers, until at last they were forced to migrate westward and ally themselves with the Tuscaroras. Where these Indians had their camping-grounds, archæological treasures in great abundance have been recently found, such as pestles, clubs, stone axes and arrowheads, clay and soapstone pottery, and numerous articles of utility and ornament. Many of the specimens of clay pottery and the ornamental work exhibit considerable skill and taste, and give evidence that the aboriginals of the District had attained some degree of civilization.

In 1623-5 Henry Fleet, the hardy and adventurous English fur trader, thoroughly explored the Potomac borders. He had many exciting adventures with the wild tribes, and was often in deadly peril. At one time he suffered a long captivity among the Indians, but he fortunately escaped harm and succeeded in obtaining a large amount of information concerning the new southern country. He wrote of the tract around Washington: "This place is without question the most healthful and pleasant in all this country and most convenient for habitation; the air temperate in summer and not violent in winter. The river aboundeth in all manner of fish, and for deer, buffaloes, bears and turkeys the woods do swarm with them, and the soil is exceedingly fertile." Fleet's enthusiastic description of the country watered by the Potomac was published in England, and may have influenced many of the emigrants to America at that time to direct their steps toward Maryland and Virginia. A company of

Scotch and Irish people from the mother-country made a settlement, about the close of the seventeenth century, within the limits of what is now the District of Columbia. They obtained patents for a large amount of land, divided it into a number of good plantations, and designated their adopted home "New Scotland." For nearly a century this colony lived in rural solitude, enjoying the fruits of their labor. Some of the descendants of these early settlers were among the original proprietors of the land on which the city of Washington was eventually built.

It is told of a member of this colony, by the name of Pope, that he set up his lares and penates on the top of the hill where the Capitol now stands. He called his plantation "Rome," and a little stream that meandered along the base of the hill, "the Tiber," believing that in the course of time a capital city greater than imperial Rome would arise on the spacious plateau where he cultivated his crops. To his friends and companions he was known as "Pope of Rome." This simple farmer was endowed with prophetic vision. Busy streets

THE DAVIE BURNS COTTAGE.

now entirely cover the Tiber creek, and above its bank is the majestic legislative building of a vast continental nation, looking down upon
a city that in the near future may be even greater than Rome in its
proudest days.

The laying out of Georgetown was authorized by the Maryland
Assembly in 1751, and some time later this attractive suburb of
Washington began existence. It soon grew into a town of importance. During the Revolutionary War it was one of the places of
deposit for military stores. The troops of both armies marched
through its streets and encamped on its steep hills. A small ferry
connected it with the Virginia shore. In Suter's tavern, a favorite
resort in those days, the wealthy land-holders of the neighborhood
met on business and for merry-makings, and they made its rude
walls ring with their jovial songs and stories. Whenever Washington came up the river from his Mount Vernon estate he enjoyed the
good cheer of this ancient hostelry, and in Suter's he held many of
his deliberations with the first commissioners engaged in the laying
out of the Federal city. Small settlements were started on the Maryland banks of the Potomac just below Georgetown, and several thriving plantations tilled by slaves dotted the site of the future capital.

In 1785 Washington made an extended and careful exploration of
the upper Potomac, in order to ascertain if the river could be navigated
above tide-water at Georgetown. A canoe or pirogue was expertly
hollowed out of a large poplar tree, hauled to the river bank and
launched, and Washington with several friends, among whom was
Governor Johnson, of Maryland, a gallant soldier of the Revolution,
started on the important survey. The party sailed for a number of
days in their humble bark amid the sublime scenery of the upper
Potomac, and made a complete exploration, the result of their work
being that a company was finally organized for the improvement of
the river, and nearly a million dollars expended in a series of years.
During this unique voyage the distinguished party would seek quarters for the night at the houses of well-to-do planters who lived near
the river, and everywhere they were received as highly honored guests,
and a most generous hospitality was dispensed. One night they were
compelled to lodge at the house of a planter whose accommodations
were rather scanty, and Washington, Governor Johnson, and another
gentleman were given a room with two small beds. The great chief-
tain with a smile turned to his companions and said, " Come, gentlemen, who will be my bed-fellow?" They both declined the honor,

SEVENTH STREET, NORTHWEST.

however, and the Maryland governor, in relating the incident afterward, said, "Greatly as I should have felt honored by such distinction,
yet the awe and reverence which I always felt in the presence of that
admirable man prevented me from approaching him *so nearly*."

There was a severe contest over the selection of the Federal Territory. In the Congress of the Confederation the question of a permanent seat of government was broached, and propositions to establish a "Federal town, a Federal house for Congress and for the Executive officers," on the banks of the Delaware River near the Lower
Falls, and also at Georgetown on the Potomac, were entertained, but
did not receive special sanction. The matter was somewhat discussed
in the convention held in Philadelphia in 1787, to revise the Federal
system of government, but it was not until the second session of the
First Congress of the United States under the Constitution, held in
New York in the summer of 1790, that it was finally decided. The
discussion was long and earnest, and a strong sectional feeling was
developed. New York, Philadelphia, Baltimore, Trenton, Harris-

burg, and many other places urged their claims upon Congress to be made the capital city, and for a time it seemed as if it would be impossible to make any selection. Maryland and Virginia had offered the necessary territory for the Federal District, but the former state strongly favored its location at the thriving "Baltimore town." Many votes were taken, and finally an act was adopted by Congress which received executive sanction in July, 1790, giving the sole power to President Washington to select a Federal Territory "not exceeding ten miles square on the river Potomac at some space between the mouths of the Eastern Branch and the Conogocheague for the permanent seat of the government of the United States." The new territory was to be ready for the use of the government in 1800, and in the mean time the "Federal town" was to be Philadelphia.

The final adoption of the Potomac site for the national territory was brought about by a stroke of policy contrived by Jefferson and Hamilton. In an article upon Congress, Garfield speaks of the matter as follows: "It dampens not a little our enthusiasm for the superior virtues of the fathers to learn that Hamilton's monument of statesmanship, the funding bill, which gave life to the public credit and saved from dishonor the war debts of the states, was for a time hopelessly defeated by the votes of one section of the Union, and was carried at last by a legislative bargain which, in the mildest slang of our day, would be called a 'log-rolling job.' The bill fixing the permanent seat of the government on the banks of the Potomac was the argument which turned the scale and carried the funding bill. The bargain carried them both through."

Jefferson was appealed to by Hamilton to give his aid to the scheme for the assumption by the general government of the debts incurred by the states during the Revolutionary War, which amounted to $20,000,000. The bill had been defeated in the House after an obstinate struggle, and Hamilton was earnestly seeking to have it reconsidered, believing that the Eastern or creditor states would secede from the Union if their claims were not allowed. Mr. Jefferson says in his *Ana:* "I proposed to him (Hamilton) to dine with me the next day, and I would invite another friend or two and bring them into conference together, and I thought it impossible that reasonable men consulting together coolly could fail, by some mutual sacrifices of opinion, to form a compromise which was to save the Union. The discussion took place. It was finally agreed that, whatever importance had been attached to the rejection of the proposition, the preservation of the Union and of concord among the states was more important, and that therefore it would be better that the vote of rejection should be rescinded, to effect which some members should change their votes. But it was observed that this pill would be peculiarly bitter to the Southern States, and that some concomitant measure should be adopted to sweeten it a little to them. There had been before, propositions to fix the seat of government either at Philadelphia or at Georgetown on the Potomac; and it was thought by giving it to Philadelphia for ten years and to Georgetown permanently afterwards, this might act as an anodyne, and calm in some measure the ferment which might be excited by the other measure alone. So two of the Potomac members agreed to change their votes, and Hamilton undertook to carry the other point. In doing this the influence he had established over the Eastern members effected his side of the engagement, and so the Assumption was passed."

Thus it was, that a good dinner and the sagacity of two able men healed a serious breach in the affairs of the Nation, and placed the capital city on the banks of the "River of Swans," as the Indians called the Potomac.

The selection of the permanent seat of the government of the United States, so bitterly opposed at the time, particularly by the members of Congress from New York, Pennsylvania, and New Jersey, and so ardently favored by the members from the Southern States, and by President Washington, has proved with the passage of years a most judicious one. Originally the boundaries of the Federal Territory were "located, defined, and limited" as follows: "Beginning at Jones' Point, being the upper cape of Hunting Creek, in Virginia, and at an angle in the outset of forty-five degrees west of the north, and running in a direct line ten miles for the first line; then beginning again at the same Jones' Point, and running another direct line at a right angle with the first, across the Potomac, ten miles for the second line; then from the termination of the said first and second lines, running two other direct lines, of ten miles each, the one crossing the Eastern Branch of the Potomac, and the other the Potomac, and meeting each other in a point." This territory was ten miles square, or one hundred square miles, and comprised sixty-four thousand acres of fertile lands situated between 38°, 48′ and 38°, 59′ north latitude.

WASHINGTON IN 1810 — THE OLD CAPITOL.

CHAPTER II.

WHEN President Washington returned from his tour of the South in the summer of 1791, and the wheels of the famous cream-colored chariot in which he had taken the memorable ride of 1,900 miles rolled up to the western door of the Mount Vernon mansion, he found a visitor awaiting his coming. The visitor was Maj. Pierre Charles L'Enfant, a skillful French engineer, who had been chosen to draw the plan of "the new Federal town." The site of the Federal District had been selected by Washington in the January previous, after long and careful delibera-tion, from the 105 miles of territory embraced in the boundary defined by the act of Congress locating the permanent seat of government. The act was amended by request of the President so as to include the city of Alexandria and adjacent country. Three commissioners, Gov. Thomas Johnson and the Hon. Daniel Carroll, of Maryland, and Dr. David Stuart, of Virginia, were appointed to have entire charge of the surveying and laying out of the district, and on April 15, 1791, they had laid the first boundary stone at Jones' Point on the Virginia side of the Potomac, with impressive Masonic ceremony, in the presence of a large assemblage. The commissioners had decided to call the district the "Territory of Columbia," which name it bore for some years; and the new city to be established on the river bank, "the city of Washington," in honor of him who was at that time, and who

in all time shall be, the "first in the hearts of his countrymen."
Satisfactory terms had been arranged with the proprietors of the land
lying within the bounds of the proposed city, and an agreement had
been signed by the commissioners and the land-holders. All the land
used for streets and squares was to be relinquished to the government
without cost, and all the land taken for public buildings was to be
paid for at the rate of £25 an acre. One-half of the proceeds of all
lots offered at public sale was also to go to the original owners, and
the remainder was to be expended in the erection of the government
edifices.

Major L'Enfant was cordially received by Washington, and remained at Mount Vernon in consultation with him for nearly a week,
during which time the plan of the Federal city was thoroughly ma-
tured. L'Enfant, who was an educated soldier, had come to America in 1777 from Paris, and had commended himself to Washington
by his patriotic zeal while serving as major of engineers during the
Revolutionary War, and a warm friendship had sprung up between
them. He had designed the insignia of the Society of the Cincinnati at Washington's special request, and in various ways had
demonstrated the possession of marked ability. His plan of the city
was very elaborate and magnificent, and it was duly set forth on a
finely drawn map. It is believed he partially followed the work of
Le Notre in Versailles, the seat of the French government buildings.
Broad, transverse streets and avenues, numerous open squares, parks,
circles, and triangular reservations were marked on the plan, the
places for the public buildings were indicated, and everything was
designed upon a spacious scale.

Washington desired that "the Capitol" should occupy the centre
of the city, and it was accordingly located on the broad plateau in
the eastern section, and the Executive Mansion and the other public
buildings were located in the western section, more than a mile distant. In one of his letters Washington says that this wide separa-
tion of Congress and the Executive departments was intended to
prevent members of Congress from too frequently visiting the various departments. L'Enfant's design meeting the full approval of
Washington, and also of Jefferson, then Secretary of State, of whom
it was said that "he almost monopolized the artistic taste and knowledge of the first administration," it was formally adopted, and the
young Frenchman was engaged to superintend its execution. He
had as assistant, Andrew Ellicott, a bright Pennsylvanian, who with

THE VAN NESS MANSION.

his brother had established the town of Ellicott Mills, in Maryland. Ellicott was a competent surveyor, and a young man of remarkable intelligence. Later in life he became professor of mathematics at West Point. The streets and squares of the city were chiefly laid out by him, and under his direction the work progressed quite rapidly. Before the erection of any building was allowed an exact survey was made and properly recorded, and all subsequent building operations had to conform to this survey.

The states of Maryland and Virginia were greatly interested in the founding of the seat of the national government within their borders, and generously voted a large sum of money as a gift to the United States, to aid in the erection of the public edifices. Afterward, when it was necessary to obtain more money to carry on the work, and Congress was strangely dilatory in making an appropriation, and European bankers had declined to advance funds to the commissioners, the legislature of Maryland promptly authorized a loan of $100,000 in response to the appeal of President Washington.

The most prominent proprietors of the land taken for the city were Daniel Carroll, David Burns, Notley Young, and Samuel

Davidson. The Carroll estate very nearly covered all that part of Washington known as Capitol Hill, and was called Duddington manor. Daniel Carroll was a gentleman of culture and high social standing in Maryland. He had been a delegate to the Philadelphia Convention that framed the Federal Constitution, and a member of the First Congress of the United States. He was a brother of the Rt. Rev. John Carroll, the first Catholic bishop of Baltimore, who founded the great college of the Jesuits, at Georgetown, and was a cousin of Charles. Carroll, of Carrollton, one of the signers of the Declaration of Independence. As the Capitol was to be located adjacent to his estate, he believed that section would become the most desirable part of the city, and immediately demanded exorbitant prices for building-lots. Speculators, possessed with the same idea, bought a number of his acres, largely with " promises to pay "; and Stephen Girard, the richest man in Philadelphia in those days, even offered Carroll $200,000 for a certain portion of his estate, but the offer was refused, five times the sum being demanded. The high prices for lots on Capitol Hill compelled many who wished land for the erection of houses and stores to settle in the northern and western parts of the city, and the tide of population rapidly turning that way, forever decided the fate of the eastern quarter. The city developed on its northwestern side, which to-day is the most populous and fashionable section.

Carroll's dream of great wealth was never realized. At his death he was in embarrassed circumstances, and his estate for a long time after was encumbered with heavy obligations. Recently a portion of the Carroll tract, upon which his descendants had paid $16,000 in taxes during the past eighty years, keeping its possession so long in hope of an advantageous sale, was finally disposed of for $3,600. The spacious " Duddington House," erected in the early days of Washington for the residence of the Carroll family, still remains on North Carolina Avenue, southeast, in a good state of preservation.

An interesting story is told of this ancient brick mansion. Shortly after the streets of the city were marked out strictly in accordance with L'Enfant's plan, Daniel Carroll, who was one of the commissioners, assumed the right to begin the erection of his house in the middle of New Jersey Avenue, near the Capitol grounds. L'Enfant vigorously protested against its location, as it would close the avenue and destroy the symmetry of the general plan of the city; but his protests not being heeded, he gave orders one morning to his assistant to demolish the structure. Carroll hurried to a magistrate, obtained a warrant and stopped the demolition before it had proceeded very far. That night, when L'Enfant returned to the city from Acquia Creek, where he was working busily getting out sandstone for the new Capitol, he was much chagrined to find his orders unfulfilled. He vowed the house should come down, and, organizing a gang of laborers secretly, he took them quietly up the hill after dark, and set them at work. By sunrise, not a brick of the obnoxious dwelling was left standing. Carroll was very indignant at this arbitrary act, and made complaint to the President, who ordered the reconstruction of " Duddington House," precisely as it was before, but, very wisely, not in the middle of New Jersey Avenue. This house was the first fine one erected in the city. It is surrounded by a high brick wall, enclosing grounds full of majestic trees, and even now, in its partially dilapidated condition, shows considerable of its former elegance.

A very fortunate man was David Burns, another of the original land-holders. His property was situated largely in what is now the

THE DUDDINGTON HOUSE.

fashionable northwest quarter of the city. Burns—"crusty Davie
Burns," as he was called—was a very bigoted, choleric Scotchman,
fond of controversy, and never known to agree with any one in the
slightest particular. He lived in a rude cottage near the river, and
cultivated a large plantation extending over the spot where the White
House now stands. The demand for his land made him very wealthy,
and his only child, Marcia Burns, was known in all the country
around as "the beautiful heiress of Washington." For some time
Burns was opposed to the projected transfer of land to the government, and the President and the commissioners had several confer-
ences with him in his cottage to explain the advantages of the plan.
On one of these occasions, so the tradition runs, the testy old planter
answered one of Washington's arguments by this outburst: "I suppose, Mr. Washington, you think people are going to take every grist
from you as pure grain; but what would you have been if you hadn't
married the rich widow Custis!" The usually sedate Washington at
this audacious remark is said to have actually lost his temper, and
left the house in indignation. He afterward spoke of the impertinent Scotchman as "that obstinate Mr. Burns," and would never
meet him again.

Miss Burns was placed by her father in a cultivated Baltimore
family, where she received an excellent social and literary training.
When she returned to Washington after several years' schooling she
became the belle of the embryo city, and attracted many admirers.
She was lovely in person, and gracious and winning in her manners.
Her father could not be induced to leave his old house—a small,
rudely-fashioned structure, with only two rooms on the ground floor,
and but little better than the cabins of the slaves who tilled his plantation—and, with all his great wealth, would not change his plain
way of living. The girl uttered no complaint, but came from the
refined Baltimore home at her father's bidding, and resumed her former life with the lonely man. Her mother had died when she was a
child, and for years she had been her father's sole intimate companion.

Troops of gallants began to seek the favor of the beautiful heiress. The wooers were generally treated to cutting remarks from
Burns, and promptly shown the door. Dashing young members of
Congress—gay fortune-seekers who saw in Marcia a splendid prize
—picked their way across the marsh to Burns' hut on fine evenings,
craftily allowed the old Scotchman to win their gold at cards, and
awakened good feeling by generous gifts of mellow usquebaugh,

for which he had a notorious fondness. Gen. John P. Van Ness, a young, well-born, jovial New Yorker, was a frequent visitor. Of an ancient Dutch family prominent in politics and society, a congressman of some brilliancy, with a very handsome face and agreeable deportment, ever full of song and story, he soon succeeded in winning Marcia's affection and her father's sanction, and they were married. Van Ness became a resident of Washington, living at first with his bride in the old cottage, and afterward in a costly mansion erected on the Burns estate. He became mayor of the city, and was eminent in business and social affairs. Gilbert Stuart painted his portrait, and it was said of him that he was " well fed, well bred, and well read." When David Burns died he left his daughter the sole owner of a great estate, yearly rising in value. On his death-bed he said to her, " Marcia, you have been a good daughter; you'll now be the richest girl in America."

The Van Ness mansion was constructed by the celebrated Latrobe, one of the architects of the Capitol, and he expended many thousands of dollars in trying to make it the finest private residence in the country. The grounds were enclosed with a brick wall, trees and flowers planted, and fountains and statuary added adornment. Close to the great house, in the same enclosure, stood the old cottage of David Burns, and Mrs. Van Ness would never permit her father's humble home to be taken down. For a number of years the Van Ness mansion was the resort of the distinguished people of Washington, and presidents and eminent statesmen were entertained within its walls. The last acre of the Burns property passed out of the possession of the heirs fifteen years ago, and now all that remain to tell the story of the Burns and Van Ness families are a great monumental tomb at Oak Hill Cemetery, and the two houses by the river — father's and daughter's — decaying, neglected ruins. The tomb was erected by Van Ness at a cost of over $30,000, and is constructed in imitation of the temple of Vesta. The legend is, that on each anniversary of the death of Van Ness his favorite " troop of six white horses" make a ghostly midnight gallop around the old mansion, and that supernatural sounds are heard within its deserted halls.

The third largest land-holder was Notley Young, who held nearly all the land in the centre of the city and on the river front between Seventh and Eleventh streets. Carroll owned the land to the east and Burns to the west of him. He, too, acquired wealth from sales and leases of his property, and erected a substantial residence on

G Street south, overlooking the Potomac. The house was taken
down thirty years ago to give room for the extension of the street.
Of Samuel Davidson, the fourth largest proprietor, scarcely anything
is known.

When the time approached for the first public sale of lots by the
commissioners, a difficulty arose between them and Major L'Enfant.
After the demolition of Carroll's house by L'Enfant, he was not in
good favor, and as he refused to allow his maps of Washington to be
published as a guide to the purchasers of lots, he was dismissed from
the service of the government. L'Enfant claimed that, if his maps
were published, speculators would know all about his plan, and
would build unsightly edifices on the finest streets. He continued to
live in the city, and in his old age became a claimant for compensation for his services as the original designer of Washington —
constantly haunting the committee-rooms of Congress, a poor but
rather courtly, feeble old man, attired in a long blue coat closely but-
toned high on his breast. His claim was never considered, and it
was quite the fashion in those days to laugh and sneer at what was
called " L'Enfant's extravagant plan." He died in 1825, and was
buried by charitable hands on the Digges farm, a short distance from
the city. No stone marks his grave. L'Enfant's design has been
fully vindicated by time, and to-day the beautiful capital city owes
much of its beauty and fascination to the broad streets, the great
squares, the parks, the wide, straight avenues, the location of the
public buildings, for which he contended with the sublime energy of
a liberal, far-sighted man, in an age of restricted views and small
things.

The first public sale of lots was held by the commissioners at
Georgetown, Oct. 17, 1791, and was mainly attended by speculators
from the large cities, who were eager to obtain what they considered
the best lots, in the belief that Washington was to become the great
city of the country. At that time there were less than 60,000 people
in New York; and predictions were freely made that in ten years
after Congress begun its sessions in Washington, the national city
would have a population of at least 150,000. Even a rumor, indus-
triously circulated at the sale by enemies of the new capital, that
Congress never would remove from Philadelphia, made no impression on the confident purchasers of the land. The commissioners
executed a number of contracts for the sale of lots in parcels on easy
terms, on condition that the buyers should erect " brick houses, two

H AND SIXTEENTH STREETS, SHOWING ST. JOHN'S CHURCH.

stories high," on the property within a certain time. These contracts, entered into with enthusiasm, were mostly repudiated afterward, and the brick houses were not built. Many lots were sold, and at good prices, but prior to the removal of the government to the city the actual residents were few, and the "new national settlement" was very insignificant.

The formal transfer of the government from Philadelphia to Washington took place in October, 1800. That it was indeed the day of small things, is evident when we read that "a single 'packet' sloop brought all the office furniture of the departments, besides seven large boxes and five small ones, containing the 'archives' of the government." The officials numbered fifty-four persons, including President Adams, the secretaries, and the various clerks. They came to the city by different conveyances, and as they had left pleasant, comfortable quarters in Philadelphia, the crudeness and discomfort of Washington produced a feeling of disgust. Mrs. Adams spoke of Washington as "this wilderness city"; and Secretary Wolcott in a letter to his wife said, "There are but few houses in any place, and most of them are small, miserable huts, which present an awful contrast to the public buildings. The people are poor, and, as far as I can judge, live like fishes, by eating each other."

The best description extant of the city, as it appeared at the time the government took possession, is found in a letter written by Hon. John Cotton Smith, then a member of Congress from Connecticut. He says : " Our approach to the city was accompanied with sensations not easily described. One wing of the Capitol only had been erected, which, with the President's house, a mile distant from it, both constructed with white sandstone, were shining objects in dismal contrast with the scene around them. Instead of recognizing the avenues and streets portrayed on the plan of the city, not one was visible, unless we except a road, with two buildings on each side of it, called the New Jersey Avenue. The Pennsylvania Avenue, leading, as laid down on paper, from the Capitol to the Presidential mansion, was nearly the whole distance a deep morass covered with elder bushes, which were cut through to the President's house; and near Georgetown a block of houses had been erected which bore the name of the 'six buildings.' There were also two other blocks consisting of two or three dwelling-houses in different directions, and now and then an insulated wooden habitation ; the intervening spaces, and, indeed, the surface of the city generally, being covered with scrub oak bushes on the higher grounds, and on the marshy soil either trees or some sort of shrubbery. The desolate aspect of the place was not a little augmented by a number of unfinished edifices at Greenleaf's Point, and on an eminence a short distance from it, commenced by an individual whose name they bore, but the state of whose funds compelled him to abandon them. There appeared to be but two really comfortable habitations in all respects, within the bounds of the city, one of which belonged to Dudley Carroll and the other to Notley Young. The roads in every direction were muddy and unimproved. A sidewalk was attempted in one instance by a covering formed of the chips hewed for the Capitol. It extended but a little way and was of little value ; for in dry weather the sharp fragments cut our shoes, and in wet weather covered them with white mortar. In short, it was a new settlement."

Such was the capital city in which President John Adams, Secretary of State John Marshall, Secretary of the Treasury Oliver Wolcott, Jr., Secretary of War Samuel Dexter, Secretary of the Navy Benjamin Stoddart, and the other officials of the government took up their abode in the fall of 1800, twenty-four years after the Declaration of Independence. Congress began its session a few weeks later, and many and loud were the complaints of the new capital uttered by all the assembled statesmen.

Newspapers in New York, Philadelphia, and New England, and satirists everywhere, cracked many amusing jokes at the expense of the infant city. The Capitol was called "the palace in the wilderness," and Pennsylvania Avenue "the great Serbonian Bog." Georgetown was declared "a city of houses without streets; Washington, a city of streets without houses." Only one favorable thing seems to have been said, and that was, "Washington is the happiest region of flowers, and a garden here might be made to yield something for the basket of Flora for nearly three-quarters of the year."

FORD'S OLD THEATRE, IN WHICH PRESIDENT LINCOLN WAS SHOT.
(*Now the Army Medical Museum.*)

Thomas Moore, just coming into prominence as a poet, visited the city in 1804, and was hospitably entertained. He afterward used his splendid talent to compose this satire of Washington :

> "In fancy now beneath the twilight gloom,
> Come, let me lead thee o'er this modern Rome,
> Where tribunes rule, where dusky Davi bow,
> And what was Goose Creek is Tiber now.
>
> This fam'd metropolis, where fancy sees
> Squares in morasses, obelisks in trees ;
> Which traveling fools and gazetteers adorn
> With shrines unbuilt, and heroes yet unborn."

The Abbé Correa de Serra, the witty Minister from Portugal, bestowed upon Washington the famous title of " the city of magnificent distances," referring to the great spaces between the scattered houses. There was considerable talk of removing the capital, and a motion to that effect in Congress was lost by only two votes. A clever Scotch artist made a good deal of fun by drawing a caricature representing the congressman who had made the motion of removal, with the Capitol strapped on his back, all ready to start as soon as he should know which way it was to go.   But some wanted it to go north, others west, and others south.

When we consider the jealousy and opposition displayed toward the city, it is small wonder that it required the fostering hand of several kindly administrations before it appeared likely that Washington would remain the permanent seat of the government.   During the administrations of Adams, Jefferson, and Madison, the city improved considerably.   Jefferson secured money from Congress for the public buildings, planted poplar trees on Pennsylvania Avenue, and did what he could to make that " Appian Way of the Republic" something better than a " slough of despond."   He applied his artistic skill and taste to the work of beautifying the capital.   Population increased at the rate of about eight hundred a year ; and when, after the invasion by the British in 1814, the vexed question of removing the capital was settled by Congress appropriating liberal sums to restore the public buildings damaged during the invasion, the city had nothing to hinder its steady growth.

The invasion of Washington by the British troops under General Ross, Aug. 24, 1814, was a severe blow to the weak and slowly growing city.   It had been apprehended for some weeks that the city would be attacked, and President Madison had taken various pre-

A SCENE IN THE COLORED QUARTER.

ventive measures, which, however, proved futile. The British fleet, under command of Admiral Cockburn, sailed up Chesapeake Bay, and 4,500 men were landed on the left bank of the Patuxent River on the 21st of August, with orders to march on Washington. The residents of the city were warned of the approach of the British, and many of them hastily left their homes and found refuge in Virginia. The invaders marched across Maryland to Bladensburg, five miles from the capital, without hinderance; but at this place their advance was stopped by a body of raw militia, organized from residents of Maryland and the District, under command of General Winder, and a few hundred seamen with field-pieces under Capt. Joshua Barney, the celebrated privateersman. The American troops numbered about seven thousand, but they were so badly handled that almost at the first fire from the British the militia broke in disorder and could not be rallied again. Barney's sailors stood their ground and fought desperately for nearly three hours, but at last were compelled, from sheer lack of numbers, to abandon their position on the Bladensburg turnpike, and fall back to Georgetown Heights. President Madison and other prominent officials of the government had sought safety at Montgomery Court House, in Maryland.

The way to Washington now being open, the British continued their march, and on the evening of August 24, they halted in front of the unfinished Capitol. Orders were given to burn all the public edifices, and in a short time the Capitol, the White House, and the Executive buildings were in flames. The troops dispersed throughout the city, burning and destroying a large amount of private as well as public property. They visited the arsenal on Greenleaf's Point and

attempted to destroy several large cannon left by the garrison in
the haste of their departure, by discharging one against the others.
When the piece was fired, some of the wadding fell into a well in
which a large quantity of powder was secreted, and a tremendous
explosion ensued, killing a number of the British. The records of
the War, Treasury, and Navy Departments were nearly all burned,
and the records of the State Department were only saved by the
energy of several clerks, who packed them into bags and transported
them to a secure place in the country.

While the public buildings were burning a severe storm began,
and the drenching rain fortunately extinguished the fires at the Capitol and White House, and saved them from total destruction. The
enemy left the city late that night, fearing an attack under cover of
the darkness, and in a few days the British fleet, which had come as
far as Alexandria, sailed down the Potomac. The amount of damage done by the invasion was estimated at $1,000,000. About sev-
enty-five Americans were killed and wounded, and the British suffered a loss of several hundred men.

At this period nearly all the field and domestic labor in and around
Washington was performed by slaves. The rich planters employed
hundreds of negroes to cultivate their fertile acres, and the relations
between the slaves and their masters were very different from what
they were in the regions farther south. The slaves were usually
treated with kindness, well clothed and fed, and were apparently as
happy and contented as human beings could be in bondage. They
were very civil and well behaved, and took great pride in ornament-
ing their little cabins, and many of them had very neat and comfortable homes. They were allowed, on many plantations, good pay
for extra labor, and often saved money enough by industry to purchase their freedom. The culture of tobacco made many of the
planters very wealthy, some of them raising one hundred hogsheads
yearly of the " Indian weed that from the devil doth proceed," as the
quaint old poem has it. The tobacco was largely shipped to Europe.
It was brought to the place of shipment in this way : A hole was bored
in the heads of the hogshead, and an axle placed in it from end to
end. A shaft was attached to the axle like the shaft of a cart, and
horses and mules hitched to it. The tobacco was then drawn along
the streets, up and down the hills, rolling and bumping over the stones.

An ancient register has the following estimate of the yearly expenses of a slave : " His price about $500, which at 6 per cent., the

FAMOUS STATUES.

1. The Bartholdi-Fountain in the Botanical Garden.
2. Statue of General Scott at the Soldiers' Home.
3. Mills' Statue of General Washington.
4. Marble Group on the Portico of the Capitol.
5. Statue of General Greene.
6. Mills' Statue of General Jackson.

lawful interest, is $30; for risk or accident, $30; for a peck of Indian meal per week or 13 bushels per year at 50 cents, $6.50; two pounds of salt meat per week, $7.50; a barrel of fish per annum; $4; fowls, vegetables and milk per annum, $5; for clothing, $15 — total for the year, $98; or daily expense of 27 cents." The slaves assumed the names of their masters, and many of these old family names are continued to-day among the negro population of the city. In April, 1862, slavery was abolished in the District of Columbia.

It is interesting to learn the rates of free labor in those days. A shoemaker who could make one good pair of shoes daily was paid $1.50, and in the other trades wages varied from 75 cents to $1.25 a day. Laborers obtained 50 cents a day. A seamstress received $4.50 a month and board; female servants, from $2.00 to $4.00 a month, with the exception of cooks, who were paid from $15 to $20. Coachmen who could handle two and four horses expertly, demanded $10 a month and board. Food was cheap, land easy to obtain, and houses could be built for little money of brick made from the finest clay, abundantly found in the city. Gray and blue granite, the breccia marble, or "pudding stone," as it was commonly called, and sandstone were also to be had at comparatively little cost for public buildings. The so-called "luxuries of life" were not very plenty, with the exception of "ice and pineapples." Ice could be readily obtained in summer for fifty cents a bushel, and pineapples from the West Indies were sold for twenty-five cents apiece.

An English writer in 1816 gave the following quaint description of the state of female society in Washington: "The women have been accused of sacrificing too much to the empire of fashion, but as we have not been able to verify the truth of this charge, it would be dangerous to decide on so delicate a subject. They are certainly superior women, generally highly gifted in mental as they are adorned with personal endowments. They have hitherto withstood the lamentable ravages which art and luxury have in the great cities produced upon their sex. There is an evil, however, which is deeply lamented. It is natural to love those who are made to love; and no sooner do the young ladies of Washington arrive at the nubile state than they give their hand to some wooing stranger, or member of Congress, who carries them off in triumph to his distant home. The young citizens who have been daily contemplating the regular advances of these shoots into perfection, disappointed in their ardent intentions, sigh and exclaim (not without reason) against the corruption of the times, against family interests and an unnatural and disheartening prefer-ence to foreigners. Washington thus resembles a nursery, whose fine plants are annually transported to a foreign and less congenial soil."

The same author says: "In the Territory of Columbia women have no reason to complain of the degradation to which they are ex-posed by the tyrant, man. They go where they please, both before and after marriage, and have no need to have recourse to dissimula-tion and cunning for their own repose and that of their husbands. Any particular attention to a lady is readily construed into an inten-tion of marriage. At dinner and tea parties the ladies sit together, and seldom mix with the gentlemen, whose conversation naturally turns upon political subjects. Gentlemen wear their hats in a car-riage with a lady, as in England. In almost all houses toddy is of-fered to guests a few minutes before dinner. In summer, invitations to tea-parties are made verbally, by a servant, the same day the party is given. In winter the invitation is more ceremonious. The parties at the house of the President of the United States unite simplicity with the greatest refinement of manner. The inhabitants are social and hospitable, and respectable strangers, after the slightest introduction, are invited to dinner, tea, balls, and evening parties. Tea-parties have become very expensive, as not only tea, but coffee, negus, cakes, sweetmeats, iced creams, wines and liquors are often presented ; and, in a sultry summer evening, are found too palatable to be refused. In winter there is a succession of family balls, where all this species ot luxury is exhibited."

This intelligent Englishman, in speaking of some of the peculiar customs prevailing in Washington at the time of his visit in 1816, says : " Both sexes, whether on horseback or on foot, wear an um-brella in all seasons : in summer, to keep off the sunbeams ; in win-ter, as a shelter from the rain and snow ; in spring and autumn, to intercept the dews of the evening. Persons of all ranks canter their horses, which movement fatigues the animal, and has an ungraceful appearance. The barber arrives on horseback to perform the opera-tion of shaving, and here, as in Europe, he is the organ of all news and scandal. Boarders in boarding-houses, or in taverns, sometimes throw off the coat during the heat of summer ; and in winter, the shoes, for the purpose of warming the feet at the fire — customs which the climate only can excuse."

During the administration of Monroe extensive improvements were made in all parts of the city, and large sums of money expended

for public works. Several fine residences were erected by high officials of the government and wealthy citizens. The sales of government lots realized nearly $500,000. Public spirit began to be
manifested. In a statistical record bearing date of 1821 is this entry:
" Eighty-eight buildings were commenced up to June; a new bridge
built, the Center Market enlarged, much progress made in the City
Hall, an addition made to the Infirmary, the new theatre finished and
the old one rebuilt for assembly rooms; Unitarian Church erected
and a Presbyterian Church completed; and a fountain of water opened
that yields 60 gallons a minute." In 1822 the city contained nearly
fifteen thousand people, and taxes were assessed upon property valued
at $6,668.726. There were 2,229 dwellings, numerous churches,
hotels, and stores, and several large public buildings.

In the fall of 1822 a race between two celebrated Virginia horses,
" Sir Charles " and " Eclipse," was the leading topic of conversation
in Washington for weeks, and ten thousand people assembled at the
trotting-park to witness the contest. President Monroe, and the leading government officials, were among the spectators. It is said that
more than a million dollars were wagered. Planters staked their
slaves, and in one case eight hundred negroes changed owners after
the race. People of high and of low degree were intensely excited,
and a great amount of money was lost by men " who were unable to
pay their honest debts to mechanics, grocers, and even washer-
women." " Eclipse " easily distanced " Sir Charles," and its owner
received the stake of $5,000, and in addition made a considerable
fortune from his wagers.

Another odd scrap of history is worthy of mention. In March,
1823, a great excitement was created in the city by the absconding of
the manager of the " Grand National Lottery," after refusing to pay
the principal prize of $100,000, and several smaller ones. The city
corporation, under whose auspices the lottery was carried on, claimed
not to be responsible for the default, and those who held the tickets
for the prizes had to go without their money. An article in the *National Intelligencer* about the affair was headed in large letters: " So
We Go! "

During the administration of John Quincy Adams, from 1825 to
1829, Washington had a population of nearly twenty thousand, but it
was a slow-going, uninteresting city, with very few signs of promise.
Its social life, however, was very agreeable. Society at that time
was said to have " all the hues of many colored life from the highest

THE HOUSE IN WHICH PRESIDENT LINCOLN DIED.

polish of polite France to the rude dignity of untutored nature. Parties were numerous in the winter months, and were well attended by all who were or wished to be thought fashionable." The popular hotel was the "Indian Queen," on Pennsylvania Avenue, and its great swinging sign, with a highly-colored picture of Pocahontas, was a conspicuous object. The hotel was noted for its good living, and many members of Congress resided in it. A large part of the city was occupied by market gardens and brick kilns, plentifully interspersed with ponds and marshes. There were no public schools; what were known as "Gadsby's Row" and the "Seven Buildings" were the "architectural palaces," and stray cows and pigs the statuary that adorned the squares and parks. In the sandstone Capitol with a wooden dome, great statesmen were invoking the Goddess of Liberty; and at the slave-pen in the centre of the city, unfeeling auctioneers were selling men, women, and children to the highest bidder.

Even in 1840, M. de Bacourt, the French Minister wrote: "As for Washington, it is neither a city, nor a village, nor the country: it is a building-yard placed in a desolate spot, wherein living is unbearable." About this time there was a general renewal of the public buildings, and after 1850 the city began to wear a somewhat brighter, more enterprising appearance. Population increased about two thousand a year; many substantial business blocks and private residences were constructed; more energy was displayed by the residents; and, although it was still a "city of magnificent distances," many of the unsightly spaces were filled, and the former barren, desolate aspect had changed to something better. When the Civil War began, in 1861, Washington had 62,000 people, and was described as "a big, sprawling city, magnificent in some parts, dilapidated and dirty in others."

During the years of the Rebellion the city was an extensive military encampment. Its streets resounded with the march of troops, and all its available buildings were used for military purposes. Everywhere "war's stern alarums" were heard. Over Long Bridge thousands of brave men went to battle on the soil of Virginia. Formidable lines of defenses enclosed the capital, and apprehensions of an attack were constantly felt. In July, 1864, General Early made a demonstration on Washington, hoping thereby to induce General Grant to raise the siege of Richmond. He crossed the Potomac with 12,000 men, defeated General Wallace at Rockville, sixteen miles from the city, and marched on Fort Stevens, on the Seventh Street road. The guns of the fort checked his advance until the Sixth Corps from Petersburg arrived, when he was driven back across the Potomac.

On the evening of the 10th of April, 1865, Washington was brilliantly illuminated in celebration of the close of the war, and there was great rejoicing among its loyal people. Four nights after, the city heard with pallid cheek and bated breath that President Lincoln had been stricken down at Ford's Theatre, on Tenth Street, by the bullet of a cowardly assassin. The rejoicings at the return of peace were changed to bitter lamentations. The colored people were almost wild with grief at the death of the great Emancipator.

President Lincoln was removed from the theatre to the Peterson house, nearly opposite, where he died early on the morning of April 15. The theatre was purchased by the government in 1866, and is at present used for the Army Medical Museum and the record and pension division of the Surgeon General's Department. The interior was entirely reconstructed, and no trace now remains of the scene of the assassination. On the Peterson house a marble tablet has been placed, bearing the record of Lincoln's death. The small bed-room in which the President died suggests little now of the sad scenes of that night. The original furniture has been removed, and the pretty, flaxen-haired children of the present owner of the house use the apartment for a play-room. It is proposed that the government purchase the house and make it a museum for the exhibition of articles belonging to President Lincoln.

In May, 1865, the troops under the command of Generals Grant and Sherman marched in grand review through the streets of Washington, prior to their disbanding. Two days were taken for the review, which was witnessed by many thousands of people from all parts of the North and the West. During this final march of " the largest army of volunteers ever organized in the history of the world," the city was full of patriotic enthusiasm. As the various generals with their divisions, all wearing the actual accoutrements of the war —the boys in blue stained with the soil of Virginia and of Georgia, and bearing proudly the tattered banners which had waved on many hard-fought battle-fields — passed up Pennsylvania Avenue, they were the recipients of long-continued and enthusiastic cheers, and were literally covered with garlands.

For a few years after the war Washington continued to be a very unattractive city. At this time an English tourist wrote of it: " The whole place looks run up in a night, like the cardboard cities Potemkin erected to gratify the eyes of his imperial mistress on her tour through Russia; and it is impossible to remove the impression that, when Congress is over, the place is taken down and packed up till wanted again."

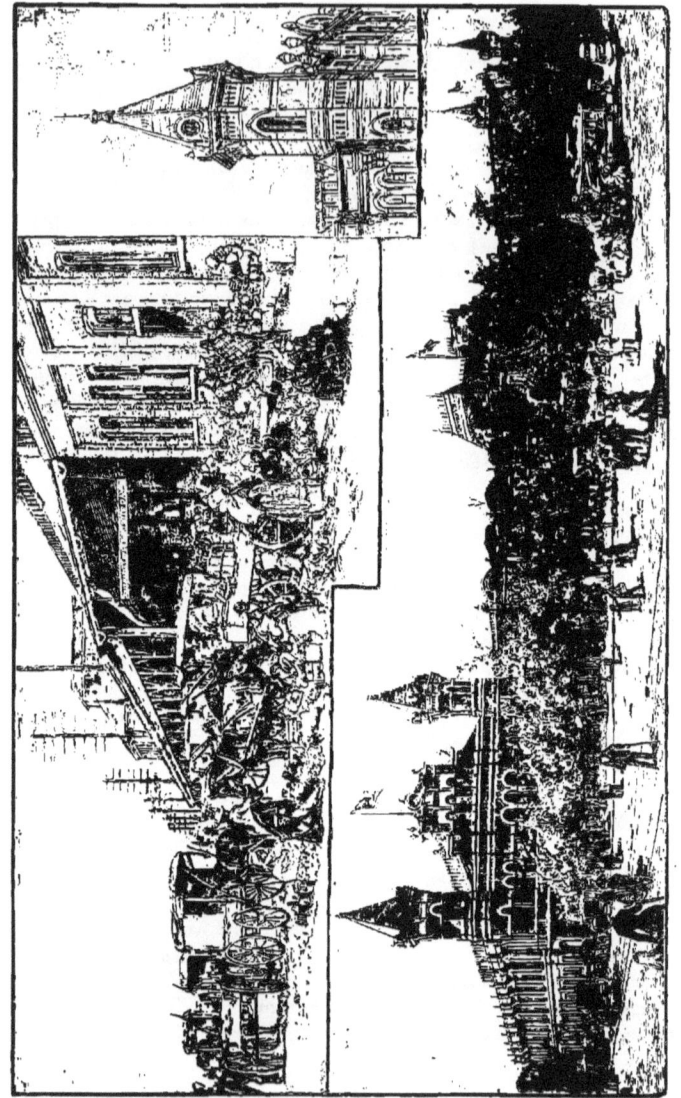

THE CENTER MARKET — GROUP OF HUCKSTERS.

CHAPTER III.

IN the year 1870 Washington was suddenly aroused from its leth-
argy. After seventy years of existence it had not realized the
expectations of its friends, or greatly lessened the opposition of
its enemies. It was in a critical condition. Its use by the Federal soldiers in the Civil War had made thousands of intelligent Northern men familiar with its discomforts, its shiftlessness, and its entire
lack of the desirable qualities that the seat of government of the
American Nation should possess. There was nothing hopeful or
promising about it. Young cities in the West had grown important
and prosperous by their own exertions; old cities in the East had
advanced steadily with the enterprise of the age; but Washington,
with the strong aid of the government, and many years of life, had
failed to be a credit, much less an object of pride, to the American
people.

The project to remove the national capital to St. Louis, vigorously started by a Western man of rare energy and persistency, gave
Washington at this time a great fright. The proposition of removal
received the hearty indorsement of the West, and a large delegation
in Congress was pledged to its advocacy. Prominent newspapers
in New York and elsewhere favored it, and the scheme began to grow
rapidly in public estimation. St. Louis was ready to expend millions
to obtain the splendid prize, and the other large Western cities came

4

forward with offers of their influence and money, enthusiastic over the plan to have the capital city located in "the great golden harvest land," as the West is glowingly described.

At this juncture a strong man came into leadership, and turned aside the current that was flowing perilously against the city. He thoroughly believed in Washington, and was determined to aggrandize it, and at the same time that he improved and built up the city he proposed to enrich himself. This man was Alexander R. Shepherd, well known afterward to the country by his sobriquet of "Boss Shepherd." General Grant was President, and his friendship for Shepherd was marked and enduring. Congress finally disposed of the question of removing the capital by appropriating $500,000 to begin the erection of the grand State, War, and Navy Building, which has cost $12,000,000; and the city, through the efforts of Shepherd, began at once to assume a better appearance. Shepherd at that time was thirty-eight years old. He had realized a fortune of $100,000 from plumbing contracts, and was known as the leading plumber of the District. He had a large political friendship, was an alderman of the old city government, and was noted for his immense energy and invincible determination.

In describing Shepherd's career a well-informed writer says : "He and his friends conceived the idea of making a great and beautiful city out of the slovenly and comfortless Southern town which the capital of the country then was. They first abolished the old municipal government, and ended once for all the conservative *régime* of the past. In its place they put a territorial government with a legislature, which by means of the universal suffrage in the District, then recently established, they were easily able to control. The territorial government was merely a cover for the Board of Public Works, and of this board Shepherd was the head. Eighty miles of the three hundred miles of half-made streets and avenues were improved, and nearly all the thickly-settled streets of the city were paved with wood or concrete. A general and very costly system of sewers was begun. The grades of many of the most populous streets were radically changed. Scores of new parks were graded, fenced, and set with trees and fountains. The old Tiber Canal was filled up, and the greatest nuisance of Washington was thereby shut out of sight. From $15,000,000 to $20,000,000 were swallowed up in this vast undertaking. Congress appropriated at least $5,000,000 in cash, and $2,000,000 more in cash were raised on improvement bonds, which

were put on the market at a very large per cent. The remainder of
this great indebtedness took the shape of sewer bonds, floating loans,
and other securities. Nearly all of this money was disbursed by
Shepherd. It was he who determined to whom all these millions
should go. He had his circle of friends among the contractors, and
it was charged that he shared in the profits; but of this charge there
was no evidence, and probably it was not true. Shepherd must be
credited with an ambition which was much more than a merely selfish one. It cannot be charged against him that he diverted the funds
of the District to improve his own property as distinguished from the
property of others. The street improvements were almost universal,
and his building operations extended to every part of the city. When
the Board of Public Works began operations and property rose in
value all over the city, his real estate and building enterprises (dating
back to 1865) were largely augmented."

During ten years Shepherd erected over one thousand buildings,
and was the first man to build blocks of dwellings in Washington,
after the plan common in Northern cities. His building operations
exceeded those of any other man in the United States, and comprised
total values of $10,000,000; and in land he handled other millions.
He secured large amounts of money from Northern capitalists, carried heavy financial burdens, and exhibited wonderful capacity in ob-

ENTRANCE TO LONG BRIDGE.

taining the credit necessary for his innumerable enterprises. In 1873 he became governor of the District, and ruled its affairs with an imperious hand. He was, in truth, the "Boss" of Washington, and forced the public improvements against all opposition, determined that the city should no longer be a reproach to its people, and a disgrace to the Nation. He was the latter-day L'Enfant, with more brains and more power. In 1876 he became financially embarrassed, and his audacious, extraordinary business and political career came to an end.

The queenly Potomac City, secure now from fear of the removal of the capital, owes its grand renovation largely to this man; and to-day in the city he beautified and raised to a prosperous, distinguished position, thousands of hearts go out in gratitude and well wishes toward the exile from home, as he labors in far-off Mexico to repair his shattered fortune — grateful that he compelled them, even by arbitrary acts and extravagant expenditures, to make Washington the fit place for the seat of government.

In ten years from the time the Board of Public Works began its improvements, the city was transformed. The streets were covered with an almost noiseless, smooth pavement. Fifty thousand shade-trees had been planted; the old rows of wooden, barrack-like houses had given place to dwellings of graceful, ornate architecture; blocks of fine business buildings lined Pennsylvania Avenue and the other prominent thoroughfares; blossoming gardens and luxuriant parks were to be seen on all sides; the squares and circles were adorned with the statues of heroes, and bordered with costly and palatial mansions; splendid school-houses, churches, market buildings, newspaper offices had been erected. The water-works and sewer system were unequaled in the country. Washington had risen fresh and beautiful, like the Uranian Venus, from stagnation and decay.

THE population of the city in 1880 was 147,293, and with Georgetown added, 159,885. It is believed that since the last government census was taken there has been a large yearly increase in population, and that the city now contains quite 240,000 permanent residents. There is also a floating population in the winter months estimated at 50,000, which is composed in part of congressmen and employés of Congress and their families, and people of wealth from various portions of the United States, who spend the winter in the city. There is a constant growth in enterprise and public spirit, and year by year the capital increases in prosperity and importance.

THE DISTRICT COURT HOUSE.

The government business in Washington necessitates the disbursement of a vast amount of money yearly to the residents of the city. All the great departments of the United States government are located there, and the number of persons who perform service in them is estimated at 20,000. The Treasury Department has on its pay-rolls 3,504 persons who do work in Washington; the Interior Department, 2,949; the War Department, 1,686; the Post-Office Department, 544, and the many other departments, divisions, subdivisions, and offices of the government employ from 100 to 2,500 persons each in transacting the immense business of the states and territories included in the American Republic. Many millions of dollars are annually paid as compensation to the government employés in Washington, and, in good times or bad, these enormous disbursements are made with the regularity of clock-work. The government is generally a liberal paymaster, as it is obliged to employ the best talent in all of its difficult and complicated business. Year by year, as the country increases in population and wealth, the affairs of the government greatly increase, and additions to the employés in Washington have constantly to be made to keep up the work of the departments. In some of the important departments, even with the large force employed — with every room in a huge building crowded with clerks attending to their duties with an energy and faithfulness that the people of the country scarce give government employés credit for — the business is often many months behind.

The wholesale and retail trade of the city is steady and flourishing. The vast sums disbursed by the government flow easily and regularly into the currents of trade, and in addition, Washington has within a few years developed a very lucrative traffic with the rich and populous country to the south and west of it, whose people heretofore were accustomed to go to Baltimore for goods. The ample salaries of government employés, the majority of whom receive larger compensation than the same class of workers in any other city, enable them to live well, to purchase many articles of taste and luxury, to enjoy public entertainments, and to gratify their desires in literature and art. The rates of government pay tend also to increase, by comparison, the wages of those engaged in private business. The popular fallacy that when the session of Congress is over each year, the city becomes dull and depressed, is entirely groundless. Congress now merely adds so much to the continuous busy life of Washington — accelerates trade and society in a certain measure while it remains; but when Congress is not in session the streets are lively, trade flourishes, amusements are plentiful and well supported, and social events are brilliant and numerous. The old notion that because Washington is the seat of government commercial interests are out of the question, is rapidly fading away, as the city has advanced a long way in ten years toward that importance to which it is entitled as the centre of a large and flourishing territory, yearly increasing in population.

The city is also fortunate in the strong attraction it has for strangers. Every day hundreds of tourists from all parts of the world visit Washington, to enjoy its sights and objects of interest, which are exceedingly numerous and of great fame; and every day hundreds of people from all sections of the United States arrive to transact business with the various departments of the government. Thus the city is constantly full of visitors who spend their money freely, and consequently add in a large degree to the prosperity of its merchants.

The extensive libraries and scientific collections, open to everybody, attract to the city many students and those engaged in special researches. The Congressional Library, with 500,000 miscellaneous books; the complete Medical and Surgical Library, with 50,000 volumes pertaining to medicine and surgery; the great Law Library of the government; the valuable library of the Patent-Office, for the use of inventors; the libraries of the State, War, and Navy Departments, rich in government records and historical works; the vast collections of natural history in the Smithsonian Institution and the National Museum,— all present to scholars and professional men and women superior facilities for the prosecution of their studies, and they are largely used by persons from every part of the United States.

From the census report devoted to the statistics of manufactures it appears that in the District of Columbia there are at the present time 971 manufacturing establishments employing 7,145 persons, and using an aggregate capital of $5,552,526. Of the employés, 5,495 are males above sixteen years, 1,389 females above fifteen years, and 261 youths and children, who receive annually in wages $3,924,-612. The value of material annually consumed is $5,365,400, and the value of the annual product is $11,882,316. The manufacturing establishments are mainly devoted to the production of various small wares. There are, however, iron works, brick, marble and granite companies, lithographic, book-binding, bank-note, and other establishments of considerable importance.

The real and personal property in the District of Columbia is valued at $254,189.536, and is thus classed: Taxable real property, $112,802,101; belonging to United States, $120,589,684; belonging to District government, $2,258,872; churches, etc., exempt, $6,604,-634; taxable personal property, $11,934,245. The yearly expenses of the District government are about $4,800,000, of which the United States pays one-half. Three commissioners, appointed by the President, consisting of two resident civilians and one army officer of the Corps of Engineers, have charge under Congress of the District affairs. They appoint the various officials, and serve three years. Each commissioner receives $5,000 per year. The District had formerly a delegate in Congress, but at the present time has no voice in legislation. It is governed principally by the old laws of Maryland.

The Constitution of the United States (Art. I., Sec. 8,) gives Congress the authority "to exercise exclusive legislation in all cases

whatsoever over such district (not exceeding ten miles square) as
may by cession of particular states and the acceptance of Congress,
become the seat of the government of the United States." The legal
jurisdiction of the District of Columbia was assumed by Congress
Feb. 27, 1801, and on May 3, 1802, the city of Washington was incorporated. At first a mayor was appointed yearly by the President,
and a city council was elected by the people. After some years the
mayor was chosen by the people. In 1871 the charter of the city
was repealed by Congress, and a territorial government established,
with a governor and legislature. The present permanent Commissioner's government was established in 1878. From 1874 to 1878
there was a provisional government of three commissioners.

WASHINGTON, in its general plan, has been called a combination of
ancient Babylon and modern Philadelphia, with much of the grace
and beauty of Versailles. L'Enfant's design has been closely followed, and the result is a broad, spacious city, pleasing in all its parts.
Within its boundary are 6,111 acres, and of this amount 3,095 acres
are used for public purposes. There are more than one hundred
streets, and twenty-one avenues, the latter named after the states.
The avenues extend from one end of the city to the other, and those
that lead to principal points are from 130 to 160 feet wide, and have
sidewalks from 20 to 38 feet wide. The streets and avenues in
general are of greater width than those of any other city in the
world. They are mostly paved with concrete or asphalt, and are very
smooth and well kept. Carriage-riding through the centre of the
city and on the principal streets of residences is delightful, because
the smooth, elastic pavements prevent jolting. The heavy traffic is
confined as much as possible to certain streets which have stone
pavements, which prevents the concreted streets from being rapidly
worn out.

The streets are laid at right angles from the Capitol, which is
located in nearly the centre of the city; the avenues cross the streets
diagonally. North Capitol, South Capitol, and East Capitol streets,
and the Mall, which extends from the Capitol grounds west to Fifteenth Street and takes the place of West Capitol Street, divide
Washington into four cardinal sections. The streets extending north
and south of the Capitol are designated by numerals, and are known
as First Street east, First Street west, etc. Those extending east
and west are lettered, and are known as A Street north, A Street

THE BALTIMORE AND POTOMAC RAILROAD DEPOT.

south, etc. The aggregate length of streets is 279 miles; of avenues, 65 miles.

The wide avenues, with their concrete pavement, the principal ones extending in an almost straight line for several miles, are among the prominent attractions of Washington. On pleasant days they are full of gay equipages, and present a very brilliant appearance. They command extensive prospects, and on many of them the view is unbroken as far as the eye can reach.

Pennsylvania Avenue is one of the longest in the city, and the most prominent. It is four and one-half miles in length, but its continuity is twice broken, once by the White House and Treasury, and again by the Capitol. It begins at Rock Creek, which separates Washington from Georgetown, passes the Washington Circle, the State, War, and Navy Building, the Corcoran Gallery of Art, the White House, Lafayette Park, and the Treasury. From Fifteenth Street to the Capitol it extends a mile through the finest business

section. East of the Capitol it continues to the banks of the Anacostia River. From Rock Creek to the Treasury, at Fifteenth Street,
the avenue is 130 feet wide; from Fifteenth Street to its terminus at
the Anacostia it is 160 feet. Many of the leading business establishments, several prominent hotels, the Center Market, and the newspaper offices are located on it, and the theatres are adjacent to it. It
is the fashionable thoroughfare, and during most hours of the day it
is bright and lively with thousands of pedestrians and carriages. A
number of parks are situated on " the avenue," and its broad walks
are lined with trees.

The longest unbroken avenue is Massachusetts Avenue, which is
four and one-half miles in length, and 160 feet wide throughout. On
its course through the northwest quarter of the city are many elegant
residences, and several squares and circles. It is finely concreted,
and is shaded by a variety of trees with expansive foliage. New
York, Connecticut, New Hampshire, Vermont, and Rhode Island
avenues also traverse the northwest quarter, and are 130 feet wide,
with the exception of New Hampshire Avenue, which is 120 feet.
They are of great length, and admirably laid out. Maryland Avenue begins at Long Bridge and continues to the Baltimore turnpike;
New Jersey and Delaware avenues intersect each other at the Capitol.
They are each 160 feet wide.

In addition to the fashionable avenues there are numerous streets
extensively built up with costly dwellings of brick and stone, and
comparing favorably in elegance with the avenues. Seventh, Ninth,
and F streets are thriving business sections, filled with fine buildings.
On both sides of Seventh Street, above Pennsylvania Avenue, are
continuous blocks of business establishments for over a mile, and
there is an enormous daily traffic in this quarter. During the past
ten years many thousands of shade-trees, comprising twenty different sorts, selected for their handsome foliage and symmetry, have
been planted on the streets and avenues, and their growth will give
Washington in a few years a distinction as a sylvan city.

The " parking system " is in common use. This system was introduced to lessen the width of the sidewalks, many of which were
much too wide. By it the owner of a house is allowed to enclose,
but not to build upon, all the space in front of his house except twenty
or thirty feet of the sidewalk. On the majority of the streets the
houses stand from forty to fifty feet back from the curbstone, and by
the parking system each house has about twenty feet of garden in front

of it. As the system is almost universally taken advantage of, the result is, that in the vernal season Washington is dotted by innumerable gardens filled with lovely southern flowers.

WHEN the city was first laid out, President Washington selected certain districts for public purposes. These government reservations are used for the buildings of the United States, and for the squares and circles. The small spaces at the intersection of streets are termed triangular reservations, and most of them are planted with trees and shrubs, and ornamented with fountains.

The squares and circles are numerous and exceedingly attractive. Directly opposite the White House, on Pennsylvania Avenue, is Lafayette Square, a tract of seven acres laid out as a park, with choice varieties of shade-trees and flowering plants. Here is Clark Mills' famous equestrian statue of Gen. Andrew Jackson, which was erected in 1853 at a cost of $50,000. It was constructed of cannon captured by the gallant soldier in his various battles. It stands on a white marble pedestal, around which are field-pieces and piles of cannon-balls. General Jackson is represented in complete military uniform, mounted on a rearing horse, which is poised high in the air without the aid of rods.

The space at the intersection of Massachusetts and Rhode Island avenues, Sixteenth and N streets, is known as Scott Square. It is about one acre in extent, and in its centre is an equestrian statue of Lieut.-Gen. Winfield Scott, which was modeled by H. K. Brown, and cast of cannon taken during the Mexican campaigns. The figure is ten feet high, and the total height of the statue is twenty-nine feet. Five enormous blocks of granite compose the pedestal. The statue was ordered by Congress, and was erected in 1874. Its cost was about $45,000. General Scott appears in the full uniform of his rank, seated on his favorite war-horse.

Farragut Square is on Connecticut Avenue, between I, K, and Seventeenth streets. It covers a little more than an acre, and contains a small park in which is a colossal bronze statue of Admiral David Glasgow Farragut, which was modeled by Mrs. Vinnie Ream Hoxie, and cast at the Washington Navy Yard of metal taken from Farragut's flag-ship, the "Hartford." Congress appropriated $20,000 for the purpose. The figure is ten feet high, and the granite pedestal on which it stands is twenty feet, and has an ornamental base holding several mortars. Farragut is portrayed in naval uniform, standing with one foot resting on a block, telescope in hand, watching the enemy's movements. The statue was unveiled on April 25, 1881.

On Vermont Avenue is McPherson Square, which is adorned with a pretty park, in which is an equestrian statue of Maj.-Gen. James B. McPherson, modeled by James T. Robisso. It was erected at a cost of $23,500, by the Society of the Army of the Tennessee, from cannon allotted by Congress. The pedestal is composed of five massive blocks of granite appropriately decorated, and cost $25,000. Congress appropriated this amount. The figure is fourteen feet high, and the horse twelve feet long. General McPherson is represented surveying the field of battle.

On the south side of Pennsylvania Avenue, between Eighth and Ninth streets, is a bronze statue of Brig.-Gen. John A. Rawlins, Secretary of War in 1869, which was ordered by Congress, and cost $10,000. It is in a small park containing choice plants, evergreens, and trees. The figure was modeled by J. Bailey, is eight feet high, and weighs 1,400 pounds. It stands on a granite pedestal, twelve feet in height. General Rawlins is represented in uniform as chief-of-staff to General Grant.

A mile directly east of the Capitol is Lincoln Square, formed by the intersection of East Capitol, Eleventh, Twelfth, and Thirteenth streets and Massachusetts, Kentucky, North Carolina, and Tennessee avenues. It is a space of six acres, in the centre of which is a bronze group called "Emancipation," which represents Abraham Lincoln standing at a small pedestal, holding the Proclamation of Emancipation in one hand, while the other is extended in a protecting manner over the crouching form of a negro with his fetters broken — a slave no longer. It is a notable work, and clearly expressive of the momentous event in American history which it commemorates. The group was designed by Thomas Ball, and cast in Munich. It is twelve feet in height, and stands upon a granite base which rises ten feet. The statue weighs 3,000 pounds, and cost $17,000. When it was unveiled, on April 14, 1876, there were imposing ceremonies, and the Hon. Frederick Douglass was the orator of the occasion. This memorial was erected from contributions received from the freed people of the South, the initial contribution, a five-dollar greenback, coming from an aged colored woman of Virginia.

Northeast of the Capitol, at the intersection of Massachusetts and Maryland avenues, is Greene Square. Here is an equestrian statue of Maj.-Gen. Nathanael Greene, of the Continental Army. It stands in

GARFIELD MEMORIAL TABLET IN THE BALTIMORE & POTOMAC R. R. DEPOT.

the centre of a plat of three and one-half acres, and is thirty-three and one-half feet high. It was modeled by H. K. Brown, and erected in 1877 by authority of Congress, and its cost, including the granite pedestal, was $50,000. General Greene is represented as if issuing orders on the battle-field.

Between Thirteenth and Fourteenth streets west, and I and K streets north, is Franklin Square and Park, comprising four acres planted with luxuriant trees and shrubs. The grounds are surrounded by elegant dwellings, and are charming in their arrangement and ornamentation.

The largest square in the city is Judiciary Square, which contains nineteen acres. It is located between Louisiana Avenue and G Street north, and Fourth and Fifth streets west. It contains the new Pension Building, and the District Court House. In front of the Court

House is a plain marble column, crowned with a full-length statue of Lincoln by Lot Flannery.

Washington Circle is at the intersection of Pennsylvania and New Hampshire avenues. In this circle, within a spacious park, is Clark Mills' equestrian statue of Gen. George Washington, which was unveiled in 1860. It was ordered by Congress, and cost $50,000. Washington is clad in continental uniform, and is represented as at the battle of Princeton.

Thomas Circle is formed by the intersection of Massachusetts and Vermont avenues and Fourteenth Street. Here, on the 19th of November, 1879, was unveiled the equestrian statue of Maj.-Gen. George H. Thomas, which was erected by the Society of the Army of the Cumberland at a cost of $50,000. The statue is the work of J. Q. A. Ward, and was cast from new material. It is sixteen feet high, and the pedestal is also sixteen feet. Congress appropriated $25,000 for the pedestal, which is constructed of Virginia granite, handsomely designed, and bears bronze tablets representing the badge of the Society of the Army of the Cumberland. Four bronze lamp-posts, costing $4,000, surround the base. General Thomas is represented in field dress, observing the tide of battle.

Dupont Circle is at the intersection of Massachusetts, Connecticut, and New Hampshire avenues and P and Nineteenth streets. A statue of Admiral Dupont is to be erected here.

Iowa Circle is at the intersection of Vermont and Rhode Island avenues and P and Thirteenth streets.

WASHINGTON is divided into four distinct sections or quarters. The Northwest quarter has the largest population, and is the most fashionable. In it are the President's House, the Executive Departments of the government, the Foreign Legation buildings, the principal hotels, the theatres, the largest business establishments, and the majority of the finest residences.

The Southwest quarter is extensive and populous, but it is mainly occupied by small places of business and the residences of persons of moderate means. Some of the streets are, however, being taken up for very fine houses, particularly those in the vicinity of the National Museum. The wharves of the river transportation lines are in this quarter.

The Northeast quarter is sparsely settled, but it increases yearly

THE WASHINGTON MONUMENT.

in population. On some of the streets there are numerous blocks of fine dwellings, those located near the Capitol being notable for elegance.

The Southeast quarter, with a portion of the Northeast, is called Capitol Hill, as the Capitol stands on the western brow of this extensive plateau. Although not as fashionable as the Northwest quarter, it yet has a numerous population of people of large means, and many elegant residences, together with blocks of plain, neat houses and places of business. Within a few years it has developed considerably.

Long Bridge extends from the southwestern terminus of Maryland Avenue across the Potomac River to the Virginia shore, and is a mile in length. It was completed in 1835 at a cost of $100,000, and, singular as it may seem, only one-third of the money appropriated by Congress to build it was expended. It is doubtful if there is another case on record of a public work being constructed for less than the original appropriation. President Jackson formally dedicated the bridge in the spring of 1836, and, after nearly fifty years of hard service, it is now in a substantial condition. It is an unsightly wooden structure; one side of it is used by the railroads running south from Washington, and toward the Virginia end is an extensive draw, to admit of the passage of vessels to Georgetown. Before many years it will doubtless give way to the march of improvements, and a bridge better adapted to the needs of the capital will take its place. During the Civil War thousands of Northern soldiers tramped over its dusty road, and a large part of the vast quantities of supplies for the Federal army in the field was transported over it. At present it is largely used by the farmers of Virginia who bring their produce to the Washington markets, and daily hundreds of vehicles and several thousand people cross the old structure.

Many years have passed since the corner-stone of the Washington Monument was laid with imposing ceremonies on an anniversary of the Nation's Independence Day. This grand memorial to him who was called " the pride of our land and the glory of our race," progressed in an exceedingly tardy manner, but was finished in December, 1884, and dedicated February 22, 1885, the one hundred and fifty-third anniversary of the birth of Washington. The cost of the monument has been about one million, two hundred thousand dollars.

This monument has been called " the world's greatest cenotaph." It is a plain obeliscal shaft, rising to the height of 555 feet from the base of the shaft, and 572 feet above the natural surface of surrounding ground. Around the base a mound of earth has been graded, sloping in all directions to meet the natural surface at distances of 350 to 450 feet from the shaft. The foundation of the shaft is 126 feet square and is thirty-seven feet below the base of the shaft. The shaft, at the base, is fifty-five feet square, and at its top it is about thirty feet square. The lower portion is constructed of blue gneiss, faced with large crystal marble, and the upper portion is of similar marble, with cut granite backing. In the interior lining are set numerous blocks of stone, presented by the states and cities of the United States, by foreign countries, and by various societies. They are properly inscribed, and are arranged to be plainly seen in ascending the monument.

An elevator, and also a spiral staircase, is used for the ascent, and the interior of the shaft is illuminated by electricity, as the only openings, except the entrance doors, are small windows at the top.

This shaft is the loftiest artificial structure in the world. It rises many feet above the Capitol, and above any of the cathedral spires and monuments in Europe and the East. It is fifteen feet higher than the main tower of the new city hall in Philadelphia, thirty feet higher than the great cathedral at Cologne, and ninety-five feet higher than St. Peter's, at Rome. The prospect from the top is sublime beyond conception. On the west the range of vision is bounded by the Alleghany Mountains, and on the south it extends to the Chesapeake Bay, and across it to the ocean. The prospect on the north and east comprises the city of Washington, and far beyond over the District and Maryland Hills.

The site of the monument was designated by act of Congress in 1848, and is said to have been originally chosen by President Washington. It occupies the government reservation, bounded by Fourteenth Street west, and the Potomac River. All of this tract is to be included in the extensive harbor improvements in progress, and it is believed will eventually be a portion of a beautiful park, with drives extending a long distance on the river bank.

The subject of a national memorial to the Father of His Country was early discussed. The Continental Congress, in 1783, adopted a resolution for the erection of a statue "in honor of George Washington, the illustrious Commander-in-Chief of the United States Army during the war which vindicated and secured their liberty, sovereignty and independence"; but the resolution was not carried into effect, as it was understood that Washington did not desire a statue while he was living. After his death one branch of Congress, in 1800, passed an act to erect to his memory "a mausoleum of American granite and marble in a pyramidal form," but it failed of passage in the other branch. Some years afterward an attempt was made to erect a national monument by private subscriptions after the plan of the Timoleonton of Syracuse, but very little was done toward carrying out this plan, and it was not until 1833 that the monument project assumed definite form. In September of that year the citizens of Washington had a meeting and formed the "Washington National Monument Society," with Chief Justice John Marshall as president. An appeal was made to the country for subscriptions, and $230,000 were obtained. The corner-stone of the monument was laid on the 4th of July, 1848, in accordance with Masonic rites, the Hon. Robert C. Winthrop delivering an oration on the life and character of Washington. The society proceeded with the work of construction until 1854, when it was compelled to suspend operations on account of its inability to obtain money. The monument was left but a little way above its foundation walls until 1878, at which time the government undertook its completion. The work was performed by Col. Thos. Lincoln Casey, under the direction of the joint commission created by Congress, with the Washington Monument Society in an advisory capacity.

THE city of Washington has passed beyond the possibility of decadence, and doubtless will have, before many years, a population of half a million people. Sagacious men are of the opinion that eventually the vast and unequaled water-power of the upper Potomac will be utilized for manufacturing purposes, and that the city will then become the centre of a great industrial district, producing goods for the southern and southwestern markets. From a city of malaria and large death rate, it has become, by wise sanitary measures, a salubrious place of residence, and its death rate, despite a large floating population, is very low, averaging about 17.48 per 1,000. Its climate in winter is usually mild and genial, the spring months are delightful, and the heat in summer rarely exceeds that in the cities several hundred miles to the northward. There is no reason to believe that it will not always remain the national capital, and as the country increases in greatness and opulence, this city, the seat of government, is likely to fully share in the general prosperity.

A FEW MOMENTS OF LEISURE.

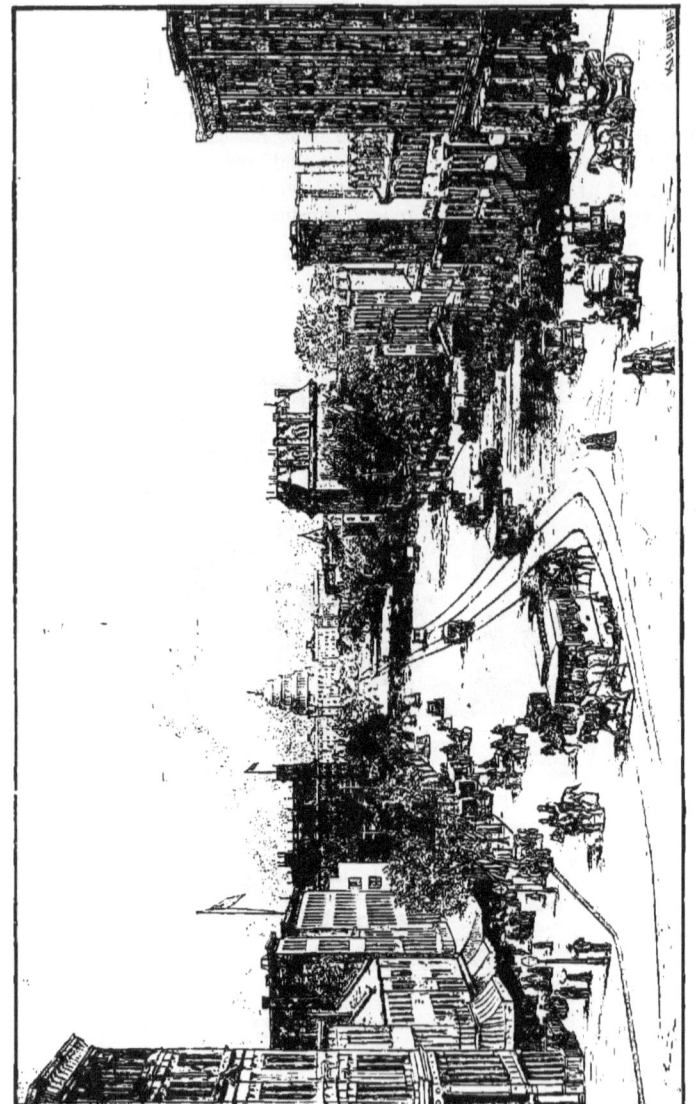

PENNSYLVANIA AVENUE, FROM TREASURY BUILDING.

CHAPTER IV.

THE commissioners appointed to lay out the capital city were
directed to " procure suitable buildings for the accommoda-
tion of Congress, and of the President, and for the public
offices of the government of the United States "; and, shortly
after the city was surveyed, they entered upon this portion of their
duties. On L'Enfant's design the " Federal House for Congress "
was designated as " the Capitol," and this name, meeting with the
approval of President Washington, was adopted. It had been ascertained that the hill in the eastern section was " the central point ' of
the city, and therefore it was decided to erect the Capitol there, with
its front toward the east, where a spacious level plateau extended for
two miles. It was believed that on this plateau the best houses would
be erected. To the westward were swamps and woods, hillocks and
creeks, and it was apparent that the eastern section was in every way
better adapted for the homes of the cultivated and wealthy people
who were expected to settle in the national city. But the city's growth
was almost entirely toward the west; and to-day the Capitol stands
with its back to the populous and fashionable part of Washington.
It has been humorously said that " the Capitol is like the Irishman's
shanty, which had the front door on the back side." It is proposed
to reconstruct the western façade and make it similar to the eastern,
and doubtless this will be done before many years.

A premium of $500 and a building-lot was offered by the commissioners for the best design of the Capitol, and in response to their advertisement sixteen designs were submitted by architects in the principal cities. These designs were carefully examined by Mr. Jefferson, the Secretary of State, and promptly rejected by him, being mostly beneath serious consideration. Mr. Jefferson had early expressed a preference for " the adoption of some of the models of antiquity, which have had the approbation of thousands of years." In July, 1792, a French architect residing in New York, named Stephen L. Hallet, or Hallate, as it was sometimes written, sent a sketch of a design to the commissioners which met with favor, and he was invited to come to Washington and examine the locality chosen for the Capitol, in order that he might fully perfect his design, which, in many particulars, was satisfactory. About this time an amateur draughtsman, named Dr. William Thornton, an Englishman who had come to the United States after residing for some years in the West Indies, presented a highly colored and elaborated design to Washington and Jefferson, which so greatly pleased them that the President sent a communication to the commissioners requesting the adoption of Thornton's design in place of Hallet's, but suggesting that they " do it with delicacy." It was advised, however, that Hallet be engaged as supervising architect, as Thornton had no practical knowledge of architecture.

Hallet was informed of this request, doubtless " with delicacy," and immediately began to develop and improve his design. Thornton also improved his, and for several weeks these aspirants for the distinguished honor of designing the Capitol of the new and vigorous American Nation, worked with intense rivalry and bitter feeling. A charge was made by Hallet that Thornton had stolen the major part of his design from his (Hallet's) rough sketches, and had merely drawn out in detail the plans he had thus obtained. This charge was stoutly denied by Thornton, and his denial being satisfactory to the commissioners, they finally accepted his design, and awarded the premium to him. Although Hallet demurred at this award, and was greatly aggrieved by it, he was partially appeased by receiving the appointment of supervising architect of the Capitol, with a salary of £400 per year, and began work on the edifice.

On the 18th of September, 1793, the corner-stone was laid in the southeast corner of what was to be the north wing of the Capitol. In an ancient account of this event it is stated that " a grand Masonic, military and civic procession was formed on the square in front of the President's grounds, from whence it proceeded to the Capitol with martial music and flying colors, attended by an immense concourse of spectators. The ceremony was grand and imposing, and large numbers from various parts of the country attended." On the corner-stone was placed a large silver plate, which was inscribed as follows :

"This southeast corner-stone of the Capitol of the United States of America in the City of Washington was laid on the 18th day of September, 1793, in the 13th year of American Independence, in the first year of the second term of the Presidency of George Washington, whose virtues in the civil administration of his country have been as conspicuous and beneficial as his military valor and prudence have been useful in establishing her liberties, and in the year of Masonry 5793, by the President of the United States in concert with the Grand Lodge of Maryland, several Lodges under its jurisdiction, and Lodge No. 22, from Alexandria, Virginia."

President Washington delivered an oration, it is believed, although no record of it can be found, and the Grand Master of the Maryland Masons made an impressive address. After the ceremony "the assemblage retired to an extensive booth, where they enjoyed a barbecue feast."

A few months after the corner-stone had been laid, a serious quarrel began between Architect Hallet and Dr. Thornton, who had been appointed one of the commissioners. Hallet was requested to furnish the commissioners with his various drawings and designs, but he peremptorily declined, and, in consequence, was dismissed from the public service. George Hadfield, an Englishman, who came highly recommended by Benjamin West, and also by James Hoban, the architect of the White House, was appointed in Hallet's place, and remained until he, too, had a quarrel with the commissioners, and was forced to give up the position. Hoban continued the work, and finished the north wing in 1800.

In 1803 the construction of the south wing was placed in the hands of Benjamin H. Latrobe, who had come from London, where he had thoroughly studied architecture with Cockrell, one of the leading architects of his day. He arrived in the United States in 1796, and in Norfolk, Va., was introduced to Judge Bushrod Washington, a nephew of the President, who took him to Mount Vernon to form the acquaintance of Washington. Latrobe made a favorable impression upon the President, and was frequently consulted by him in regard to the public buildings. When he was engaged as the architect of the Capitol, the commissioners gave him full power to construct the south wing, and also to remodel the north wing, which had been very poorly constructed, in accordance with his own plans. He finished the work in 1811, and then connected the wings by a large wooden scaffolding, or bridge, which occupied the place of the present Rotunda. The walls of the wings were constructed of sandstone, quarried on an island in Acquia Creek, a small stream that empties into the Potomac River about forty miles below Washington; and the bricks used for the interior work were made in kilns, erected on the Capitol grounds. Congress had occupied the building since 1800, and at the time the British troops invaded the city, on Aug. 24, 1814, the new Capitol looked quite imposing on its hill-top.

The British army, commanded jointly by General Ross and Admiral Cockburn, reached Capitol Hill early in the evening, flushed and excited by their victory at Bladensburg. As General Ross rode toward the Capitol his horse was killed by a shot fired from a house in the vicinity. The shot was apparently aimed at the British general, and it so enraged the troops that, after setting fire to the house containing the sharpshooter, they marched quickly to the Capitol, and fired several volleys into its windows. A regiment then marched into the hall of the House of Representatives, "the drums and fifes playing 'The British Grenadiers,'" and the soldiers were formed around the Speaker's chair. Admiral Cockburn was escorted to the post of honor, and, seating himself, derisively called the excited assemblage to order. "Shall this harbor of Yankee Democracy be burned? All for it say aye!" he shouted. There was a tumultuous cry of affirmation, and then the order was given to fire the building. The pitch-pine boards were torn from the passage-way between the wings, the books and papers of the Library of Congress were pulled from their shelves and scattered over the floor, valuable paintings in a room adjoining the Senate Chamber were cut from their frames, and the torch applied to the combustible mass. Presently clouds of smoke and columns of fire ascended from the Capitol, and it seemed doomed to destruction. The soldiers discharged army rockets through the roof of each wing, and when the fire was burning furiously, left the building and marched up Pennsylvania Avenue to fire the other public edifices. The wooden passage-way, and the roofs and interiors of the wings were burned, but the walls were saved, as the flames were

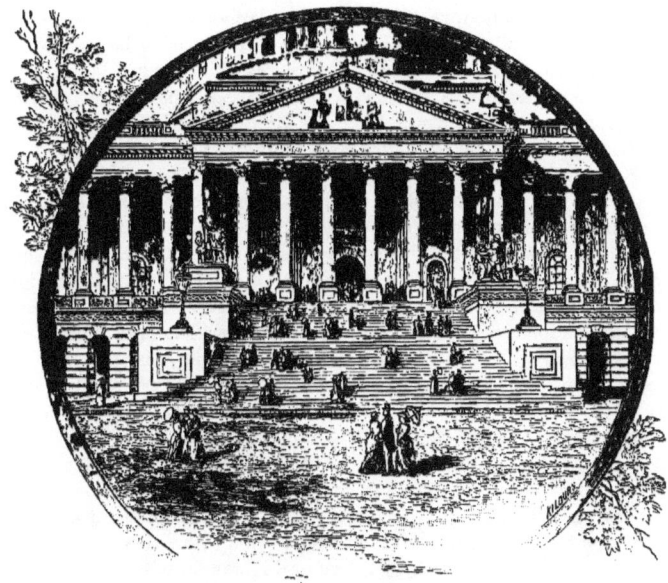

MAIN ENTRANCE, CAPITOL.

extinguished in time by a severe rain which set in within half an hour after the fire had begun, and continued all the evening. .

Congress held its first session after the British invasion in Blodgett's Hotel, which occupied the site of the present Post-Office building. The Capitol was ordered rebuilt, and in December, 1816, Congress leased a building which the citizens of Washington had erected near the eastern grounds of the Capitol, and held its sessions in it for several years. This building has always been known as the "Old Capitol." In it John C. Calhoun died on the 31st of March, 1850; and during the Civil War it was used as a prison for Confederates. Henry Wirz, the keeper of Andersonville prison, was hanged in its yard on Nov. 10, 1865. It is now standing, and is used for business purposes and for residences.

At the time the Capitol was burned, Latrobe, its real architect, was in Pittsburg, aiding in the construction of a steamboat for Robert Fulton. He was immediately recalled to Washington, and, after a thorough examination, reported that the Capitol could be easily restored, as its foundations and walls were unimpaired. Latrobe was a man of infinite resource. He could speak five modern languages fluently, and was also familiar with Latin, Greek, and Hebrew. He was an inventor, and a discoverer. In the Loudon Hills, in Virginia, he discovered the beautiful mottled marble, known as "breccia," which he used extensively in the interior of the Capitol. He invented what President Madison called "the American order of architecture," using designs of Indian corn, the cotton blossom, and the tobacco-leaf for columns and capitals instead of the acanthus. Until 1817 he labored assiduously to restore and improve the Capitol, and to him the credit is due for the old hall of the House of Representatives, now the National Statuary Hall; the old Senate Chamber, now used by the Supreme Court; the Law Library Chamber, and the old lobbies. When he resigned, and Charles Bulfinch was engaged as the architect, the understanding was that the Capitol should be completed in accordance with the designs he had made.

Bulfinch was a native of Massachusetts. He had constructed the old State House in Boston, and had performed other notable work. For ten years he devoted himself to the Capitol, following Latrobe's plan to a great extent. He completed what were then called the wings, and connected them by the central Rotunda, with a low dome, and also built the main hall of the Library of Congress. In 1827 he reported to Congress that the Capitol was finished, and three years later, resigned the position of architect and returned to Boston. The edifice was declared "majestic," and "perfect in all its adaptations." It covered about one and one-half acres, and was three hundred and fifty-two feet long, and seventy feet high to the top of the balustrade. To the top of the dome it was one hundred and forty-five feet high. Its construction had cost $2,433,814.

DURING the twenty years ensuing, the Capitol was considered sufficient for the use of the Nation. Robert Mills, a Washington architect, was placed in charge of it, and made sundry small improvements from time to time. In 1850 the necessity for better accommodations for both Houses of Congress, the number of members having greatly increased, compelled an enlargement of the building. It was decided to "extend the wings by greater wings, called extensions," which were to be constructed of marble, and connected with the original Capitol by wide corridors. Thomas U. Walter, of Philadelphia, who had built Girard College, was secured as architect, and he retained the position until 1865. He arranged a plan for the extensions, and immediately began the work of construction. Gen. Montgomery C. Meigs, the accomplished engineer, was appointed as the superintendent and inspector.

On the 4th of July, 1851, the corner-stone of the south or House extension was laid by President Fillmore, assisted by the Grand Lodge of Masons of the District of Columbia, the Grand Master wearing the regalia worn by President Washington as Master Mason when he laid the corner-stone of the original edifice, nearly fifty-eight years before. An eloquent oration was delivered by Daniel Webster, Secretary of State, which was listened to by a vast assemblage. Beneath the corner-stone this record was deposited:

" On the morning of the first day of the seventy-sixth year of the Independence of the United States of America, in the city of Washington, being the 4th day of July, 1851, this stone, designated as the corner-stone of the Extension of the Capitol, according to a plan approved by the President, in pursuance of an act of Congress, was laid by Millard Fillmore, President of the United States, assisted by the Grand Master of the Masonic Lodges, in the presence of many members of Congress; of officers of the Executive and Judiciary Departments, National, State, and District; of officers of the Army and Navy; the corporate authorities of this, and neighboring cities; many associations, civil, military, and Masonic; officers of the Smithsonian Institution, and National Institute; professors of colleges and teachers of schools of the District of Columbia, with their students and pupils; and a vast concourse of people from places near and remote, including a few surviving gentlemen who witnessed the laying of the corner-stone of the Capitol by President Washington, on the 18th day of September, 1793. If, therefore, it shall be hereafter the will of God that this structure shall fall from its base, that its foundations be upturned, and this deposit brought to the eyes of men, be it known that, on this day, the Union of the United States of America stands firm; that their Constitution still exists unimpaired, and with all its original usefulness and glory, growing every day stronger and stronger in the affections of the great body of the American people, and attracting more and more the admiration of the world. And all here assembled, whether belonging to public life or to private life, with hearts devoutly thankful to Almighty God for the preservation of the liberty and happiness of the country, unite in sincere and fer-

vent prayers that this deposit, and the walls and arches, the domes
and towers, the columns and entablatures, now to be erected over it,
may endure forever!   God save the United States of America!

DANIEL WEBSTER,

Secretary of State of the United States."

The extensions were constructed of white marble, tinged with blue,
from quarries at Lee, Mass.; and the one hundred massive columns
around them, each consisting of a single block of marble, were quarried in Cockeysville, Md.

It was proposed to construct a new and grander dome to take the
place of "the small wooden thing" that surmounted the Capitol, and
the way in which the first appropriation of $100,000 was obtained for
the purpose is described thus: "Mr. Walter prepared plans for a complete extension of the Capitol — new wings, new dome, and a new
marble front for the middle or sandstone building, and as he knew very
well that Congress would never vote the great sum required in the
most economical way, that is in bulk, he first submitted the wings.
Next, as Congress was about adjourning at the end of a session, and
they were all very merry at a night session — ladies on the floor, and
everything lively — the new dome was presented splendidly painted
in a picture, and adopted at once."   The money first appropriated was
barely sufficient to remove the old dome, which was constructed of
wood, brick, and stone, with a sheathing of copper.   The new dome
required nine years for its construction, and cost $1,250,000.

The extensions were finished in November, 1867, and the Capitol
then presented the stately appearance it has to-day.   Nearly $10,-
000,000 had been expended for its reconstruction, which, with the cost
of the original edifice, made the total expenditure a little less than
$13,000,000.   General Meigs, the superintendent, made a report to
Congress, in which he said, "I have labored faithfully and diligently
to construct this building in such a manner that it would last for ages
as a creditable monument of the state of the arts at this time in this
country."

From 1867 to the present time nothing of consequence has been
done to the exterior of the Capitol.   Edward Clark, of Philadelphia,
is the architect in charge.   The interior has been variously adorned,
and the grounds greatly improved.   Walter's plan included the extension of the eastern façade so as to cover the "deep cuts" made by the
Senate and House extensions, which would give an unbroken series

of columns; and it is proposed to rebuild the front and the back of the main or original building with marble, to take the place of the sandstone, which requires very careful painting every year to prevent it from crumbling. These changes will doubtless be made, in time.

On the brow of a hill which rises ninety feet above the Potomac River is the majestic Capitol, one of the grandest structures in the world. It covers an area of six hundred and fifty-two feet more than three and one-half acres, and the grounds around it comprise forty-six acres. Its total length is seven hundred and fifty-one feet four inches, and its greatest breadth, including the porticoes and the steps, is three hundred and twenty-four feet. It has a principal story, and an attic story, which rest upon a rustic basement. The basement supports an ordonnance of pilasters rising to the top of the two stories above, on which is the entablature, and a marble balustrade surmounts the whole. The basement story is devoted to committee-rooms of Congress, the Law Library, the document and folding rooms, the House post-office, the Senate and House restaurants, and offices. The principal story contains the Rotunda, the National Statuary Hall, the Supreme Court Chamber, the National Library or Library of Congress, and the halls of the Houses of Congress, with various rooms for the members and the officials. The attic story contains committee-rooms.

The main building, or original Capitol, is three hundred and fifty-two feet four inches long, and one hundred and twenty-one feet six inches deep. On the eastern façade is a portico one hundred and sixty feet wide (the grand central portico); and on the western façade is a projection of eighty-three feet, which forms a recessed portico of ten coupled columns. The extensions, or north and south wings, occupied by Congress, are connected with the centre building by corridors, each forty-four feet long, and fifty-six feet wide. Each wing is one hundred and forty-two feet eight inches in length, and two hundred and thirty-eight feet ten inches in width. The wings have porticoes of twenty-two columns on their eastern façades, and porticoes of ten columns on their ends and western façades. The north wing is occupied by the Senate, and the south wing by the House of Representatives.

On the tympanum of the grand central portico, at the main entrance to the Capitol, is a colossal allegorical group representing the "Genius of America," which was designed by John Quincy Adams.

when Secretary of State, after he had rejected various designs submitted in competition for a premium. It comprises three figures, the Goddess of Liberty, with Justice and Hope, executed in sandstone by Persico, an Italian sculptor, at a cost of $1,500. At the sides of the entrance doors are niches in which are huge statues of Carrara marble, representing War and Peace, also executed by Persico. They cost $12,000. War is portrayed by the figure of Mars, attired as a Roman soldier, with sword and shield; and Peace by the figure of Ceres, in flowing robes, holding fruits and an olive-branch in her hands. Above the door is a bust of Washington, laurel-crowned, cut in stone by Capellano.

On the top of the broad stone steps of the portico are two huge groups in marble, designated as "The Discovery of America," and "Civilization." The first group is the work of Persico, and represents Columbus holding the globe aloft " in the hollow of his hand," while an Indian maiden crouches in alarm and amazement at his side. This sculpture is said to give a faithful copy of the armor worn by Columbus when he discovered America. The other group was executed by Horatio Greenough. It represents a desperate encounter between an American pioneer and an Indian. On one side is the wife of the pioneer, holding her babe pressed to her bosom, shrinking from the contestants, fearful of the result. These groups cost $48,000.

The twenty-four massive monolithic columns of sandstone, each thirty feet high, which constitute the portico, were placed in position in 1825. They were quarried on an island in Acquia Creek, and transported to Washington in flat-boats, which were brought to the foot of Capitol Hill by means of the Tiber Creek. Ropes were then attached to the columns, and they were dragged up the hill by long lines of men, and every day many congressmen were to be seen pulling at the ropes, laughing and shouting like school-boys.

On the steps of this grand portico the oath of office has been administered by the Chief Justice of the Supreme Court to all the Presidents of the United States, from Andrew Jackson in 1829 to Grover Cleveland in 1885. Before the portico, in the eastern park, 100,000 people can witness the inauguration ceremony. When the President has taken the oath, the guns of the Arsenal, the Navy Yard, and the forts around Washington fire the Presidential salute.

The famous Rogers bronze door is placed in the main entrance to the Capitol. On it are designs in high relief representing events in

THE ROGERS BRONZE DOOR.

the life of Columbus, and the discovery of the American continent. The door is nineteen feet high, and nine feet wide, and is folding or double. It is within a bronze casing, on which are emblematic figures of conquest and navigation in the four quarters of the globe. It is constructed of solid bronze, and weighs 20,000 pounds. There are nine panels, in which the scenes are arranged in regular order, beginning with the examination of Columbus before the Council of Salamanca, and following with his departure from the Convent of La Rabida to visit the Spanish court. Then are shown the "Audience at the court of Ferdinand and Isabella"; the " Starting of Columbus from Palos on his first voyage"; the "First landing of the Spaniards at San Salvador"; the " First encounter of the discoverers with the Indians"; the "Triumphal entry of Columbus into Barcelona"; "Columbus in chains," and his " Death scene." Each scene is very clearly and effectively delineated. Between the panels, and on the sides and the top of the door are sixteen small statues of the eminent contemporaries of Columbus, together with ten projecting heads of the historians of his voyages; and on the transom arch is a bust of the great navigator, beneath which the American eagle spreads its wings. The door was modeled by Randolph Rogers in Rome, in 1858, and cast in Munich in 1860, by F. von Muller. Its cost was $30,000.

Broad flights of marble steps lead to the eastern porticoes of the Senate and House extensions. On the tympanum of the Senate portico is a group of figures in marble, executed by Thomas Crawford, illustrating " American Civilization and the Decadence of the Indian races." Fifty thousand dollars were paid for this work. America is the central figure; on the left are figures representing War, Commerce, Education, and the Mechanical Arts; on the right are pioneers, Indians, and an Indian grave. Above the Senate door is a marble group representing History and Justice.

A bronze door, modeled by Thomas Crawford, and cast in Chicopee. Mass., by James T. Ames, was placed at the entrance to the Senate extension in 1868. It was executed at an expense of nearly $57,000, and is a notable specimen of American art. It portrays events in the Revolutionary War, and in the early history of the Republic. The panels contain representations of the "Battle of Bunker Hill and death of General Warren"; the "Battle of Monmouth and rebuke of Gen. Charles Lee, the traitor, 1778"; "Yorktown —the gallantry of Hamilton, 1781"; a " Hessian soldier in death-struggle with an American"; an allegory of the "Blessings of Peace"; the "Ovation to Washington at Trenton, 1789"; the "First Inauguration of President Washington, 1789"; and the "Laying of the Corner-stone of the United States Capitol." The door is the finest example of bronze-work ever cast in the United States, and compares favorably with the Rogers door in design and execution.

It is proposed to place a bronze door at the main entrance to the House extension, and also to adorn the portico with marble groups. Designs for a door were made some years ago, but as yet Congress has taken no action in the matter.

RISING far above the Capitol is the great dome, an object of imposing beauty, to be seen for miles around. No edifice in the world possesses a dome equal to it in grand, classic symmetry, and in size it is only equaled by the domes of St. Peter's in Rome, St. Paul's in London, and the *Hôtel des Invalides* in Paris. It was designed by Thomas U. Walter, and erected by Charles Fowler. The most beautiful forms of classical architecture are embodied in it. It is of cast iron, and is a vast sphere nearly 3,576 tons in weight. The builder states that it was constructed on a series of ribs which give support to the large outer plates, which are bolted together. It is nearly all of one metal, and the plates are so arranged that they will expand and contract "like the folding and unfolding of a lily, all moving together." Any atmospheric change that will move one part will also move all the others — the plates, the bolts, and the other mechanism, and "the Rocky Mountains will budge as quickly" as this ponderous iron structure, which is likely to endure for ages. It is prevented from rusting by covering it yearly with white paint in solid coatings. It rises from a colossal peristyle, with tall, fluted columns, above which is a balustrade, and above this an "attic." On its top is a "lantern," fifteen feet in diameter, and fifty feet high, which is crowned by a huge bronze statue of Freedom. This statue stands three hundred and seventy-seven feet eleven inches above the level of the Potomac River. From the base line of the eastern front of the Capitol to the top of the statue it is two hundred and eighty-seven feet eleven inches. Thomas Crawford modeled the figure, which is that of the Goddess of Liberty, with a "liberty cap" of eagle's feathers, suggested to the sculptor by Jefferson Davis, when Secretary of War. The figure is nineteen and one-half feet in height, and weighs 14,985 pounds. It was cast at a foundry in Bladensburg, Md., and cost nearly $25,000.

6

The body of the statue was raised to the lantern on the dome a few days previous to the 2d of December, 1863, and on that day the head was placed on the body with patriotic ceremony. All the forts around Washington fired rapid salutes as the head of the goddess was carefully hoisted over the vast iron sphere, and when it had reached the summit and was securely fastened to the body, flags were dipped on every public building, and in every encampment in and near the city, and a hundred guns on the District and Virginia hills rang out deeptoned salutations to the glorious emblem of liberty.

THE grounds of the Capitol comprise an open court on the eastern, and a grand terrace on the western side — in all, forty-six acres of park, laid out in an attractive manner, and planted with a great variety of luxuriant trees and a wide range of shrubbery, which afford pleasing contrasts of form and color. The design has been to arrange the grounds for convenience of business with Congress and the Supreme Court, and also to fitly support and present the Capitol to advantage. When the government first took possession of the tract it was overgrown with " scrub oaks," and had a soil of stiff clay, dusty in dry, and like mortar in wet weather. For many years it was merely an open common, with roads and paths crossing it in all directions. At the base of the hill, on the west, flowed the Tiber Creek, a little stream with rugged sycamore trees overhanging its banks. In the early spring it was not fordable, and the small bridge was often washed away by freshets. Congressmen in riding to the Capitol were frequently compelled to secure their horses on the farther side, and to pick their way across the swollen stream on fallen trees. Ten years ago the Tiber Creek was utilized for the sewer system of the city, and now forms a natural sewer much larger than the famous sewers of Paris. It runs through the city and empties into the Eastern Branch of the Potomac. Its course is covered by streets, under which the tide ebbs and flows.

President Washington planted a number of trees in the park on the north of the Capitol, and one of these, known as the " Washington Elm," still remains. It is likely to outlive many more Presidents, as it is well cared for and in a flourishing condition. In 1825 the grounds were laid out for the first time with some attempt at system. Rows of trees, flower-beds, grass-plats, and gravel walks were arranged. A few years later, more land was enclosed, and numerous trees planted. In the eastern court two "barbecue groves" were made, one for the Democrats, and the other for the Whigs, to hold their meetings and jubilations in. The system of landscape gardening now in use was begun soon after the Capitol was reconstructed. Around the building on the western side an architectural terrace is to be constructed, which will greatly add to the ornamentation of the grounds. There are forty-six carriage and foot entrances from the streets on all sides, well paved with concrete and smooth stone, and the entire park is enclosed by low walls, with handsomely ornamented coping, posts, and gateways. Many trees and shrubs from foreign countries are growing vigorously. They are properly described by means of labels attached to them, and visitors are thus enabled to gain accurate knowledge of the varieties. The park is largely used as a place of public resort in spring and summer, and the government has provided pretty rustic arbors and resting-places, drinking-fountains of pure spring water, and plenty of wide, comfortable seats under lofty trees for the use of all who seek this pleasant, sylvan retreat.

In the eastern court, fronting the central portico, is a colossal marble statue of Washington, by Horatio Greenough. The statue was executed in Italy, and its cost, including the pedestal and transportation, was nearly $45,000. Congress ordered it in 1832, and ten years later it was placed in the centre of the Rotunda of the Capitol. Subsequently it was removed to its present location. Greenough was a native of Boston, and died near that city in 1852, after a long residence abroad. In writing of the statue he said, "It is the birth of my thought, and I have sacrificed to it the flower of my days and the freshness of my strength; its every lineament has been moistened with the sweat of my toil and the tears of my exile. I would not barter away its association with my name for the proudest fortune avarice ever dreamed of." Washington is represented seated in a Roman chair adorned with lions' heads and the acanthus leaf. The figure is nude to the waist, with a mantle draped round the lower part and extending over the right shoulder. The right hand points toward heaven, and the left holds a sheathed sword. On the sides of the chair are allegories of Phœbus-Apollo driving the chariot of the sun, and Hercules strangling the serpent. On the back is a Latin inscription, which is freely translated, "This statue is for a great example of liberty, nor without liberty will the example endure." The granite pedestal is inscribed with the famous eulogy on Washington, uttered by Gov. Henry Lee, of Virginia: "First in war, first in peace, first in the hearts of his countrymen."

At the foot of Capitol Hill, near the main entrance to the western park, is the Naval Monument, or Monument of Peace, executed in Italy by Franklin Simmons. It is inscribed, "In memory of the officers, seamen, and marines of the United States Navy, who fell in defence of the Union and liberty of their country, 1861–1865." It is of pure Italian marble, and rises to a height of forty-four feet, and rests on an elaborate granite pedestal, which contains a fountain. It cost $21,000, and the pedestal cost $20,000. At the top are large figures representing America, and History. America is weeping, while History holds a tablet on which she has written, "They died that their country might live." A figure portraying Victory stands below the other figures, holding aloft a wreath of laurel in her right hand, and at her feet are miniature images of Mars and Neptune. On the back of the monument is a figure of Peace bearing an olive-branch, and surrounding the figure are models of agricultural implements and products. This fine memorial was erected from funds contributed by members of the navy, and the pedestal from an appropriation by Congress.

THE National Botanical Garden adjoins the Capitol grounds on the west, and is part of the government reservation, known as the Mall. It was originally an alder swamp, with the Tiber Creek flowing through it. . The first attempt to establish a garden here was made about fifty years ago. It was begun with a small collection of trees and plants carelessly brought together, and of no special value, and it was not until 1850, when the first building was erected, that it began to claim attention. At that time Congress commenced to make annual appropriations for it, and it was enriched by having placed in it the extensive and valuable botanical collections brought to Washington by the Wilkes Exploring Expedition from southern climes. Nothing now remains of these collections save a Jujube tree. During the past twenty years the rarest and most beautiful plants have been gathered from all parts of the world, and the national garden is at present the equal in many respects of the famous gardens of Europe. Within the enclosure of ten acres are small houses for the growing of plants, and a grand central conservatory three hundred feet in length, with a huge dome — a veritable palace of glass and iron, with large transept halls and octagonal pavilions, filled with the choicest floral productions. It rivals the great conservatory in the Royal Kew Garden in London, or that on the Chatsworth estate of the Duke of Devon-

STATUARY HALL.

shire, and in its architectural design and proportions it is finer than either. In the avenues of the garden is an extensive scientific collection of trees, consisting of the best American and foreign varieties, and everywhere about the grounds the most valued flowers and shrubs are cultivated. North of the main conservatory is the celebrated Bartholdi fountain, which was exhibited at the Philadelphia Centennial.

Visitors throng the garden in winter as well as summer, and it is regarded as one of the attractions of Washington. It is often jocosely called the "bouquet garden" for congressmen. During the annual session of Congress as many as two thousand bouquets are sent from it to the wives and fair friends of the statesmen, and when the session is finished, each congressman is entitled to take to his home one large box of choice plants, which privilege is seldom neglected, particularly as the government pays the cost of transporting the "botanical specimens" anywhere throughout the United States. The garden is under the control of the Library Committee of Congress, and a liberal appropriation is annually made for it. Its superintendent receives a salary of $1,800, and the employés are paid nearly $10,000 per year.

Up to the present time, good judges have estimated, the Capitol has had expended upon it not much less than fifty millions of dollars. Its works of art and the interior decorations and improvements have cost millions, and an enormous amount of money has been expended upon the laying out and ornamentation of the grounds. The annual cost of caring for the Capitol is very large. Even to light it and the grounds requires the yearly expenditure of $25,000; and the yearly compensation of its engineers, firemen, laborers, and other employés will aggregate nearly one hundred thousand dollars. The special Capitol police are paid $36.600 per year. There are thirty policemen, commanded by a captain and three lieutenants. They preserve order, protect the public property, and give information to visitors. The architect of the Capitol receives a salary of $4.500, and his office is provided with several well-paid employés. The building is open daily from 9 A. M. until 5 P. M., and in the evening whenever Congress has a night-session. Then the lantern on the dome is lighted, and the light can be seen from every part of Washington, shining like a great brilliant star in the heavens.

A visit to the Capitol is not complete without ascending the dome and taking the wonderful and charming view from the top of this mighty iron globe. It is a toilsome ascent, and when the balustrade above the peristyle is reached, many people are content to stop at this point, where the view is exceedingly beautiful. But here the dome only really begins, and those who persevere in the ascent, and finally arrive at the summit just below the lantern on which the figure of liberty rests, will be amply repaid for all their toil. Here is a circular landing with a strong balustrade, from which can be viewed at an elevation of about three hundred feet, the city of Washington, the Potomac River, and the hills and valleys of the District of Columbia and the states of Maryland and Virginia for many miles. No words can express the grandeur of this scene. The city is sharply outlined on all sides, each prominent building standing out in high relief. Murmurs of its busy life come faintly to the ear, but on its broad streets, filled with innumerable moving things, no motion is apparent. You know that thousands of changes are being made each moment, but you cannot perceive the slightest movement anywhere, although you can look from end to end of the thoroughfares. To the west, beyond the city, the hills of Georgetown and of Arlington rise blue and misty, with fields beyond fields spreading out to meet the sky. Along the Virginia shore the silver thread of the Potomac can be seen stretching far to the southward in sparkling loveliness, till it is hidden by jutting banks. The green plateau of the Soldiers' Home stands out boldly to the northward, and seemingly within easy distance is Howard University, on the brow of its high hill. Fertile plains, rising into wooded heights, are to the east and south, and directly downward are the streets and buildings of Capitol Hill, the ships of war in the Navy Yard, and the waters of the Anacostia. It is a sight long to be treasured in the memory, and ever recalled with delight.

From the dome one is enabled to obtain a better realization of the solidity of the Capitol than from the ground below. The massive edifice, composed of marble, sandstone, and iron, is spread out directly to the eye, and its huge proportions are clearly revealed in all their strength and grand symmetry. One can see that faithful, honest work has been done in constructing this greatest and most beautiful of American edifices — work that will certainly bear the test of time. Every part of the Capitol has a very substantial appearance, and looking at it from the elevation afforded by the great iron sphere, no one can fail to be impressed with its solidity. Around the " tholus " or lantern of the dome are placed numerous electric lights, which have a greater elevation than any similar lights in the country. They illuminate the dome at night in a magnificent manner. A large electric light, with a strong reflector, is placed at the base of the dome on the western side, and this light each evening casts its powerful rays far up Pennsylvania Avenue.

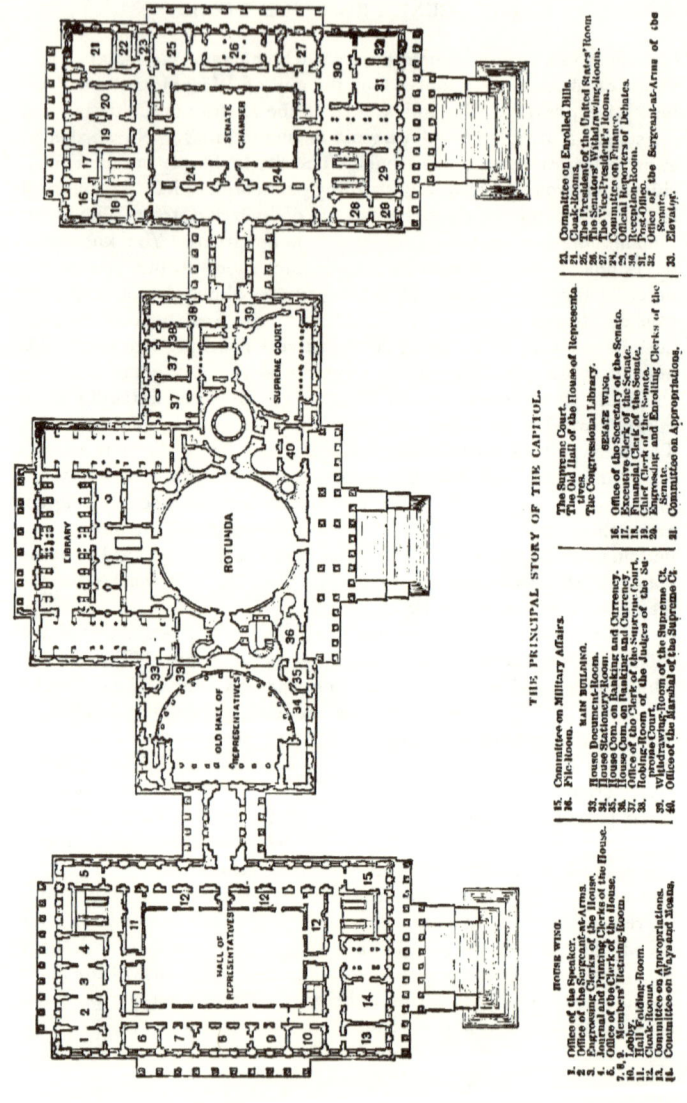

THE PRINCIPAL STORY OF THE CAPITOL.

HOUSE WING.

1. Office of the Speaker.
2. Office of the Sergeant-at-Arms.
3. Engrossing Clerks of the House.
4. Journal and Printing Clerks of the House.
5. Office of the Clerk of the House.
6. Member Retiring-Room.
7, 8, 9.
10. Lobby.
11. Cloak-Room.
12. Cloak-Room.
13. Committee on Appropriations.
14. Committee on Ways and Means.

15. Committee on Military Affairs.
16. File-Room. MAIN BUILDING.

33. House Document-Room.
34. House Stationery-Room.
35. House Com. on Banking and Currency.
36. House Com. on Banking and Currency.
37. Office of the Clerk of the Supreme Court.
38. Robing-Room of the Justices of the Supreme Court.
39. Withdrawing-Room of the Supreme Ct.
40. Office of the Marshal of the Supreme Ct.

The Supreme Court.
The Old Hall of the House of Representatives.
The Congressional Library.

SENATE WING.

16. Office of the Secretary of the Senate.
17. Executive Clerk of the Senate.
18. Financial Clerk of the Senate.
19. Chief Clerk of the Senate.
20. Engrossing and Enrolling Clerks of the Senate.
21. Committee on Appropriations.

22. Committee on Enrolled Bills.
23. Cloak-Room.
24. The President of the United States' Room.
25. The Senators' Withdrawing-Room.
26. The Vice-President's Room.
27. Committee on Finance.
28. Official Reporters of Debates.
29. Reception-Room.
30. Post-Office.
31. Office of the Sergeant-at-Arms of the Senate.
33. Elevator.

CHAPTER V.

T HE ROTUNDA, which occupies the centre of the interior of the
Capitol, is a grand circular hall, ninety-five feet six inches in
diameter, and three hundred feet in circumference. From the
floor to the canopy over what is called " the eye of the dome,"
it is one hundred and eighty feet three inches in height. Looking
upward, you see at first the thirty-six long windows of the peristyle of
the dome, which admit a flood of light, and then the gigantic iron ribs
and frame of the dome itself, gradually curving to the "open eye,"
which is fifty feet in diameter. The canopy suspended directly overhead appears very small, yet it is an immense sheet of metal and
plaster, covering an area of 4,664 feet, and is two hundred and five
feet four inches in circumference, and sixty-five feet four inches in
diameter. From the base to the top it is over twenty feet.

On this canopy is an allegorical painting by Constantino Brumidi,
designated as "The Apotheosis of Washington." It was executed at
a cost of $39,500, and is a remarkable work in many respects. It
represents Washington seated in majesty, with the Goddess of Liberty
at his right, and Victory at his left hand. Encircling the central
group are thirteen female figures, portraying the thirteen original
states, holding a banner on which is inscribed, " E Pluribus Unum."
Around the border of the canopy are six groups of figures, emblematic of the Fall of Tyranny, Agriculture, Mechanics, Commerce, the

Marine, and the Arts and Sciences. Each figure is of great size, and most carefully finished. The artistic merit of this painting cannot, of course, be appreciated from the floor, but when one ascends the dome and inspects the canopy from the gallery directly under it, the massive figures, the glowing colors, and the exceeding beauty of the design can be seen to advantage. From the gallery a downward view of the Rotunda can be obtained, almost startling in its effect. The height and extent of the grand hall will be better realized from this position than from the floor below. The canopy is a perfect "whispering gallery," fully equal to that in St. Paul's, in London. Persons conversing from opposite sides of the gallery over which the canopy hangs, can distinctly hear the slightest whisper across the huge concave.

Eight oil paintings, each eighteen by twelve feet, are set in panels round the walls of the Rotunda. The first of the series depicts the "Landing of Columbus at San Salvador," and was painted by John Vanderlyn at a cost of $10,000. Then follow "De Soto's Discovery of the Mississippi," painted by William H. Powell at a cost of $12,000; "The Baptism of Pocahontas," by John G. Chapman, and "The Embarkation of the Pilgrims from Delft-Haven," by Robert W. Wier, each costing $10,000.

The four other paintings are by Col. John Trumbull, a son of Gov. Jonathan Trumbull, of Connecticut, and an aide-de-camp to General Washington during the Revolutionary War. They faithfully represent important scenes of the struggle for American independence. Trumbull studied art in Europe after leaving the army, and was engaged for nearly thirty years in gathering material and executing the paintings. Washington gave him several sittings, attired in full uniform as Commander-in-Chief of the Continental Army, and many other distinguished persons represented in the series were painted from life. The paintings were finished in 1824, Trumbull receiving $32,000 for them.

The first painting of the Trumbull series is a representation of the "Signing of the Declaration of Independence, July 4th, 1776." This contains life-size figures of the signers, each face being regarded as a correct likeness. John Hancock is represented sitting at a table on which rests the Declaration, and standing near him are Jefferson, Adams, Franklin, Sherman, and Livingston, the committee who had reported the draft of the instrument. Disposed in chairs about the room are the members of the Continental Congress.

The second painting depicts the "Surrender of General Burgoyne, Saratoga, October 17th, 1777." General Gates is represented surrounded by his officers, receiving the defeated British general and his staff. General Burgoyne tenders his sword, but General Gates declines to take it, and instead invites him and his companions to enter his tent and partake of refreshments.

The third of the series represents the "Surrender of Lord Cornwallis at Yorktown, October 19th, 1781." It shows the principal British officers passing before the American and French generals, and the troops drawn up in line. It is a spirited delineation, and the canvas seems to reflect the glory of the great triumph.

The "Resignation of General Washington at Annapolis, December 23d, 1783," is the subject of the fourth picture. Washington is portrayed as he appeared before Congress to resign his commission as Commander-in-Chief of the Continental Army. Many figures are introduced, and Mrs. Washington and her grandchildren are represented among the spectators. This painting fitly closes a series distinguished for exquisite coloring, accuracy and faithfulness of historical details, and strong effects.

Above the paintings are arabesque designs executed in low relief, and panels containing medallion heads of Columbus, Sir Walter Raleigh, Cabot, and La Salle. Over the four entrance doors of the Rotunda, in oblong panels, are *alto relievos* cut in stone, representing "Penn's Treaty with the Indians," by Gevelot; "The Landing of the Pilgrims," and a "Conflict between Daniel Boone and the Indians," by Causici, a pupil of Canova; and "The Preservation of Captain John Smith by Pocahontas," by Capellano. The *relievos* cost $14,000, and the arabesque designs and heads, $9,500.

Within the sunken space about nine feet wide which encircles the Rotunda above the architrave, is a series of frescos in light and shade illustrating the principal epochs of American history. The work was begun by Brumidi, and after his death was continued by Castigini. Each fresco is broad in its effect and of sufficient size to be clearly seen from the floor.

The Rotunda has a freestone floor which is supported by brick arches resting upon peristyles of forty Doric columns. These columns form the subterranean chamber called the Crypt, in which it was proposed to place the body of Washington when the Rotunda was originally designed. The plan was to have a galleried opening in the centre of the floor through which the sarcophagus could be seen. Mrs.

Washington consented to the proposition, but after her death Washington's heirs decided that by the terms of his will the body must remain at Mount Vernon. Henry Clay, Daniel Webster, John Quincy Adams, and other distinguished men endeavored for a long time to secure the removal of the body to the Crypt, but as the Washington family were firm in refusal, the project was abandoned in 1832. When the Crypt was first constructed, Congress appointed a keeper of it, and ordered a light to be kept burning continuously within it. This light was not extinguished for over fifty years, and it was not until after the Civil War that the office of "Keeper of the Crypt" was abolished.

THE NATIONAL STATUARY HALL is entered at the south door from the Rotunda. This beautiful hall was occupied by the House of Representatives until the new legislative hall, in the House extension, was completed. It is ninety-five feet long, and sixty feet high to the top of its magnificently painted dome. It has a colonnade of twenty-six massive columns and pilasters of the variegated Potomac marble called "breccia," and a wide, sweeping arch. It was designed by Latrobe to resemble the ancient Greek theatres, and for its ornamentation he secured the services of a number of prominent Italian artists, among whom were the Franzoni brothers, and Valperti and Causici. After the British troops had partially burned the hall, Latrobe reconstructed it in finer proportions, adding the marble columns and works of art. It was declared "so perfect and so grand" that a writer early in the century quaintly said, "Its defects of construction with reference to acoustics, is a happy circumstance for the worthy fellowship of fault-finders, who would otherwise have to hang themselves from the galleries in despair." The congressmen who used it found it was a badly constructed hall for public speaking, as it had very provoking echoes, and at certain points "a whisper scarcely audible to the ear into which it was breathed, would resound over the entire hall." But with all its bad acoustic properties, many of the most eloquent and effective speeches ever heard in the halls of Congress have been delivered in this old legislative chamber, by renowned statesmen, whose names will live forever in the annals of the Republic.

Under the arch near the dome is a large plaster figure of Liberty, by Causici, and beneath it is the American eagle with outspread wings, sculptured in stone by Valperti. Over the main entrance is a marble statue of History recording the events of the Nation, while rolling over the globe in a winged car, the wheel of which serves as a clock. This

THE CAPITOL — WEST FRONT.

was executed by Carlo Franzoni, and is known as "Franzoni's Historical Clock."

When the House of Representatives removed to its new hall it was suggested by Senator Morrill, of Vermont, then a member of the House, that the old hall should be taken for a National Gallery of Statuary, and that "each state should be permitted to send the effigies of two of her chosen sons, in marble or in bronze, to be placed permanently here." The suggestion was adopted, and the states were invited to send contributions of statues.

The first to respond to the invitation was the State of Rhode Island, which contributed a statue of Roger Williams, her "great Apostle of Religious Freedom," and a statue of Gen. Nathanael Greene, a distinguished soldier of the Revolutionary War. Connecticut followed with statues of Gov. Jonathan Trumbull, the last colonial governor of the State, to whom Washington familiarly applied the sobriquet of "Brother Jonathan"; and Roger Sherman, one of the signers of the Declaration of Independence. New York sent statues of George Clinton, Vice-President of the United States in 1804; and Robert R. Livingston, who, as Chancellor of the State of New York, administered the oath of office to President Washington. Massachusetts contributed statues of Gov. John Winthrop, of colonial fame, and Samuel Adams, who was called "The Father of the Revolution." Vermont is represented by statues of Col. Ethan Allen and Jacob Collamer; Maine by a statue of Gov. William King, her first governor; and Pennsylvania by a statue of Robert Fulton and Muhlenberg, the heroic Revolutionary Minister; Ohio by a statue of Garfield, and one of Governor Allen. Doubtless before many years all the states will be represented in this silent assembly of "chosen sons."

The statues are regarded as fine works of art, and as highly creditable to the states which have placed them in the care of the Nation. They are supplemented by statuary and portraits purchased by the government. Prominent in the collection is a plaster copy of Houdon's famous statue of Washington, carefully taken from the original in Richmond, Va. Here also is Mrs. Vinnie Ream Hoxie's statue of Lincoln.

THE SUPREME COURT of the United States has occupied the old Senate Chamber, north of the Rotunda, since December, 1860. Previous to that time it held its sessions in what is now the Law Library, in the basement story of the Capitol. From the second Monday in

October until the first week in May in each year, with short intermissions, the court sits to hear cases on appeal, and to decide constitutional questions. The court consists of a Chief Justice, with a salary of $10,500 per year, and eight Associate Justices with salaries of $10,000. The justices are appointed by the President, and " hold their offices during good behavior." The court officials include a clerk and deputy clerk, a marshal, and a reporter. During a portion of the year the justices act as circuit justices in the nine judicial circuits of the United States, each justice being assigned to a particular circuit, in which he receives the assistance of the specially appointed circuit and district justices. The Federal courts have jurisdiction of all constitutional questions, and of all offences against the laws of the United States not within the jurisdiction of the state courts.

The chamber of the Supreme Court was the first portion of the Capitol that was finished, and in 1800 it was occupied by the Senate. It was reconstructed by Latrobe after the British invasion, and until the winter of 1859, when the Senators left the familiar, classic chamber for their new hall, " all gold and buff," it was the place where some of the most important contests in the history of American legislation occurred. The chamber is semi-circular in form, and of pure Grecian design. The ceiling is part of a low dome, the greatest elevation being forty-five feet. The greatest width of the floor is seventy-five feet. Ionic columns of Potomac marble, with white marble capitals, form a screen at the back of the long judicial bench, and around the walls are marble pilasters, and marble busts of deceased Chief Justices. There is a small gallery over the bench, with windows through which the daylight streams. The justices sit with their backs to a large crimson curtain, and in front of them is a curtained bar with a railing. In the central area are mahogany chairs and tables for the use of lawyers and others having business with the honorable court. Outside of the area are rows of comfortable seats, cushioned in red velvet, for spectators. The chamber is a very beautiful example of classical symmetry.

Promptly at noon of each day that the court is in session the crier requests all persons in the chamber to rise, and then announces in measured, solemn tone, "The Honorable Chief Justice and the Associate Justices of the Supreme Court of the United States." Nine dignified gentlemen, attired in long silken robes, march in from the "withdrawing-room," and take their places upon the bench with the Chief Justice in the centre. They bow all together very courteously to the members of the bar, who return the polite salutation, and then seat themselves in their wide, comfortable chairs. The crier then opens the session in the usual form: "Oyes! Oyes! Oyes! All persons having business with the honorable the Supreme Court of the United States are admonished to draw near and give their attention, as the court is now sitting. God save the United States and this honorable court."

Usually the decisions of the court are read by one of the justices at the beginning of the day's session. Until four o'clock in the afternoon the business continues without intermission. The chamber is free from disturbing noise. Cases are argued by the lawyers in a low, conversational tone, save when some legal luminary from the backwoods, sent to Washington by admiring clients, tries to make an impression on the court by means of artful tricks and mannerisms successful with a jury, and declaims at the top of his voice, strides back and forth, and sets out the merits of his cause with emotional and gymnastic effect. But usually the counsel who appear before this high tribunal are gentlemen of skill and discrimination, who know that solid arguments, stated quietly and easily, are all that is necessary here. The thick carpet on the floor entirely prevents the sound of footfalls as people come and go, and a high screen hides the entrance door from the view of the bench and the bar. Gray-haired colored attendants guard the door, and inform visitors in a whisper where to sit. And so all the afternoon the legal stream flows along as placidly as the waters of the Potomac. The chamber gives you a drowsy feeling. You listen to the "lawyers with their endless tongues," and in following the droning arguments soon feel so inclined to sleep that you wonder how the honorable justices manage to keep their eyes open during the four hours of the sitting. Indeed, members of the court have said that the room was so "full of repose" that they often had to struggle to keep from sleeping while a dull argument was going on.

Some of the justices sit very quiet and appear to pay a great deal of attention to the lawyers. Others are nervous and uneasy, and twist about in their chairs constantly. One justice has the habit of getting up and standing behind his chair to rest himself. They turn over the pages of the briefs, consult books brought to them by attendants, and now and then put pertinent questions to the counsel. Sometimes a justice, by a few keen remarks, will show the matter under consideration in such a clear light, that the lawyer who is trying to muddle it will

CHAMBER OF THE SUPREME COURT OF THE UNITED STATES.

become quite embarrassed, and abruptly close his argument. The justices are complaisant in manner, and there is no stiffness, no assumption of superiority, often seen in very ordinary tribunals. They
address the lawyers pleasantly, and are patient in hearing even the
most tiresome discussion. The two senior justices sit at the right and
left of the Chief Justice, and the others are disposed on the bench in
the order of their appointment. In their consultation-room the same
order is observed at the table around which they sit.

The black silk robes worn by the justices are nearly like those
used by clergymen of the Episcopal church. They reach to the feet,
and have capacious sleeves. Before entering the court chamber the
justices are dressed in their "sheeny gowns," in the robing-room, by
colored attendants. In the first part of the century it was customary
for the members of the court to wear wigs, and to cover their nether
limbs with small-clothes. Lawyers were expected to appear in court
in full suits of black, with ruffled shirts, small-clothes, silk hose, and
low shoes with silver buckles. It is the court custom now for lawyers
to wear black and a frock coat, but occasionally a "business suit"
will be seen.

There was a great deal of formal ceremony in the court some years
ago, most of it, doubtless, taken from the English courts, but it has
been gradually abandoned, and now very little is left. The early
justices were treated with high respect, not unmingled with a certain
amount of awe, and members of the bar seldom attempted to be familiar with them either on or off the bench, unless they were in intimate
social relations. It is related of Henry Clay, who was noted for
suavity, that he stopped one day when arguing a case before the court,
and advancing to the bench in graceful manner, took a pinch of snuff
from the box of a justice, saying, "I perceive that your honor sticks
to the Scotch," and then resumed his argument. This excited much
astonishment at the time, and Justice Story said, "I do not believe
there is a man in the United States who could have done that but Mr.
Clay."

The first Chief Justice was John Jay, of New York, who was ap-
pointed when the court was organized, in 1789, and served until 1795.
A portrait of him, painted by Gilbert Stuart, hangs in the robing-room.
Following Jay were John Rutledge, of South Carolina, and Oliver
Ellsworth, of Connecticut. Then John Marshall, of Virginia, became
Chief Justice in 1801, and remained on the bench for thirty-four years.

Chief Justice Marshall has been placed in the front rank of American magistrates for profound learning, inflexible honesty, and a rare genius for logical argument. He was called "the great Chief Justice." He was dignified, but very kind in manner. He was tall and ungainly, and noted for wearing very shabby clothes. In the coldest weather he never wore an overcoat, and was often seen on winter days walking at a rapid pace through the streets of Washington, clad only in his rusty, thin black suit. He was very fond of society, was exceedingly hospitable, and frankly acknowledged he enjoyed the pleasures of the table. He took infinite delight in playing billiards and quoits, and even when over seventy-five years old was always ready, in his leisure moments, to play these games, and whenever he scored good points he would shout with childish glee. In addition to his severe labors as Chief Justice, he found time to write a very excellent life of Washington.

During his time one of the associate justices was Bushrod Washington, a nephew of President Washington. He was on the bench for thirty-one years, and achieved a fine reputation as a learned and industrious magistrate. He was a small, thin man, of rather insignificant appearance. Severe study had deprived him of the use of one eye, but it was commonly remarked that "he could see more with one eye" than most men with two. He had a great fondness for Virginia tobacco, and was continually smoking or taking snuff. He was never known to become tired at the most protracted sittings of the court, and once greatly astonished the people of a town where he was holding a circuit court by having a continuous session for sixteen hours.

The early justices were not allotted to certain circuits, as they are now, but each in turn traveled over the entire country, often meeting with very interesting adventures. Justice Wilson always made the grand tour in a huge lumbering coach and four, with dashing outriders; Justice Todd, in one year, rode over two thousand miles on horseback in performing his judicial duty. Some of the justices traveled in open phaetons with two horses.

From 1835 to the present time there have been four Chief Justices — Roger B. Taney, Salmon P. Chase, Morrison R. Waite, and Melville W. Fuller. Taney served twenty-eight years, Chase a little less than ten years, and Chief Justice Waite served fourteen years. The present Chief Justice is Melville W. Fuller, appointed in 1888. There have been forty-four associate justices. Justice Joseph Story was a member of the court for thirty-four years, and quite a number of the justices served more than twenty years. By the law of 1869 a justice may retire with full salary when seventy years old, if he has given ten years of service.

The docket of the court is always crowded with cases, most of them involving questions of great importance, and suitors are compelled to wait generally for two or three years, and sometimes longer, before they can have a hearing. Not more than four or five hundred cases can be disposed of in a year, and as there are usually over one thousand cases on the docket at each term, the unavoidable "law's delay" is very trying to the patience and the purses of litigants. Several plans of relief have been proposed, but as yet Congress has considered none of them.

The official etiquette of Washington requires that the Chief Justice and the associate justices shall pay an official visit to the President and to the Vice-President annually, on the day of the opening of the court session. They are also required to call on the President on the first day of January. During the winter the President entertains the court at a ceremonious dinner.

A VISIT to the Library of Congress, or, as it is frequently and perhaps more properly called, the National Library, will enable one to better realize King Solomon's saying — "Of making many books there is no end." In the beautifully decorated library halls, occupying the entire central portion of the western front of the Capitol, there are 580,000 books and 180,000 pamphlets. They are in many languages — a vast store of literature, representing the researches and product of the mind in every conceivable field of human knowledge. The library is now one of the five great libraries of the world, and at its present rate of increase will number a million books and pamphlets in about ten years. The halls are crowded to repletion with publications — books in every available space; closely packed two deep on the shelves which extend tier after tier through the storied rooms; lying in great heaps on the floors; loading the railings of the galleries — half a million volumes crammed into quarters originally designed for less than half that number. An appropriation act has been passed to construct a large building adjacent to the Capitol, to cost about $3,000,000, for the use of this inestimable National Library. This new library edifice will be located at the junction of East Capitol and First streets, directly opposite the House of Representatives, and fronting the Eastern Capitol Park. It will measure 460 feet front by 310 feet in depth, and will cover about

three and a half acres, being designed to store about three million volumes. On the second floor an art gallery will be provided, 300 feet long by 35 wide, for the arrangement and exhibition of the extensive collection of works of graphic art which

THE NATIONAL LIBRARY.

the National Library has accumulated.

The western door of the Rotunda leads to the main hall of the library. This hall is 91 feet long, 34 feet wide, and 38 feet high. It is flanked by two others, each about the same size as the main one. They are lighted by windows and crystal roofs, are constructed of iron, with floors of marble, and are entirely fire proof. They are painted in light, delicate colors, and adorned with gold-leaf, and present an elegant appearance. The book-cases are of iron, and iron railings protect the alcoves. Small galleries extend along the stories. It is estimated that the halls contain nearly five miles of book shelving, yet the library increases yearly at such an enormous rate, that these miles of shelving have long since proved insufficient to hold the literary collections. In the main hall is the desk of the librarian, at which all applications for books must be made. Tables and chairs are placed in two of the halls for readers, and one hall is used almost entirely by the employés engaged in cataloguing publications and attending to the copyright business.

The library force consists of a librarian, whose title is the " Librarian of Congress," and twenty-three assistant librarians. The compensation of the librarian is $4,000 per year, and the assistants receive $32,640 in all. Congress annually appropriates about $12,-000 for the purchase of books of reference not published in the United States, files of newspapers, etc. Only members of Congress, and about forty high officials of the government, have the right to take books away from the library, but all persons over sixteen years of age have the privilege of freely using the collections inside the halls. This great privilege is taken advantage of by thousands of people from all portions of the United States, who desire to investigate certain subjects, and every day the halls contain several hundred readers.

In some cases a person seeking the widest information of a special matter can have spread before him, within a short time, many books and pamphlets bearing on the subject, which have come from American, English, French, and German presses for over a century — pages dim and yellow with age, or bright and fresh from the publisher's hands. The collections are rich in ancient and rare historical works, in books and pamphlets pertaining to the history of states, counties, and towns, and the files of American and foreign newspapers and magazines are very extensive. There are files of the principal newspapers printed in New England, New York, Pennsylvania, Maryland, Virginia, and other states, from 1735 to 1800; and from the latter date to the present time the collections of newspapers and periodicals are unrivaled. Among very rare works are two great volumes written on vellum, issued in the thirteenth century, a copy of Eliot's Indian Bible, and the various volumes written by Cotton and Increase Mather. The departments of miscellaneous literature are very full. Many an old novel, forgotten long ago; many a poem, many a song or play, dead and buried for two or three score years, can be exhumed from this vast literary storehouse. The aim always has been to collect *everything* published in the United States that could be obtained, and as much of foreign literature as possible, in order that the library should be complete in the full meaning of the term.

By law the Librarian of Congress has charge of the copyright business, and all applications for copyrights of books, maps, dramatic or musical compositions, and works of art, have to be made to him. Copyrights are granted for twenty-eight years, and then may be renewed for fourteen years. Some figures of the copyright business may be interesting, as they show the great mental activity of the people of the United States. During the year 1886 there were granted 31,241 copyrights, and the government received in fees the sum of $25,421. Of the articles copyrighted there were 11,136 books, 6,089 periodicals, 7,514 musical, and 672 dramatic compositions. Two complete copies of each publication copyrighted must be deposited in the Library of Congress to perfect the copyright. Thus the library is enabled to possess copies of all printed matter issued in the country on which a copyright is granted.

The library exchanges many of its spare copies of publications with the libraries of foreign governments, obtaining much valuable foreign literature in this way. All the publications and exchanges of the Smithsonian Institution are deposited here. Many donations of books are received from institutions and individuals all over the world, and purchases of thousands of volumes are made. Whenever a famous private library is sold, bids from this library are generally forwarded, and many rare books are purchased.

In 1800 Congress established this literary treasure-house with a number of books obtained from London. This was the list: " 212 folios, 164 quartos, 581 octavos, 7 duodecimos, and 9 magazines. It was the only library of reference the government then possessed. In 1814 the collection had increased to about 3,000 volumes, which went to feed the fires started by the British troops in the Capitol. The next year Congress purchased President Jefferson's private collection of about 7,000 books, considered the finest in the country at that time, for $23,950, and this was the nucleus of the present Library of Congress. In 1851 there were 55,000 volumes on hand, but in December of that year nearly 35,000 were destroyed by a fire in the library hall. The fire also consumed a number of valuable paintings, including Gilbert Stuart's portraits of the first five Presidents. The main hall was soon restored in fire-proof, after designs by Walter, and the two iron extensions added, the work costing $280,500. Congress yearly appropriated large sums of money for the purchase of books. Through the efforts of ex-President Hayes, then a member of Congress, and chairman of the Committee on the Library, the invaluable historical collections belonging to Peter Force, of Wash-

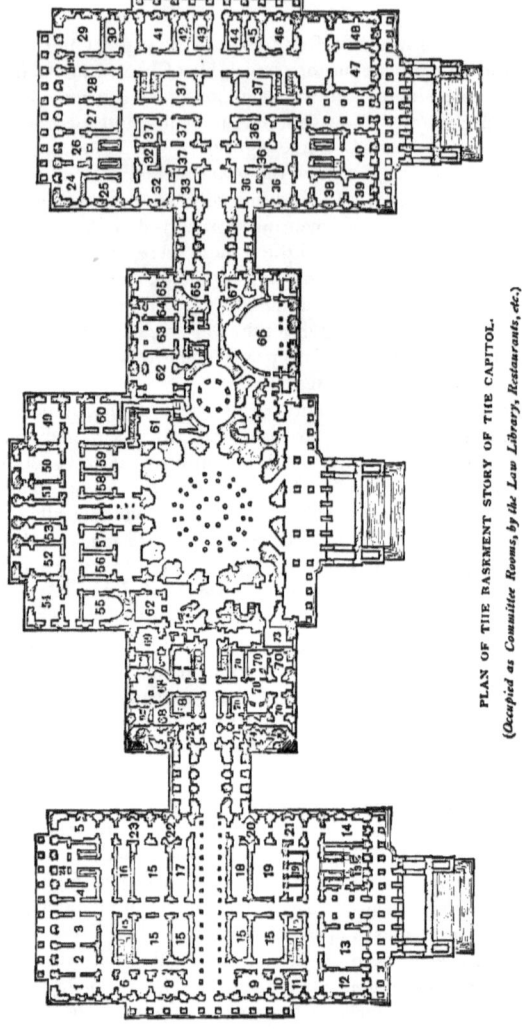

PLAN OF THE BASEMENT STORY OF THE CAPITOL.

(Occupied as Committee Rooms, by the Law Library, Restaurants, etc.)

ington, were purchased for $100,000, and deposited in the library. These collections of books, pamphlets, prints, etc., pertaining to early American history, are of inestimable value. They were accumulated during many years of earnest and enthusiastic antiquarian labor. In 1866 the library of the Smithsonian Institution was added to the Library of Congress.

The law department contains nearly 70,000 volumes, and is considered very complete. Every volume of American, English, Irish, and Scotch court reports is to be found here, together with the statutes of all countries, from 1649 to the present time. From 2,500 to 3,500 volumes are added yearly.

This collection of works relating to jurisprudence, which is the largest and most valuable in the country, is contained in the basement story of the Capitol, in what was formerly the chamber of the Supreme Court of the United States. The chamber is directly underneath the present court chamber, and is a notable example of classical architecture. It was designed and constructed by Latrobe, and was occupied for court purposes from the early part of the century until the winter of 1860. In the vestibule Latrobe placed his celebrated "cornstalk columns" with capitals of ears of corn, which have been described as the "American order of architecture."

There have been many important suits at law heard in the old chamber—suits concerning the disposition of vast properties, and the settlement of complicated questions of rights and privileges, every step of which has been earnestly contested by lawyers of rare ability and great distinction. Clay and Webster, and numerous other advocates of eminence in the history of American jurisprudence, have pleaded here with eloquent tongues and strong arguments—bright lights of the age that has gone. Here the renowned Chief Justice, John Marshall, of Virginia, whose effigy in bronze now adorns the western grounds of the Capitol, presided for many years, and here most of his decisions upon vital constitutional questions were given—decisions which have remained to this day as the law of the land. Here the early justices—men of sound and extensive learning—served long terms. The old chamber, now crowded with volumes of law, is indeed an historic place.

The law library is extensively used by lawyers every day, and is also of great service to the justices of the Supreme and District courts in preparing their decisions. Many members of the legal profession from distant parts of the country frequently visit Washington to consult its rare volumes.

THE SENATE CHAMBER.

CHAPTER VI.

THE First Congress of the United States, under the Constitution, began its session in New York on the 4th of March,
1789. In 1790 Congress removed to Philadelphia, and for
ten years thereafter held its sessions in that city. On November 17, 1800, the Sixth Congress convened in Washington in the
unfinished Capitol, and on the 22d of that month President John
Adams appeared before both houses, in joint session in the Senate
Chamber, and made the customary "annual speech." Vice-President Thomas Jefferson presided over the Senate, and the Hon.
Theodore Sedgwick, of Massachusetts, was the Speaker of the House
of Representatives.

When Congress began its sessions in Washington, only the north
wing of the Capitol was finished, and that was badly constructed.
The Senate Chamber was mostly of wood and plaster, and was not
completed in its present substantial, symmetrical manner until after
Latrobe had reconstructed the building in 1815–17. The House of
Representatives at first was crowded into a room intended for the
Senate officials, but a temporary apartment was soon arranged for it
in the south wing of the Capitol. This apartment was facetiously
called "the oven," and was used until 1804, when the House removed
to another apartment and remained there until it took possession in
1808 of its beautiful, classic hall. When the Capitol rose stately

and capacious after the British conflagration, both Houses of Congress were amply accommodated in fine halls.

Many exciting and important parliamentary battles took place in these old halls of legislation. The momentous political questions of the times — the United States Bank, the Missouri Compromise, the protective tariff, the Mexican War, the annexation of Texas, nullification, the fugitive slave bill, and other issues as grave and significant — were debated by Congress, often with fierce wrangles which aroused high excitement and wrath. There was malevolent sectional feeling, and the harmony of the country was frequently disturbed. Indeed it continually required the greatest efforts of the wisest men to preserve the union of the states, and it was then that the grand statesmen and orators — the glory of American legislation — were developed, and they held the Ship of State firmly and steadily on its course.

The Senate for a time sat with closed doors, after the manner of the Continental Congress, but as there was decided objection to this secrecy, the chamber was opened to the public, except during executive sessions. The House of Representatives always transacted its business openly. In the early sessions the Senators discussed the matters before them in a colloquial way, and set speeches were rarely made; but in the House there was considerable formal speaking. Many of the early congressmen wore powdered wigs, and retained the European fashions in dress which had been in vogue in 1700. Their wigs were curled and powdered every day with great care, and the barber was an important individual.

It was thought necessary for the Speaker of the House to have a symbol of authority, and the sergeant-at-arms was directed to procure the mace, which is "a bundle of ebony rods, fastened with silver bands, having at its top a silver globe surmounted by a silver eagle." When the mace was placed on the Speaker's table it signified that the House was in session and under the authority of the Speaker; when it was placed under the table, that the House was in committee of the whole. The sergeant-at-arms was required to bear aloft this glittering mace when executing the commands of the Speaker, and in many of the sessions in the old hall he was often compelled to brandish it in the flushed faces of angry debaters, and bid them to "be still." An attempt was made to abolish the mace, but it was vigorously resisted, and failed, and the time-honored symbol is placed to-day at the Speaker's right hand whenever the House is sitting.

For some years there was an official pen-maker in each house, whose duty it was to mend the goose-quills commonly used. Many of the congressmen were exceedingly particular as to the " degree of flexibility and breadth of point" of their quills, and while some would use nothing but " broad nibs," others required the finest of " fine points," and the pen-makers had no easy task in trying to suit the different writers. There were also official sealers, who were entrusted with the sealing of letters and packages with red wax. The " stationery" used in both houses included pen-knives, scissors, razors, pocket-books, kid gloves, bottles of perfumery and bear's grease, and numerous other little articles which the officials would purchase " by request" whenever they went to New York to get their supplies. For a number of sessions " an innocent beverage called swichell, composed of molasses, ginger, and water," was largely consumed by the Representatives, and it was popularly supposed that among its " innocent" ingredients were good French brandy and Jamaica rum. It was always charged in the appropriation for stationery under the head of " syrup."

Previous to 1816 the compensation of members of Congress was six dollars per day, and when a bill was passed in that year to raise the compensation to $1,500 a session, a sum barely sufficient to pay the expenses of a decent living in Washington, it aroused great excitement throughout the country. In an ancient record it is stated that "the whole nation was shaken to its centre ; parties were formed and political armies marshaled, and the patriotism of the country was aroused to ebullient indignation at the bare proposition that a member of Congress should dare to take thought for what he should eat and drink, or wherewithal he should be clothed, and the liberties of the country where menaced with destruction when Congress ventured to demand the necessaries of life in payment of its thankless services." So great was the feeling that Congress, at its next session, repealed the obnoxious bill, and made the compensation eight dollars per day.

It was customary for the Representatives to wear their hats in the House during the sessions, and it was not until 1828 that the practice was discontinued. Ladies were excluded from the galleries for a time, but at last, after some discussion of the " momentous question," they were admitted, and even had seats reserved for them. As many congressmen were inveterate snuff-takers, urns filled with " old Scotch" were placed in each house, and officials were charged with the duty of keeping them filled. Even to this day, in the Senate Chamber there is a large box containing choice snuff, which is freely used by the " most potent, grave, and reverend" Senators.

Duelling was quite common in the early days of Washington, and the Western and Southern congressmen usually had a case of duelling pistols as an important part of their outfit.   In the museum of the Patent-Office there is a case of pistols owned by Andrew Jackson while he was in Congress, and the heavy, cruel-looking weapons bear the appearance of having been frequently used.   The "code" was a matter of general conversation, and was carefully studied. Truculent congressmen were prompt to resent insulting words spoken in debate, and occasionally pistols would be drawn in the House during a session.   Then the sergeant-at-arms would seize the mace and hasten to the contestants, hold the official symbol high over their heads, and command them to take their seats under penalty of being arrested for contempt of the House.   Henry Clay and John Randolph once fought a duel.   Randolph was always abusive in his remarks about Clay, and in debate one day referred to him in a very insulting manner.   He declined to apologize for his words, and Clay sent him a challenge.   They fought, but without injury to either.

There were many exciting scenes in the House in those "good old days."   The debates were full of virulence, and the Speaker frequently had to exert his authority to the utmost to check the passionate members.   Those who have looked on the House in these "piping times of peace," when an animated debate was going on — when all over the great legislative hall there was a furious din and babble; members rising much excited and uttering sarcastic and exceedingly impertinent remarks, and apparently confusion worse confounded — can form some idea of how the old House appeared while debating the vexed questions in the turbulent times of the first part of the century, when congressmen had a "code of honor" which necessitated the carrying of pistols, and when there were numerous "crested jay-hawks of the mountains" threatening violence to those who spoke the truth too plainly.

MANY able men gave strength and character to the national legislation for half a century, and made the old halls of Congress memorable.   John Quincy Adams, who enjoys the distinction of being the only son of a President of the United States who has ever occupied the Presidential chair himself, began his congressional career in 1803 as a Senator.   After his term as President he was elected to the House of Representatives in 1831, and became one of its leading members. He was bold, experienced, and learned, but exceedingly frigid in his

THE ROTUNDA.

manner, and was never on terms of familiarity with any member.
The "old man eloquent," as he was styled, was seldom absent from
his seat in the House, and day after day was fully prepared to discuss
every matter that came up. It was his delight to start a stormy debate, and then he would throw off his frigidity, and become very excited. One who knew him well wrote as follows of his manner of
speaking: "He rises abruptly, his face reddens, and in a moment
throwing himself into the attitude of a veteran gladiator, he prepares
for the attack; then he becomes full of gesticulation — his body sways
to and fro — self-command seems lost. His head is bent forward in
his earnestness till it almost touches the desk; his voice frequently
breaks, but he pursues his subject through all its bearings. Nothing
daunts him — the House may ring with the cry of ' Order'; he stands
amid the tempest, and like an oak that knows its gnarled and knotted
strength, stretches his hand forth and defies the blast."

It is related that when he was canvassing his district in Massachusetts for election to the House, his cold, apathetic way of dealing
with influential people often created for him a great deal of unpopu-
larity. On one occasion he was introduced to a farmer of considerable political influence, who cordially shook his hand and said,
"Mr. Adams, I am very glad to see you. My wife, when she was
a girl, lived in your father's family; you were then a little boy, and
she has often combed your head." "Well," replied Mr. Adams in
a harsh tone, "I suppose she combs yours now."

On the 21st of February, 1848, Mr. Adams was stricken with
apoplexy while sitting in his seat in the House. He was removed to
the Speaker's room, and in about an hour regained consciousness for
a few moments. Looking at those around him, he said in a whisper,
"This is the last of earth, but I am content." Then he closed his
eyes and never spoke again. He died on February 23.

John Randolph, the "Lord of Roanoke," as he was generally
called, was a member of the House from Virginia before Congress
began its sessions in Washington. He served until 1825, and then
was a Senator for two years, but afterward returned to the House for
one term. It was his boast that he had descended from Pocahontas.
He was very tall and thin, and had a small, round head and sallow
face. His eyes were black, keen, and expressive, his nose and chin
long and sharp, and his hair, which was brushed back and tied in a
queue, was as black, straight, and coarse as that of the race from
which he claimed descent. On his daily trips to the Capitol he

always rode a fine, high-blooded horse, whose sleek, plump body was in marked contrast to his own leanness. He was usually dressed in a long surtout coat of drab English broadcloth, buckskin knee-breeches and top-boots.

Randolph always attracted great attention in the House, and it is said that "his speeches were reported more fully than any other member of Congress." His powers of sarcasm and invective were remarkable, and as he had "a tongue with a tang," his wrath was avoided as much as possible. He was selfish, exclusive, contemptuous; he had no popular sympathies, and was never known to approve of anything favored by other men. He was full of "quarrel and offence," and spared no one from the copious shower of his epithets. Garland, his biographer, says, "He was like an Ishmaelite, his hand against every man, and every man's hand against him."

In 1806, Henry Clay, the great Kentuckian, began his long career in Congress. He first served in the Senate for one session to fill a vacancy, and again in 1809 he became a Senator for two years. He entered the House of Representatives at a special session on the 4th of November, 1811, and "on the very day he made his first appearance on the floor he was elected Speaker by a vote of 75 out of 128 cast—the only instance on record in which the confidence of Congress has been yielded in so marked a manner to any person on his entrance as a member." He retained the speakership during five Congresses, and was a member of the House for about fourteen years. He was elected to the Senate in 1831, and served until 1842, when he resigned his seat, and retired to private life for seven years. In 1849 he was again elected as Senator. His last speech in the Senate was delivered on the 1st of December, 1851, and on the 29th of June, 1852, he died in the National Hotel in Washington. His large experience in state craft, his preëminent intellectual strength, and his wonderful gift as a popular orator, admirably fitted him to play an important part in the legislative arena. He was of commanding height, and had a pleasant face lighted by sparkling gray eyes. He was courtly in manner, and thoroughly understood the difficult art of being easy at all times and in all places. When he spoke, a winning smile would give effect to his words. Few orators of his day could so enchant an audience, and his speeches in Congress and on the platform were listened to with deep interest, and always made a marked impression. He was the recognized leader of the Whig party, and ruled its affairs with an iron hand.

Clay was sincere and liberal, and ardent in his devotion to the things he considered right and just. He was the champion of the system of protection to American industry, and made many powerful speeches and assiduously labored for it. Sometimes for weeks when he was in the Senate he would take very little part in the proceedings, but would sit quiet in his seat, day after day, eating candy and taking snuff, and jocosely commenting in a low tone on the speeches of others. He relished a good joke, and nothing pleased him better than a bright repartee, even if it was against himself. When he was ready to engage in debate he would spring to his feet and hold his auditors fascinated by his eloquent language and graceful delivery.

Daniel Webster entered the House of Representatives in 1813, as a Representative from New Hampshire, his native state, and served until 1817. About this time he took up his residence in Boston, and thereafter Massachusetts claimed him as her foremost orator and statesman. He was elected to the House in 1823, and to the Senate in 1827. He continued as a Senator until 1841, and then went into President Harrison's Cabinet as Secretary of State, which position he held until May 9, 1843. In 1845 he was again chosen to the Senate, serving until 1850. He had a massive form, and his large, finely developed head was covered with hair " as black as the raven's wing." His face was full of character, and his eyes were deep set, large, and melancholy in expression. He was always carefully dressed, and, as a writer has said, " in the old Whig colors of blue and buff." For years he was a leader in the great debates, and his speeches gave him national fame and influence. Visitors to the Senate Chamber would eagerly watch his movements, and listen to his words with rapt interest. Whenever it was announced that he intended to speak upon any question the crowd to hear him would fill every part of the chamber, and hundreds would be unable to gain admission. His speeches were always prepared with great care, and he would never permit them to be published until he had thoroughly revised them. Many of his eloquent sentences were composed after days and even weeks of study. He had a good deal of humor, which now and then would be displayed in the Senate, although generally he was very dignified while engaged in his legislative duties.

Quite often in his private hours he would be gloomy and despondent about his political career. At one time when he was feeling depressed a friend said to him that he should not feel so, as his fame was made.

THE SENATE RECEPTION-ROOM.

"Fame," replied Mr. Webster; "and
much for fame! Let me give you a striking
illustration of this fact. I was traveling in a railroad car a short time
ago, and it so happened that I was located by the side of a very old
man. I soon found that this old man was from my native town in
New Hampshire. I asked him if he was acquainted with the Webster
family up there. He answered that he and old Mr. Webster, in his
life-time, were great friends. He then went on to speak of the children. He said Ezekiel was the most eminent lawyer in New Hampshire, and his sisters, calling each by her christian name, were married to most excellent men. I then inquired if there was not another
member of the family. He said he thought not. Was there not

one, I asked him, by the name of Daniel? Here the old man put on his thinking-cap for a few moments, and then replied: 'O, I recollect now. There was one by the name of Daniel, but he went down to Boston, and I have not heard of him since.'"

Thomas Hart Benton, of Missouri, entered the Senate in 1821, and served for twenty-nine years and seven months continuously — the longest continuous service ever given. He was not a pleasing speaker, being noted for long, bombastic speeches, delivered in a loud, imperious manner. In debate he was passionate, and would often "launch thunderbolts of hatred, jealousy, and rage" at the heads of those who opposed him. His stalwart body was always attired in a long, double-breasted frock-coat of antique fashion, and as he walked to and fro on the floor of the Senate, he would assume a martial bearing, and his eyes would flash with arrogance. Although a man of marked ability, his displeasing manner and lack of tact and grace in speech prevented him from obtaining popularity.

One of the group of great statesmen was John C. Calhoun, of South Carolina, who began his congressional career in 1811, as a member of the House of Representatives, serving for six years in that body. He was elected Vice-President in 1825, when John Quincy Adams was President, and in 1831 went into the Senate, where he remained for twelve years. He took a leading position, and was fully the peer of the remarkable men who composed the Senate of his day. In 1843 he became Secretary of State, but returned to the Senate in 1845, and served until his death in 1850. He was tall and slender, and had a sombre face, on which a smile was rarely seen. As an orator he was logical and forcible, and in all the prominent debates his voice was often heard. Very ambitious, with his "whole mind and soul given to politics," he yet would never descend to trickery or baseness to accomplish his purpose, and he has gone into history as one of the purest of public men.

Martin Van Buren, who was President in 1837, was for some time in the Senate. He was a wily politician — shrewd, capable, and ingenious. He was rather under medium height, and had a high forehead and comely features. He was exceedingly courteous, and made as much study of "deportment" as Mr. Turveydrop, and he is said to have diligently practiced all his graceful attitudes before a large mirror in his room.

Then there were Silas Wright, the influential Democrat, who invariably carried conviction by his sound logic; Henry A. Wise, who

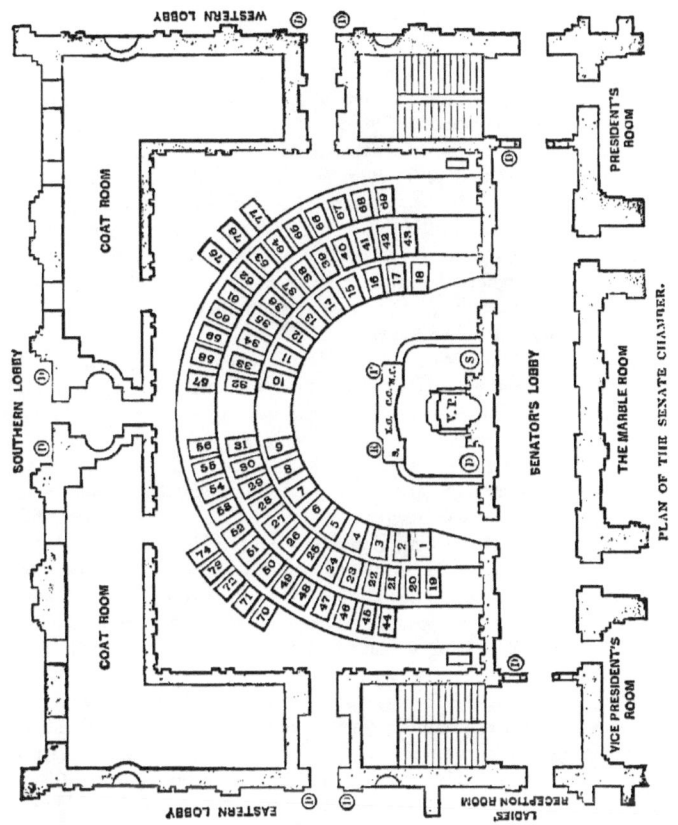

PLAN OF THE SENATE CHAMBER.

could startle the House by a perfect hurricane of passionate words;
Edward Everett, noted for his captivating speech and great learning;
Charles Sumner, polished and graceful as an orator, sincere and sagacious as a statesman; John Forsyth, a superb debater, and remarkable
for his accomplishments; Tristam Burges, called "the man of the
iron heart"—strong and brave, whose keen wit and eloquent tongue
made even the "Lord of Roanoke" tremble; David Crockett, from
the mountains of Tennessee, always ready with his rifle to shoot for
prizes, and noted for quaint, common-sense speeches; George Mc-
Duffie, Thomas Corwin, Lewis Cass, and innumerable others of great
ability and marked individuality.

The present hall of the House of Representatives was occupied on
the 16th of December, 1857, and the present Senate Chamber on the
4th of January, 1859.

THE north wing of the Capitol is known as the Senate extension.
The principal story contains the Senate Chamber, the Senate post-
office, the office of the sergeant-at-arms, the reception-room, the
Senators' withdrawing-room, the rooms of the President and Vice-
President of the United States, the office of the secretary of the Senate,
and the offices of the Senate clerks and official reporters. Around
the Senate Chamber is a grand corridor adorned with marble columns
and pilasters. The wing is constructed entirely of marble and iron,
and is very magnificent.

At the back of the Senate Chamber is the Senators' lobby, and
opening from it is the withdrawing-room. or, as it is generally called,
"the marble room," as it is made entirely of marble. Senators use
it for consultation. The President's room is on one side of it, and
the Vice-President's room on the other. Medallion portraits of Washington and the members of his first Cabinet cover the walls of the
President's room, and it is sumptuously decorated. Here the President comes on the last day of the session of Congress, to sign the bills
passed by both houses. When the Senate is not sitting the various
rooms can be inspected, and the floor of the Senate Chamber is also
open to the public.

The Senate Chamber is one hundred and twelve feet in length,
eighty-two feet in width, and thirty feet high. The ceiling is composed of large iron girders and cross-pieces, in which are panels of
glass containing painted emblems representing the Union, Progress,
the Army and Navy, and the Mechanical Arts. At night hundreds

of gas-jets, arranged back of the ceiling, throw a flood of softened light into all portions of the chamber. The walls are painted in exquisite tints and decorated in gold, and have buff panels. Arranged on the floor in concentric semicircles are mahogany desks and chairs for the Senators. On a dais is the chair of the President of the Senate, and in front of it is a broad mahogany desk. To the right of the president's chair is the chair of the sergeant-at-arms, and to the left that of the assistant door-keeper. In front of the president's desk are the desks of the Senate clerks and the tables of the official reporters. Galleries with seats for 1,000 persons extend around the chamber. Above the president's chair is a gallery for reporters of the press, and

THE PRESIDENT'S ROOM.

directly opposite is one for the diplomatic corps. The others are for the public.

Two grand staircases of highly polished marble lead to the Senate galleries from the public corridor. The eastern staircase is constructed of variegated Tennessee marble, with white marble steps. A stained glass skylight set in a paneled iron frame is placed overhead. From the main floor a broad flight of sixteen steps leads to the first landing; thence the ascent is by a double flight of eighteen steps. In a niche at the foot of the staircase is a marble statue of Benjamin Franklin, by Hiram Powers, executed at a cost of $10,000. On the wall above the first landing is a large painting of "Perry's Victory on Lake Erie," Sept. 10, 1813. It was painted by W. H. Powell, and cost $25,000. Commodore Perry is represented in a boat, making the perilous transfer of the flag from the disabled "Lawrence" to the "Niagara," during a tremendous cannonading.

The western staircase is constructed entirely of white marble, and is similar in design to the eastern. At the foot is a marble statue of John Hancock, by Horatio Stone, which cost $5,550. Over the main landing is a painting of "The Storming of Chapultepec" by General Scott's troops, Sept. 13, 1847. It was painted by James Walker, from sketches taken on the battle-field, the artist receiving $6,000 for the work. The staircases, with their massive pillars and balustrades, are very beautiful.

THE south wing of the Capitol, or the House extension, is similar in design and construction to the Senate extension. It has a grand corridor or lobby, and a vestibule with fluted columns. In the principal story is the great hall of the House of Representatives, and surrounding it are the Speaker's room, the retiring-room, the office of the sergeant-at-arms, the offices of the House clerks, and committee-rooms. The retiring-room is large and richly furnished, and the other rooms are of good size and elegant in their ornamentation and furniture. Opening from the rear of the legislative hall is the members' lobby, which is finely decorated and hung with portraits of past Speakers of the House.

The hall of the House of Representatives is one of the largest and finest legislative halls in the world. It is one hundred and thirty-nine feet in length, ninety-three feet in width, and thirty-six feet high. The chairs and desks of the Representatives and Delegates are arranged on the floor in concentric semicircles. The chair of the Speaker is placed on a platform three feet from the floor, and in front of it is a large marble table, and in front of that are marble desks for the House clerks and official reporters. At the right of the Speaker's chair is a stand on which the mace is placed when the House is in session, and close by is the chair of the sergeant-at-arms; on the left is the chair of the assistant door-keeper. A portrait of Washington, by Vanderlyn, hangs on one side of the Speaker's chair, and a portrait of Lafayette, by Ary Sheffer, on the other. Two paintings by Bierstadt, for which he received $20,000, are set in panels near the south doors. They represent the " Settlement of California," and the " Discovery of the Hudson River." A fresco by Brumidi, of "Washington at Yorktown," adorns a panel. Over the main entrance door is a large clock, supported by figures of an Indian and a pioneer, and surmounted by an eagle. The ceiling is similar in construction to that in the Senate Chamber. It is profusely gilded and ornamented, and the panels are filled with panes of painted glass bearing the arms of the states and other emblems. Back of the ceiling are 1,500 gas-jets, which at night illuminate the hall in a very brilliant manner. The galleries will seat nearly two thousand people, and they are often filled during the progress of an important debate. The press gallery, back of the Speaker's chair, has accommodation for sixty reporters. Two galleries are reserved for the diplomatic corps and the leading officials of the government; the others are open to the public.

The eastern and western grand staircases, leading from the corridor of the House to the galleries, are exactly like those in the Senate extension. At the foot of the eastern staircase is a marble statue of Thomas Jefferson, by Hiram Powers, executed in Italy at a cost of $10,000. On the wall of the landing is Francis B. Carpenter's famous painting of " President Lincoln signing the Proclamation of Emancipation," which was purchased of the artist for $25,000, by Mrs. Mary Elizabeth Thompson, and presented to the United States in 1878. While making studies for the work Mr. Carpenter resided in the White House as the guest of President Lincoln.

At the foot of the western staircase is a bronze bust of a friendly chief of the Chippewa Indians, called Bee-She-Kee, the Buffalo. The wall of the landing is embellished with an immense chromo-silica, by Emanuel Leutze, representing an emigrant train crossing the Rocky Mountains. It is bold in drawing and brilliant in color. Leutze received $20,000 for the work.

THE HALL OF THE HOUSE OF REPRESENTATIVES.

CHAPTER VII.

CONGRESS CONTINUED—MANNER OF LEGISLATION IN BOTH HOUSES—THE ENORMOUS COST OF A SESSION—HOW MILLIONS ARE SPENT—SENATORIAL SKETCHES—A GLANCE AT THE HOUSE OF REPRESENTATIVES—CLAIMANTS AND LOBBYISTS—THE CONGRESSIONAL RECORD—THE DISTRIBUTION OF PUBLIC DOCUMENTS.

THE Congress of the United States is the supreme legislative body, and has full authority under the Constitution to make all laws " which shall be necessary and proper " for carrying on the national government. It is composed of seventy-six Senators (two from each state), and three hundred and twenty-five Representatives, apportioned to the various states according to population. There are also eight Delegates who have seats in the House of Representatives and represent the territories, but who have no vote. The legislative period of each Congress extends through two years, and is divided into two regular sessions. The first session is termed " the long session," as it begins in December and continues until June or July, or even later, at the option of Congress. The second session, termed " the short session," begins in December and ends at noon on the 3d of March. Congress assembles annually on the first Monday in December. Senators are chosen by the legislatures of the states for a term of six years, and Representatives are elected by the people for a term of two years. Each member of Congress receives a compensation of $5,000 per year, and is also allowed mileage at the rate of twenty cents per mile, with $125 annually for newspapers and stationery. The President *pro tempore* of the Senate and the Speaker of the House of Representatives have an additional compensation of $3,000 per year each.

As a matter of reference, the apportionment of Representatives in Congress is herewith given: Alabama has eight Representatives; Arkansas, five; California, six; Colorado, one; Connecticut, four; Delaware, one; Florida, two; Georgia, ten; Illinois, twenty; Indiana, thirteen; Iowa, eleven; Kansas, seven; Kentucky, eleven; Louisiana, six; Maine, four; Maryland, six; Massachusetts, twelve; Michigan, eleven; Minnesota, five; Mississippi, seven; Missouri, fourteen; Nebraska, three; Nevada, one; New Hampshire, two; New Jersey, seven; New York, thirty-four; North Carolina, nine; Ohio, twenty-one; Oregon, one; Pennsylvania, twenty-eight; Rhode Island, two; South Carolina, seven; Tennessee, ten; Texas, eleven; Vermont, two; Virginia, ten; West Virginia, four; Wisconsin, nine.

The two Houses of Congress exercise joint legislation, but all bills to raise revenue for the government must originate in the House of Representatives. The Vice-President of the United States acts as President of the Senate, but has no vote unless the Senate is equally divided; then he casts the deciding vote. The Senate elects a president *pro tempore*, who, in the absence of the Vice-President, presides over its sessions. The House elects a Speaker to preside. All the officials of the Senate and House serve two years, or during the legislative period of each Congress.

The bills introduced in either house are first referred to proper committees; they are printed and placed on the files of the committees. Afterward, when any committee reports a bill for action, it is read by title and then is assigned a place on a calendar until it is called up for discussion in what is known as the "committee of the whole," which is constituted of all the members of either house acting as a committee, and not as a house. When the Senate, or House, goes into committee of the whole, the presiding officer calls a member to the chair to preside. If a bill is adopted by the committee of the whole it is reported and ordered engrossed. After another reading it is debated, and then is voted upon, and if it receives a majority of all the votes cast, it is declared adopted, and is sent to the other house, where it is referred to the committee of the whole. If the second house adopts the bill it is transmitted to the President of the United States for his approval. If he signs the bill it becomes a law, and if he vetoes the bill it may still become a law if both houses pass it again, over the veto, by a two-thirds vote. If the bill is retained by the President for ten days after Congress has presented it to him, it becomes a law without his signature.

A statement of the cost of the sessions of Congress may be interesting and very astonishing to many readers. As the national legislature is very expensive, the details of its principal expenditures can be properly given for the information of those who pay the bills — the people of the United States. In the first place, the annual compensation and mileage of the members amount to $2,188,624. The Senators receive as compensation $380,000, and the Representatives and Delegates, $1,665,000. There is appropriated for mileage the sum of $143,624.

The miscellaneous expenses of the Senate are very large. The secretary of the Senate has a salary of $4,896 per year, and is also allowed $1,200 for the hire of a horse and wagon. The chief clerk and the financial clerk have $3,000 each. Then there are five other clerks who have $2,592 each, six clerks who have $2,220 each, and five more clerks who have $2,100 each. The librarian has $2,220, and the assistant librarian, $1,440. The keeper of the stationery has $2,102, and two assistant keepers, $1,800 and $1,000. For making a five minutes' prayer each day in the Senate at the opening of the session, the chaplain has a salary of $900. The sergeant-at-arms and door-keeper has $4,320, and his clerk, $2,000. The assistant door-keeper and the acting assistant door-keeper have $2,592 each, and three other door-keepers, $1,800 each. The principal book-keeper has $4,320, and two assistant book-keepers, $2,592 each. For reporting the proceedings of the Senate in short hand, the four official reporters are paid $6,250 each. The Senate postmaster has $2,250, his assistant, $2,088, and five mail-carriers, $1,200 each.

Nor is this all. The secretary to the President of the Senate has a salary of $2,102, and the messenger to the President's room, $1,440. There are thirty-six messengers, for various purposes, whose aggregate salaries amount to $50,000 per year; and there are eighteen pages who receive $2.50 per day each during the session. The numerous clerks to committees are paid, some $6 per day, and others from $2,220 to $2,500 per year. The other expenses of the Senate are considerable, and the total yearly expenditure is about $370,000, exclusive of the compensation and mileage of Senators.

The House of Representatives, being a much larger body than the Senate, has expenses which swell into an enormous aggregate. In addition to the great sum of money annually paid as compensation to the Representatives and Delegates, the salaries of the House officials and the other expenses will amount to nearly $550,000.

. The chief clerk of the House has a salary of $4,500. To assist
him there are five clerks with salaries of $3,000, one clerk with $2,-
500, and three clerks with $2,240. These clerks have seven assist-
ants who are paid $2,000 each, and three assistants who are paid
$1,440 each. In addition there are five book-keepers who have sal-
aries of $1,600. The private secretary of the Speaker has $1,800,
the Speaker's clerk $1,600, and the clerk to the Speaker's table $1,-
400. The principal door-keeper has $2,500, with $500 allowed him
for horse hire, and the two assistant door-keepers have $2,000 each.
Forty messengers, some of whom act as door-keepers, receive salaries
aggregating $50,000. There are thirty-two clerks to committees who
are paid $6 per day each, and numerous committee clerks who have
salaries from $2,000 to $2,500. Thirty-one pages are employed at
$2.50 per day each, and in the short session they also receive a gra-
tuity of $75 each. There is an " upholsterer and locksmith," whose
duty it is to keep the chairs and desks of the Representatives in good
order, and for this work he is paid $1,440 per year.

The sergeant-at-arms, who disburses the funds of the House, has
a salaried force equal to that of some national banks. His salary is
$4,000, and $500 are allowed him for a horse and wagon, and $300
for postage-stamps. He has a deputy at $2,000, a cashier at $3,000,
a paying-teller at $2,000, a book-keeper at $1,800, a messenger at
$1,200, a page at $60 per month, and a laborer at $660 per year.
His office is furnished in an elegant and costly manner.

There are five official short-hand reporters who have salaries of
$5,000, and two stenographers for committees, who also receive $5,000
each. The chaplain has $900, the postmaster, $2,500, and the assistant postmaster, $2,000. In the House post-office there are nine
clerks with salaries of $1,200, and two clerks with $800. An employé known as "the conductor of the elevator" has a salary of
$1,200. The stationery and newspapers for the House cost $47,500
per year ; $10,000 are paid for repairs to the furniture, the expenses of
special committees are $50,000, and contingent expenses many more
thousands. If the amount of the compensation and mileage of the
members is added to the amount expended for miscellaneous expenses,
it will be found that the aggregate yearly cost of the House is more
than $2,300,000.

Each annual session of Congress costs the country all of three
millions of dollars, and if this vast sum is divided by the number of

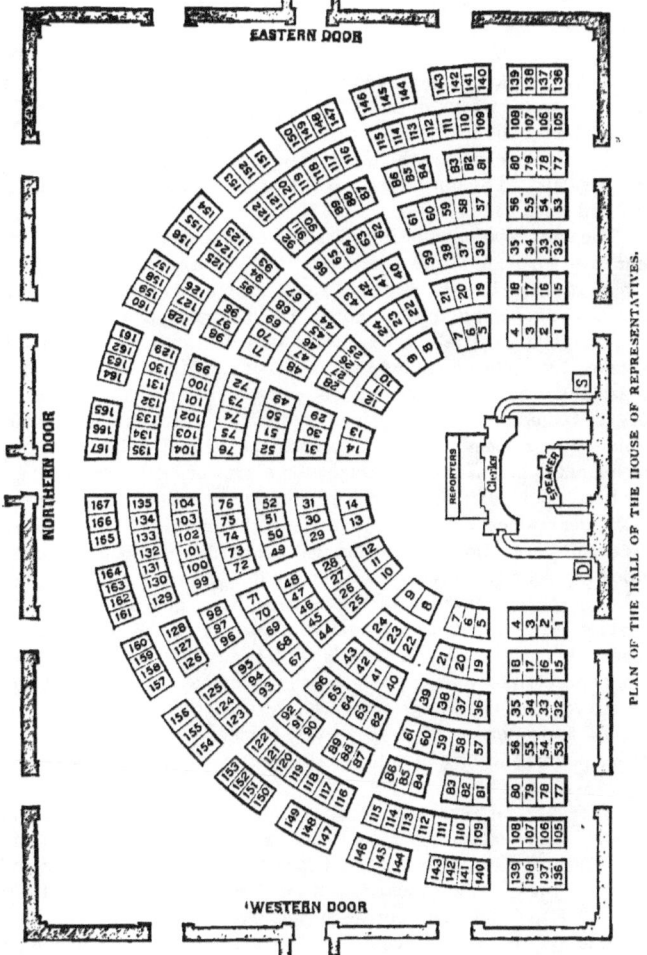

PLAN OF THE HALL OF THE HOUSE OF REPRESENTATIVES.

days or weeks of the session it will give a really startling result. For instance, the short session, deducting the usual holiday recess, is of less than twelve weeks' duration. If the session is estimated at twelve weeks the cost of it will be $250,000 per week, and if Congress sits six days in each week, which is a rare occurrence, very nearly $42,-000 per day. The long session will cost about one-half as much per day and week as the other.

The daily sessions of Congress begin at noon and continue until four or five o'clock in the afternoon. During the first weeks of the annual meeting both houses have short sittings, as there is very little that can be done until the committees get in working order, and report bills for action. The last weeks are crowded with business, and it is generally necessary to hold night-sessions. Much of the work of legislation is done in the committee-rooms, and some of the committees are tasked to the utmost with a multiplicity of affairs, while others seldom have a meeting. Each house is opened daily with prayer by the chaplain, and after the journal of the previous day's proceedings has been read, petitions and bills are introduced and referred to appropriate committees during what is called "the morning hour." Various reports are also made by committees, with accompanying bills, which are usually placed on a calendar for consideration in regular order. At the expiration of the morning hour, bills are taken from one or more of the calendars and considered until the adjournment. Whenever Congress sits on Saturday, it is generally "for debate only." The appropriation bills, or bills providing money for the support of the government departments, are usually taken up near the end of the session, and often occasion very lively debates. There is always a strong political feeling in both houses, and much of the legislation is tinged with it.

Whenever the Senate receives a communication from the President of the United States, it goes into what is called "executive session" to discuss it. The galleries and floor are cleared of spectators and reporters, the doors are locked, and the Senators then feel at liberty to express themselves freely upon the President's communication, which is usually in reference to appointments which are presented for confirmation by the Senate.

The Senate is quite a dignified body, and generally adheres to certain rules of decorum. It is rarely that there is a very noisy debate in this branch of Congress. In fact, the proceedings during the greater part of a session might be characterized as " dull." Now and then a matter will come up which will arouse party feeling, or perhaps sectional prejudice, and then earnest words will be spoken, and some flushed faces will be seen. Occasionally rather impertinent remarks are made. One Senator, during a debate, said of another whose speech had proved very irritating, that " It is generally believed the gentleman from —— rests his mind while talking "; to which saucy remark the Senator alluded to replied, " The gentleman from —— reminds me of that sterile tract of land in Virginia which was said to be poor by nature and exhausted by cultivation." But these "little pleasantries" are to be expected during the conflicts of the powerful opposing interests represented in the Senate.

The Senators have the right to speak as long as they please on most matters under consideration, and although long speeches are not the rule, occasionally one will be delivered of very great length. If the matter is not particularly interesting, or the speaker gifted as an orator, the Senators will retire from the chamber, or busy themselves at their desks over their correspondence or the newspapers, and the visitors in the galleries will gradually depart until few or none remain. But the Senator who has the floor goes on entirely regardless of the lack of listeners, as in most cases the speech is intended for the country, and an arrangement has been made with the correspondents of the press to give it a wide circulation.

One day during a debate a Senator who was known to have aspirations for the Presidency was addressing the Senate, and in the course of his remarks shouted in an impressive manner, " I would rather be right than be President ! " To this remark a Senator quickly retorted, " The Senator from —— will *never* be either ! " This retort was so applicable that the Senators burst into roars of laughter, and the presidential aspirant abruptly concluded his speech in a very embarrassed manner.

Not a few of the Senators have risen to eminent position from humble life, and they are often quite proud of the fact that they fought their way to prominence by the hard road of poverty and drudgery. It is related of two Senators of national fame that they worked together when young men on the same farm for several years. When they met in the Senate one said to the other, after congratulating him upon his election as Senator, " Well, John, when we used to drive old Brown's oxen we never expected to meet in the United States

9

Senate." " No, Henry," replied the other, "we didn't know there was such a place."

In the Senate Chamber are some of the chairs used in the old chamber by the famous Senators of years ago — Webster, Clay, Benton, McDuffie, Cass, and others. These historic chairs have been carefully preserved, and once they were pointed out to visitors, but as relic hunters began to mutilate them, it was thought best to keep their identity a close secret, and now only Capt. Isaac Bassett, the venerable assistant door-keeper, and two or three of the oldest Senators know which they are. But few of the Senators and officials of the Senate who served in the old chamber are living. Mr. Bassett is the only official of those days at present connected with the Senate. He began his service in 1831 as a page, and has continued in various positions ever since.

The late Senator Henry B. Anthony, of Rhode Island, gave the longest continuous service of any Senator except Thomas Hart Benton. He entered the Senate in 1859, and served for twenty-five consecutive years, until his death in September, 1884.

THE House of Representatives, with its great hall and throng of members, is in marked contrast to the Senate. Apparently the House cares very little for dignity or decorum, and sometimes there is considerable confusion on the floor. There are many days when the proceedings are proper even to extreme dullness, but on other days, when an important matter is under consideration, the House is brimful of animation. Until one becomes accustomed to its bewildering noises, its manifold and complicated rules and practices, and its peculiar kind of speech-making, frequently broken by sarcastic retorts and impertinent interjections, it is very difficult to understand much of its legislation.

A glance at the House will show members absorbed at their desks over piles of books and documents; some are writing letters, others are reading newspapers. Groups here and there are conversing in animated tones, and before the cheerful grate fires in the corners of the hall are other groups comfortably seated, joking and laughing. Pages are running to and fro with their arms full of papers, and responding to members as they clap their hands. On the floor there may be a running fire of debate, with keen, experienced debaters shouting at the top of their voices, for it is necessary to shout to be

heard half-
way across this
huge hall,
while others
are standing in
readiness to
join in the dis-
cussion as soon
as they can
catch the
Speaker's eye.
Cries of "Mr.
Speaker!"
"Mr. Speak-
er!" "Mr.
Speaker!" go
up from all
sides. The
Speaker has a
difficult task.
He strikes his
marble table
with the gavel
almost inces-
santly to call
the House to
order, and oc-
casionally is
compelled to

THE RETIRING-ROOM OF THE HOUSE.

stop all business and to peremptorily command every member to take
his seat or retire from the hall.

One is never at a loss for amusement while watching the House
during a spirited session, and it does not take long to understand why
it is that only a few men, and those the ablest and strongest, ever
attain to any degree of prominence as Representatives. Even to be
heard in the hall requires lungs of iron, and to stand against the free
and often exceedingly insolent comments and personal remarks, the
continual strife for mastery, and the shrewd political manœuvering, a
member who makes speeches and aims to be prominent must have

great courage, much endurance, a ready wit, and a very practical way of meeting all difficulties. It is little wonder that many men who go into the House with the belief that they can make a reputation in national legislation are soon content to remain " mute, inglorious " members, ambitious only to obtain the privilege of printing their undelivered speeches in the *Congressional Record*, for circulation among their constituents. The House is no respecter of persons, and a man to win success in it must be made of sturdy metal.

The business yearly brought before Congress is so enormous that it has become impossible to dispose of a quarter of it. The files of the principal committees will contain thousands of bills at each session, and on the calendars of both houses there will be long lists of important matters waiting consideration. Yet hardly three hundred bills will be disposed of, and all the rest must go over, greatly to the loss and injury of many persons in different sections of the country.

In the room of the House Committee on Claims hundreds of claims are always on file, some of which have been pending for years. One claim for half a million dollars is twenty years old, and at nearly every session during that time something has been done about it. It has been reported a number of times, but was not reached on the calendar, and consequently died with the session, and had to be introduced over again. There are claims for the relief of public officials, for compensation for damages, and for all sorts of things, many of them just and proper, but it is found to be impossible to dispose of any considerable number. Claimants throng the lobbies of Congress, and use all the means in their power to have their claims acted upon, but the majority have to go away unsuccessful.

As there is great necessity for personal action and influence to expedite matters before Congress — to persuade the committees to report, and then to persuade either house to act — it naturally follows that there must be considerable " lobbying." This practice is very ancient, and from the early Congresses to the present one, the lobbyist has been an important factor of legislation, and the Third House almost a recognized branch of the national legislature. The lobbyists thrive at each session, and the shrewd, worldly-wise men, and even women, who make lobbying a business, usually have all they can do in assisting the reporting and passage of bills. The methods employed are numerous and diversified, and great care is taken to prevent a knowledge of them coming to the public. Some lobbyists work on contingencies — that is, they receive so much if the business they are charged with is accomplished; while others will do nothing without money in advance. Great corporations that desire the passage of certain bills bearing directly and profitably upon their business; claimants who have become discouraged at the failure of their own efforts to advance their claims; the organizers of "jobs" to take millions out of the Treasury — seek the lobbyists and make terms with them for their peculiar and mysterious services. Stories are told of fortunes made by the members of the Third House who have been very successful, and it is generally understood that the wily, ingenious, persistent lobbyists are pretty sure to gather a lucrative harvest.

The official reporters of the Senate and House take down in short hand the proceedings of each day's session, and they are printed the following morning in the official publication known as *The Congressional Record*. The reports are presumed to be verbatim, but they are far from that. Few, if any, of the sarcastic and impertinent remarks made by members during the debates are ever printed, and many of the speeches undergo substantial change, passages being stricken out and new ones added on the proof-slips sent out from the Government Printing Office to members who desire to make corrections. There are also very many speeches printed in the *Record* which were never delivered. A congressman who wishes to gain in an easy way the reputation of having "made a great speech in Congress," will obtain "the permission to print," and then will have inserted in the official publication his so-called speech. This saves all the trouble of delivering it before an ungracious house, and the member's constituents, afar off, will not be aware of the fact that the "eloquent words" were never uttered in the legislative hall.

Members frequently withhold their speeches from publication in the *Record* for a number of days in order to obtain the place of honor, the conspicuous first page. Each member of Congress is entitled to twenty-four copies of the *Record* daily, and can purchase as many more as he desires. After Congress has finished its annual session the publication is usually continued for a month to "work off" all the speeches, previously crowded out, that members had received permission to print. The yearly cost of the *Record* is about $200,000.

In the basement of the Capitol are many committee-rooms, the House post-office, the restaurants, and the document and folding rooms. About thirty rooms are used for the enormous business con-

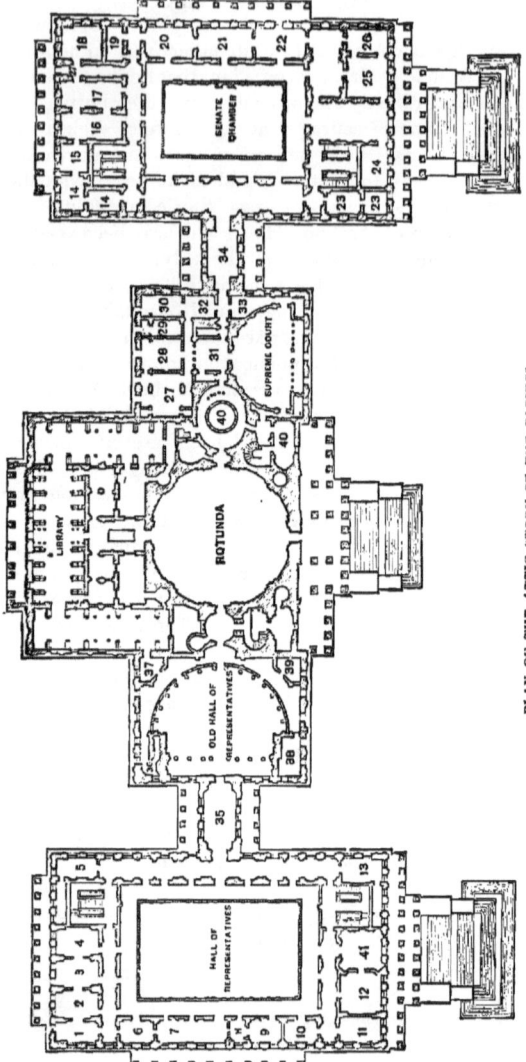

PLAN OF THE ATTIC STORY OF THE CAPITOL.

(Used for Committee-Rooms, the Senate Library, Document-Rooms, Etc.)

nected with public documents. The government issues yearly nearly three hundred different books — reports of departments and special reports on home and foreign matters, mostly bulky volumes, and many of them illustrated in the finest and costliest manner — besides a large number of pamphlets. The Government Printing-Office is constantly engaged in many of its departments in printing and binding these publications. A large force is employed in the document and folding rooms in wrapping and addressing the books and pamphlets, and nearly every day in the year one hundred large mail-sacks of public documents are sent out over the country. It is estimated that the printed matter annually distributed will fill two hundred and fifty mail-cars, and will weigh six millions of pounds. More than a million bound volumes are distributed, and an immense number of pamphlets. Each congressman is entitled to a certain number of copies of all the works, and he furnishes the list of people to whom they shall be sent.

Thousands of copies of *The Congressional Record* are distributed over the country every day, and during the progress of an exciting and important debate the number will swell into tens of thousands. Some congressmen expend a large amount of money in the purchase and mailing of their speeches, and in one case it is known that a very ambitious speechmaker expended five thousand dollars, his entire compensation for the congressional year, in sending his " great speech " to his constituents and to others far and wide throughout the United States. In another case a speech on the tariff had a circulation of one hundred thousand copies.

The report of the Department of Agriculture has the largest circulation of any of the public documents, and it is greatly appreciated by enterprising and progressive farmers, as its fund of information concerning the agricultural interests is accurate and complete, great pains being taken by the department with all the subjects treated of. Within a few years the farmers of the great southwestern region of the country have taken many thousands of the reports, and the demand from that section yearly increases. The circulation of the report in the northwest is also very large. Reports on mines and minerals are circulated throughout the mining regions in great numbers, and are also sent to the financial centres. The reports of some of the departments are distributed among the state and public libraries, and are found to be very useful for reference. Many of the public documents are of much value to specialists, and the demand for them generally exceeds the supply.

THE WHITE HOUSE, FROM PENNSYLVANIA AVENUE.

CHAPTER VIII.

FROM the beginning of the century to the present time the Presidents of the United States have resided, during their official life, in the Executive Mansion, popularly known as the White House, and as one walks through the rooms of the ancient mansion recollections of these historic characters throng the memory. Here the men chosen to guide the affairs of the Nation have lived from day to day, have had their joys and their sorrows, their domestic felicity, the honors of high position, and the cares and burdens which accompany great office. Here have been many brilliant scenes of festivity—the joyous nuptial ceremony, the pomp and glitter of fêtes and receptions; and here, likewise, have been scenes of anguish—the lights and shades of human existence. Nearly a hundred years ago Washington was present at the laying of the corner-stone, and month by month watched the beautiful structure rise, and on one day, but a few weeks before his death, he walked through the house with his beloved wife. It was then the only completed public building in the new capital city, and its pure classic elegance won the admiration of the first President and all who looked upon it. The tradition is that it was called the "White House" out of respect for Martha Washington, whose early home on the Pamunkey River, in Virginia, was known by that name; but as its color was always white, it is more probable that the popular name came into use from that. It is always officially styled "The Executive Mansion," but this dignified appellation is seldom heard outside of government circles.

The first commissioners of the city of Washington advertised on the 14th of March, 1792, for a design of "The President's House," offering a premium of $500 for the best one. Among the number submitted was one by a talented young architect named James Hoban, and his design being approved, the premium was awarded to him, and he was engaged at a salary of one hundred guineas per year to superintend the construction of the mansion. Hoban had resided for some years in Charleston, South Carolina, before he came to Washington to enter the ranks of the contestants for the honor of designing the White House, and was considered one of the leading architects in the country. He had studied in Europe, and was familiar with the most notable examples of foreign architecture. In his design he followed that of the palace of the Duke of Leinster, in Dublin, and the White House, as it stands to-day, bears a marked resemblance to its foreign prototype. Hoban resided in Washington until his death in 1831, and accumulated a large estate by the practice of his profession.

On the 13th of October, 1792, the corner-stone of the White House was laid, in accordance with the rites of Masonry. It was an important event to those who were deeply interested in the embryo capital, and several thousand people assembled to witness the ceremony. President Washington, the commissioners, the architect, the Masons, and others formed a procession and solemnly marched to the spot, and there held formal and impressive exercises. The work of construction was begun at once, but on account of some difficulty in raising money the building was not entirely completed until 1799. Up to 1814, when the interior was partially burned by the British troops, the total cost of construction was $333,207. The reconstruction and re-furnishing, after the fire, cost about $300,000, and since then many thousands of dollars have been expended in various improvements, and in the laying out and ornamentation of the spacious grounds. When the house was re-opened on the 1st of January, 1818, it was pronounced "a grand edifice"; and from that day to this it has been an object of admiration.

The White House is situated on the government reservation called "The President's Grounds," and fronts on Pennsylvania Avenue at Lafayette Square. It is in the centre of an enclosed plat of twenty acres, and the main entrance is reached by two broad semi-circular driveways lined with noble trees. The grounds are filled with flower-beds and well-kept lawns, and adorned with marble fountains, and at the back of the house is a park sloping gradually to the river bank, which opens a far-reaching prospect of the Potomac and the blue hills of Virginia. Stately oaks, sycamores, and poplars give the grounds in summer a most beautiful sylvan appearance, and the official mansion then is almost hidden by expansive foliage. The building is constructed of Virginia freestone, painted white. It is of the Grecian order of architecture, has two stories and a basement, and is surmounted by a wide balustrade. It is one hundred and seventy feet in length and eighty-six feet in width. At the main entrance is a grand portico of Ionic columns, and at the rear is a semi-circular colonnade. Adjoining the house on the west is a large conservatory containing a choice and varied collection of plants.

The state parlors on the first floor are usually accessible to the public during certain hours of each week-day. The main entrance door opens into a spacious vestibule which is elegantly frescoed. From the vestibule the great East Room is reached. This is the largest apartment in the house, and until 1837 it was used as a banquet hall. It is eighty by forty feet, and is designed in Grecian style and richly ornamented. Its lofty ceiling is composed of three large panels, profusely decorated, and in the centre of each panel hangs a massive crystal chandelier. Eight long, magnificent mirrors, supported on carved mantels, in white and gold, are placed around the room, and a costly velvet carpet covers the broad floor. The hangings and upholstery are exceedingly rich and handsome. A full-length painting of Washington, by Gilbert Stuart, purchased in 1803, hangs on the walls, and also one of Martha Washington, by E. F. Andrews, purchased in 1878. When evening receptions are given by the President, the room is fragrant and beautiful with masses of flowers. Festoons of smilax encircle the chandeliers, the mantels are banked with precious roses, and the windows and angles are filled with tall-palms and comely exotic plants, the luxuriant floral display adding a charming effect to the gay and brilliant surroundings.

Leading from the East Room is the Green Room, in which all the furniture and decorations are pale green. In this room hangs the life-size painting of Mrs. Rutherford B. Hayes, which was presented to the government in May, 1881, by the National Temperance Union. It is by Huntington, and the canvas is over seven feet high, and the elaborately carved oaken frame, made by the Cincinnati School of Design, is nearly ten feet high. Mrs. Hayes is represented standing in a graceful attitude, holding a bunch of roses. She is attired in crimson velvet, and has white lace around her neck and arms.

The Blue Room is the next in the suite. It is here that the President receives his guests at public and private receptions. The room is oval, and is decorated and furnished in light blue. The walls are profusely yet very tastefully embellished, and the upholstery, consisting of delicate silk with gilt trimmings, is unique and attractive.

It is in the Red Room, the last of the apartments on the first floor open to the inspection of the public, that the President sits at night, and it is furnished and arranged as a family parlor. Here are books and periodicals, numerous bric-à-brac, a mahogany table over one hundred years old, a fine portrait of Lincoln above the mantel, and elegant red plush furniture. The walls and hangings are red, and the room has a cheerful, cosy appearance — an atmosphere of home life about it.

The state parlors open into a long corridor, which is used on the occasion of fêtes as a grand promenade for the guests. Paintings of the Presidents cover the wall of the corridor, and here and there on the floor are placed tropical plants. The corridor is separated from the vestibule by a handsome sash screen.

The state dining-room, in which the President gives ceremonious dinners during the winter to the members of the Cabinet, Senators and Representatives, the Justices of the Supreme Court, the diplomatic corps, and other distinguished personages, is at the western end of the corridor. It is magnificently furnished, and at its table over fifty persons can dine. When state dinners are given, the White House is brilliant with lights and flowers, with court costumes and splendid toilets, with fair women and stately men. The table is set with the sumptuous state china, on which is finely depicted the fauna and flora of America, and with masses of silver and delicately cut glass. Gold and silver candlesticks and mirrored sconces in broad silver frames contain wax-lights, which brightly illuminate the table, and special floral designs of exquisite beauty add rich color and perfume to the banquet. Corsage bouquets are provided for the ladies, and *boutonnières* for the gentlemen. The President leads the way to the table at eight o'clock, and the dinner of many courses continues for three hours, during which time the Marine Band, stationed in the vestibule, discourses soft, delicious music.

THE WHITE HOUSE, FROM THE SOUTH.

In the second story are the executive offices, the President's reception-room, where he receives those who call during the day on business or to pay their respects; the Cabinet room, and the various family rooms. All the rooms on the east side of the house are used for the government business, and all on the west are private.

The Cabinet room is spacious and well arranged. Here the President meets the members of his Cabinet every Tuesday and Friday at noon, and around a long table, covered with books and documents, they discuss affairs of state. The President sits at the head of the table, with the Secretary of State at his right, and the Secretary of the Treasury at his left hand. The Cabinet meetings usually continue for two hours.

The President's reception-room is a large, finely furnished apartment, oval in shape. The windows are hung with silk curtains, and the furniture is of mahogany, upholstered in red leather. At the sides of the room are long, low book-cases, filled with richly bound volumes, and before these are chairs for persons waiting to be received. In front of the windows is the President's desk, a massive oak structure of historic interest. It was constructed of timber which formed part of Her Majesty's ship "Resolute," sent to the Arctic Sea in 1852 by the English government, to search for Sir John Franklin. The ship was abandoned in the ice, but afterward was discovered and restored by an American whaler. This souvenir was expressly made for the White House, and came into it in 1881. The room has a pleasant appearance: portraits of the first five Presidents look down from the walls, and disposed in various nooks are bronzes and art decorations.

It is proper to call on the President on any public business, or simply to pay respects, and he is "at home" to visitors from ten A. M. to one P. M. on Wednesdays, Thursdays, and Saturdays, and at such hours on other days as suit his convenience. Visitors are shown into a waiting-room at the head of the stairs leading from the first story, and their cards taken to the private secretary. Afterward they are escorted to the reception-room, where the President receives each person in turn. The customary form of address is "Mr. President."

The President receives a compensation of $50,000 per year. He furnishes his personal servants, all household supplies, and horses and carriages. The government provides the furniture for the White House, keeps the house and grounds in order, and pays the salaries of the private secretaries and clerks, and other employés. The private secretary has a salary of $3,250 per year, and the assistant secretary $2,250. Two executive clerks have salaries of $2,000, and a stenographer is employed at a salary of $1,800. There are also six clerks, a steward, three ushers, five messengers, two door-keepers, a watchman and a fireman. The total compensation of the household force provided by the government amounts to $36,000 per year. There are $8,000 allowed for the contingent expenses of the executive offices, $15,000 for lighting the house and grounds, which require considerable illumination every evening; $5,500 for the care of the conservatory, and $25,000 for the other expenses. Thus it will be seen that it costs the government $89,500 per year to maintain the Executive Mansion.

Every morning the private secretary examines the enormous mail which comes to the White House from all parts of the world, selects the letters which it is necessary for the President to see, and turns the

others over to the clerks who have charge of the correspondence.
He also arranges the details of the social life which forms no small
part of the duty of the President, especially during the congressional
season, and in many ways relieves him of official burdens. His relations with the President are very confidential. The assistant secretary has charge of all papers concerning Presidential appointments,
and also of all matters between the President and Congress. A complete record is kept of the appointments, the confirmations and rejec-
tions by the Senate, and the removals from office, and the history of
every appointment or removal can be readily ascertained from the
record-books.

A large part of each day's mail consists of letters relating to the
affairs of the various departments of the government. These letters
are recorded, and then are transmitted to the departments to which
they belong, to be answered. From two hundred to three hundred
newspapers are received daily from all sections of the United States
and from Europe. Editors who desire that the President should see
certain political articles send marked copies of their publications, and
many others favor him with printed matter. He subscribes for the
leading newspapers and periodicals. A clerk is specially detailed to
carefully examine all the newspapers, and to cut out the articles he
thinks the President would like to read. The cuttings are put in a
scrap-book, which is laid before the President every morning. He
looks it over, and thus is enabled, in a half-hour, to become familiar
with the good things and the bad things printed of his administration,
and also with the general drift of political affairs.

The President's business day begins at ten o'clock in the morning,
and an hour before he has entered his office, the outer waiting-room
will contain a number of persons seeking an interview with him. He
first reads the many letters on his desk, and to the least important of
them rapidly dictates answers, keeping his private secretary and his
stenographer busy for some time. The letters requiring careful
attention are put aside to be attended to when the stress of business is
over for the day, and he has time to properly consider them. When
the correspondence is disposed of visitors are admitted.

The visitors are always numerous. They come on all sorts of
business, with all sorts of stories, from the east and west, from the north
and south, and from lands beyond the sea. As the President has the
appointment of a vast army of office-holders — nearly 100,000, it is estimated — much of his time in the morning hours, and for that mat-

ter in all hours, has to be given up to the seekers for office and their friends. He has to listen to all the urgent claims, all the requests of statesmen and politicians, that this or that office shall be awarded to this or that patriot whose valuable services to the country (that is "the party") have entitled him to feed at the public crib. Aspirants for every office in his gift are at hand — for bureau offices, for first-class and second-class or any class missions, for judicial offices, for marshal-ships, for post-offices, for collectorships, for territorial commissions, for the army and navy, and, in fact, for everything in the long list. They throng around the President day after day and insist, with many strong reasons, that their claims shall be allowed — insist with indom-itable perseverance. Delegations from various states arrive in the city and hurry to the White House, eager in the hunt of some good office which has just become vacant, each delegation striving to be in advance of the other, so as to influence the President in making up his mind as to the new appointment. Senators and Representatives send in their cards with requests for "a few minutes' interview on import-ant business." High officials, diplomats, eminent strangers, seek an audience, and until the President closes his doors at luncheon-time his reception-room is constantly full of visitors, and he is entirely occu-pied in attending to them.

The hours of the afternoon are devoted by the President to study-ing the questions of state which have been brought to his attention. As he is charged with the duty of ascertaining if the immense and important business of the government is properly conducted, it is necessary for him to continually review the work of the department officials. Certainly a day of arduous toil at its best. And then there is the pain of disappointing many whose desires cannot be gratified, and there is the difficulty in arriving at the exact truth in order that justice may be done, and withal the need of making momentous decisions which are likely to be criticised harshly in every section of the coun-try, howsoever they are made. This is the President's usual routine of life, commingled with incessant social duties, no portion of which can be remitted in any way.

The regular dinner hour at the White House is seven o'clock, and at this meal the President usually has a few intimate friends at his table, and for a while banishes the cares of his position. He rarely accepts invitations to dinner, except with the members of his Cabinet, and never makes ceremonious calls; but he invites officials and friends to dine with him, and visits in official circles without ceremony at his

FAMOUS STATUES.

1. Statue of General Rawlins.   2. Ward's Statue of General Thomas.   3. Statue of Emancipation.
4. Statue of General McPherson.   5. Statue of Admiral Farragut.

pleasure. An invitation to dine with the President must be always accepted, unless illness compels declination. No previous engagement has precedence, and when it is absolutely necessary to decline it is customary to send a full explanation in writing.

The etiquette regulating the social intercourse of the President and his family with officials and the public has been in vogue since the administration of Washington, modified more or less by the different Presidents, but retaining its salient points to the present day. In the early years of the White House there were many courtly ceremonials, but they have been long since laid away with the powdered wigs, the lace ruffs, and all the ancient styles of dress, and the certain polite forms now prescribed, the careful observance of which is expected, are very simple in comparison with the ceremony once prevailing.

The annual series of presidential receptions begins on New Year's day, and continues until spring. On New Year's day the President has a public reception. The first to pay their respects to him are the members of the Cabinet, the Justices of the Supreme Court, the Senators and Representatives, and the high officials of the government. Then the diplomatic corps, in court costumes, and the officers of the army and navy, in full uniform, present themselves. Afterward the public are admitted. From this time until the season wanes there are fêtes and grand dinners at the White House every week.

The President usually gives a number of public evening receptions during the winter, which are open to everybody of respectability. Although there is no rule about the matter, it is customary to appear at these receptions in full evening costume, and the finest of toilets are always to be seen. On these occasions the White House assumes a fascinating appearance. The grounds are brightly illuminated, long lines of carriages fill the great driveways, and throngs of people assemble on the walks, and are slowly admitted into the house. The interior is lavishly adorned with flowers, the state apartments and the conservatory are open, and are dazzling with a thousand lights. Ushers conduct the guests to the cloak-rooms, and thence to the Blue Room, where presentations are made to the President by the Marshal of the District of Columbia. A brilliant and distinguished group always surrounds the President — members of the Cabinet, famous generals and congressmen, diplomats, high officials, with their wives and daughters. After the presentation, which is necessarily brief, the guests can stroll through the gorgeous rooms and down the floral pathways of the conservatory, and for two hours enjoy the music, the gay conversation, and the brightness of the festival.

The ladies of the presidential household have weekly afternoon receptions during the winter, generally on Saturday, from two to five o'clock. No invitations are issued, and every one is at liberty to attend. Prominent society ladies assist at these receptions, and the President is often present. The dress is that customary for morning calls.

DURING the two official terms of the first President he resided in plain, comfortable, but not over-large houses in New York and Philadelphia, which were rented by the government and furnished in a suitable manner. In these houses Washington and his wife held what has been described as a "Republican court," and established the official ceremony which, in part, has come down to this age.

When the government removed to the capital city in October, 1800, the White House was ready for occupancy, and President John Adams and family at once took up their residence in it. The first public reception was given on the 1st of January, 1801, and the guests were received in the room in the second story in which the President now receives his business callers. The East Room was then unfurnished, and Mrs. Adams used it as a drying-room, for lack of a good yard, the grounds of the White House being rough and exposed at that time, and in this spacious state parlor the presidential linen was hung on wash-days. In writing to her daughter, Mrs. Adams said of her new residence: "The house is on a grand and superb scale, requiring about thirty servants to attend and keep the apartments in proper order and perform the ordinary business of the house and stables. The lighting of the apartments, from the kitchen to parlors and chambers, is a tax indeed, but the fires we are obliged to keep to secure us from daily agues are cheering. Bells are wholly wanting; not one hung through the whole house, and promises are all we can obtain."

Abigail Adams is credited with a strong intellect and extensive culture. Although in feeble health, she zealously and faithfully performed all her social duties, aided her husband in his official work, and carefully attended to the household affairs. She is the only lady of the White House who reared a son to become President.

During President Adams' residence in the official mansion he gave many splendid state dinners and receptions, but his own way of living was very plain. His invariable luncheon consisted of oat-cake and lemonade, and the family dinners were simple. He was in the habit of taking long walks, and was quite unassuming in manner. In fact, his wife, it is said, occasionally had to remind him, when he was somewhat free and sportive in his intercourse with people, that he held a high and dignified office. Like all persons of rank in those days, he wore richly embroidered coats, silk stockings, huge silver buckles on his shoes, and a powdered wig, but is said to have preferred a plainer garb. He was frugal, and went out of office with a good sum of money saved from his salary.

Thomas Jefferson, the third President, entered the White House in 1801. When he appeared before Congress to deliver his " annual speech " every one was astonished at his simple attire, which was in great contrast to that of his predecessors. He wore a blue coat with gilt buttons, blue pantaloons, and serviceable American shoes tied with leather strings. He had entirely discarded the " aristocratic foppery," as he termed it, of official life. He adopted the plainest style of living, and appeared in public either on foot or mounted on a sedate, slow-going horse, instead of in a showy presidential coach with liveried servants and outriders. Usually he wore a large felt hat, pulled down nearly over his eyes. With the stiff, formal customs then in vogue he would have nothing to do, and he set himself to the pleasant task of making all the callers at the White House " perfectly at home." He liked to be surrounded by poets and painters, singers and musicians, and every genial denizen of Bohemia that he could secure. As his wife had died some time before he became President, his two daughters, assisted by Mrs. Madison, the wife of the then Secretary of State, conducted the social affairs of the White House during his administration.

Jefferson was noted for his exalted ideas of equality. He was sincere and unaffected, and made it a rule to be courteous and companionable to all men. One day while riding with a grandson, named after him, an old slave they met in the road raised his cap and bowed very obsequiously. Jefferson returned the salute in a polite manner, but his grandson took no notice of it. Turning to the boy he said, " Thomas, do you permit a poor slave to be. more of a gentleman than yourself ? "

On one occasion when Jefferson was returning from a horseback ride in Virginia, with two of his nephews anc a party of gentlemen, he and the young men rode somewhat in advance of the others, and coming to a swollen stream they found the water was up to their saddle-girths. A countryman was on the bank, waiting to get across, and when the young men had ridden over, he stepped up to the President and requested a ride. " Certainly," said Jefferson ; and he reined

up to a rock, bade the stranger mount his horse, and then took him
over the stream. The party in the rear noticed the occurrence, and
when shortly after they overtook the pedestrian, one of them asked
him why he did not request one of the young men instead of the elderly gentleman to take him over the water. "Well," he replied, "if
you want to know I'll tell you. I reckon a man carries yes or no in
his face. The young chaps' faces said no; the old 'un's said yes."
"But it isn't every man that would have asked the President of the
United States for a ride behind him," said the other. "You don't
say that's Tom Jefferson, do you?" cried the astonished countryman, adding, "He's a fine old fellow, anyway!" Then he laughed
heartily, and said, "What do you suppose my wife Polly will say
when I get back home and tell her I've ridden behind Jefferson?
She'll say I voted for the right man!"

When James Madison became President, in 1809, he restored in
full the stately ceremonies of the White House, disregarded by Jefferson, and court costumes were again seen at the levees. Madison
always wore his hair powdered, but his dress was usually plain, except
when he gave official receptions and dinners, when he would don a
very magnificent suit. He was a small man, with a mild, pleasant
face, and was quite overshadowed by his tall, elegant wife. At the
inauguration ball "Mrs. Madison ' looked and moved a queen.' She
wore a buff-colored velvet dress with pearl ornaments, and a Paris
turban with a bird of paradise plume." Dolly Madison was a widow
when she married Madison, and was known in Philadelphia society
for her beauty and accomplishments. She had a happy, buoyant
nature, and during her reign of five years filled the great mansion
with merriment and good-cheer. Dancing-parties were frequent, and
innumerable gay social events delighted the fashionable circles of
Washington. At the levees Mrs. Madison is said to have "made a
most magnificent appearance, her stately and Juno-like form towering above the rest of the ladies." She was often styled "the queen,"
and the White House was generally called "the palace."

The first marriage which ever took place in the White House was
during Madison's administration. In the winter of 1811 Miss Todd,
a relative of Mrs. Madison, was married to Congressman Jackson,
of Virginia. The nuptial ceremony was very brilliant, and was attended by nearly all the select society of the capital.

When the British troops entered Washington and fired the Capitol, the inmates of the White House made a hasty flight. President

Madison with his Cabinet had retired from the city after the battle of Bladensburg, but he had left his wife and her companions to follow as soon as it should be necessary. Mrs. Madison had issued invitations for a dinner-party, and as it was not believed that the enemy would reach the city that evening, she had the preparations for the dinner go on. When the news was brought that the British were on Capitol Hill, she collected a few personal articles, cut from its frame the famous painting of Washington hanging in the East Room, that it might not fall into the hands of the invaders, and with her friends fled from the house to a place of safety.

The British soldiers, when they marched into the White House, found, to their great surprise, a bountiful dinner all spread, with covers for thirty guests. The meats were ready to be served, and on the sideboard the wine was cooling. It is almost superfluous to say that the soldiers made a good meal before they fired the " Yankee palace."

ST. DOMINICK'S R. C. CHURCH.

CHAPTER IX.

THE WHITE HOUSE CONTINUED—SKETCHES OF THE PRESIDENTS AND THEIR MANNER OF LIVING—THE BRILLIANT SOCIAL EVENTS—DISTINGUISHED WOMEN WHO HAVE PRESIDED OVER THE HOUSEHOLD—SCENES AND INCIDENTS FROM THE BEGINNING OF THE CENTURY TO THE PRESENT TIME.

CONGRESS authorized the restoration of the White House in 1815, and Hoban, its architect, had it ready for occupancy in the early part of James Monroe's administration. When it was re-opened in 1818 it was more beautiful than before the British conflagration, and the fifth President, in a short time, made it quite a splendid court. Washington society at that period was exceedingly brilliant with lavish displays of wealth. The South sent its beauty and its culture to adorn the capital, and the great sugar and cotton planters, who had obtained opulence in a few years, used their means freely, during their residence in Washington, in entertaining and living in a gay and costly manner. The State of Virginia was proud of the fact that four of the five Presidents were from her people, and claimed the rare distinction of being "the mother of Presidents." Her lovely women and distinguished men thronged the city, and invested its society with a refined and courtly tone. The Northern element was also large, and some of the most intellectual people of the prominent cities were among the leaders of the social life.

President Monroe was a stately Virginian, nearly six feet in height. He was polished in manner, and was always carefully dressed in a dark blue coat, buff vest, small-clothes, and top-boots. He wore a cocked hat of Revolutionary style, and he has been called "the last of the cocked hats," for he was the last of the Presidents to adhere to the fashions of the past century. His face was mild and grave, and, although he was very courteous, he was never familiar in his intercourse with men, and was given to a liking for the strict observance of official ceremony. He had been in public life from youth, and was highly esteemed for his true, gentle nature, and it has been recorded of him that he was " one of the purest public servants that ever lived."

His wife, Elizabeth Kortright Monroe, was a highly accomplished lady of New York. She had a beautiful face, a tall, graceful person, and elegant manners. She was familiar with fashionable life abroad, and introduced into the White House many English forms of etiquette. Her receptions were numerous, and were attended by the highest and most exclusive classes of the city. She held them in the East Room, which was also used for the state dinners, and full dress was always required. The fêtes were given in a style of unusual splendor, and the most ceremonious usages were prescribed. Mrs. Monroe inaugurated the custom of the President's wife returning no calls, which custom has been very generally followed to the present time. She had several children, and her oldest daughter, Maria Monroe, was married in the White House in 1820, to Samuel L. Gouverneur, of New York. Monroe's administration was marked by harmony, his domestic life was happy, and he retired from office in 1825 with the respect of his countrymen.

When John Quincy Adams, of Massachusetts, became President the sum of $14,000 was appropriated by Congress to refurnish the White House, and the East Room in particular was fitted up in a superb manner. President Adams was a perfect host. His long and varied experience of men and affairs, at home and abroad, enabled him to preside at the state dinners and to conduct the official ceremonies with infinite grace. To people outside of the highest circles he was apt to be cold and forbidding, and his repellant manner often created hard feeling. No more precise and methodical man ever occupied the White House. His life was regulated by the clock. He rose at four in summer and at six in winter. After a cold bath he would take a long walk, generally to the Capitol and around the Capitol park and back, a distance of nearly four miles. Then he would read precisely two chapters in the Bible, and then look at the newspapers until breakfast, at nine. He went into the executive office at ten, and remained there absorbed in work until four; then would come another walk, and then dinner, at six. In the evening he attended to public business, unless social duties intervened. He was

THE FAMOUS ROOMS OF THE WHITE HOUSE.

an untiring worker, and was ever acquiring information from all sources, which he carefully stored away for future use.   In person he was short and inclined to corpulency ; his eyes were bright and expressive ; he always had good health, and his face was full of wholesome color.   At times, with those he dearly loved, he would display a surprising playfulness, laughing merrily, uttering odd jokes, and even singing snatches of old songs learned in his youth ; but these sunny moments were too infrequent.   His manner of living was marked by a certain degree of elegance, but it was not ostentatious.   In 1826 his son, John Quincy Adams, Jr., was married in the White House to his cousin, Miss Johnson.

It has been declared that the fashionable circle Mrs. Louisa Katharine Adams drew around her was far superior in elegance, refinement, beauty, and worth " to that which has appeared at any period since."   She greatly aided her husband, by her fine manners, kindliness, and varied accomplishments, in meeting the requirements of his position, and often displayed consummate tact in her efforts to make his administration popular.

A great crowd attended the inauguration of Gen. Andrew Jackson, of Tennessee, on the 4th of March, 1829, and the gallant soldier was lustily cheered as he rode up Pennsylvania Avenue on a spirited horse after the inaugural ceremony.   The people followed the President into the White House, filling the state parlors to overflowing. In the East Room a banquet had been spread, and the tables were laden with choice viands, but no one appearing to serve the guests, there were many clamors of impatience, and, finally, the crowd, without ceremony, surrounded the tables and began a tumultuous attack on the food.   In the struggle ice cream was scattered over the costly carpet, glass and china dishes were broken, coffee was spilled on the satin furniture, and a great deal of damage was done. The President at one time was violently pressed against the wall by the surging mob striving to reach the tables, and was only saved from injury by some officials who linked their arms, and in this way formed a living barrier around him.   Surely it was a strange scene to witness in the White House.

After this occurrence the practice of serving refreshments at public receptions, introduced in Monroe's administration, was speedily discontinued.   Although Jackson was profuse in his hospitality, and quite willing the public should enjoy good food in the White House, yet the throngs at his receptions were so great, and generally so unmannerly, that he was compelled, after providing refreshments several times and seeing his guests "rush at and strip the salvers in the corridor long before they reached the banquet-room," to cease the practice, and it never has been resumed.

Jackson opened the doors of the White House to everybody, and visitors of all sorts poured in and roamed through the rooms at will. The hearty old soldier disliked ceremony even more than Jefferson, and saw no reason why the presidential abode should be hedged about with formal etiquette. He was a man of the people, and it has been said that "all his vices were of the popular sort." He went about the house and grounds smoking a corn-cob pipe, and, as may be supposed, others availed themselves of the privilege of smoking, even in the state parlors. He called his friends by their christian names, and they invariably addressed him as "General"; he slapped people on the back familiarly, joked about his position, and would say, "By the Eternal," whenever he desired to emphasize a sentence. His hospitality was so bountiful that the proceeds of his "Hermitage" farm in Tennessee had to be constantly used to pay the expenses of his entertainments. At his dinners there was no special ceremony, and guests were simply expected to be social and merry, and have a good time. After dinner they did not immediately depart, as had been customary in Adams' time, but remained to dance or otherwise enjoy themselves.

Many of his dinners to intimate friends were notable for fun and frolic at the table. On one occasion Webster and Van Buren were present, and the latter proposed that Webster should favor the company with a song. To this he agreed, if the President would sing one first. Nothing loath, Jackson immediately began, in quaint, discordant notes, his favorite song of "Auld Lang Syne," singing for a few minutes without interruption; but the strange discord was too much for the company, and he was forced to stop by reason of the uproarious laughter that went round the board, and in which he heartily joined. Webster and Van Buren then attempted to sing, but their efforts produced so much merriment that they ceased, and gracefully acknowledged that Jackson was the better vocalist.

Jackson was more than six feet in height, but was very slim, not weighing over one hundred and forty pounds during the time he was President. He had strongly marked features, bushy, iron-gray hair, brushed high above his forehead, and dark blue eyes, which would snap and sparkle with peculiar lustre whenever he was excited. He was usually plainly and rather negligently dressed, and when out of doors carried a stout cane, with which he would strike the ground incessantly when engaged in earnest conversation. He went about unattended, and liked to talk freely with every one he met. When saluted by the highest or the humblest a winning smile would light up his strong face, and he would say in cordial tones, " How do you do, sir ; glad to see you." He was fond of children, and would stop them on the street and chat familiarly, patting their heads and taking great delight in their innocent prattle. One day a friend met him entering the White House grounds carrying a little girl on one arm and a dog on the other. In explanation he said that the child was crying because her dog was cold, and he was taking them into the house to the fire.

His wife, Rachel Donelson Jackson, with whom he had lived happily for nearly forty years, died shortly before he became President, and was laid to rest in the dress she had made to wear at his inauguration. It is related that " he wore her miniature next his heart day and night until his death." Her place in the White House was filled by Mrs. Emily Donelson, the general's niece, who was assisted by the wife of his adopted son, Mrs. Andrew Jackson, Jr. They were charming women. and performed their duties in a manner winning universal praise.

When Jackson held his farewell reception, Feb. 22, 1837, he presented his visitors with a parting gift. Friends and admirers in New York had sent him a monster cheese, larger than a hogshead in circumference, and nearly a yard thick. This cheese was cut by two men with huge knives manufactured from saw-blades, and distributed in an ante-room, each person receiving a piece weighing about three pounds. Everybody was very merry over the cheese, and most of the visitors carried home this remarkable presidential souvenir.

Martin Van Buren, of New York. who succeeded Jackson as President, had almost lived in the White House before he went there in 1837 as master for four years. He had been Jackson's Secretary of State, and was always believed to be " the power behind the throne." He had been constantly at Jackson's elbow, and as a reward for his valuable services. the gallant commander had worked hard to make him his successor. Van Buren was a little, dapper gentleman, elegant and refined, the pink of fashion and politeness, but withal remarkably shrewd as a politician, and full of tact and practical busi-

THE WHITE HOUSE, FROM THE EAST.

ness capacity in dealing with public affairs. It was customary to call him the American Talleyrand, and his cleverness in political management was much discussed in those days. He was a widower, having lost his wife nearly twenty years before he became President, and his household affairs were directed by his son's wife, Angelica Singleton Van Buren, a sweet young Southern beauty, whose grace and amiability won the hearts of all who met her in the White House. Her social duties were performed in such a pleasant manner that she gained extensive popularity. No more gracious woman ever has been at the head of a President's household.

Gen. William Henry Harrison, of Ohio, "the hero of Tippecanoe," was only one month in office. He became President in 1841, with John Tyler as Vice-President. "Old Tip," as he was affectionately called, it is believed, "was worried to death" by importunate office-seekers, not having the faculty of repressing them possessed by some of the latter-day Presidents. He died on the 4th of April, and his funeral was the first to occur in the White House.

He was tall and graceful, and had keen black eyes and a face beaming with good nature. Like Jackson, he was thoroughly conscious that the White House was the property of the Nation, and one day when a servant showed a plain, humble caller into a room without a fire, he took him to task for it. "Why did you not show the man into the other room, where it is warm and comfortable?" he asked. The servant thought the man might soil the carpet with his muddy boots. "Never mind the carpet another time," said Harrison; "the man is one of the people, and the carpet, and the house, too, belong to the people."

John Tyler, who succeeded Harrison, was a Virginian—an intellectual, high-bred gentleman, tall and slender, with a light complexion, brown hair, blue eyes, and prominent features. He was very courteous to all classes, but particularly favored men of learning and polite letters, and the Executive Mansion was much frequented by this class during his administration. He appointed Edward Everett Minister to England, Washington Irving to Spain, Caleb Cushing to China, and made John Howard Payne consul to Tunis. His tastes were polished, and he had the urbanity of refined culture and association. His first wife, Letitia Christian Tyler, appeared at but one reception, and that was on the occasion of the marriage of her daughter. She died in Washington in 1842, and Tyler lived in retirement for some time. Eight months before the expiration of his official term he married Miss Julia Gardiner, of New York, and the wedding reception was held in the White House. Mrs. Julia Tyler was the first woman who ever entered the house as a President's bride. Her receptions were notable for elegance and refinement, and her short career as the "first lady of the land" was a very brilliant one.

James K. Polk, of Tennessee, the eleventh President, was inaugurated in 1845. He was rather below the medium height, and excessively thin. He had a large, angular brow, and sharp gray eyes. His face was grave and sad, and his hair was nearly white. In regard to his thinness a writer of that date said, "If his clothes were made to fit he would be but the merest tangible fraction of a President. He has them, therefore, especially his coat, made two or three sizes too large in order to hide his spareness." His wife, Sarah Childress Polk, was an agreeable hostess. Her dress was always magnificent, and her presence commanding. A gentleman said to her one day, "Madam, there is a woe pronounced against you in the Bible; for it is written there, 'Woe unto you when all men shall speak well of you.'"

In 1849 Gen. Zachary Taylor, of Louisiana, was inaugurated, but he remained in office only sixteen months and five days. He died July 9, 1850, of cholera morbus, after a few days' illness. He was a portly gentleman, with a pleasant face and a well developed head crowned with pure white hair. He had mild, beautiful eyes, and a soft, pleasing voice. His manner was kind, and whenever he appeared in public and was greeted by applause he would wave his hand and say, "Your humble servant, ladies; Heaven bless you, gentlemen." His wife, Margaret Taylor, took scarcely any part in the round of ceremonies pertaining to official life, but left everything to the direction of her daughter, Betty Taylor Bliss, a bright, dainty little lady, who won golden opinions for her performance of the rôle of hostess, and the White House was a very attractive place during her reign.

The Vice-President, Millard Fillmore, became President after the death of General Taylor, taking the oath of office on the 10th of July, 1850. Fillmore was an eminent lawyer of Buffalo, and had worked his way to prominence from poverty and obscurity. He was tall and finely proportioned, and was considered a very handsome man. He was agreeable in manner, and made friends readily by his charming simplicity and frankness, and his manifest desire to do what was right. During his administration he gave many grand entertainments, and in the congressional season always had weekly morning and evening receptions. His wife, Abigail Powers Fillmore, had a fine erect figure, a delicate, intellectual face, and silky auburn hair hanging in ringlets about her head. She was an exemplary wife and mother, and had been a strong support to her husband when he was a young lawyer, "to fortune and to fame unknown." She was rather shy of society, much preferring the companionship of a few friends and the solace of her books to the ceremonious social practices of the White House. At President Fillmore's request Congress appropriated considerable money to furnish the oval sitting-room in the second story of the mansion as a library, and Mrs. Fillmore selected the books to fill the cases. She was a reader and a student, and in the library spent many happy hours.

Franklin Pierce, of New Hampshire, became President in 1853. He came to Washington in very simple style, and when his baggage was carried into the White House it was found to consist of "a

couple of old hair trunks, which might have been the property of a
veteran of 1812, and two portmanteaus scarcely less venerable in
appearance." At his first reception a great throng of office-seekers
appeared and pressed their claims on him. "One ambitious fellow
stepped up with the prefatory remark : 'I'm an applicant for office.'
'Glad to see you, sir,' was the reply ; 'good morning,' and off glided
the President. One applicant managed to thrust his memorial into
the President's hands, but it was dropped like a hot coal."

Pierce was nearly six feet in height, and a man of fine presence.
There was a keen, bright expression to his face, and his eyes were
dark and penetrating. He delighted in horseback riding, and nearly
every day rode long distances in the country unattended. Mrs. Jane
Appleton Pierce was an invalid, but she faithfully endeavored to perform her social duties as the lady of the White House. She was a
highly cultivated woman, and was ardently beloved by her husband.

The fifteenth President was James Buchanan, of Pennsylvania, a
large, muscular man, six feet in height, with light complexion, hair
and eyes, and a serious face. He was a bachelor, and the first
one to occupy the Executive chair. During his administration,
which began in 1857 and continued to the commencement of the
Civil War, the social life of the White House was very brilliant
under the inspiration of his niece, Miss Harriet Lane. The city was
exceedingly gay, although the black and angry clouds of war were
gathering in the political sky. As one has said, "people danced on
the edge of a volcano, with the crust heaving under their feet." Miss
Lane made the White House more nearly like a Republican court
than it had been since the ancient régime—the days of powdered
wigs, embroidered satins, and "aristocratic foppery." The President was very ceremonious, and largely retained the form and color
of his life among the English nobility while Minister to England.
He exacted strict, formal etiquette, and was displeased at familiarity.
Miss Lane was a beautiful woman, and finely educated and accomplished. She has been described as "tall and commanding, with a
perfectly molded shape, with a faultless head, finely poised and
crowned with a mass of golden-brown hair, with large dark blue
eyes, handsome features, the mouth particularly lovely, and a skin of
milk and roses." Her taste in dress was exquisite, and in all social
observances she was perfectly schooled.

Buchanan's last reception was given on the 12th of February,
1861, and was attended by a large number of people. The Presi-

FAMOUS STATUES.

1. Statue of Civilization.
2. The Naval Statue, or Monument of Peace.
3. Greenough's Statue of Washington.
4. Brown's Statue of General Scott.

dent received his guests in a very amiable manner, and Miss Lane, elegantly arrayed in pure white satin, charmed everybody by her graciousness. The state parlors were decked with fragrant flowers, the ladies present made a lavish display of magnificent toilets, bright uniforms of the army and navy were to be seen, the band played patriotic airs, and apparently every one was joyous.

In a short time after this night of pleasure the lurid flames of civil war burst forth, and Abraham Lincoln, of Illinois, the sixteenth President of the United States, was compelled to enter Washington secretly, like a thief in the night, to assume his place as the head of the Nation.

At the first evening reception held by President Lincoln there was a notable gathering. It took place on March 8, 1861, and long before the doors of the White House were opened, the grounds were filled with ladies and gentlemen patiently waiting for the hour of the reception to arrive. From eight until eleven o'clock the state apartments were crowded to overflowing with a brilliant assemblage, comprising all the prominent officials of the new administration, the diplomatic corps, the leading officers of the army and navy, the *élite* of Washington society, and hundreds of people who had come from distant states expressly for this occasion. The tall, grave President, towering above the majority of his guests, was incessantly engaged in shaking hands and acknowledging the congratulations and promises of support, and his countenance would brighten now and then with pleasure as he greeted old friends and heard their fervent "God bless you, Mr. President." Mrs. Lincoln stood at the side of her husband, a proud and happy woman, cheerful, smiling, and attractive to all who sought her acquaintance.

No man was ever more courteous, sympathetic, and considerate in high office than President Lincoln, and the humblest persons could approach him with the feeling that he would sympathize with their troubles, and relieve them if it was possible. The years of war caused him to have an anxious face, save when he was telling a story or engaged in a frolic "to get the kinks out," as he used to say. He liked all innocent pleasures, and was occasionally very jolly when he had dropped his cares for an hour or two and was enjoying himself with his family and friends. He was never known to speak harshly of any one, not even of those who were supposed to give him much annoyance, and when it was absolutely necessary for him to give a reprimand he would do so in a sort of serio-comic way, but effectively. As everybody knows, he was very fond of a good story, and possessed an inexhaustible fund of anecdotes and apt illustrations, which he was in the habit of using on many occasions to make his meaning plain to those who were rather dull of comprehension, or when he was in a sportive mood among friends. A little story from him would sometimes have a volume of significance. He was a diligent worker, spending many hours of the day at his desk, and oftentimes half the night. Frequently he would sit in profound thought, completely abstracted from outward things, or he would rise from his chair and slowly pace the floor while meditating, his lips moving, and his long, bony hands pointing here and there as his thoughts prompted. No one was permitted to disturb him, and back and forth he would walk, back and forth, until suddenly he would seem to wake from his abstraction, his sombre, rugged face would become almost beautiful by a tender smile, and he would turn to the person nearest to him and begin to relate a humorous anecdote.

An old resident of Washington who was an intimate friend of Lincoln, in speaking of the proclamation of emancipation, has said: " It is hard to believe now that very nearly half of the Republicans were opposed to the issue of that proclamation, and that half embraced the most active politicians. A strong effort was made to induce the President to withdraw the proclamation. It was issued in the summer of 1862, and was to take effect on the 1st of January, 1863, provided the rebels did not in the mean time lay down their arms. I never felt more anxious during the war than at that time, for fear that Lincoln would be induced to recall the proclamation. About Christmas time, 1862, a week or so before the proclamation was to take effect, if not recalled, I called on the President's private secretary in his room adjoining the President's room. We were sitting conversing before the fire, when Lincoln's door opened, he walked into the room and took a seat before the fire at my right hand. He slapped me on the shoulder and said, ' Well, my friend, the important day draws near.' ' Yes,' I replied, ' and I hope there will be no backing out or backing down.' ' Well,' he said, ' I don't know about that. Peter thought he would not deny his master, but he did.' I replied, ' I think you will do better than Peter did.' And he did."

Lincoln took great delight in theatricals, and said they rested and refreshed him more than anything else. Whenever he could leave his harassing business he would visit the theatre for an hour or two of recreation. He occasionally went behind the scenes and watched the actors at their work, and would seem to greatly enjoy all he saw in that curious mimic world. He had a box at Ford's old theatre, and on many evenings sat in it alone, hidden by the curtains, the audience having no suspicion that he was present. On one evening "Tad" Lincoln, the President's jolly little boy, whom everybody loved, accompanied his father to the theatre and went in among the actors. One of them dressed him in a ragged suit and sent him on the stage in a certain scene. The President, who was in his box, looked at the boy in astonishment for a few moments, and then threw up his hands, leaned back in his chair, and burst into a roar of laughter which was heard all over the theatre, thus revealing his presence to the audience. Instantly there was a round of applause, and he was compelled to acknowledge it. Tad ran off the stage when the applause began, changed his dress and went to his father's box, and the President put his arms around him and lovingly kissed him over and over again.

The mighty concerns of the war interfered with the social life of the White House, but there were some magnificent fêtes, and the occasional public receptions were very agreeable. There was always a proper amount of etiquette, but none of the "court ceremony" introduced by the former President. At all the entertainments Lincoln endeavored to make everything pleasant for his guests, and was quite successful as a host, his manner having a quaint simplicity which was very charming. He was six feet four inches in height, and his strong, sinewy body was capable of great endurance. His arms and legs were very long, and he was awkward in his movements. His face was thin and sallow, his forehead high and well developed, and his hair black and abundant. Usually his dark gray eyes had a sad expression, but now and then they would sparkle with roguish fun.

A sagacious critic of Lincoln's administration has said that "during all the perilous years of civil war he managed the Ship of State with remarkable skill, prudence, and wisdom." Second only to Washington in the hearts of his countrymen, his "great name will flow on with broadening time forever."

Mrs. Mary Todd Lincoln shared the anxieties of the war with her husband, rejoiced in every success, and was a loving companion to the great-hearted President. She was a frequent visitor to the hospitals in which scores of wounded soldiers were lying in pain and distress, and gladdened their lonely hours by her presence and tender solicitude for their comfort. The conservatory of the White House was stripped of its flowers, that the "poor sick boys" might have them by their bedsides, and delicacies of all sorts were taken from the White House kitchen to many a hospital, to tempt the appetites of the soldiers. Day by day the President's carriage, filled with flowers, fruits, and baskets of delicacies, conveyed the sympathetic, devoted woman to the scenes of suffering. She affectionately bathed the brows of the hapless ones stricken down in battle, consoled them as best she could, wrote letters to parents and friends in far-off states, and was indeed a blessed ministering angel at many a sorrowful couch. For this, if for nothing more, she should be held in loving remembrance : gentle, compassionate one, whose own bitter sorrows made her after years dark and comfortless.

Vice-President Andrew Johnson, of Tennessee, became President at the death of Lincoln, and was sworn into office by Chief Justice Chase on Saturday morning, April 15, 1865, at the Kirkwood House, in Washington. After a proper period of mourning President Johnson opened the White House to society, and made constant efforts to dispel the gloom arising from Lincoln's death, believing that " the new glad days of peace " should be joyously celebrated. During the greater part of his administration he entertained liberally, and introduced the pleasing feature of children's parties. The White House was often filled with little ones enjoying " a real party," with pretty flowers, fine music, and refreshments, and with the President to do them honor. Their young, gleeful voices rang through the ancient halls, and their blithesome games and frolics greatly delighted the elders.

As the President's wife, Mrs. Eliza McCardle Johnson, was an invalid, the management of the house was given over to her daughters, Mrs. Patterson and Mrs. Stover, who successfully carried out the customary social practices. President Johnson was above the medium height, and rather stout. He had brown hair, and light, expressive eyes, and a face denoting decision of character.

The White House was completely refurnished when Gen. Ulysses S. Grant, of Illinois, became President in 1869, and for eight years it was the scene of unceasing festivity. President Grant and family sought in all ways to make the house attractive to the gay society of " the city of palaces," and the dinners and fêtes were upon a splendid scale. Mrs. Julia Dent Grant proved an admirable hostess, easily winning the esteem of all who enjoyed her hospitality.

In 1877 Rutherford B. Hayes, of Ohio, began his term as President. At his first reception there was a very large assemblage. Mrs. Lucy Webb Hayes " received " in a plain black silk dress, and it was said that "Mrs. Madison in her time, in her pink satin and feathers, commanded hardly more admiration." On the 31st of December, 1877, President Hayes and wife celebrated the twenty-fifth anniversary of their marriage — the first "silver wedding" ever held in the White House. One hundred guests were present, and the "happy pair" received many hearty congratulations.

James A. Garfield, of Ohio, assumed the Presidency in 1881. His interesting family included his venerable mother, Mrs. Eliza Garfield, who was the first mother of a President to have a residence in the White House during the whole period of its existence. It is not necessary to relate the story of the sudden closing of Garfield's promising career, for it is firmly impressed on the memory of the American people.

Chester A. Arthur, of New York, Vice-President, succeeded to the Presidency on Sept. 19, 1881, and served to the end of the presidential term, 1885.

The list of occupants of the White House ends at present with Mr. and Mrs. Grover Cleveland, of New York. Mr. Cleveland became President on the 4th of March, 1885. The marriage of President Cleveland and Miss Frances Folsom on the evening of June 2, 1886, was an event of great interest to the people throughout the country. It was the first marriage of a President in the history of this famous residence of the Presidents.

ALONG THE CHESAPEAKE AND OHIO CANAL.

CHAPTER X.

THE Department of State is the first of the executive departments of the government. It has the supervision of all foreign affairs, and of all affairs concerning the states of the Union. It directs the diplomatic and consular service, has charge of all international claims commissions, issues passports, publishes and preserves all the laws enacted by Congress, and has other important duties. At first the foreign affairs of the government were directed by commissioners, but in 1789 Congress passed an act creating the Department of State, and authorizing the appointment of a chief official with the title of Secretary of State. For a time the department issued all patents and copyrights, had charge of the work of taking the census, and supervised the affairs of the territories. As now constituted it has a Diplomatic Bureau, a Consular Bureau, a Bureau of Indexes and Archives, a Bureau of Accounts, a Bureau of Statistics, a Bureau of Rolls, and several minor divisions. The entire business is carried on in a strictly confidential manner, and all persons connected with it are required to maintain the closest secrecy in regard to every matter which comes to their knowledge.

The Secretary of State is the first in rank of the members of the President's Cabinet, and on account of his office, and from long custom, his relations with the President are very intimate. His compensation is $8,000 per year. He has the general supervision of the

Department of State, and, under the direction of the President, nego-
tiates treaties with foreign powers, decides the various questions arising from the relations of the United States with other countries, and
is charged with the execution of all the state business.   There is a
first assistant Secretary of State, who has a compensation of $4,500
per year, and there are two other assistant secretaries who have $3,-
500 each.   The assistant secretaries have the supervision of the diplomatic and consular correspondence, and perform other duties assigned them by the Secretary of State.   There is a chief clerk, with
a salary of $2,750, who is in charge of the employés of the depart-
ment; and there are six chiefs of the bureaus, with salaries of $2,-
100, and nearly seventy clerks and employés.   Congress annually
appropriates $113,000 for the compensation of the officials and others,
and about $20,000 for the miscellaneous expenses of the department.

Since 1875 the department has occupied the southern portion of
the imposing State, War, and Navy Building, which stands directly
west of the White House, on part of the government reservation
called " The President's Grounds."   This building, in massive proportions and architectural beauty, has few equals in the world.   It
was begun in 1871, and has cost very nearly $12,000,000.   It was
designed by A. B. Mullett, and was constructed in the style of the
Italian renaissance, the material being Maine and Virginia granite.
Over a sub-basement and basement are four stories, surmounted by a
mansard roof of artistic design.   From north to south, including the
projections, the building is five hundred and sixty feet; exclusive
of projections, four hundred and seventy-one feet.   From east to
west it is three hundred and forty-two feet; exclusive of projections, two hundred and fifty-three feet.   Its greatest height is one
hundred and twenty-eight feet.   There are four façades, alike in
design and construction, and four grand entrances through lofty
pavilions reached by broad flights of stone steps.   Huge blocks of
granite, each over twenty tons in weight, form the platforms to the
entrances.   The greatest possible care has been taken in the construction, and the building is entirely fire proof.   All the parts are
in harmony, the ornamentation is a tasteful combination of the classic
and modern methods, and the result is an almost perfect specimen of
architecture.

The interior of the building has been constructed in a very magnificent and yet entirely substantial manner.   There are wide staircases of granite with bronze balusters, long, spacious corridors, and

THE STATE, WAR, AND NAVY BUILDING.

innumerable apartments, richly frescoed and adorned, and furnished
with every convenience that could be suggested for the transacting
of the business of the three departments for which the building was
erected.   The War Department occupies the whole of the northern
and western portion, and the Navy Department the eastern.

Very large and elegant apartments are occupied by the Department of State.   On the second floor are the apartments of the Secretary of State and his assistants.   They are finely painted in dis-
temper, and splendidly furnished.

The diplomatic reception-room, in which the foreign ministers
have audience with the Secretary of State, is sumptuous in its appointments.   It is sixty feet long, and twenty feet wide.   A great
mirror in an ebony and gold frame reaches from the floor to the ceiling; the furniture is of ebony, and the upholstery of bluish-brown
brocade.   The walls are painted in Egyptian style, and the floor is
tessellated and partially covered by oriental rugs.   Paintings and
busts adorn the walls and mantels, and two large chandeliers hang
from the ceiling.   The ante-room is also richly decorated and furnished.

The Bureau of Indexes and Archives occupies large apartments
excellently arranged for its business.   This bureau has charge of all
the letters and documents of the department, and hundreds of official
papers are carefully examined and filed every day by its employés.
A most perfect system is used, and although the accumulation of
state documents during the past century is vast almost beyond belief,
anything that is wanted can be produced in a very short time.
Whenever the officials of the department desire certain papers they
apply to this bureau.   The demand is constant, and embraces an
extensive range of subjects daily.   Papers of the widest variety and
character in reference to every country in the world with which the
government has official relations, and also to all parts of the United
States, are called for to be used in the settlement of the multifarious
questions under consideration.   The correspondence with foreign
ministers and consuls is enormous, and the miscellaneous correspondence is also large and important.   All the letters are opened
and indexed in this bureau before they are delivered to the chief
officials for their inspection.

Several apartments of the bureau contain many precious archives
of the Nation.   The first draft of the Declaration of Independence
and of the Federal Constitution are here carefully preserved.   Wash-

ington's commission as Commander-in-chief of the American Army, and a host of documents pertaining to the Revolution and the early days of the government, are to be seen. The letters and papers of Washington, Jefferson, Madison, and Monroe, and some of the other Presidents, are preserved in large volumes, many of the manuscripts appearing as clear and distinct as if written yesterday. Autograph letters from kings and queens, princes, statesmen, and historical personages who have flourished during the past one hundred years, are to be found in these collections. Here are the original copies of all the laws enacted by Congress, and of all the treaties made by the United States with foreign nations, from the first, with France in 1778, and the second, with England — the treaty of peace, bearing date of Sept. 3, 1783 — down to those of recent years. One treaty with Turkey is gorgeously embellished with golden letters; but the most unique treaty in the collection is one with Japan, which is contained in a costly lacquered case covered with silk. The quaint Japanese characters, covering many pages of fine paper, are clearly and boldly portrayed. The royal signature appears at the top, and you read from the bottom. The treaty was brought to Washington by two officials of high rank, who were charged with its safe delivery on peril of their lives. One day they triumphantly marched into the Department of State bearing aloft on long bamboo poles a queerly-constructed box, in which was the important document. Glad, indeed, were they to have escaped the "disastrous chances" of land and sea, and when the royal agreement finally passed into the hands of the Secretary of State they appeared greatly relieved, for their heads were no longer in danger.

The great seal of the United States is kept in one of the apartments. This seal is affixed to all executive proclamations, to all warrants of extradition or pardon, and to all commissions issued to ministers and consuls to foreign countries.

The library of the department is in the third story. It is in a spacious room with three balconies, and is well lighted by a dome of glass. The room is constructed entirely of iron, wrought in graceful forms, and beautifully decorated in pearl and gold tints. Jefferson established the library, and many of the oldest books contain his autograph. On the shelves are over thirty thousand volumes, comprising the laws of all the states, and works relating to history, diplomacy, and international affairs. They are in many languages, and are extensively used by the members of the foreign legations in Washington, and by the officials of the department.

The diplomatic and consular service requires a large force of officials stationed in the important cities and towns throughout the world. The expenditure for this service—for what is termed "the foreign intercourse"—is about $2,500,000 per year. Thirty-three legations, with ministers, secretaries, and attachés, and more than nine hundred consular offices, are maintained by the United States. The ministers at London, Paris, Berlin, and St. Petersburg receive salaries of $17.500 per year; those at Vienna, Rome, Madrid, Peking, Rio de Janeiro, Tokei, and the City of Mexico, $12,000; those at Guatemala, Santiago, and Lima, $10,000; those in minor countries, $7,500 and $5,000. The consuls-general at London, Paris, Havana, and Rio de Janeiro receive $6,000.

There are twenty-five foreign legations in Washington, most of them occupying large, finely furnished mansions. They represent all the prominent countries, and have many attachés, and a throng of servants. Numerous receptions and dinners are given by the diplomatic corps, and at certain seasons the members are entertained at the White House. Then they wear their gaudy court costumes, and display their glittering orders and decorations. By the United States statutes they are exempt from arrest, and no process of law can reach them. This immunity extends to all the members of a diplomat's family, and even to the servants, if they are not citizens of the United States.

The Chinese Legation occupies a fine mansion, in which there is ample room for the grand entertainments given by the Chinese Minister during the winter. It is furnished entirely in the Mongolian style of high official life, and its apartments are filled with rare and curious articles. The walls of the parlors are hung with Chinese tapestry of delicate texture, elegantly embroidered with the sacred maxims of Confucius upon the virtues of charity, honesty, and justice; and massive oriental vases of peculiar design mingle their bright colors with the gold and scarlet of the unique and magnificent furniture. One strangely fashioned vase has been in the possession of the minister's family for more than two centuries. There are silk-embroidered screens, worked by Chinese ladies, and in various nooks are well-filled book-cases with costly volumes of the Chinese classics. The parlors, and many of the other apartments, are the very perfection of bric-à-brac and oriental adornment, and are very attractive to guests. The smoking-room is furnished with a varied collection of Chinese pipes, and has comfortable divans, and, in fact, is a ver-

FRENCH LEGATION.

RESIDENCE OF THE GERMAN LEGATION.

itable smoker's paradise. In the halls are groups of Chinese statuary, some being of a humorous character, modeled with much skill and fidelity to nature. At the minister's banquets the tables are spread in grand style, with exquisite oriental ware, silver and gold dishes, and many unique articles of table service. Numerous Eastern delicacies are furnished, and first chop Chinese tea, rarely to be had in the United States, is served in quaint wicker-covered pots. The minister receives his guests attired in his gorgeous court dress of colored silks, and the attachés of the legation, numbering more than a dozen, appear in silken robes of superb quality and brilliant hues.

The Japanese Minister has a large residence furnished in the picturesque fashion of his country, and within its walls are many quaint and beautiful articles. There are a number of young Japanese gentlemen of good education and refined manners attached to the legation. The minister gives brilliant receptions and banquets, and is fond of society.

Fêtes are frequently given by the English, French, Spanish.

Russian, and Mexican legations. The residence of the English Minister was erected by his government, and is one of the notable mansions of Washington. It has broad halls, a great ball-room illuminated by three chandeliers, a spacious dining-room, and elegant parlors. It is situated on Connecticut Avenue.

Upon their arrival in Washington the members of the diplomatic corps present themselves to the President and the Secretary of State, and then make ceremonious calls upon the Vice-President, the Speaker of the House of Representatives, the members of the Cabinet, the Justices of the Supreme Court, and the Senators. They call on the President on New Year's day. During the winter the Secretary of State gives a series of dinners, at which all the foreign ambassadors appear.

MASSACHUSETTS AVENUE, SHOWING CHURCH OF THE ASCENSION.

CHAPTER XI.

DURING the session of the First Congress under the Constitution, in 1789, an act was passed to establish the Treasury Department, which was to have the entire charge of the finances of the government. Previous to that time commissioners had performed the duties appertaining to the collection of public moneys and the settlement of public accounts, but there had been no well-regulated and competent system. By the new act the officials authorized were a Secretary of the Treasury, who was to be the financial head of the government, and to have a seat in the President's Cabinet; an assistant secretary, a comptroller, an auditor, a treasurer, and a register. When the government removed to Washington in 1800, a small wooden building was erected for the Treasury, but it was burned to the ground by the British troops in 1814. Another building was speedily constructed, and remained until March 31, 1833, when it was entirely destroyed by fire. It was proposed to locate the present Treasury Building farther down the tract on which the other buildings had been erected, in order that the White House might be seen from the Capitol; but the story is that President Jackson became impatient at the delay of Robert Mills, the architect, in selecting a location, and walked over the ground one morning, planted his cane in the extreme northeastern cor-

ner, and said, "Here, right here, I want the corner-stone laid!"
And the stone was laid there, and the huge structure was erected
where it breaks the continuity of Pennsylvania Avenue, and prevents
the President from looking toward Capitol Hill from the windows of
his residence.

In 1841 the Treasury Building was completed. It was constructed
of Virginia freestone, and on its eastern façade a lofty colonnade of
thirty Ionic columns was placed. In 1855 it was found necessary
to add extensions, and designs for these were made by Thomas U.
Walter. The extensions were constructed of Maine granite, and
were finished in 1869. At that time the total cost of the building was
nearly $7,000,000, and since then large sums have been expended
in alterations and interior decorations. The building extends four
hundred and sixty feet on Fifteenth Street, and has a frontage of two
hundred and sixty-four feet on Pennsylvania Avenue. It is Grecian
in architecture, with various modifications. Over a rustic basement
are three stories, surmounted by a balustrade. There are four façades, those on the north, west, and south having massive porticoes
of Ionic columns. The walls of the extensions are composed of
pilasters, with belt courses, resting on the basement story. The
massive pilasters, monolithic columns, and blocks of granite were
quarried on Dix Island, near Rockland, Maine, and brought to Washington in vessels of peculiar construction. Each portico has a broad
flight of steps descending to a spacious platform, on each side of
which is a flower-garden. The northern front is ornamented with a
stone fountain. The building is very substantial, and its great size
and the superb architectural design of its extensions, give it a majestic appearance. Seemingly, it should be large enough for any
possible business that the Treasury Department might have to do,
but this is not the case. It is far too small, and at present some of
the Treasury bureaus have to be accommodated elsewhere for lack
of room in this vast structure.

If the business of the department continues to increase during the
next ten years as rapidly as it has the past ten, greater extensions to
the Treasury Building will be necessary to accommodate the force
of employés which will be required for the financial service of the
government. The country is growing so fast that, year by year, the
business of the Treasury increases enormously. Fifty years ago a
few men were able to attend to everything connected with the finances
in quite an easy manner; now an army of officials, clerks, and em-

THE TREASURY BUILDING.

ployés drive the work to the utmost of their strength, but are unable to dispose of it promptly, and there are many embarrassing accumulations. The settlement of some public accounts is often delayed for months, from sheer inability to cope with the work. Army paymasters' accounts will average two years in settlement, so that a paymaster cannot know how he stands on the Treasury books until two years after he renders his accounts, and neither does the Treasury Department know until after the same period whether the paymaster has properly accounted for the thousands of dollars advanced to him for disbursement.

The Treasury Building contains nearly two hundred rooms, exclusive of the basement. Most of the rooms are spacious and well arranged, and those occupied by the principal officials are handsomely furnished. The halls and corridors are wide and well lighted, and all of the interior furnishing is substantial and often elegant. There is such a constant pressure of work, and so much of it is necessarily of a private, confidential nature, that but few of the rooms are accessible to visitors. Business with the divisions is usually done through the chief clerks, whose offices are open to the public. To inspect the money-vaults it is necessary to obtain a permit from the Treasurer of the United States. The building is crowded with employés, nearly three thousand persons performing service in it daily. Stringent rules are enforced for the government of this host of workers, and a rigid business system prevails in every division.

The rooms occupied by the Secretary of the Treasury, and the numerous divisions appertaining to what is called "The Secretary's Office," are large and finely furnished. The Secretary, as a member of the Cabinet, has a compensation of $8,000 per year. There are two assistant secretaries who receive $4,500 each, and in the Secretary's office are a chief clerk at a salary of $2,700, a stenographer at $2,000, and several chiefs of divisions at salaries averaging $2,500. There are also one hundred and thirty clerks, fifty of whom are women, and a large force of book-keepers, messengers, and others. The salary list is $495,000 per year. The Secretary's office may be called "the official division" of the Treasury Department. It has special duties connected with the Secretary's supervision of the sub-departments of the Treasury, but it is in a certain sense independent of them.

The sub-departments are large and important. They occupy

special suites of rooms, and have many officials, clerks, and employés, whose total compensation amounts to $2,500,000 per year. These are the principal divisions: The offices of the First Comptroller and Second Comptroller, the Commissioner of Customs, the Commissioner of Internal Revenue, the Treasurer of the United States, the Register of the Treasury, the Comptroller of the Currency, the Director of the Mint, and the First, Second, Third, Fourth, Fifth, and Sixth Auditors. Then there are the offices of the Supervising Architect, who has charge of the erection of public buildings throughout the country; the Light-house Board, the Bureau of Statistics, the Bureau of Engraving and Printing, the Life-Saving Service, the Secret Service, the Coast and Geodetic Survey, the Revenue Cutter and Marine Hospital Service, the Construction of Standard Weights and Measures, and the Steamboat Inspection Service.

All the sub-departments are under the general supervision of the Secretary of the Treasury, and it must be admitted that this distinguished official has a great deal to engage his time and attention if

THE BUREAU OF ENGRAVING AND PRINTING.

he faithfully performs his duty. If a secretary carefully verifies everything in the sub-departments; if he is determined to know all about the official acts of his subordinates — and many secretaries have been scrupulously particular in this respect — he must give all his time to the work, and even then he can hardly master the full details of the colossal transactions of the Treasury Department.

There are sub-treasuries in New York, Philadelphia, Boston, Baltimore, Cincinnati, New Orleans, St. Louis, and San Francisco; and mints in Philadelphia, San Francisco, New Orleans, Carson, Nevada; and Denver. Colorado. Assay offices are also located in New York, Helena, Montana; Boise City, Idaho; Charlotte, North Carolina; and St. Louis. All these financial institutions are under the supervision of the Secretary of the Treasury. They are of great importance, and transact a very large business. They are sustained at a yearly cost of $1,556,000.

The First Comptroller is familiarly called "the autocrat of the Treasury," as he has been given remarkable power by Congress. He countersigns all the warrants on the Treasury for the payment of money, and not a dollar can be obtained unless his signature is on the warrant. He decides every matter of payment, and even if a claim has been passed by a department of the government, the claimant, be he the highest official, even the President of the United States, cannot receive what is due him unless the First Comptroller is satisfied that the claim is correct. It is supposed that this official was created when the Treasury Department was first organized, as a check upon the officials whose duty it was to audit claims; and from time to time additional power has been given him by statute, so that now he has the final decision in regard to all payments, and can reverse the decision of any official, and even refuse his signature to a warrant signed by the President or the Secretary of the Treasury. There is no appeal from his decision except to the courts. In fact, through the laws which give him absolute power, he can stand before the government money-vaults, and allow only what he thinks is proper to be paid out of them. The President can remove him from office, but he would find it difficult to explain why he removed an official for doing what Congress has authorized him to do, and particularly as Congress has deemed it necessary to make this official a check upon the Executive.

The salary of the First Comptroller is $5.000 per year. He has

a deputy with a salary of $2,700, four chiefs of divisions with sala-
ries of $2,100, and fifty-one clerks. Eighty-three thousand dollars
are yearly expended for the maintenance of his office. The Second
Comptroller has a salary of $5,000, and his office is provided with
a large force of clerks.

In the offices of the auditors the accounts of the various departments of the government are examined, after which they are transmitted, with the vouchers, to the offices of the First Comptroller and
Second Comptroller for final examination and approval. Each auditor examines the accounts of certain departments, and has full authority to approve or reject any account, subject to the final decision
of the First Comptroller. The auditors have salaries of $3,600,
and employ many clerks.

The Treasurer of the United States is in charge of the government funds. He receives and disburses all the public moneys, has
the custody of the great money-vaults, holds the bonds deposited by
the national banks to secure their circulating notes, issues new treasury notes and redeems old ones, is the custodian of the Indian trust
funds, pays the interest on the public debt, and has numerous other
duties. His salary is $6,000, and he is required to give a bond for
the faithful performance of his duties in the sum of $150,000. There
is an assistant treasurer with a salary of $3,600, and in the six
divisions of the department there is a large force of accountants,
cashiers, and clerks.

The money-vaults in which the government keeps its reserve
funds are located in the basement of the Treasury Building. They
are massive iron and steel structures, which are faithfully guarded
night and day. There are other vaults on the first floor, near the
cash-room, which contain the funds for current payments. In the
different vaults and safes are millions of dollars in treasury notes,
in gold and silver coins, and in United States bonds — "wealth beyond the potential dream of avarice!" The Treasurer of the United
States is the custodian of this vast sum, is solely responsible for its
safe keeping and proper disbursement; and it can be truly said of
him, that he can day by day indulge in the sight and touch of a
larger amount of money than any other person in the country. If
we could examine the great pile of bank-notes and bonds, and the
bags of coins in the compartments of the vaults, we should find that
they represented between four and five hundred millions of dollars.

In the first place, there are bonds held in trust for various purposes to the amount of about four hundred millions. Then there is national currency of the value of fifty or sixty millions — to-day more, to-morrow less, as the payments and receipts cause the fund to increase or diminish. In the coin sections there are usually from twenty to forty millions in gold and silver, and this represents but a small fraction of the specie the government has on hand, as the greater portion is deposited in the sub-treasuries in other cities. Sometimes the vaults will contain many tons of the precious metals.

There never has been an attempt made to rob the Treasury, and it is believed that it would be an impossibility. A guard of sixty men, nearly all old soldiers, patrol the building day and night. The men are commanded by a captain and lieutenant, and are armed with revolvers of the largest and best variety. When the building is closed at night, every room is inspected, and if a safe is found unlocked an officer is placed in charge of it, and the person whose duty it was to lock it is sent for. After the inspection the guard is set, and a rigid discipline maintained until morning. The men patrol their beats every ten or fifteen minutes, and the lieutenant goes the rounds every two hours.

The redemption and counting division is a busy and interesting place. Here worn and mutilated bank-notes, retired from service, are examined and counted, previous to being destroyed. Every year national currency of the value of two hundred millions is counted, canceled, and destroyed. The counting is done by female clerks, many of whom acquire marvelous skill, and seldom, if ever, make a mistake in manipulating the great piles of valuable paper. Some of the clerks have been at the work for eight or ten years, and in that time have handled many millions of dollars. They sit at long tables, on which bank-notes are spread as thick as leaves in a forest. Package after package is opened, the notes are closely scrutinized and rapidly counted, and are then turned over to officials who cancel them by means of machines which punch them full of holes. Afterward the " dead " currency is placed in water and thoroughly macerated, nothing remaining but a mass of paper-pulp. It is then given into the hands of a special officer, to be burned. The national currency received from the Bureau of Engraving and Printing, and from government depositories throughout the country, is also carefully counted and verified before it is accepted, and the amount certified to as correct.

THE MASONIC TEMPLE.

In the redemption bureau a great deal of delicate work is done in verifying currency which has been partially destroyed by fire or other causes, and which has been sent to the Treasury to be exchanged for new notes. Ladies who are expert in this business take the mass of burned or otherwise damaged currency in hand, and with long, thin knives and powerful magnifying-glasses slowly and cautiously separate the pieces, and then endeavor to trace out each note alleged to be in the collection. Sometimes the entire amount can be thus verified, even if the notes were badly burned; but usually from ten to thirty per cent. is lost to the owner from sheer inability to distinguish in the mass of *débris* anything that bears the slightest resemblance to a bank-note. Hundreds of thousands of dollars — in fact, an astonishing amount — rendered worthless by various accidents are received every year, and the greatest of care is taken to redeem as much of the money as possible. One day a mass of cinders, the remains of a package of bank-notes of the value of $1,700, was received from Missouri for redemption. The money had been placed

in a stove over night for safe keeping, and was entirely forgotten the
next morning until after the fire was lighted. The charred fragments
were carefully collected, brought to the Treasury, and placed in the
hands of one of the most expert ladies of the redemption bureau.
She succeeded, after ten days of arduous labor, in identifying nearly
eighty per cent. of the notes, and when their owner received the new
money he was so delighted at his good fortune that he presented the
skillful lady with a brand new one hundred dollar bill.

A curious case is related of the redemption of notes amounting to
$2,091, which were found in a secret pocket in the undershirt of a
German, who had died in a New York almshouse and had been buried
in a pauper's grave for three months. A relative of the supposed
pauper arrived from Europe, and had his body disinterred, when the
money was discovered. The condition of the notes, after they had
been in contact with a decomposing body for such a length of time,
can be imagined, and the lady to whom was assigned the duty of
examining and verifying them was speedily deserted by her companions, and had the entire end of the apartment to herself. The work,
although very disagreeable, was satisfactorily accomplished, and clean,
new notes were returned to the German's heir.

The cash-room of the Treasury is a large apartment on the first
floor, beautifully constructed of polished marbles of a wide variety.
It is a palatial banking-office, all its appurtenances being sumptuous
and ornate. Here are a dozen cashiers who daily disburse great
sums of money in the payment of warrants and checks to the cred-
itors of the government. Usually there are ten or fifteen million dollars in the vaults to meet the requirements of the daily business. The
cashing of a warrant for one million dollars is no unusual thing, and
warrants for several millions are occasionally presented. On one
occasion the pension office presented a warrant for ten millions,
which was promptly cashed. Members of the Secret Service are
constantly in the room to guard the treasure. By ascending to the
second floor, visitors can enter the balcony which extends around the
cash-room, and watch the cashiers make the payments, enjoying, if
only for a few moments, the sight of a great deal of money.

The national currency is manufactured at the Bureau of Engraving and Printing, which is located in a large brick building on the
Mall at the corner of Fourteenth and B streets southwest. The
building is of the Romanesque style, and was erected at a cost of

$300,000. It has three stories and a high basement, and on the northeast end is a tall tower of handsome design. The interior is constructed in a very elaborate and elegant manner. Visitors are permitted to inspect the different divisions of the bureau, and a guide is provided to conduct all who apply on "the grand tour" of the rooms.

The entire third story is devoted to the printing division. Here are two hundred and fifty plate-presses, worked by hand, and a force of about five hundred men and women constantly engaged in printing sheets of bank-notes, bonds, and internal revenue stamps. Intense activity prevails throughout the long, spacious room. Those who have the idea that government employés "take things easy," should look at this host of energetic workers who waste not a moment, but with the untiring movement of a great machine, drive on the work they have to do. Each employé has to perform a certain fixed amount of work in a day—and the same is true of the employés in most of the departments of the public service—and if it is not done the failure is recorded, and the employé stands in danger of dismissal. Six hundred sheets a day must be printed on each press, and when it is considered that every time an impression is taken the delicate copper and steel plate has to be removed from the press, carefully wiped dry, then polished with whiting, then inked, and all the ink rubbed off save that contained in the minute lines of the engraving, then put on to the press and the fibre paper laid on it expertly, some idea may be obtained of the labor necessary to print the number of sheets required each day. There is, indeed, no time allowed for loitering. To print a bank-note, three impressions are necessary. First, the centre picture or design on the back is printed; then the border for the back, and then the face of the note. The sheets printed on each press bear the name of the pressman, and all bad impressions—those too light or too dark, or defaced in any way—are thrown out by the examiners, and recorded to the discredit of the pressman.

In the second story are the examining, lettering and numbering, and counting divisions. When the sheets of currency come from the press-room they are closely inspected by the examiners to detect imperfections, and those that are imperfect are thrown out and sent to the redemption bureau of the Treasury to be finally counted and destroyed. The perfect sheets are passed over to the employés in

charge of the lettering and numbering machines, and the letters and
numbers belonging to the series are printed on each note. When
this process is finished the clean, crisp notes are given into the hands
of a large force of women, who count them with marvelous celerity,
after which they are taken to the basement story, where the red seal
of the government is stamped on them. The new-made paper dollars are then deposited in the vaults of the bureau until they shall be
conveyed to the Treasury in the guarded treasure-wagons. It requires about twenty-eight days to complete a lot of bank-notes of
small denominations, aggregating five million dollars — certainly a
very short time to make so much money. The government is continually obliged to print new currency with which to redeem the worn-
out notes that are all the time being sent to the Treasury by the
national banks to be exchanged.

While the employès in the several divisions of the bureau are
working, they are under the strict surveillance of officials stationed
here and there throughout the rooms. Around each room is a high,
closely-woven wire screen, completely enclosing the employés, and
rendering it impossible for any of them to pass the sheets of currency to persons who may come into the corridors, even if they were
so disposed. At the close of working hours no one is permitted to
leave the building until the heads of the divisions have reported to
the chief of the bureau that every printed and unprinted sheet, and
every stamp. die, and plate have been properly accounted for.

The engraving division, in the basement, is fitted up with the best
appliances for executing the fine plates required. Here is a massive
vault used as a depository for all the plates and rolls, which at night
are securely locked in it. The engravers are guarded by watchmen,
lazily sitting in comfortable arm-chairs a few steps off, who keep their
eyes fixed on the blocks of steel and copper being engraved, for
here. as in the other divisions, all the employés are under surveillance very much as if they were inmates of a prison.

The Register of the Treasury, who has charge of the account-
books wherein all the receipts and expenditures of the government
are recorded. and the Comptroller of the Currency, who has charge
of the national banks and their circulating notes, are important officials. and their divisions have numerous officials and employés. The
Register has a salary of $4,000 per year, and the assistant register
$2,250; the Comptroller has $5,000, and the deputy-comptroller,

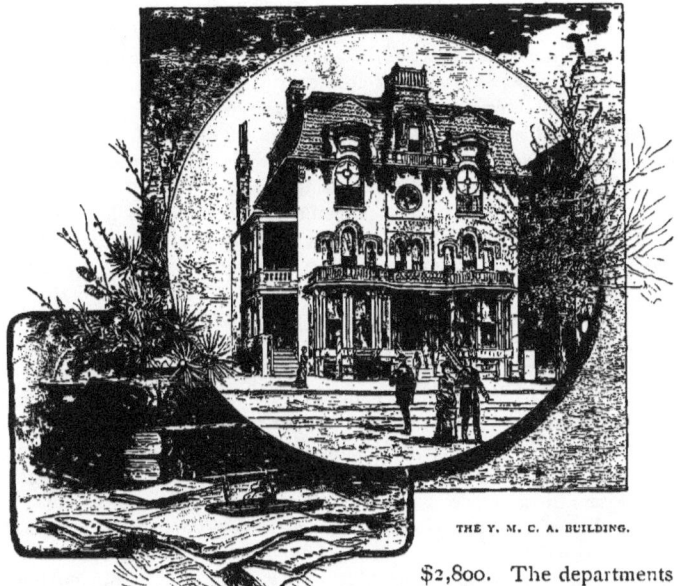

THE Y. M. C. A. BUILDING.

$2,800. The departments of Customs and Internal Revenue are very extensive. The Commissioner of Customs has a salary of $4,000, and the Commissioner of Internal Revenue, $6,000. The Director of the Mint, who has the supervision of the mints and assay offices, has a salary of $4,500.

A large amount of important and very beneficial work is performed by the Secret Service Office, which is in charge of a chief with a salary of $3,500, who reports to the Solicitor of the Treasury. Counterfeiting, and the numerous cunning devices employed to fraudulently obtain money and lands from the government, are investigated by the Secret Service agents, and evidence obtained to convict offenders. The office rooms in the Treasury Building contain an extensive museum of counterfeit bank-notes and coins, and the plates, dies, and moulds used by counterfeiters, and there are also collections of photographs of the fraternity. The office keeps a thorough record of cases and of men, and it can furnish the fullest information concerning hundreds of persons who are ranked among the dangerous classes. It is thought that the Secret Service does remarkably good work in the suppression of counterfeiting, when the extent of the country and the wide variety of the government money are considered. Many of the most skilled bank-note counterfeiters have been given long terms of imprisonment, and those who are at liberty are kept, as far as possible, under close surveillance. The greatest difficulty the Secret Service now has to contend with is the counterfeiting of silver coins, which is largely increasing, and proving very annoying to the government, as well as a matter of considerable loss to the public. Counterfeiters of silver money now pay great attention to the mixing of their metals, and the plating of the coin, and consequently the detection of the counterfeits is very difficult. There are imitations of the silver dollar and half-dollar in the possession of the Secret Service which are almost as perfect as the coins made in the United States mints, in weight, size, ring, and general appearance.

Unceasing efforts are made to discover the counterfeiters who work so much mischief. Not long since an entire family was captured in Vermont,—father, mother, sons and daughters, and even the aged grandsire,—all diligently laboring at the nefarious business. The coin-testers in the mints, whose duty it is to test each coin received, furnish a good deal of the information as to the counterfeits, particularly those which deceive bank officials and experts. A coin must be quite perfect to pass their test. They balance the coin on the top of the middle finger, and lightly tap its rim with the forefinger. Thousands of coins are tested by them, and they acquire wonderful skill, readily detecting the slightest false ring or "rote," as they term it. Counterfeit coins are also analyzed in the Treasury assay office, and their qualities given to the Secret Service agents, to aid them in their work.

The attic of the Treasury Building consists of a series of capacious rooms, halls, and corridors. Many of the rooms are filled with documents relating to the department and its multifarious transactions during the past threescore years. There are tons of written and printed papers — cases reaching to the roof filled with reports, vouchers, letters, books, records. certificates of deposit, some of them yellow with age. In this vast documentary museum are hundreds of curious relics of by-gone days.

CHAPTER XII.

THE War Department has charge of the military service of the government, and is under the direction of the Secretary of War. It occupies the northern portion of the State, War, and Navy Building, with several divisions located elsewhere in Washington. It has been an executive department since 1789. The divisions are, the office of the Secretary of War, the Headquarters of the Army, the departments of the Adjutant-General, Inspector-General, Quartermaster-General, Commissary-General, Surgeon-General, and Paymaster-General; the Corps of Engineers, the Ordnance Department, the Bureau of Military Justice, the Signal Office, the Bureau of War Records, etc. The department, in addition to the charge of military affairs, has the management and control of numerous matters that are not strictly warlike. Among the number are the manifold river and harbor improvements throughout the United States, the government explorations and geographical surveys, the various public works, the gathering and promulgation of the weather reports, and the national cemeteries and asylums. It is a vast establishment, requiring a host of workers and an enormous yearly expenditure to maintain it. In some recent years the disbursements have amounted to about fifty millions of dollars. Every year the army and its adjuncts require the expenditure of nearly $29,000,000, the salaries and expenses of the department amount to $2,400,000, and from ten to twenty millions are expended for public works.

The Secretary of War is a Cabinet minister, and receives $8,000 per year. He has a chief clerk with a salary of $2,500, a disbursing clerk with $2,000, a stenographer with $1,800, and three chiefs of divisions with $2,000 each. His office is provided with fifty-six clerks and numerous other employés. The chief clerk has the general superintendence, is in charge of the correspondence, and acts as a medium between the Secretary and the heads of the sub-departments. The several military bureaus have many employés, and are part of the army establishment, the chiefs being officers of the regular army.

The old War Department building, so familiar to thousands of soldiers of the volunteer army during the Rebellion, was demolished in 1879. It stood where the northern wing of the State, War, and Navy Building now stands, and had a history going back to President Monroe's time. It was a three-story brick structure with a huge portico of marble pillars, and in front of it were a number of grand old trees, among the largest and finest in Washington. When it was proposed to cut down these trees there was an earnest protest from army officers, but the new building required the space, and the woodman could not " spare the axe."

In the present palatial building the department offices are all very spacious and magnificent. The apartments used by the Secretary of War are artistically decorated and richly furnished. They are in the second story, fronting on Pennsylvania Avenue. The Secretary sits at a handsomely carved mahogany desk, with his private secretary and his stenographer near at hand. In the early part of the day he receives members of Congress, the chiefs of the sub-departments, and those whose business renders an interview necessary. The afternoon is devoted to an examination of the reports and papers submitted to him for approval. It is his duty to make a careful study of the public business pertaining to the important department he controls, and to ascertain the most correct and efficient methods of doing it. No man, it is declared, can master the details of this department who does not give his nights, as well as his days, to their study; and unless the details are mastered, a Secretary of War can never fully understand the questions he has to decide, or be competent to give proper advice to the President.

In one of the rooms of the Secretary's office is a collection of portraits of past Secretaries of War, and in other rooms are portraits of famous soldiers and a series of well-painted battle-scenes. The

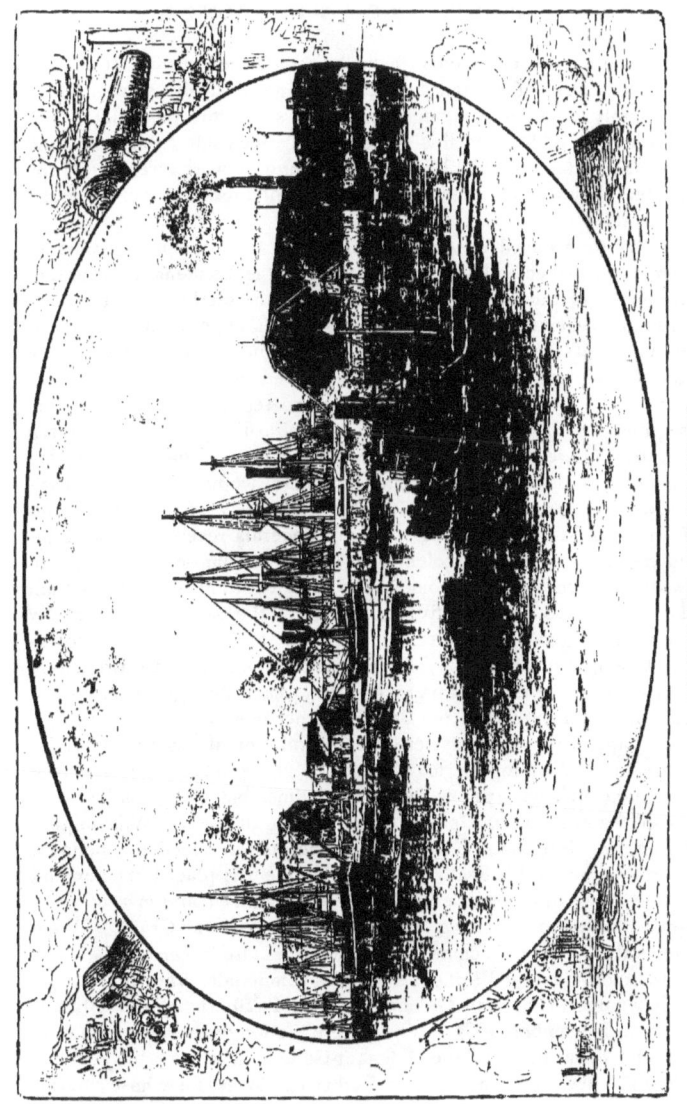

THE NAVY YARD, FROM THE POTOMAC.

office library is contained in a finely embellished room. It consists of 3,000 works of reference, and 15,000 miscellaneous works, which are freely circulated among army officers and the department employés. In addition to this library, the various sub-departments and bureaus all have special libraries, consisting of works treating of the matters they are occupied with, and many of these libraries are large and valuable.

The rooms used for the headquarters of the army are very handsomely furnished. They are occupied by the Lieutenant-General in command of the army, his aides-de-camp, and clerks. Here reports are daily received, and the numerous details appertaining to the supervision of the military force are attended to. The regular army consists of over two thousand commissioned officers, and 23,000 enlisted men, and is divided into twenty-five regiments of infantry, ten regiments of cavalry, and five regiments of artillery. Three hundred scouts, engaged in Indian warfare on the plains of the far West, are also part of the army organization. There are nine military departments throughout the United States. The pay of the Lieutenant-General is $11,000 per year. Major-generals receive $7,500, brigadier-generals $5,500, colonels $3,500, lieutenant-colonels $3,000, majors $2,500, captains from $1,800 to $2,000, and lieutenants from $1,400 to $1,600. After five years' service the pay of officers below the rank of general is increased from ten to forty per cent., according to length of service. All commissioned officers are retired from service on three-quarters pay when they reach the age of sixty-two. Enlisted men are paid from $13 to $21 per month.

In the army headquarters are portraits of the commanders-in-chief, from Washington to Sheridan. There have been nineteen commanders from 1775 to the present time, but Congress has conferred the full title of General on only three of them — Washington, Grant, and Sherman. General Washington received the honor a short time before his death, in 1799, when he was placed in command of the army, in expectation of a war with France; and in 1866 Congress revived the title as a special honor for General Grant. When General Sherman became commander he also received the title. Lieutenant-General Winfield Scott was commander from June, 1841, to November, 1861, and General William T. Sherman from March, 1869, to November, 1883. These were the longest terms of service.

The department of the Adjutant-General is a very busy place. Here are five hundred clerks and other employés, for whose salaries the sum of $691,000 is annually appropriated. Two hundred of the clerks are constantly engaged in preparing reports to expedite the settlement of pension claims. The muster-rolls and papers relating to enlistments and discharges are kept in this department. The Adjutant-General publishes the orders in regard to military affairs, issues commissions, and has charge of the army discipline. There are four assistant adjutants-general.

Another large and important department is that of the Quartermaster-General, which provides the means of transportation by land and water of troops and the materials of war. It furnishes horses for the artillery and cavalry, and all the clothing, tents, camp and garrison equipage for the army; builds barracks, hospitals, store-houses, bridges, etc., and also has charge of the eighty-one national cemeteries in various parts of the country, in which soldiers are buried. It yearly expends from ten to fifteen millions of dollars.

The Paymaster-General is charged with paying the army and the military academy. He has an office force of fifty persons, and annually disburses over thirteen millions of dollars.

The Bureau of War Records has published seven volumes of records of the Civil War, and has other volumes in course of preparation. Records of the Union army, from 1861 to 1865, have been gathered from all sources with diligent and persevering labor, and a great collection of records of the Confederate service has also come into the possession of the bureau. Search is constantly being made throughout the Southern States by special agents, for original documents relating to the war, and frequently very valuable Confederate papers are discovered.

Carefully preserved in the Bureau of Military Justice are a number of relics of the Lincoln assassination. They include the pistol with which the President was shot, the fatal bullet, flattened by contact with his skull, the bowie-knife that the assassin brandished, and the hat he wore, and other articles associated with the historic event. The bureau is under the supervision of the Judge-Advocate-General, and has charge of the proceedings of courts-martial and courts of inquiry, and furnishes reports on various matters submitted to it by the Secretary of War.

The department of the Surgeon-General is very extensive, and his offices are full of industrious workers. He has over four hundred clerks, the majority of whom are engaged upon matters concerning the settlement of pension applications. Besides having the care of the health of the army — the medical and hospital department — the Surgeon-General has possession of the enormous collection of records relating to the disability and the death of soldiers, from the first organization of the army of the United States to the present time, and from these records are compiled the reports used by the Commissioner of Pensions in determining the merits of claims for pensions. There are nearly nineteen thousand volumes of hospital registers, classified and indexed; and thousands of volumes of records containing the names of deceased soldiers, as well as an immense collection of documents pertaining to the medical and surgical history of every war that this country has known. The records of the Civil War are very complete. They were begun during its progress, and were continued afterward for a number of years, requiring in their compilation remarkable patience, perseverance, and skillful application to details. The registers in the possession of the Surgeon-General contain the names of more than seven millions of sick, wounded, and deceased soldiers, and nearly half the names are arranged in convenient form for every-day reference.

The record and pension division of the Surgeon-General's department is located in the historic building on Tenth Street, formerly known as Ford's Theatre, and now as the Army Medical Museum. In this building President Lincoln was assassinated by John Wilkes Booth, on the evening of April 14, 1865. The government took the building for its present purpose at the suggestion of the late Surgeon-General Joseph K. Barnes, who founded the Army Medical Museum, and began the great *Medical and Surgical History of the War of the Rebellion*, three volumes of which have been published. On the second floor is the library of the department, which is considered to be the largest and best collection of medical works in the world. In the cases are over fifty thousand volumes and nearly seventy thousand pamphlets, some of them very ancient. They are in many languages, and constitute a thorough history of medicine and surgery, from the earliest times. The library can be used gratuitously by physicians, and is much resorted to, many physicians coming from distant parts of the country to consult its rare and precious books.

On the third floor is the Army Medical Museum, an institution which has no counterpart in Europe or America. It has obtained great celebrity, and is visited by thousands of people every year. Visitors are freely allowed to inspect its immense collections, and in one recent year the names of 13,250 people were registered. The

THE SIGNAL OFFICE, OR THE WEATHER BUREAU.

museum contains thorough illustrations of the diseases of armies, of the casualties of battle, and of military surgery. The illustrations comprise over twenty thousand specimens taken from life, and arranged in systematic series. It is a very interesting exhibition, even to the non-professional, and furnishes many instructive object-lessons. The display of surgical instruments and appliances is very large, and includes the ancient as well as the modern; and there is a large collection of models of barracks, ambulances, railroad cars for the sick and wounded, etc. The anatomical divisions are full and finely arranged. A great deal of pains is taken with the museum, and yearly its unsurpassed collections are considerably increased.

In Winder's Building, on Seventeenth Street, opposite the State,

War, and Navy Building, is the Ordnance Museum, which contains a large, novel, and interesting exhibit of military articles, including many relics of the Civil War. Here the instruments of war can be studied to advantage, and much useful information readily obtained. The collections of arms comprise everything known to America, with considerable of foreign manufacture, and fully illustrate the various stages of advancement.

The Signal Office, better known as the "Weather Bureau," is located on G Street northwest. It occupies a brick edifice, which is conspicuous by reason of the numerous appliances on its roof, used for registering the velocity of the wind, for ascertaining the rain-fall, etc. This bureau is in charge of a chief signal officer, who is a brigadier-general of the regular army. He has several officers of the army as assistants, a chief clerk, a force of scientific experts, draughtsmen, and others, together with many clerks, copyists, messengers, etc. Throughout the United States there are three hundred and seventy-six signal stations, in charge of nineteen officers and five hundred men of the signal corps of the army, and each station is provided with the best instruments for the "weather service"—for observing and accurately recording the constant variations of the weather. From one hundred and thirty-nine of these stations telegraphic reports are sent daily to Washington; the others report by mail.

The Signal Office receives reports from the trained observers three times in every twenty-four hours — at 7 A. M., 3 P. M., and at midnight. These reports contain full particulars of the weather in the different districts. Seventeen stations in Canada, one in St. Johns, Newfoundland, and one in another part of British America, send reports; and, in the seasons of tropical storms, reports by telegraph are daily received from six stations in the West Indies. Over three hundred voluntary observers also send reports by mail. The lines of the regular telegraph companies are used, and besides, various military and sea-coast telegraph lines owned by the government. The reports from all the stations in the United States, Canada, and the West Indies, which give telegraphic service, are received inside of thirty minutes, Washington time. The first synchronous weather reports were made on the first of November, 1870, and since then the service has reached a high state of perfection. The display of cautionary signals at American ports was begun in October, 1871.

The weather reports are telegraphed from the signal stations to

Washington by means of a secret code, a few figures conveying a large amount of information. A "translator" takes the telegrams in hand and carefully reads them off to eight clerks, each of whom has a special weather map before him, on which he marks the particular readings he has been instructed to take. Afterward these eight maps are combined in one general map, which will fully represent all the phases of the weather in the United States and Canada at the hour the reports were sent. This map is closely studied by the assistant signal officer detailed for the purpose,—the assistants alternating in the work, each one serving thirty days at a time,—the "storm-centre" is located, the probable course of storms determined, and finally the "weather indications" are made up for the East and West, the North and South, and given to the agent of the associated press for transmission to the newspapers of the country.

The completed weather map, which is the finest of the kind issued in the world, is lithographed by the Signal Office, and copies of it

THE SOLDIERS' HOME.

are distributed every morning in the sections easily reached from Washington. In order that the map may have a more extended circulation, certain parties in prominent cities east, west, and south are also charged with its publication by authority of the War Department, and the daily "plan of make-up" is telegraphed to them by an efficient system, which enables them to issue an exact copy of the map printed in Washington. Thus it is possible to obtain a weather map hundreds of miles from the Signal Office, by noon of the day of its date.

A large amount of meteorological work is done by the Signal Office, and its records are very precise and voluminous. It publishes a magazine called *The Monthly Weather Review*, which contains papers on meteorology by eminent scientists, and much valuable information for those interested in "the weather."

The United States Barracks (formerly known as the Arsenal) are situated on a tract of sixty-nine acres in the southerly part of Washington, at Greenleaf Point, where the waters of the Anacostia flow into the Potomac River. This military station was established in 1803. The grounds are finely laid out.

A SHORT distance from Washington, on the Rock Creek road, is the Soldiers' Home, a most beautiful sylvan retreat where the aged and invalid soldiers of the regular army can pass their days in peace and comfort. There are few finer rural estates in the land, and it is often called "the Central Park of Washington," as it is constantly open to the public, and over its five hundred acres of beautifully diversified hill and dale, every one can wander at will, enjoying the charming views and attractive surroundings. Within the grounds there are seven miles of drives on broad, well-made roads, shaded in summer by gigantic oaks with luxuriant leafage ; and there are lakes with swans, long stretches of meadow-lands, handsome arbors perched on hills, whence can be obtained delightful prospects of the country for several miles; ornate villas, statuary, and various adornments. It is, indeed, a pleasing spot, with plentiful means for peaceful enjoyment, and, doubtless, many a "weary pilgrim on life's devious course," as he strolls through these grounds almost envies the superannuated warriors their privilege of residing here.

The Soldiers' Home was founded in 1851, not long after the Mexican War, and was suggested by Gen. Winfield Scott. Congress appropriated $118,719, the balance remaining of the sum General

Scott had obtained from the City of Mexico as indemnity for the violation of the truce, for a fund to establish the institution, and the fund was further augmented by levying a tax of twelve cents a month on the pay of the enlisted men of the regular army. The money received by the government from fines, forfeitures of pay, etc., of the soldiers was also devoted to the purpose. At present the fund amounts to over $800,000, and the yearly receipts from all sources are nearly $150,000. The government also holds more than one million dollars accruing from forfeitures of pay of deserters from the army, and from the money of deceased soldiers which has remained unclaimed for three years, and as soon as the complicated army accounts can be adjusted, this great sum will be turned over to the Home. Soldiers of the regular army who have served faithfully for twenty years, or who have been disabled in service, are entitled to a residence in the Home for the remainder of their lives. There are over six hundred inmates, who are not subject to any strict regulations, but are well fed and clothed, tenderly cared for while sick, and who spend their time in a very comfortable, pleasant manner. The institution is directed by a superintendent and various officials, and is under the supervision of a board of high army officers, at the head of which is the Lieutenant-General of the Army.

The main building is of white marble, and has a frontage of two hundred feet, with a wing of sixty feet, and a tall central tower. It is two stories in height, and is fashioned after the Norman order of architecture. On the grounds are several elegant marble cottages, occupied by the officials; a pretty church of Seneca stone; a capacious hospital building with wide piazzas, from which charming views of Washington and the Potomac can be had; a fine library building, well stocked with books and periodicals, and numerous other structures. On the brow of one of the hills stands a bronze statue of General Scott by Launt Thompson, erected in 1874 at a cost of $18,000. The entire estate is enclosed by a low stone wall, surmounted by a small iron fence of handsome design. Fifty acres are under cultivation, and fine crops of fruits and vegetables are raised.

Near the main building is a large cottage used by the Presidents of the United States as a summer residence. It is surrounded by noble trees, and has a very attractive appearance. Buchanan was the first President to pass the summer here, and Lincoln, Johnson, Hayes, and Arthur have lived on this grand estate.

THE NAVY DEPARTMENT is directed by the Secretary of the Navy, who is a member of the Cabinet, and is required to execute the commands of the President in regard to the naval establishment. Like the other Cabinet ministers, his compensation is $8,000 per year. He has a chief clerk at a salary of $2,500, a disbursing clerk at $2,250, a stenographer at $1,600, and other clerks and employés whose total salaries amount to $40,000 per year. The department occupies the eastern portion of the State, War, and Navy Building, and has finely embellished suites of rooms. The Secretary's office is decorated in Greek style, and furnished very handsomely. During the customary business hours the Secretary is to be found at his desk attending to the many affairs with which he is charged, receiving callers, and listening to reports from the different bureaus of the department. These bureaus are as follows: Yards and Docks, Navigation, Ordnance, Provision and Clothing, Medicine and Surgery, Construction and Repairs, Equipment and Recruiting, and Steam Engineering. Each bureau is in charge of a high officer of the navy, and is provided with a numerous force of officials and employés.

At present the navy consists of thirty-seven cruising war-vessels, "creditable in their appearance, well adapted for ordinary naval exercises, and useful for displaying the national flag upon the seas and in the harbors of the commercial world." But they are of low speed and mostly built of wood, and gradually will be replaced by new iron or steel ships, constructed in the very best manner. There are also numerous steamers and small craft, and thirteen monitors, or armored vessels, mostly laid up since their use in the Civil War, but kept in good condition. In the service at sea and on shore there are over eighteen hundred naval officers, and there are also over three hundred officers on the retired list. The seamen number over seven thousand, and the apprentices 950. The marine corps has 2,077 officers and enlisted men. The pay of the Admiral of the Navy is $13,000 per year, and of the Vice-Admiral, $9,000. Rear-admirals are paid $6,000, commodores $5,000, captains $4,500, commanders $3,500, and lieutenant-commanders from $2,800 to $3,000. Lieutenants are paid from $2,000 to $2,600, and masters from $1,800 to $2,000. The pay of seamen is $258, and of ordinary seamen $210. Over seven million dollars are annually paid to the naval force.

The maintenance of the Navy Department requires the yearly expenditure of from fifteen to twenty million dollars, the amount depending very much on the construction of new vessels. Provisions

THE NAVAL OBSERVATORY.

for the navy cost $2,200,000 per year; coal and various articles of equipment, $1,000,000, and the expenses of the bureaus of the department are $250,000.

The hydrographic office, under the direction of the Bureau of Navigation, supplies the navy with charts, its surveying work covering all the navigable waters of the globe, with the exception of those of the United States, which are surveyed and chartered by the United States Coast Survey, a bureau of the Treasury Department. It publishes a series of charts for the benefit of navigators, and also numerous volumes of sailing directions, and other information of great value to those whose business is on the mighty deep. A large force of draughtsmen, engravers, and copper-plate printers is employed in producing the charts and volumes. One of the largest chart printing-presses in the world is to be found in this office.

In 1855 the Bureau of Navigation began the publication of the *American Ephemeris and Nautical Almanac*, which is regarded as a standard authority, both here and in Europe. It is published three years in advance of the time for which it is required. An able staff of scientists devote themselves to the difficult labor of making the computations. The first part of the work is designed for the use of navigators, and is adapted to the meridian of Greenwich. It contains ephemerides of the sun, moon, principal planets, and fixed stars. The second part is for the use of astronomers on land, for surveyors and scientific men generally, and is adapted to the meridian of Washington.

The Bureau of Yards and Docks has charge of the navy yards throughout the United States. There are eight of these yards, the principal one being at Brooklyn, New York. They have great docks, work-shops, and store-houses, and the most approved machinery for constructing and repairing ships, and for the manufacture of ordnance, cordage, and all naval equipments. The yard in Washington was established in 1804, and for many years some of the best ships in the navy were constructed in it. Of late, however, it has been chiefly used for the manufacture of naval supplies. Here are manufactured all the chain cables and anchors used in the navy, and all the ordnance, such as rifles, breech-loading guns, howitzers and boat-guns, and many other articles entering into the construction and equipment of vessels of war. The yard is situated at the termination of Eighth Street east, about a mile from the Capitol, and covers nearly twenty-eight acres. It lies on the banks of the Anacostia River, and has a fine water frontage. It is in charge of a commodore, who has a staff of naval officers as assistants. Visitors will find numerous objects of interest in the yard. The work-shops, museum, laboratory, monitors and ships of war can be inspected. The museum contains many naval relics, and a large collection of arms, torpedoes, and maritime appliances.

The extensive Marine Barracks are situated on Eighth Street, a short distance from the navy yard. They were constructed at a cost of $350,000, and are the headquarters of the marine corps, which is an adjunct to the naval force.

LOCATED on the hill where General Braddock's troops encamped in 1755, is the United States Naval Observatory, or, as it is also called, the National Observatory. It is on the government reservation of nineteen acres bounded by Twenty-third, Twenty-fourth, and Twenty-fifth streets and the Potomac River, and stands about ninety-six feet above tide-water. The structure is surmounted by a large dome, and has two wings. The observatory is in charge of the Bureau of Navigation, and its superintendent is a rear-admiral of the navy. It was established in 1842, and now ranks among the foremost observatories in the world. Here is the great twenty-six inch equatorial telescope, one of the largest and most powerful ever constructed. It was mounted in 1873, and cost $47,000. It rests upon a solid foundation of masonry deeply imbedded in the earth, and, with its base, weighs six tons. The dome in which it is placed is forty-one feet in diameter, and forty feet in height. The observatory has also a nine and one-half inch equatorial telescope, set in a dome twenty-three feet in diameter, and twenty feet high. These far-reaching instruments are used for much of the difficult and important astronomical work for which this observatory is famous. A transit circle, with an object-glass of 8.22 inches, is used for observations of the sun and moon, and some of the planets. The best apparatus is to be found in the observatory, and from month to month a large amount of labor is performed in the way of astronomical researches and computations.

G STREET, SHOWING FOUNDRY AND EPIPHANY CHURCHES.

THE METROPOLITAN M. E. CHURCH.

CHAPTER XIII.

THE Post-Office Department occupies a marble building situated on the square between Seventh and Eighth, and E
and F streets northwest. The building is of the delicate
Corinthian order, and is a notable example of architectural
grace and beauty. Its façades are ornamented with monolithic columns and pilasters, with beautiful capitals, and the architrave, frieze,
and cornice are designed in pure classic style. It is three hundred
feet from north to south, and two hundred and four feet from east to
west. It has two stories resting upon a rustic basement, with deep,
spacious vaults below. That portion on E Street was erected of New
York marble in 1839, from designs by Robert Mills. In 1855 the
building was extended over the entire square, the extensions being
designed by Thomas U. Walter, and constructed of Maryland marble. The cost of construction was nearly two million dollars. The
building contains eighty-five apartments excellently arranged for the
postal business, and most of them are elegantly decorated and furnished.

By the Constitution of the United States, Congress was given the
right "to establish post-offices and post-roads." The office of Postmaster-General was created in 1789, and the General Post-Office was
established in 1794. On the 2d of March, 1799, Congress passed an
act to establish the General Post-Office in Washington. The depart-

ment has had a marvelous growth. Fifty years ago there were 10,693 post-offices throughout the country, and the revenue from them was only $2,823,749. At present there are 47,863 post-offices, and the yearly revenue of the department is over $45,000,000. To carry on the postal service requires the assistance of 67,000 persons.

The site of the Post-Office Building was originally occupied in the early days of Washington by a large brick structure erected for a hotel by a sanguine speculator, who believed that the new capital would rapidly become a great city. Before the hotel was finished his funds gave out, and the building was offered as a prize in a lottery, and drawn by two orphan children to whom the lucky ticket had been presented by a friend. They were without means to finish it, and it was suffered to remain in an unfinished state for nearly ten years. Here the first play ever given in the city was performed by a troupe of strolling players, some of whom afterward achieved distinction on the American stage. It was used now and then as a theatre until 1810, when the government purchased and completed it, using it for the post-office, and also to store the first collections of patent models ever made. When the British invaders burned the public buildings in 1814, this one was spared through the efforts of Dr. William Thornton, then in charge of the patent business. He appealed to the soldiers sent to destroy it, who were his countrymen, and succeeded in persuading them to stay the work of destruction until the next day. Then the troops had left the city, and this building was the only public one to which the incendiary torch had not been applied. Congress held one session in it after the burning of the Capitol, and the post-office occupied the first story until Dec. 15, 1836, when a fire completely destroyed it. In the fire were consumed the collections of the patent office, stored in the second story, which numbered over four thousand models, the accumulation of nearly half a century. A private building was then rented for the post-office, and was used until the present building was erected.

The Postmaster-General, who has the supervision of the affairs of the Post-Office Department, is a member of the Cabinet, and receives $8,000 per year. There are three assistant postmasters-general, appointed by the President, who receive $4,000 each. The Postmaster-General has a chief clerk at $2,200, a stenographer at $1,800, an appointment clerk at $1,800, a law clerk at $2,500, and a dozen or so other employés for the special business of his office. He appoints all postmasters for offices to which a salary of not more than $1,000 is attached. The other postmasters come within the "Presidential classes," and are appointed by the President. They number 2,175, with total salaries of $3,750,000. The office of the Postmaster-General is a richly furnished apartment; near it are the offices of the assistant postmasters-general — large, elegant apartments.

The bureau of the first assistant postmaster-general has five divisions, viz.: the appointment division, the bond division, the salary and allowance division, the free delivery division, and the blank agency division. The bureau acts upon the establishment of new post-offices, and the appointment of postmasters, postal clerks, agents, and others; attends to the bonds required, has the supervision of the free delivery system, adjusts the salaries of postmasters, considers allowances for the various expenditures of post-offices, and furnishes the greater part of what are called "department supplies." A large amount of business is transacted in the different divisions, and seventy-five officials and clerks are employed. In regard to the free delivery system it may be said that it is now in use in one hundred and fifty-four cities, and requires the services of 3,680 letter-carriers, whose yearly salaries amount to more than $3,000,000. The postmasters of the country are annually paid over $12,000,000, and postal clerks, $4,900,000.

Few persons are aware of the magnitude of the postal business, particularly that portion of it relating to the transportation of the mails. The transportation service is in charge of the second assistant postmaster-general, and the three divisions of his bureau are known as the contract division — familiarly called the "contract office," — the inspection division, and the mail equipment division. To transact the business of this bureau requires one hundred employés.

The "star service," or the "star routes" as they are usually called, is that portion of the mail transportation not covered by railroads and steamboats. In the endeavor of the Post-Office Department to furnish all communities with mail facilities, use is made of private conveyances in sections of the country, particularly in the far West, where there are no railroads or steamboats. The mails are carried over these special or star routes by contractors who make bids for the service, and furnish the horses and wagons and the persons required. These routes number very nearly 8,000, and are mostly in the western and southwestern states and the territories. Their yearly cost is upwards of five million dollars, and their aggregate length is 226,865 miles.

By these routes mails are carried to the mining camps, to the interior villages, and to communities located away from the great highways of travel. The service is very useful and important, and has largely aided in the settlement of the western country.

The contract office attends to all the mail lettings. The country is divided into four postal sections, and bids are received and contracts made for carrying the mails in one section every year. As many as 100,000 bids will be received in some years. The department has no discretion in the matter of mail lettings, as the law directs that the routes shall be awarded in all cases to the lowest bidders, if their bids are in proper form. Contracts for mail transportation, after the acceptance of bids, must be filed in the department within a certain time. If an accepted bidder fails to file his contract by the time specified, he becomes a "failing bidder," and the route is awarded to the next lowest bidder.

On the day fixed for closing the bids the Postmaster-General assigns three officials of the department to open and stamp all those received. In the basement story of the post-office is a massive vault in which all the bids are kept, and near at hand is a printing-press. The three officials, aided by a force of clerks, first assort the bids by states; then the bids are opened and passed through the press, and have imprinted on them the special seal of the department, which shows the date they were opened. When all the bids have been opened and stamped they are taken to the room of the chief clerk of the contract office, where they are examined by clerks detailed for the purpose, to see if they are proper in form. The amount is then indorsed on the back of each bid, and then the bids are "listed" or classified according to the routes, after which they are recorded in route-books specially prepared.

After all this tedious and laborious work is done, the chief clerk goes over the route-books and designates the lowest bidder for each route. An acceptance is then prepared by the Postmaster-General and sent to each lowest bidder, who executes a contract according to the terms of the bid. The contracts are made in duplicate, and when received, one is retained by the Postmaster-General, and the other is sent to the Sixth Auditor of the Treasury, who has charge of the disbursements of the Post-Office Department.

The railroad mail routes number nearly 1,400, and the yearly expenditure for the transportation of mails over them is $13,000,000.

THE GENERAL POST-OFFICE.

There are more than one hundred steamboat routes, which cost $625,-000. The mail messenger service on the railroads is performed at a cost of $800,000, and the railroad postal clerks are paid $3,700,000. At present the railroad mail service is 110,208 miles in length.

The third assistant postmaster-general has charge of the following divisions: The division of finance, the division of postage-stamps and stamped envelopes, the division of registered letters, and the division of dead letters. It is the duty of this official to pay the mail contractors, to collect the postal revenues, to issue postage-stamps, stamped envelopes, and postal cards to the post-offices, and to attend to the business connected with registered letters and dead letters.

The Dead-Letter Office occupies a spacious apartment in the F Street portion of the department building, and can be inspected by visitors. The apartment has a wide gallery, and is well lighted by a glass roof and high, broad windows. The office has a chief with a salary of $2,250, and a force of one hundred male and female clerks.

About 15,000 dead letters are received every day from the post-offices of the country, and a great quantity of other mail-matter. All the "dead mail" is first examined by the chief clerk and his assistants, in order to ascertain if there is anything in it which has been improperly sent to the office. This is a very needful practice, as every day a number of letters are discovered properly addressed and stamped, and which should have been delivered. By carelessness on the part of postmasters and postal clerks, a letter plainly addressed to a place, say in Pennsylvania, will be sent to a place, say in Texas. The postmaster there, instead of forwarding it to the place to which it is addressed, will retain it the customary time, and then send it to the dead-letter office. These letters are taken out of the dead mail and forwarded by the department to the post-offices to which they should have gone in the first place, accompanied by an official order to the postmasters that they shall request the parties claiming the letters to allow the envelopes to be returned to Washington. The envelopes thus obtained are put on record, and a reprimand is sent to the postal officials through whose carelessness the mistakes occurred. Upon an average, four thousand of these "careless letters" are discovered every year.

When the dead letters have been examined by the chief clerk and his assistants they are given into the hands of men sitting at long tables, who deftly cut open each envelope with a sharp, long-bladed knife, and examine the enclosure to ascertain if it contains any valuables. If anything is found the finder makes a detailed record of it in a small book lying at his hand, and the letter is put aside. Those letters which contain nothing of value are passed over to a force of women in the gallery, who search them to ascertain if they bear an address by which they can be returned to the writers. If one is found the department sends the letter back to the writer. The others are consigned to the waste matter, which is taken at certain intervals to West Washington, to a government structure, cut up, and thoroughly reduced to pulp.

If a letter or parcel with anything of value contains an address it is returned at once, but if there is no address the property is retained for six months, and then is disposed of at auction, at what are termed "sales of unclaimed and undeliverable mail-matter." A careful record is made of the sales, and the amount received for any article can be recovered upon application any time within four years.

A peculiarity of the dead-letter office is, that the letters are all opened by elderly men, quite a number of whom áre in the "sere and yellow leaf" time of existence, with hair and beards fully frosted by many winters. The parcels are all opened by elderly women. It is only for the other work that young persons are employed. The reason for this, it is said, comes from a belief that men and women of mature age will be more conscientious in regard to valuables found in the letters and parcels—that is, will not secrete anything they find. It would be quite an easy matter for a person opening a letter or parcel which contained a bank-note, or something else of value, to slyly pocket it, and in a majority of the cases it would be difficult, if not impossible, to detect the theft.

Great quantities of money are found. In one recent year 20,000 letters were opened that contained $45,000 in bank-notes. The articles found are of most every sort, and quite often they are of considerable value. Checks, drafts, and money-orders yearly discovered represent a value of more than two million dollars. Between thirty and forty thousand photographs come into the office every year; and, strangest of all, nearly ten thousand letters annually appear in the dead mail which have no address upon their envelopes.

The Money-Order Office is located in a high brick building adjacent to the Post-Office. It is in charge of a superintendent who has a salary of $3,500, and employs numerous clerks. Here the money-orders that have been paid are received from all the money-order offices in the United States, and from foreign countries. They are classified, and then the accounts of postmasters in reference to the money-order business are verified and audited. As the business is very extensive and complicated, the accounts require the greatest of care in their settlement. Over nine millions of American and foreign money-orders are issued in a year, representing a value of $125,-000,000.

No department of the government is better managed than that of the post-office. The details of its immense business are thoroughly attended to, its expenditures are usually very judicious, and its working system is constantly being improved to meet the public requirement.

THE NEW PENSION BUILDING.

CHAPTER XIV.

THE Department of the Interior was created by act of Congress in 1849. It is an extensive and important branch of the public service, and comprises the Patent Office, the Pension Office, the General Land Office, the Census Office, the Bureau of Indian Affairs, the Bureau of Education, the Office of the Commissioner of Railroads, and the Office of the Geological Survey. It is under the supervision and control of the Secretary of the Interior, who is a Cabinet minister, and has a compensation of $8,000 per year. The Secretary has also the general supervision of the Capitol (through the office of the architect), the Government Printing-Office, the Government Hospital for the Insane, and the Columbia Institution for the Deaf and Dumb. Each office and bureau of the Department of the Interior is managed by a commissioner or director, who has his own force of officials and clerks.

The colossal structure known as the Patent Office, which extends from Seventh to Ninth streets, and from F to G streets northwest, is occupied by the Secretary of the Interior, and sundry bureaus of the department. It stands upon a government reservation of four acres, which was set apart by L'Enfant in his plan of Washington for a great national church, and is four hundred and ten feet from east to west, and two hundred and seventy-five feet from north to south. Its erection was begun in 1837, and the main division, which was constructed of Virginia freestone and granite, was completed in 1842. An east wing was added in 1853, and north and west wings some years late/. The east and west wings were constructed of marble from Maryland quarries, and the north wing of granite. The building is of the Doric order of architecture, has two stories and a rustic basement, and is nearly seventy-five feet high. The main entrance is on F Street, through a massive portico of two rows of huge columns, which was designed after that of the Parthenon in Athens, and is precisely of the same dimensions. A lofty flight of broad granite steps leads to the portico. On the Seventh Street side is another great portico, and smaller ones are on the north and west. There is an interior court-yard ornamented with fountains and flower-beds. The building contains nearly two hundred apartments, besides the extensive halls of the Museum of Models. The architects were Robert Mills, who constructed the original portion, and Edward Clark, who constructed the extensions. The cost of construction was $2,700,000.

There is an assistant secretary of the interior, with a salary of $4,000, and the department office is provided with a chief clerk at $2,750, a superintendent of documents at $2,000, six chiefs of divisions at $2,000 each, and many clerks and employés. The Commissioner of Patents has a salary of $4,500; the Commissioner of Pensions, $5,000; the Commissioner of the Land Office, $4,000; the Commissioner of Indian Affairs, $4,000; the Commissioner of Education, $3,000; the Commissioner of Railroads, $4,500, and the Director of the Geological Survey, $6,000.

THE PATENT OFFICE occupies many apartments of the building that bears its name, and employs a host of workers in its enormous and constantly increasing business. It is not only self-sustaining, but it is very profitable. In 1883 its receipts were more than one million dollars, and the profits exceeded $500,000. There are upwards of 21,000 patents issued annually, covering nearly every conceivable thing under the sun, and, in addition, there are hundreds of caveats filed, and trade-marks and labels registered. The office is divided into divisions, in each of which are examiners who have charge of certain classes of inventions. When a patent is applied for, these examiners make the necessary investigations, carefully examining the invention claimed to be new, and patiently and laboriously comparing it, part by part, with devices already patented, in order to determine whether or not the application for a patent can be granted. The principal examiners receive salaries of $2,400, and

THE PATENT OFFICE.

the assistant examiners from $1,200 to $1,800. Three examiners-in-chief, who supervise and finally decide as to the work of the others, receive $3,000 each. An examiner in charge of interferences receives $2,500, and a trade-mark examiner, $2,400. All applications for patents are classified as soon as received, and are taken up and disposed of in regular order, as far as practicable. A patent continues for seventeen years, unless the article patented has been previously patented in a foreign country, in which case the American patent expires with the date of the foreign one.

Since 1872 the office has issued a weekly publication called *The Official Gazette*, which takes the place of the old *Patent Office Report*. It contains the claims of every patent issued, including the reissues, with drawings illustrating the patents, the full list of designs patented, and the decisions of the commissioner. The copies of the monthly edition are authenticated by the official seal, and are received as evidence in the United States courts. One copy of this edition is sent to each state library, and one copy is deposited in the clerk's office of each United States district court, for public reference. Senators and Representatives are also entitled to designate eight public libraries in their states to which copies will be sent gratuitously.

A fine library is provided for the use of inventors, and its rooms on the first floor of the patent office are much frequented by that class. Congress annually appropriates $5,000 for the purchase of books. The library contains about twelve thousand volumes, comprising the best works published in all the lines of invention and mechanics, and the collections of foreign publications are specially valuable. The librarian has a salary of $2,000.

The numerous rooms used by the patent office are filled with officials, examiners, draughtsmen, clerks, and copyists, busy as bees investigating claims, comparing inventions, copying designs and specifications, and otherwise attending to the multifarious business. There are one hundred and forty-two examiners of patents, and over four hundred clerks and other employés. Since 1838 the patent office has accumulated a surplus of $2,700,000, which stands to its credit on the books of the United States Treasury, and this surplus eventually may be expended in the erection of a new building for its sole use, as its present quarters are inadequate for the business.

The Museum of Models is contained in four lofty, magnificent halls, extending throughout the second story of the department building. Here are to be seen 300,000 models of patented articles, arranged in classes and subdivisions, and filling hundreds of spacious cases, all properly labeled and indexed. By means of these models one can trace the progress of every line of industry, from crude designs to the perfected machine, wonderful in construction and almost human in action. Here is the result of the profound study of countless men diligently working in all the industrial fields through many years, and it is a marvelous exhibition of human capability, and can be inspected for hours, and even days, with plentiful profit and enjoyment.

The first collections of patent models, comprising everything received by the government from 1790 to 1836, were entirely destroyed by fire when the Post-Office Building, in which they were stored, was burned on Dec. 15, 1836. Shortly after this fire Congress enacted a law for the better recording of patents, requiring models in every proper case, and made the patent office a regular branch of the public service, placing it in charge of a commissioner. Previous to that time patents had been issued from the office of the Secretary of State, under the direction of a clerk, who bore the title of superintendent of patents. In 1877 a fire in the north and west halls of the present

Museum of Models, originating among a collection of ancient documents, destroyed 80,000 models. These halls were afterward reconstructed at a cost of $250,000.

The south hall of the museum is two hundred and forty-two feet in length, and sixty-three feet in width, and the north, east, and west halls are of nearly the same size. They are of handsome design, and present many pleasing architectural features. The museum is open daily, and visitors are allowed to gratuitously inspect the vast collections of models contained in it.

THE PENSION OFFICE is the largest bureau of the Department of the Interior, and its yearly business is enormous. It is a very difficult bureau to administer, as it is constantly assailed by thousands of dishonest people, whose ingenious trickery in the invention and substantiation of claims might deceive the shrewdest and most careful of officials. Bogus claims for pensions are so numerous that the proper claims are very much delayed in their settlement, in consequence of the great amount of time taken to detect the frauds. When it is considered that 510,938 claims were allowed from 1861 to 1883, and that during the time the prodigious sum of $621,073,297 was disbursed, the work of the office will be better appreciated. There are at present nearly 304,000 pensioners on the rolls, and every year the names of from 25,000 to 30,000 are added. Upwards of 275,000 claims are pending. The Commissioner of Pensions has a large working force, which is making all possible efforts to adjust the claims on file, but it must be necessarily many years before all the rightful claimants for pensions can receive what the government has directed to be paid. The claims are now taken up in regular order, and no favoritism is allowed in their consideration.

A careful estimate has been made by the pension office that there were no less than 2,063,391 persons who entered the army and navy during the Civil War. Of this number 304,369 died in battles, hospitals, or otherwise; 285,545 were discharged for disability, and there were 128,352 deserters. On the 1st of May, 1865, the number in the service was over 1,000,000, and previous to that time 328,187 had been discharged on account of the expiration of their terms of enlistment. Of this vast host applications for pensions have been made by over 500,000 rendered invalids by the war, and nearly 300,000 applications also have been made by those representing deceased sol-

diers and sailors. At present, it is estimated, that there are about 86,-
000 of this class who have not yet presented claims, and that there
are nearly 1,000,000 survivors of the war who have never made application for pensions — that is, there is this soldier and sailor population in the United States out of which thousands of claims may come
in the future.

It will be seen by these figures that the pension office has plenty
of business on hand, and to come ; that it will require a large force
of employés to attend to it, and the expenditure of hundreds of millions during many future years to pay all the claims. The office
annually disburses over $30,000,000 for pensions, and as much more
for the arrears of pensions. All this money goes through the hands
of the eighteen pension agents in various sections of the United States
to the persons entitled to it. Each agent is assigned to a certain district comprising one or more states, or parts of states. They give
bonds to the amount of $150,000, with justified security to the amount
of $300,000, and are allowed salaries of $4,000 each. They are
tried and trusty officials, and, although handling so many millions
of the government money in the course of a year, their accounts are
invariably exact to a dollar.

The pensions are from one dollar to one hundred dollars per
month, the last-named sum, however, being drawn by only one pen-
sioner. There are seven hundred and forty-five pensioners who draw
seventy-two dollars per month, and four hundred and twenty-five who
draw fifty dollars. Over seven thousand draw twenty-four dollars,
and nearly thirteen thousand draw eighteen dollars. A great number draw from eight to fifteen dollars, and nearly forty-three thousand
only four dollars. There are eighteen thousand who are paid only
two dollars, and about sixteen hundred who have to be content with
one dollar per month.

The pension office has twelve divisions, each in charge of a chief
with a salary of $2,000. Twenty-two surgeons are employed, with
salaries from $1,800 to $2,500, and there are forty-two principal examiners at $2,000 each, a number of other officials, and about fifteen
hundred clerks and employés. The annual salary list of the office
is $1,945,000.

The pension office formerly occupied a large brick building on
Pennsylvania Avenue, corner of Twelfth Street, which was rented by
the government. but early in 1885 it was removed to the new Pension

NORTH HALL, MUSEUM OF MODELS, PATENT OFFICE.

Building which was recently completed on Judiciary Square, near G Street. The new building resembles the great Italian palaces, and has many unique forms of architecture. It is constructed of fine pressed brick with terra cotta mouldings, and extends 400 feet from east to west, and 200 feet from north to south, and the walls are seventy-five feet high. The walls surround a large interior court-yard, which has a high roof of iron and glass, and is crowned with a dome. Two tiers of galleries extend around the court-yard, by which access is gained to the rooms. On the first story there is a course of terra cotta extending entirely around the building, consisting of a band three feet wide, on which various scenes and incidents of a soldier's life are represented in finely sculptured figures. The cost of the building is about $500,000.

THE GENERAL LAND OFFICE, which has charge of all the public lands in the United States, occupies a suite of apartments in the

Patent Office Building. It is a very important bureau, and that its work is extensive may be inferred from the number of its officials and clerks, some four hundred in all, whose salaries amount to nearly $500,000 per year. In fact, the pressure of business in this office is very great, and double the force could be advantageously employed, if Congress would provide for the increase and assign larger quarters for the work. New business comes in faster than the old can be disposed of, and the accumulation of affairs is very embarrassing. If the entire force of the office should be devoted to bringing up the work in arrears, in cases all prepared for final action, it would require at least two years to accomplish this result. Over two thousand contested homestead cases are pending, and there are fifty thousand others awaiting settlement. Besides all these cases there are six thousand more in the railroad division, which have to be decided in connection with the adjustment of land grants to railroads. There is also a great accumulation of business in the divisions of the office which have charge of the preëmption claims, the timber culture entries, and the claims for mineral lands, etc. The preëmption claims number over 300,000, and of these about 20,000 are awaiting final action, and final proof is likely to be offered at any time upon a majority of the others. The work is disposed of as fast as possible, but as much of it requires very close examination of a variety of complicated matters, it cannot be done properly in a hurried manner.

Few people, except those interested in the public lands, have any definite knowledge as to the territory in the United States still in the possession and subject to the control of the government. There is a comfortable feeling that Uncle Sam has plenty of land to furnish a good farm to all who would like to till the soil, but where this land is, and how much there is, the generality of people cannot tell. The actual area of the public domain once amounted to nearly two thousand millions of acres — verily a goodly property, hardly to be realized by the simple statement of the number of acres. This land was acquired by cession from the original states, by the Mexican treaty, by what is known as the Gadsden purchase, and by purchases from Texas, Florida, and Alaska. Of this vast public estate, nearly six hundred million acres have been sold, given to states for internal improvement, given to railroads, given to colleges and schools, disposed of under the homestead and bounty laws, and in various other ways have passed from the holding of the government. Forty-six million acres have been awarded to railroads by Congress, to aid in the construction of the roads, and other corporations have had enormous blocks and stretches of the public domain awarded them by special acts.

It is estimated that the area of public lands now remaining is about 1,800,000,000 acres. Taking out of this estimate the lands held for Indian and military reservations, the unexplored lands in Alaska, and all lands unsurveyed, etc., there will yet remain, in round numbers, some 650,000,000 acres to be disposed of by the government, nearly all of which can be acquired by citizens of the United States by actual settlement and cultivation. The lands are located in the states of Ohio, California, Arkansas, Alabama, Colorado, Florida, Louisiana, Kansas, Illinois, Iowa, Minnesota, Indiana, Michigan, Oregon, Wisconsin, Nevada, Missouri, Nebraska, and Mississippi, and in all the territories. Any citizen of the United States is entitled under the homestead laws to enter one hundred and sixty acres of these lands wherever unappropriated. In six months from the date of entry he must pay $16 in fees and commissions to the land office, and must live on the land and cultivate it for five

SOUTH HALL, MUSEUM OF MODELS, PATENT OFFICE.

continuous years. Then, upon proof of residence and cultivation, a
patent is issued, and he becomes the owner of the land. The soldiers
and sailors of the Civil War who enter homestead lands have the
period of their service in the army and navy deducted from the five
years' residence, provided they live on and cultivate the land for one
year. Under the preëmption laws it is necessary to live for one
year on the land preëmpted, at the expiration of which time the land
can be purchased for $1.25 per acre, if outside of railroad limits, and
for $2.50 per acre if within railroad limits. There are other ways of
acquiring lands under the timber culture laws and the desert land act.
Up to the present time about seventy million acres have been secured
by homestead settlers.

Connected with the land office are sixteen surveyors-general,
assigned to different states and territories, who have charge of the
surveying of public lands. They have their offices in the districts to
which they are assigned, and employ many clerks. About twenty
million acres of land are disposed of by the government every year
under the various land acts, and from eight to twelve million dollars
are received from sales, fees, and commissions.

THE BUREAU OF INDIAN AFFAIRS is charged with the care of
those troublesome wards of the Nation, the Indian tribes of the far
West. It has apartments in the Patent Office Building, and employs
about seventy clerks and others in its routine work. All the Indian
agents, inspectors, etc., are under the supervision of the bureau, and
it has many important duties. Clothing, food, agricultural implements, and many other things are supplied to the tribes, whose reservations extend from Lake Superior to the Pacific Ocean. Six
million dollars are annually paid to the Indians. There are fifty-
nine agencies, which have charge of 246,000 Indians, and outside of
the agencies there are 15,000 Indians. The bureau pays considerable
attention to the education of Indian children, and a number of good
schools for them have been established. In many of the schools
various industries are taught, and it is believed that in time the ex-
periment will be tried on a large scale of educating the Indian youth
to become intelligent, civilized laborers. If the boys and girls are
educated to manual occupations, it is thought they will cease to have
a desire for a savage life, and will become self-supporting and independent of government aid.

SECTION OF FRIEZE ORNAMENTATION ON THE PENSION BUILDING.

THE BUREAU OF EDUCATION has offices in a large brick building on G Street, opposite the Patent Office. It has a force of forty persons, many of whom are college graduates and practical educators, and Congress appropriates yearly a little more than $50,000 for its support. It was established in 1867, and its primary object is to collect information concerning schools and systems of education, not only in this country but throughout the world, and this information is compiled and diffused by means of reports and other publications, which are extensively circulated. A special feature is made of exhibits of foreign school systems, which are exceedingly instructive and interesting. The bureau is held in high estimation in Europe, and several countries have modeled their educational bureaus upon the American system. The statistics collected in reference to education in foreign countries have a wide range, and are of great value. An extensive correspondence is carried on, and every year thousands of letters are written in reply to inquiries from all over the country about the free schools of the South, the education of colored children, the compulsory school laws of the states, the methods of industrial schools in England and France, the organization and management of technical institutes, the normal school and kindergarten systems, the co-education of the sexes, the best training for teachers, and a host of other matters. The bureau is doing a beneficial work, the extent and value of which are hardly realized by the country.

THE GEOLOGICAL SURVEY is a part of the Department of the Interior, and has offices in the National Museum. It has a director,

a chief clerk, an executive officer, surveyors, and other employés.
It is charged with the examination and classification of the mineral
lands belonging to the United States, and performs an important
work. Within a few years the Survey has made extensive examin-
ations of the regions in the Western States and Territories which
produce the precious metals, and also of those regions which contain
valuable fields of anthracite and bituminous coal and iron ore, and
the reports and maps issued have been of great service not only to
the government, but to all persons interested in mineral lands. Before long the entire Rocky Mountain region will be carefully examined and accurately reported upon, and the vast mineral wealth of
this as yet but partially explored country thoroughly revealed. The
Survey has in course of preparation a geological map of the United
States which is intended to be very complete. The country will be
divided into seven districts, and the geological features of each district will be fully portrayed. The map will be published in atlas
sheets, each being composed of one degree of longitude by one of
latitude in area, bounded by parallels and meridians.

THE office of the Commissioner of Railroads is attached to the
Department of the Interior. It occupies a building on G Street, opposite the Patent Office. All the railroad companies to which the
government has granted any loan or credit are required to report to
this office their earnings and expenses, and general financial condition, and at certain times officials are detailed to examine the property and accounts of the subsidized roads. These roads are the
Central Pacific, the Western Pacific, the Union Pacific, the Kansas
Pacific, the Central Branch of the Union Pacific, and the Sioux City
and Pacific. The amount of their indebtedness to the government,
principal and interest, is over one hundred million dollars. The
Commissioner of Railroads is required to enforce the laws relating
to the railroads, and to give assistance in various ways to the government directors of the roads.

CHAPTER XV.

THE Department of Justice, under the direction of the Attorney-General, has charge of all prosecutions by the government, and supervises the United States courts in the judicial districts of the country. The office of Attorney-General
is as old as the present form of government, having been created in
1789; but the Department of Justice was not created until 1870, when
Congress thought best to combine all the law-officers, and all the law
business of the government in an executive department, with the Attorney-General as its head. This official is a member of the Cabinet,
and the law-adviser of the President and the heads of the executive
departments. He has a compensation of $8,000 per year.

The business of the Department of Justice is conducted, under
the supervision of the Attorney-General, by a Solicitor-General, who
has a salary of $7,000, three assistant Attorneys-General with sal-
aries of $5,000 each, a Solicitor of Internal Revenue with $4,500,
and an assistant Attorney-General of the Post-Office Department
with $4,000. There are also an examiner of claims with $3,500,
two assistant attorneys with $3,000 each, three assistant attorneys
with $2,500 each, one assistant attorney with $2,000, a law clerk
and examiner of titles with $2,700, a chief clerk with $2,200, two
law clerks with $2,000 each, a stenographic clerk with $1,800, and
forty other clerks and employés. The salaries of the department
annually amount to $109,590.

The office of the Solicitor of the Treasury is also under the supervision of the Attorney-General. The Solicitor has charge of the legal business of the Treasury Department. He has a salary of $4,500, and there is an assistant solicitor with a salary of $3,000. In the Solicitor's office there are fifteen clerks and employés, and the salary list amounts to $28,000.

The five-story building originally erected by the defunct Freedmen's Savings and Trust Company, on Pennsylvania Avenue, opposite the northern front of the Treasury Building, is occupied by the Department of Justice. In the office of the Attorney-General is a fine collection of portraits of the Attorneys-General of the United States from 1789 to the present time. The first story is used by the United States Court of Claims, which hears and determines claims disputed by the executive departments. The court consists of five judges, who receive salaries of $4,500.

The District Court House is situated on Judiciary Square. It is a large freestone structure, painted white, and was erected in 1820, after designs by George Hadfield. East and west wings were added in 1826 and 1849. Until 1871 it was used by the municipal government as the city hall. All the District courts are held here, with the exception of the police court, which is held in a building on the corner of Sixth and D streets northwest, once a Unitarian church.

The Supreme Court of the District is divided into a criminal court, a District court, a common law court, and an equity court. There are a Chief Justice and five associate justices, who receive an aggregate compensation of $24,500. Connected with the District judiciary are the offices of the United States District Attorney, the United States Marshal, the Register of Wills, and the Recorder of Deeds.

In the District Court House many notable trials have taken place during the more than half century of its existence. Here Guiteau was tried, and the notorious "star route cases" were heard. The District jail formerly stood in the rear of the court house, but it is now located on the banks of the Anacostia River, at the eastern termination of Pennsylvania Avenue. It is a large stone building, erected in 1875, at a cost of $400,000.

It has been said that "the government of the United States may take its stand among the most enterprising and prosperous of those nations in which departments are provided and supported for every purpose which can possibly increase the national wealth and intelli-

THE DEPARTMENT OF JUSTICE BUILDING.

gence, and stimulate the national enterprise." One of these beneficial, and it may be called stimulating, departments is the Department of Agriculture, which is charged with collecting and diffusing the most reliable information upon agriculture and the many important industries which cluster around it, and upon the successful prosecution of which the country's prosperity depends. It is not a costly department, as compared with other branches of the public service, its expenditure rarely exceeding $400,000 a year, but its work is of incalculable value. It has diffused definite information concerning the best methods to be employed in special branches of agriculture; it has told the farmers how to protect themselves from pestiferous insects, and how to guard against the diseases of farm animals; it has supplied the best seeds for vegetables and flowers, for cotton, corn, wheat, tobacco, medicinal herbs, hemp, flax, and jute; it has made many valuable discoveries, and diffused them so that they may benefit the greatest number; and in countless ways has been of vast service in the development and improvement of the agricultural interests of the country.

The department is under the direction of an official called the Commissioner of Agriculture. He is appointed by the President, and receives a salary of $4,500 per year. A force of talented specialists is constantly engaged in making careful and thorough investigations of agricultural matters, and in many of the divisions of the department invaluable work is done. Thus, in the microscopical division close examinations are made of food products, and new methods discovered for the detection of artificial impurities in them. Examinations are also made to discover the cause of diseases of animals and plants, with a view of providing remedies. Plants native to the United States are frequently discovered to have valuable medicinal qualities, and within a short time several of this sort have been found on the Pacific coast which have great value for medical purposes. In the division of entomology special investigations are made of insects which injuriously affect wheat, corn, rice, sugar-cane, fruit-trees, and many vegetables, and important information gained as to their habits, mode of development, and the means of destroying them. Men are sent to the districts ravaged by insects, and devote much time to their study, and the results of their studies are incorporated in special publications, which are distributed throughout the farming sections of the country. Careful examinations have been made of insects affecting the cotton plant, and they have resulted in discoveries by which the cost of protecting the crop is greatly lessened, and a good part of the loss from the pests is prevented.

The department has undertaken an extended series of experiments and investigations in regard to diseases of farm animals, greater than it has ever attempted before, which will be conducted with the view of thoroughly ascertaining the origin, cause, and nature of the Texas cattle-fever, pleuro-pneumonia in cattle, and hog and chicken cholera, diseases which cause the loss of hundreds of thousands of dollars to farmers; and it is confidently expected that means will be discovered by which these destructive diseases can be prevented and cured. An experimental farm has been established in one of the outlying sections of Washington, and stocked with animals to be used for the experiments, and all the necessary apparatus for inoculation, autopsies, and chemical analyses has been provided. Experts will here diligently labor to obtain the information so greatly needed, and the farm will doubtless become a permanent part of the department, to be used for many kindred experiments from time to time.

Located throughout the agricultural districts of the United States are hundreds of reliable and judicious correspondents, who make simultaneous report to the department on the first of each month, of the condition of the crops, the results of local agricultural experiments, and other valuable facts. These reports are constantly verified by special agents, and the greatest pains taken to secure accuracy. When the information is all at hand the statistician of the department compiles it, and makes out the full monthly crop report, which is announced through the newspapers and issued in pamphlet form. These reports have great practical value, especially to those pecuniarily interested in bread-stuffs, cotton, and other staples.

Thousands of letters are received requesting information in regard to the agricultural productions of the western states and the territories ; and information in regard to strange looking birds and insects, samples

THE DEPARTMENT OF AGRICULTURE BUILDING.

of which are sent — whether or not they are destructive to crops. Peculiar kinds of grass and plants that have poisoned cattle are forwarded, with inquiries about them ; and a thousand and one different requests for practical knowledge continually pour in. Each letter is promptly answered, and the fullest information it has been possible to obtain is given. The annual report of the department has a circulation of 300,000 copies, mostly of course among the western farmers, who prize it highly. It is a bulky volume, with a vast amount of information of importance to the agricultural interests, and is copiously illustrated with correct drawings of insects, and various other things appertaining to agriculture and horticulture, the illustrations costing in some years as much as $30,000.

The department building is situated on the Mall, facing Thirteenth Street, and is of fine pressed brick with brown-stone trimmings. It is of the renaissance order of architecture, and was erected in 1868, after designs by Adolph Cluss, at a cost of $140,000. It has three stories and a mansard roof, and is one hundred and seventy feet long, and sixty-one feet wide. That portion of the Mall on which the building is situated is beautifully laid out in spacious gardens, in which are grown over two thousand varieties of plants and flowers, arranged in strict botanical order. A portion of the ground is laid out as an arboretum, and contains a choice collection of trees and hardy shrubs. The front gardens are adorned with a low terrace wall, and numerous rustic vases and statues. About ten acres of the rear gardens are devoted to the raising of seeds, and the testing of small fruits. From the front of the building a charming view of the business section of Washington can be obtained.

Great plant-houses of glass and iron are located on the west of the building. They consist of a centre pavilion with long wings, and are nearly four hundred feet in length, and very handsomely designed. They contain all the principal varieties of tropical fruit plants, and an extensive collection of foreign grapes, and also many medical plants, and those furnishing dyes, gums, and textile fibres.

Adjacent to the department building on the east is the seed-house, used for the storing and distributing of seeds. Here nearly one hundred persons are employed, during the winter and spring, in packing garden, field, and flower seeds of the most approved varieties, for distribution throughout the country. The department raises great quantities of seeds, and also purchases of reliable firms in Europe and

THE NATIONAL MUSEUM.

America many seeds which are strictly guaranteed to be of prime quality. Seeds are sent to districts where the lands have been overflowed, and the farmers have lost all they put into the ground, thus enabling them to start again in the work of cultivation. Choice varieties of foreign seeds are given out in sections where it is believed the foreign plants can be successfully cultivated. Yearly over two million packages of seeds, and from 60,000 to 70,000 plants are distributed. The plants include many rare and exceedingly valuable species.

The interior of the department building is excellently arranged for the purposes of the business, and all the divisions are accommodated in large, well-furnished apartments. A large apartment on the first floor is used for the library, a collection of 10,000 volumes pertaining to agriculture, which is considered the most complete of the kind in the United States. It has a number of very costly and magnificent botanical works of foreign publication.

On the second floor, occupying all the space in the centre of the building, is a grand Museum of Agriculture, arranged to thoroughly illustrate the agricultural productions of the country, and the substances manufactured from them. The collections are very extensive, and include every vegetable grown from Maine to California, together with many minerals and woods. There is also a fine exhibit of the game birds and poultry of the United States. Illustrations are given of the effect produced upon vegetation by climate, birds, insects, and animals. The vegetables and fruits are skillfully modeled and colored to imitate nature, and are so perfect in most cases that they may be easily taken for the genuine.

In the third story is a large botanical museum, containing many thousand species of plants, properly arranged. Here all the botanical collections obtained by the government exploring expeditions are deposited.

In 1828 an English gentleman named James Smithson died at Genoa, leaving an estate valued at half a million dollars. By his will the estate passed to a relative for life, and afterward descended "To the United States of America to found at Washington, under the name of the Smithsonian Institution, an establishment for the increase and diffusion of knowledge among men." In 1838 this bequest, amounting to the sum of $515,169, was transferred to the United States by the Chancery Court of England. The agent of the government in obtaining the money wrote in his report of Smithson that "he was a natural son of Hugh, first Duke of Northumberland, his mother being of an ancient family in Wiltshire of the name of Hungerford. He was born in London, and was educated at Oxford, where he took an honorary degree in 1786. He took the name of James Lewis Macie until a few years after he left the university, when he changed it to Smithson. He does not appear to have had any fixed home, living in lodgings when in London, and occasionally, a year or two at a time, in the cities on the continent — Paris, Berlin, Florence, and Genoa, at which last place he died. The ample provision made for him by the Duke of Northumberland, with retired and simple habits, enabled him to accumulate the fortune which passed to the United States. He interested himself little in questions of government, being devoted to science and chiefly to chemistry."

Gentlemen of learning and distinction in the United States were invited by the government to submit their views as to the best method of applying the Smithson bequest, and many views were submitted. It was suggested that a national university should be established, to occupy the place between a college and a professional school, with public lectures on classical and oriental languages, and the principal sciences. It was urged that the money should be devoted to teaching the principles of the useful arts, to the founding of a great botanical garden, to the creating of a national free library of reference ; and, in fact, innumerable views were presented, all set forth with strong arguments. Finally it was decided to make the " Smithsonian Institution" a general scientific establishment, which should be devoted to investigations and researches in all branches of knowledge ; which should employ eminent men to study special subjects, and publish the results to the world.

In 1846 the institution was organized by act of Congress, the management of its affairs being placed in the hands of a Board of Regents, composed of the Chief Justice of the Supreme Court of the United States, members of the Senate and House of Representatives, and sundry private citizens. The President of the United States and his Cabinet were constituted members *ex-officio* of the institution. A secretary, to have the active management, was to be chosen by the regents.

The corner-stone of the building was laid by President Polk, with Masonic rites, on the 1st of May, 1847, and the building was

THE GOVERNMENT PRINTING-OFFICE.

completed in 1856, at a cost of $450,000, the accumulated interest on the bequest being sufficient to pay for its erection. Prof. Joseph Henry, of Princeton College, was chosen to be secretary, and for many years directed the institution most successfully, retaining the position until his death. In 1880 Congress appropriated $15,000 for the erection of a bronze statue of Professor Henry, and on April 19, 1883, this statue, the work of William W. Story, was publicly unveiled with appropriate ceremony. It stands northwest of the Smithsonian Building, in a prominent position on the grounds.

The building is located on that part of the Mall, between Seventh and Twelfth streets, known as "the Smithsonian Grounds," an area of fifty-two acres, finely laid out as a public park, with broad drives and footways, handsome lawns, and groves of luxuriant trees. Andrew J. Downing, the distinguished landscape gardener and horticulturist, designed and partially laid out the grounds, but he died in 1852, before the work was completed. A monumental vase of great beauty, which stands in the easterly portion of the grounds, was erected to his memory by the American Pomological Society. The building is of red sandstone from quarries near Washington, on the upper Potomac, and the style of architecture is that variously described as the Norman, the Lombard, and the Byzantine, which prevailed throughout southern Europe toward the close of the twelfth century. There are nine towers of different forms and heights. The front extends four hundred and twenty-six feet, the centre building being fifty by two hundred feet, and there are two wings, the east one having a vestibule and porch attached, and the west one a semicircular projection. It was designed by James Renwick, Jr., and was the first unecclesiastical edifice of this architectural order ever erected in the country. The interior is substantially constructed. The officials and employés of the institution have apartments in the wings, and the centre structure is mainly used for the exhibition of objects of natural history.

The institution expends about $70,000 a year in various scientific investigations conducted by its force of scientists, and publishes a series of volumes, entitled the *Smithsonian Contributions to Knowledge*, which are sent to the principal scientific societies of the world in exchange for their publications. It carries on an extensive scientific correspondence, and all letters that are received making inquiries relative to certain branches of knowledge are carefully answered.

A LANDMARK ON B STREET NORTHWEST.

It publishes accounts of the latest discoveries in science, and in many ways intelligently labors for the "increase and diffusion of knowledge among men."

In 1879 "an annex to the Smithsonian Institution" was erected by the government, and denominated "The National Museum." Originally intended to contain the splendid exhibits made by foreign governments at the Centennial Exhibition, which were presented to the United States, its scope has been enlarged, so that now it is the general depository of all the geological and industrial collections of the government, and is rapidly becoming one of the greatest and most attractive museums in the world. In the course of a few years it will contain vast collections of the products of industry, ancient and modern, the useful, the ornamental, and the marvelous; and, it may be said, representations of nearly everything of importance that prodigal nature furnishes for man's use and benefit.

The building stands directly east of the Smithsonian Institution, and covers nearly two and one-half acres. It is a fine example of the modern Romanesque order of architecture, and has a certain quaint beauty, with its numerous peaked towers, high central dome, and pavilions. It is constructed of bricks laid in black mortar, with blue and buff bricks set in the cornices, which produce a very pleasing effect. There are seventeen spacious exhibition halls within the building, and also one hundred and thirty-five rooms for other purposes. The floors are constructed of tiles laid in artistic forms, the cases are all of mahogany, and the decorations are elegant. In the offices and work-shops in various sections may be found men of extensive reputation in the world of science, with numerous assistants, prosecuting researches and preparing material to increase the treasures of the museum. The secretary of the Smithsonian Institution is the director, and there are an assistant director, eleven curators, and a large force of employés. Congress annually makes an appropriation for the museum.

Already the collections are very interesting and instructive to all who wander through the lofty and beautiful exhibition halls. The staple products of the world are shown in their varying qualities, and the articles manufactured from them are thoroughly represented. Much that is curious in American and foreign growth and manufacture — much that is specially attractive — can be found in an hour's inspection, and days can be spent in the profitable study of the thousands of articles displayed. The ethnological exhibit is particularly comprehensive and valuable. The fame of these collections is rapidly extending over the country, and students of natural history, and of special industrial subjects, are beginning to learn that the government has provided in the most liberal manner in this museum a remarkable school wherein object-lessons of the utmost practical value can be obtained gratuitously.

THE GOVERNMENT PRINTING-OFFICE occupies a four-story brick building, covering the square at the corner of North Capitol and H streets. It is interesting to visitors from the fact that it is the largest printing and binding establishment in the world, having a working force of from 2,500 to 3,000 persons, and an immense quantity of the best material known to the "art preservative of arts." This office executes all the printing required by Congress and the executive and judicial departments of the government — truly an enormous amount, which will be realized by the statement that every year very nearly $3.000,000 are expended for it. An official with the title of Public Printer is in charge, and he receives a salary of $4,500.

Visitors to this mammoth establishment enter at the main door on North Capitol Street, and are provided with guides to show them over the building. It is an interesting though a rather fatiguing journey through the great halls and apartments occupied by busy men and women, noisy with the clatter of presses and other machines, and crowded with thousands of printed volumes and documents. The finest and costliest typographical work done in the country may be seen, and scores of unique machines, found only in the most extensive printing offices. The immense press-room, with a hundred large presses in constant motion; the type-setting room, three hundred feet long, filled with compositors; the great folding and binding rooms —all excite wonder and admiration, particularly as the vast amount of work appears to be progressing smoothly and easily, and apparently without a sign of confusion. Every department has a competent foreman and manager, and there is a fixed standard of work to which all the employés must conform. The very best service is required, and a careful record of deficiencies is kept.

Practically the office is unlimited in its productive capacity. It can also do very rapid work, if so required by Congress or any of the departments. For instance, the copy of a bill of Congress, or a report, which will make fifty or sixty large printed pages, may be received at ten o'clock in the morning, with orders for immediate delivery. It will be put in type, the proof read twice and corrected, and in two or three hours the bill or report, printed and bound, will be ready to be delivered.

The finest work ever produced by this office was *The Medical and Surgical History of the War of the Rebellion.* It was printed on very costly paper, and contained a great number of magnificent illustrations, executed at a cost of many thousands of dollars. An edition of 2,000 copies was first issued, and afterward Congress ordered another edition of 10,000 copies. The work was demanded by all the principal libraries of the world.

In the bindery can be seen every process known to the trade, including marbling, embossing, stamping, and other high branches. Some of the volumes issued are bound in sumptuous style. In the foundry, electrotyping and stereotyping are done.

FARRAGUT SQUARE, SHOWING THE RUSSIAN LEGATION BUILDING.

CHAPTER XVI.

THOSE who knew Washington before the Board of Public Works, under the leadership of Governor Shepherd, began the remarkable improvements, described elsewhere, and who have not visited the city since, can hardly imagine the great change that has taken place everywhere within its boundary. The streets once filled with rude specimens of architecture, now contain very handsome structures, varied and ornate ; and in the popular resident sections the majority of the houses are notable for their pleasing and tasteful forms. In the extensive northwest quarter there have been erected during the past ten years large numbers of very costly and magnificent houses, which in variety and elegance of form, in size and in luxurious appointments, are unequaled in the country. What is known as the "West End" is more especially the fashionable locality, but in other portions of the northwest quarter, and also on Capitol Hill, are many streets of fine mansions. The city is now very largely one of brick and stone, there being but few wooden buildings, except in the sections occupied by the colored people.

The West End comprises about five miles of territory stretching east and south from the foot of Kalorama Hill, which borders on Rock Creek and West Washington. It was formerly called "The Slashes," and was a dreary, unhealthy part of the city, covered with swamps, and mainly occupied by negro squatters. During the Rebellion the government erected barracks over it, and it was largely used for military purposes. When the Board of Public Works began its improvements this marsh-land was included in the comprehensive plan. It was carefully drained and graded, and everything necessary was done to make it desirable for habitation. Many acres were purchased at a low price by a combination of real estate speculators, who were shrewd enough to see that the district was likely in a short time to become the most eligible in the city for the residences of the wealthy and fashionable class. Their sagacity was well rewarded, for the acres they had obtained so cheaply were afterward disposed of at several dollars per foot, and great fortunes realized. The land in every part of the West End is now held at very high prices, and is considered to be the most valuable in Washington.

Connecticut Avenue, with a roadway one hundred and thirty feet in width, extending from Lafayette Square to the northern boundary line of the city, is the principal thoroughfare of this district; and Massachusetts, Rhode Island, New Hampshire, and Vermont avenues — broad, beautiful highways — also cross it. There are squares and circles with parks and statues in various portions of the district, and its whole appearance is exceedingly bright and charming.

It is on this spacious plain, but a few years ago an almost valueless area of swamps, that those palatial mansions, the pride and boast of the capital, are erected. Here are the residences of the wealthiest citizens, and those of the millionaires from different sections of the United States who make Washington their winter home. Here are the grand mansions of Blaine, Windom, Cameron, Cox, Stewart, Matthews, and a large number of other prominent men, and those of most of the high government officials, and the leading officers of the army and navy. Here are the foreign legation buildings, and here the leaders of society have congregated under splendid roof-trees. On every side is a dazzling spectacle of luxury and grandeur, and one can obtain, by a stroll through the avenues and streets, a realization of the enormous wealth that is centering in Washington at the present time. Those competent to judge express the opinion that in less than ten years every portion of this district, extensive as it is, will be covered with magnificent buildings, and that it will be verily a region of palaces. Before the capital celebrates its centennial, it is likely that the West End will have obtained great fame as one of the finest resident sections in the world.

Fashion has firmly set its seal upon this district, and all those improvements which come with opulence are lavished upon it. The

THE JAMES G. BLAINE MANSION.

mansions here are constructed of marble, costly greenstone, and fine pressed brick, and are so arranged as to secure the highest quality of artistic work. The architecture includes many forms of the antique and the mediæval, and the most approved modern styles. The interiors are remarkable for special methods of ornamentation, for marbles and bronzes, for carvings and paintings, and exquisite cabinet work. Europe and the Orient are searched for designs and substances, and apparently there is no limit as to cost.

It is a common saying of the citizens that Washington is destined to be the most popular winter resort of the continent, on account of its genial climate and the host of attractions it furnishes not to be obtained elsewhere, and that year by year greater numbers of Northern people of wealth and leisure will take up their residence in it. People who wish to escape the rigorous northern winter, and at the same time have the excitement and enjoyments of a large city, will, it is believed, speedily ascertain that the capital is most desirable as a winter home. This belief is already partially realized, as every winter during the past few years throngs of strangers have sojourned in Washington, and the demand for costly dwellings has been quite remarkable.

From its early days the national capital has been noted for being a gay and pleasure-loving city, and its social life has been usually brilliant and delightful. Of late it has developed its social qualities to a very considerable extent, and society now has the claim of cosmopolitan characteristics. The city is so admirably adapted for the homes of people of refinement, culture, and leisure, that many believe it will become in a few years the social metropolis of the United States. There are receptions, dinners, balls, germans, afternoon teas, kettle-drums, and all sorts of entertainments almost without number, from the beginning of winter until late in the spring, and few American cities have such an incessant round of gayety. Properly the social season begins on New Year's day and continues till Ash-Wednesday, but of late years it has been quite customary to have society entertainments before January, and even before the session of Congress begins in the first part of December, and to continue them through Lent. Many society people do not observe Lent in a strict manner, and some not at all, and they are willing to give receptions and parties during this period. The houses of the wealthy are now constructed with special reference to the giving of grand entertainments, very large drawing-rooms and dining-rooms being made, and accommodations provided for a host of guests.

What is called the "official society" includes the President and the members of his Cabinet, Senators and Representatives, members of the Supreme Court, and of foreign legations, and persons in eminent positions in the army and navy, and in the public service generally. Retired statesmen, justices, generals, and others once prominently connected with the government, are also placed in this society. There are many social organizations, the members of which are government employés of various ranks, and state associations, which include all the persons socially inclined from a certain state who are living in the city. The wealthy residents, not connected with the public service, have sets and circles, exclusive or not, as it may be; and there are numerous literary, musical, and art societies, which have frequent entertainments.

It is said that Washington society people, during the winter, lunch in one place, dine in another, dance in several houses of an evening, and are never at home, except on their reception-days. Each week of the social season is full of events. Monday is the reception-day of the wives of the Justices of the Supreme Court, and of the General of the Army and the Admiral of the Navy. Many of the residents of Capitol Hill are also "at home" on that day. On Tuesday the prominent families of the West End have receptions, and on Wednesday the members of the Cabinet and the Speaker of the House of Representatives receive their friends and the public. On Thursday many receptions are held by Senators and Representatives. Friday and Saturday are filled out variously. There are very many pleasant " Saturday evenings "—dinners, card-parties, and meetings of social organizations. The officers stationed at the United States Barracks, and at the navy yard, give weekly receptions, at which dancing is customary.

All the official receptions are announced in the newspapers, and those in the afternoon are open to the public. The name or card should be promptly given to the usher upon entering a house, and if the name is not properly announced it should be mentioned at the presentation. If cards are left by strangers they are always honored by return cards, or calls in person, and invitations to evening receptions in official circles usually follow. Small and plain cards are used, with the name engraved or written, but never printed. The dress customary in society for morning calls should be worn at afternoon receptions, and full dress in the evening. The hours for afternoon receptions are from two to five o'clock ; for evening receptions, from eight to eleven o'clock.

It is customary for visitors to Washington to call first on the residents. If the person called upon is "not at home," turn down the upper right-hand corner of the card, thus indicating that the call was made in person. If the call is intended for the different members of the family, either leave several cards, or one with the right side entirely folded over. When making a parting call, previous to leaving the city, a card should be left with p. p. c. written on the right-hand lower corner. The time to return calls or cards is within three days. A call should be made in person after a dinner-party, but after other entertainments a card may be sent by a servant or by mail.

Invitations to dinner should be promptly accepted or declined, but with regard to other entertainments, no answer need be sent unless the letters R. S. V. P. are on the invitation. The customary form of acceptance to a dinner invitation is as follows: " Mr. R—— has the honor to accept Mr. S ——'s kind invitation to dinner for Wednesday, the 10th of February, at eight o'clock. Feb. 6, 188—." The date and hour of the dinner are mentioned in the acceptance to show that they are understood. This form, properly adapted, may be used in accepting other invitations.

PEOPLE who are unacquainted with department life in Washington are very apt to believe that government clerks, as a general thing, are indolent and improvident — a peculiar set who have obtained office by political favor, who work very little, and spend the liberal salaries they receive in extravagant living. This is a singular but by no means uncommon mistake. Of course there are " black sheep" among the clerks — those who shirk their work, are full of tricks, and are generally dishonorable — but it can be truly said that the majority are industrious, sober, economical, and, without doubt, fully on a par with similar workers in commercial lines. Clerks are required to perform a certain amount of work each day, and the work, when done, will compare favorably with that performed in private business establishments, and may even exceed it in quality and quantity. All of the government work must be done in a methodical, strictly accurate manner, and every imperfection or short-coming is recorded and serves as a bar to promotion, and also as a pretext for dismissal if the position held by the clerk of " bad record " is wanted for some one else. In some of the departments the standard of work is set so high, and the quantity required each day is so great, that it is only by the most diligent efforts, by really exhausting labor, that the best of clerks can keep their records entirely free from discredit. The idle and incompetent are constantly being dismissed, unless perchance they are able to retain their places by means of " strong influence," or by cunning devices which may serve for a time in place of honest, faithful labor.

The department clerks in reality form a solid, intelligent, important part of the population of Washington, and their influence is generally for good. Many are householders, over five thousand, it is estimated, owning comfortable homes of their own, paid for out of their savings, by the help of the greatly beneficial system of coöperative building, and also by the installment plan applied to real estate, which for the past ten years have been much in vogue in Washington, and which have done a great deal to make it a city of homes owned by those who live in them, like Philadelphia. They are not the aliens they have been represented to be, in any sense of the term. They have aided in the growth of Washington, they take pride in its beauty and prosperity, and large numbers look upon it as their permanent home. If they leave the government service they engage in general business, and some of the most successful merchants and professional men of the city were once department clerks.

There are many veteran clerks. In the Treasury Department there is one who has served since the administration of John Quincy Adams. A clerk in the Navy Department was appointed in 1843, and has given continuous service ever since. Here and there may be found those who can point to a record of ten, twenty, and even thirty years of service.

When one goes into the rooms in the department buildings, and observes the clerks working over great piles of documents with an

THE ANTHONY POLLOK MANSION.

intense, concentrated energy rarely seen in private business—each room under the vigilant eye of an official—the impression produced is that it is not, after all, such "a very fine thing" to be a government employé of the subordinate class, even if the compensation is liberal. Distance, indeed, lends enchantment to the view of service in the departments. Away from Washington the stories of the large salaries received by government employés for doing what is popularly supposed to be little work in a short day of labor, have a very beguiling effect, and thousands of persons long for positions in the public service, and regard those who obtain them as exceedingly fortunate. It is evident that there are some department positions with a compensation very much out of proportion to the work performed—easy and lucrative places; but a careful inspection of the departments will convince any one that the majority of the clerks and other employés render a full equivalent for their salaries.

A clerk's life is not an entirely roseate one. Promptly at nine o'clock each morning he must be at his desk to begin the day's labor. Until four o'clock in the afternoon the business in each division and bureau goes on steadily, and frequently very rapidly, as in most of the departments the affairs are many months behind by reason of the lack of employés. Officials implore Congress to give them more clerks, in order that they may dispose of the vast accumulation of business in their hands, but the appeals are seldom heeded, and the accumulation continues despite the most earnest efforts to prevent it. Seven hours' confinement over a desk in a close, stifling room; the difficulty very often of executing the daily task to the satisfaction of a hypercritical official; the "insolence of office," frequently displayed; the irritating system of watching and "spotting," common in many departments, which causes bitter, indignant feelings; the rigid, uncompromising adherence to strict rules in one case, and the unblushing favoritism shown in another; the demand for hours of extra work without extra pay; the promotions, not from merit, but from ability to fawn and "crook the pregnant hinges of the knee,"— these are some of the thorns on the government rose.

Many men and women thrive in this clerk-life and seem peculiarly adapted to it. They easily shed its irritations and discomforts, they like the short day of labor, and they quickly discover "where thrift may follow fawning." By degrees they ascend to the more lucrative, less restricted positions, and often are able to hold them for a long time. Others, of a different nature, try the life a while, and then retire disgusted, quite willing to work more hours, and even for less salary, in private business, where at least they will be regarded as something more than mere machines to be entirely regulated by official caprice.

There are nearly fifty-six hundred classified clerkships in the departments, and many thousands of ungraded positions. Clerks of the first class receive salaries of $1,200 per year; those of the second class, $1,400; those of the third class, $1,600; those of the fourth class, $1,800. In the ungraded positions the salaries range from $700 to $1,000. Male clerks usually begin their service for the government at $800 or $1,000, and female clerks at $700, unless they are fortunate enough to secure classified clerkships at once. Chief clerks who rank with officials have salaries from $1,800 to $2,700, and stenographers and translators of foreign languages, from $1,200 to $2,000. Copyists, who are mainly women, receive from $60 to $75 per month. Thirty days in each year are allowed for vacation, during which time the salary is continued, and in case of sickness, certified to by a physician, there is no loss of compensation.

Of course in the government service, as in affairs generally, the majority of the employés have the small places and the burden of work. Hundreds of well-educated clerks who do a great deal of drudgery are glad to get $800 or $1,000 per year, and if eventually they are so fortunate as to be placed on the list of those entitled to draw $1,200, they are happy indeed. The higher, more lucrative places are usually out of their reach, unless they are specially favored, or have distinguished themselves by thoroughly efficient work.

WHEN Washington was first occupied by the government, in 1800, there were over two thousand negroes in the city, and over four thousand in the entire District of Columbia. They were mainly slaves engaged in cultivating plantations, and in domestic service. In 1830 there were 6,512 free negroes, and 6,119 slaves. When slavery was abolished in the District, in April, 1862, some nine months before the general emancipation, there were about 3,000 slaves and 14,316 free negroes. In 1870 the colored population had increased to 43,404, of which number Washington was credited with 35,455. At the present time the city has nearly 49,000 colored people, and ranks as third among the cities of the United States in this class of population.

It has been said, apparently with a great deal of truth, that the capital has more intelligent, cultured, well-to-do colored people than any other American city. They have many prosperous churches, and literary, musical, and social organizations, and the thrifty families give very pleasant entertainments during the winter. Excellent public schools, a fine college, opportunities for lucrative government service, are among the advantages provided for the colored people, and a certain number, by no means small, carefully and thoughtfully strive to reach a good position — to become well educated, well disciplined.

But, looking at the race as it appears on the surface of Washington life, it must be admitted that many are improvident, unreliable, careless of the future, and are quite content if they have a ragged coat to wear, a crust to eat, and plenty of leisure to enjoy the sunshine. The small, dilapidated cabins occupied by this class in some sections of East and South Washington are really marvels of shiftless contrivance. Some of them are scarcely larger than " sugarboxes," and yet they will give shelter to a numerous family. About the doors of these fantastic, wretched abodes a half-dozen little curly heads usually may be seen playing.

Near Lincoln Park lives a former slave of John Randolph, the haughty " Lord of Roanoke." His cabin was constructed by his own hands, and is comfortable in its way, although rudely fashioned and sparsely furnished. The old man, over whose white head many winters have swept, is held in high regard by the colored people living in his vicinity, and gains a living by telling fortunes and prescribing simple remedies for various ailments. He is an odd character, and when in the humor will describe his former life on Randolph's plantation in quaint, vivid, and intensely interesting language. His clothes are patched and scarce hold together on his bent and tottering form. Usually he sits crouching before his hearth-stone, rubbing his thin hands and muttering to himself, and he leaves his cabin only at rare intervals to hobble a few squares.

The most ignorant of the colored people are very superstitious, and have great faith in charms and omens, and all of those singular things which have come from the South and pass current under the name of voudooism. There are voudoo doctors of their own race, who live well, dress fashionably, and apparently make a great deal of money. They profess to cure everything, from a big wart to a bad case of what they call " devilish conjuration." They are very mysterious in their practice, and use many curiously fashioned articles

MANSION BUILT BY DON CAMERON.

which they audaciously claim possess cabalistic and astonishing qualities, and utter many strange words. They impress their patients by
all sorts of tricks, such as manipulating large snakes, whispering in
the ear of a dog and pretending to receive an answer, and other silly
actions. The credulous negroes look with awe on these transparent
frauds, and do many ridiculous things at the bidding of the "doctors."

Around the great markets one will see among the hucksters whose
little stands crowd all the walks, a good representation of colored
people of peculiar characteristics. The colored hucksters offer for
sale twists of tobacco in the natural leaf, warranted to be perfectly
pure Virginia weed; many herbs, barks, and roots, and large quantities of flowers and "garden sass," and some have coops of live
chickens and ducks. There are numerous women in the groups,
wearing large bandanna handkerchiefs gracefully entwined round
their heads, turban-like, but the colors are not as gorgeous as they
were in the days "befo' the wa'." The gaudy red and yellow ban-
dannas are rarely seen, and it is said that the African dames of the

markets have resigned to the aristocratic æsthetes these glowing primary tints. By their pleasant ways, ready wit and repartee, the huckster women induce you to buy liberally. They call you "honey," in soft, cajoling tones, but do not take as kindly to the salutation of "Aunty" as they did years ago. They are an interesting study, and give a good deal of picturesqueness to the markets.

On the wharves where vessels bringing oysters to the city from the Virginia beds deposit their cargoes, will be found daily throughout the winter hosts of negroes known as "oyster-shuckers." They buy oysters from the vessels, and, seated in groups, skillfully "shuck" or remove the shells, shouting and laughing while at work. Then taking the bivalves in long tin cans, they go over the city, calling clearly and loudly as they walk, "Oys! oys! here's yer nice fresh oys!" Great quantities of oysters are sold by these vendors every day during the season.

There are manifold other occupations followed by the black man, diligently seeking the honest penny. The workers have no fellowship with the idlers to be seen on all the thoroughfares — ragged, shiftless sons of Ham, who contrive to live in some unknown way, although they toil not.

TENTH AND G STREETS N. W., SHOWING FIRST CONGREGATIONAL CHURCH.

CHAPTER XVII.

ONE of the institutions of Washington which attracts a great
deal of attention is the Corcoran Gallery of Art, presented
to the people of the United States by Mr. William W.
Corcoran. It was deeded to trustees on May 10, 1869,
and a year later was incorporated by act of Congress, the building
and grounds being forever exempted from taxation. In his deed of
gift Mr. Corcoran stated that the institution was designed for "the
perpetual establishment and encouragement of painting, sculpture,
and the fine arts generally," and the condition was imposed that it
should be open to the public without charge on certain days of the
week, and " on other days at moderate and reasonable charges, to be
applied to the current expenses of procuring and keeping in order
the building and its contents." The hope was expressed that it
would provide " not only a pure and refined pleasure for residents
and visitors at the national capital," but that it would be useful in the
development of American genius.

The gallery is situated on the northeast corner of Pennsylvania
Avenue and Seventeenth Street, directly opposite the State, War, and
Navy Building. It has a frontage of one hundred and six feet, and
a depth of one hundred and twenty-five feet. It is constructed of
fine pressed brick, with brown-stone facings and ornaments, and is of
the renaissance order of architecture. Ten feet above the ordinary
roof rises a mansard roof, with a central pavilion, and two smaller

ones. The building is two stories in height, and the front is divided into recesses by pilasters with capitals representing Indian corn, and has four niches in which are statues of Phidias, Raphael, Michael Angelo, and Albert Durer, portraying sculpture, painting, architecture, and engraving. On the front are fine carvings, the Corcoran monogram, and the inscription, "Dedicated to Art." On the Seventeenth Street side are niches containing the statues of Titian, Da Vinci, Rubens, and Rembrandt, and it is the intention to add those of Murillo, Canova, and Crawford. The statues are of Carrara marble, seven feet high, and were executed by M. Ezekiel, an American sculptor residing in Rome. The building was designed by James Renwick, of New York, and erected at a cost of $250,000. It is very attractive in appearance. The gallery was opened to the public in December, 1874.

Mr. Corcoran gave to it his private collection of paintings and statuary, valued at $100,000, and an endowment fund of $900,000. One of the trustees visited Europe and made extensive purchases of art works, being very successful in procuring a large number of notable productions. Many American works of great value were also obtained. The gallery is open daily, and on Tuesdays, Thursdays, and Saturdays is free; on other days there is an admission fee of twenty-five cents. Under certain regulations persons are allowed to draw from the casts and to copy the paintings. The annual income is nearly $80,000, the larger portion of which is used in the purchase of pictures and statues.

The lower story of the building is entirely devoted to the exhibition of sculpture, bronzes, and ceramic ware. In spacious halls are magnificent collections of casts of antique marbles, representing the best works of the great Greek sculptors. There are also many original examples of modern sculpture, including a number of celebrated works. The collections of bronzes and ceramic ware are very extensive and noteworthy.

In the second story are four galleries of paintings, the main one being ninety-five feet by forty-four and one-half feet, and thirty-eight feet high, with a richly frescoed ceiling. These galleries contain several hundred paintings carefully selected to furnish good examples of modern art, with something of the ancient. Many well-known American and European painters are represented on the walls, and most of the canvases are very valuable originals. The gallery ranks among the finest in the country, and in some particulars has no equal.

THE CORCORAN GALLERY OF ART.

With its large income to be devoted to acquiring the best art works, it must in time possess extraordinary collections.

Mr. Corcoran, the venerable philanthropist, who has given this superb gallery to the public, and whose long life has been rich in good works, is a native of Georgetown, but for many years he has been a resident of Washington. He began his business career as an auctioneer, and afterward established a banking-house, which he conducted very successfully for an extended period. By his financial operations, and by early investments in city lands which greatly increased in value when Washington developed into a thriving city, he became a millionaire. The princely fortune he possesses is constantly being used for the benefit of worthy objects.

In 1871 Mr. Corcoran founded the Louise Home, an institution designed for impoverished gentlewomen who may need the shelter of a friendly roof. It was named after his deceased wife and daugh-

ter. It has an endowment fund of $250,000, and is managed by a
board of lady trustees. The building is situated on Massachusetts
Avenue, between Fifteenth and Sixteenth streets, and cost $200,000.
It is a beautiful brick structure, four stories high, surmounted by a
mansard roof, with a central pavilion, and stands within a spacious
enclosure of lawn and garden, a conspicuous object in the fashionable West End. The interior is elegant in its appointments. The
doors of this noble institution are always open to women of refinement
and education who require assistance. Visitors are admitted every
week-day afternoon.

WASHINGTON, it may be said, can safely dispute with Brooklyn
the title of "The City of Churches," as there are at present within
its borders no less than one hundred and ninety churches, most of
them apparently in a flourishing condition. There are fifty-nine
Methodist churches, forty-six Baptist, twenty-two Episcopal, seventeen Presbyterian, thirteen Catholic, ten Lutheran, and a variety of
other denominations. Many of the church structures are large and
handsome, and some of them are remarkable for graceful, pleasing
architecture.

The oldest Episcopal churches in the city are Christ Church,
erected on G Street, near the navy yard, in 1795; and St. John's
Church on H Street, near the White House, which dates from 1816.
The distinguished Latrobe designed St. John's, which is of brick,
covered with stucco, and in the form of a Latin cross. One of its
pews is set apart for the Presidents of the United States, many of
whom, from the time of President Madison, have worshiped in the
venerable edifice. Other prominent Episcopal churches are the Ascension, corner of Massachusetts Avenue and Twelfth Street; the
Epiphany, on G Street, between Thirteenth and Fourteenth streets
northwest; the Incarnation, on N Street, corner of Twelfth northwest; St. Andrew's, corner of Fourteenth and Corcoran streets northwest; the Holy Cross, on Massachusetts Avenue, corner of Eighteenth
Street; and Trinity, corner of Third and C streets northwest.

About four miles from Washington is the oldest Episcopal church
in the District of Columbia — St. Paul's Church, of Rock Creek
Parish. It is situated adjacent to the Soldier's Home, on land given
by the colonial worthy, John Bradford, in 1719, to be held in perpe-
tuity for church purposes. St. Paul's was erected in 1719, of brick
imported from England, and although it has been remodeled, the
original walls remain, with every appearance of enduring for a

number of years longer. An extensive burial-ground surrounds the church, in which many of the first residents of Washington are buried, some of the grave-stones bearing dates of the past century.

The New York Avenue Church is the most prominent of the Presbyterian churches. It has a large membership, and is attended by many Presbyterians sojourning in the capital during the winter. The First Church, on Four and One-half Street; the Central Church, corner of Third and I streets northwest; the Fourth Church, on Ninth Street northwest, and the Metropolitan Church, on Fourth Street, corner of B southwest, are to be ranked among the prominent houses of worship.

The First Baptist Church, on Thirteenth Street northwest, began existence in 1803, and the Second Baptist Church, on Virginia Avenue, in 1810. These were the first of the numerous churches of this denomination. Calvary Church, corner of Eighth and H streets northwest; the E Street Church; the Metropolitan Church, corner of A and Sixth streets northeast, and the North Baptist Church, on Fourteenth Street northwest, are leading churches. The largest of the colored Baptist church organizations is the Nineteenth Street Church, which has a fine edifice in the West End.

There is only one Unitarian church in Washington, the All Souls Church, corner of Fourteenth and L streets northwest. This church is attended by a fashionable and distinguished congregation, comprising many persons of high official position, and of prominence in society.

Meetings of Methodists were held in Washington as early as 1805, and in 1815 the Foundry Church (where President Hayes worshiped) was established. Methodism flourishes, there being at present more churches of this denomination in the city than of any other. The principal churches are the Metropolitan Church, on Four and One-half Street; the Foundry Church, corner of Fourteenth and G streets northwest; the McKendree Church, on Massachusetts Avenue; the Hamline Church, corner of Ninth and P streets northwest, and the Fourth Street Church. The Asbury Church, corner of Eleventh and K streets northwest, has a large and influential colored congregation.

There is but one Universalist church in the city—the Church of Our Father, corner of Thirteenth and L streets northwest. The church was erected in 1883, at a cost of about $30,000. For some years the society worshiped in the Masonic Temple.

The Congregational churches are the First Church, corner of Tenth and G streets northwest, and the Tabernacle of the Congregation, on Ninth Street, between B Street and Virginia Avenue southwest. There are also two mission churches.

The Lutheran churches are divided into English and German, there being more of the latter than the former. The Memorial Church, on Thomas Circle, at the intersection of Fourteenth Street and Vermont Avenue, and St. Paul's Church, corner of Eleventh and H streets northwest, are the principal English ones.

On Vermont Avenue, between N and O streets, is the Church of the Christian Disciples, generally known as the Garfield Memorial Church. It is the leading church of the Christian faith in the United States. In the small chapel which formerly stood on the site of this church President Garfield worshiped for many years, and the pew he occupied has been placed in the new church. It is draped in black, and bears a silver tablet on which is the name of the lamented President.

There are two Friends' Meeting-Houses in the city; one, the Hicksite, on I Street northwest; and the other, the Orthodox, on Thirteenth Street northwest.

The principal Catholic churches are St. Patrick's, on G Street northwest; St. Peter's, on Capitol Hill; St. Dominick's, corner of Sixth and E streets southwest; St. Matthew's, corner of Fifteenth and H streets northwest; St. Aloysius, corner of North Capitol and I streets northwest; the Immaculate Conception, corner of Eighth and N streets northwest; and St. Stephen's, corner of Pennsylvania Avenue and Twenty-fifth Street northwest. The oldest is St. Patrick's, which was established in 1804. There are two German Catholic churches: St. Mary's, on Fifth Street northwest; and St. Joseph's, on Second Street northeast; and one church designed for colored people, St. Augustine's, on Fifteenth Street, northwest.

Two Hebrew synagogues have a large attendance. They are the Congregation Adas Israel (orthodox), corner of Sixth and G streets northwest; and the Washington Hebrew Congregation, on Eighth Street northwest.

CONGRESS annually appropriates about $500,000 for the support of the public schools of the District of Columbia. The schools are in charge of trustees, subordinate to whom are two superintendents, one having the management of the white schools, and the other of the colored schools. The salary of one superintendent is $2,700; that of the other, $2,250. Five hundred and twenty-five teachers are employed, their salaries aggregating $349,000 per year. There are twenty-four prominent school buildings, most of which are in Washington, and a number of smaller ones. The large buildings were erected at an expenditure of many thousands of dollars, and are considered models of school architecture. They have every approved appliance and convenience, and will accommodate large numbers of pupils.

The schools of Washington, up to 1864, were very poor and inadequate. In that year the Wallach School, a fine, spacious brick building, was erected on Pennsylvania Avenue, between Seventh and Eighth streets southeast. It was named after Richard Wallach, who was mayor of the city from 1862 to 1868. Other large and suitable buildings followed, and great attention was paid to educational matters, nothing being left undone which would make the school system equal to that of any city of the country. Washingtonians now point with proper pride to their splendid school buildings and admirable system of education, which furnishes equal advantages to white and

THE WINDOM MANSION.

colored children. Nearly thirty thousand pupils are enrolled in the schools.

The Franklin School is the finest of the school buildings, although some of the others approximate it in elegance of design. It is a large brick edifice, with three stories and a basement, and contains fourteen school-rooms. It stands on the corner of Thirteenth and K streets northwest, opposite a beautiful park, and in a locality filled with costly residences.

The High School, on O Street northwest; the Seaton School, on I Street northwest; and the Jefferson School, on Sixth Street southwest, are imposing buildings. The latter is the largest school building in the city, having ample accommodations for twelve hundred scholars. There are six prominent colored schools, the most notable of which are the Sumner School, corner of Seventeenth and M streets northwest, and the Lincoln School, corner of Second and C streets southeast. The former was erected at a cost of $70,000, and is a very fine building.

Among the important Catholic educational institutions is the Convent of the Visitation, or Visitation Academy, which occupies the entire square on Connecticut Avenue between L and M streets. It emanated from the famous institution in Georgetown, which is the "mother" community of the order of Nuns of the Visitation in the United States, and for twenty-seven years had its home in the old convent building on Tenth Street, recently demolished. In 1877 the community removed to the large and beautiful building it now occupies. The convent is surrounded by spacious grounds enclosed by a brick wall, and is an attractive and prominent object in the section of the city in which it is located.

On I Street, between North Capitol and First streets northwest, is the Gonzaga College, conducted by fathers of the Society of Jesus. It was incorporated as a university in 1858.

The National Medical College, connected with the Columbian University, is located on H Street, between Thirteenth and Fourteenth streets northwest. It was founded in 1824, and the present building, erected at a cost of $40,000 in 1864, was the gift of Mr. William W. Corcoran. The Law School of Columbian University, established in 1826, is located on Fifth Street, opposite Judiciary Square.

The Medical and Law Schools of Georgetown College are located in Washington, the former at the corner of Tenth and E streets

THE LOUISE HOME.

northwest, and the latter on F Street, between Ninth and Tenth streets northwest.

THE public markets of Washington are among the finest in the United States, and are objects of considerable interest to strangers. They consist of the Center Market, on the south side of Pennsylvania Avenue, between Seventh and Ninth streets northwest; the Northern Liberty Market, on Fifth Street, between K and L streets northwest; the Northern Market, on Seventh Street, between O and P streets northwest; the Eastern Market, on Capitol Hill, at the junction of Seventh Street east, and North Carolina Avenue; and the Western Market, on K Street, between Twentieth and Twenty-first streets northwest. They are supplied with a profusion of fine vegetables and fruits, game, fish, oysters, and the best qualities of meats. Washington being situated in the centre of a luxuriant agricultural region, and adjacent to the great oyster and fishing-grounds of the Potomac River and Chesapeake Bay, is enabled to have an abundance of food products in its markets. It has also special facilities for obtaining early vegetables and fruits from the South, and meats from contiguous districts and from the West.

The Center Market is the largest of the markets, and in many particulars, it is considered to be the market *par excellence* of the country. The building was begun in 1870, and opened in July, 1873, its erection having cost $350,000. It is located on one of the most central squares in Washington, which has been devoted to market purposes since the foundation of the city, and is surrounded by extensive grounds and wide streets. Here was the well-known "Marsh Market" of *ante-bellum* days — a rough, dilapidated building, or series of buildings, but filled to overflowing with good "marketing," and distinguished for its quaint, motley assemblages.

Four capacious brick buildings constitute the Center Market, those on the Pennsylvania Avenue front being very ornate and pleasing in design. They form a square and are connected, so that in going through the market they seem very much like one building. They are four hundred and ten feet in length, and their average width is eighty-two feet. The total space available for market purposes is 84,818 feet. One building is used exclusively for wholesale business in meats and produce. It is three stories high and contains fourteen large stores, with elevators to the upper stories. The other buildings are two stories in height, and have great arched roofs. They contain six hundred and sixty-six stalls and stands for the retail business, and have wide aisles and spaces. There is room for three hundred wagons around the market, and the covered sidewalks will accommodate innumerable hucksters' stands. The rents for stalls and stands are from $5 to $14 per month, and the yearly rent-roll is nearly $60,000. The market is owned by the Washington Market Company.

The daily business in and around this splendid structure is enormous. During the morning hours there are throngs of buyers of all classes of society — fashionable women of the West End, accompanied by negro servants, mingling with people of less opulent sections, all busily engaged in selecting the day's household supplies. It is a scene of wonderful variety and animation, and has much of the picturesqueness noticeable in the markets farther south. And on Saturday evenings, when the market is glowing with myriads of lights, and is lively and bustling with the excitement of a great traffic, it has peculiar interest and fascination. An extensive variety of articles, other than food products, can be purchased. Flowers and plants of numberless sorts are spread out in tempting array; tin, wooden, and crockery ware, and various household utensils; clothing, jewelry and trinkets, sweet-smelling herbs and barks, pictures and books, smokers' articles — these, and more, are to be obtained. Cooked food is offered, such as hominy, smoking hot, sold by the quart for family use; and everything in the baker's line is to be found in abundance. Indeed, the market is a vast, convenient bazar, where one can be readily supplied with innumerable things in daily demand.

The Northern Liberty Market is the second in magnitude. It was erected in 1875 at a cost of $140,000, and is an imposing brick building, three hundred and twenty-four feet in length, and one hundred and twenty-six in width, and is notable for its great height and ponderous arched roof, supported by colossal iron girders. The other markets are substantial brick buildings, excellently arranged, and of good size.

EIGHTH AND H STREETS N. W., SHOWING CALVARY BAPTIST CHURCH.

THERE are three regular theatres in Washington — Albaugh's Grand Opera House, the New National Theatre, and Harris' Bijou Opera House. In addition, there are theatres in which variety performances are given, and summer gardens where musical entertainments are the rule. The prominent halls for concerts and lectures are the Armory of the Washington Light Infantry Corps, National Rifles' Hall, Lincoln Hall, Masonic Temple, and the Grand Army Hall.

The principal hotels are the Ebbitt House, Riggs' House, Willard's Hotel, Arlington Hotel, Wormley's Hotel, Metropolitan Hotel, and National Hotel. There are numerous smaller hotels for the general public, as well as a number of what are called family hotels, many of which are very elegant in their appointments.

Four daily newspapers are published — *The National Republican* and *The Daily Post* in the morning, and *The Star* and *The Critic* in the evening. The *Post* and the *Star* occupy fine buildings of their own. There are six Sunday newspapers, and several other weekly publications.

The benevolent institutions of the city are numerous. Among the prominent ones is the National Soldiers and Sailors Orphan Home, on G Street, between Seventeenth and Eighteenth streets northwest. It was established in 1866, and is liberally supported by the government. Orphans of soldiers and sailors in the Rebellion are cared for and educated until they are sixteen years old. The institution is in charge of a board of lady managers, and is open to the public daily.

The Washington Asylum is located at the terminus of C Street southeast, on the banks of the Anacostia River. The present building was erected in 1859. It is an asylum for the paupers of the District, and is also used as a work-house for persons convicted of minor offenses.

The Freedmen's Hospital occupies the square between Fifth, Seventh, Boundary, and Pomeroy streets. It has accommodations for two hundred patients. It is supported by government appropriations, and, although designed for freedmen, all classes of patients are received.

Other prominent benevolent institutions are, the Garfield Memorial Hospital, at the head of Tenth Street; the Providence General Hospital, corner of Second and D streets southeast; the City Orphan Asylum, corner of Fourteenth and S streets northwest; St. John's Hospital, on H Street, between Nineteenth and Twentieth streets northwest; the Columbia Hospital for Women, corner of L and Twenty-fifth streets northwest; and the Home for the Aged, corner of Third and H streets northeast.

In the District of Columbia there are twenty lodges of Masons, with a membership of nearly three thousand, and the order is in a very prosperous condition. The Masonic Temple in Washington is an attractive structure. It is situated on F Street, corner of Ninth northwest, and was erected in 1868 at a cost of $200,000. It is of granite and freestone, and is four stories in height. The first floor is occupied by stores, and the sec-

ALL SOULS' UNITARIAN CHURCH.

ond floor contains a hall for public entertainments. The third and fourth floors are occupied by the Masonic lodges, chapters, and commanderies, the various apartments being furnished in a magnificent manner.

The Odd Fellows' building, on Seventh Street, between D and E streets northwest, was originally erected in 1846, but was thoroughly remodeled in 1874, and now is a convenient and handsome edifice. It is of brick, and has iron pilasters and ornaments painted white. It has three domes, the centre one rising above the others. On the

front of the building is a large balcony.   Stores occupy the ground
floor, and on the second floor is a public hall.   The lodge and encampment rooms are on the third floor, and are finely decorated and
furnished.   There are fourteen lodges and four encampments, and
the order numbers about eighteen hundred members, and is rapidly
increasing.

AT the foot of E Street southeast, is the Congressional Cemetery,
originally called " Washington Parish Burial Ground."   It was laid
out in 1807 by residents of the eastern quarter of the city, and afterward came under the control of Christ Episcopal Church.   As the
government made liberal donations of money and land to the cemetery, its name was changed to " Congressional," and freestone ceno-
taphs were erected for deceased congressmen.   A large vault was
erected by Congress near the centre of the grounds.   Among the
men of prominence buried here are Vice-President George Clinton,
of New York; Elbridge Gerry, of Massachusetts, and Tobias Lear,
for many years the private secretary and intimate companion of
George Washington.   The cemetery contains about forty acres, and
extends along the Anacostia River.

Oak Hill Cemetery is situated on Georgetown Heights, and is
peculiarly arranged on a series of terraces rising from the western
bank of Rock Creek.   It is unique and beautiful; noble oaks cover
its ground, and exquisite taste has been used in its adornment.   Here
is the Van Ness mausoleum, containing the remains of General Van
Ness and family.   Here Lorenzo Dow is buried, and here also John
Howard Payne rests at last in his native land, no longer an exile
from the " Home, sweet home," he sang of in immortal words.

ABOUT $340,000 is annually appropriated for the police force of
Washington.   The force is known as the Metropolitan Police, and
consists of a superintendent with the title of major, who receives a
salary of $2,600 ; a captain at $1,800, two lieutenant-inspectors at
$1,500 each, ten lieutenants at $1,320 each, twenty sergeants at
$1,140 each, and two hundred and fifty-five privates at salaries
from $900 to $1,080.   There are also seventeen station-house keepers
who are paid $720 each, and numerous clerks, messengers, and
laborers.   There is a mounted force of twenty-seven men.   The
police duties extend throughout the District of Columbia.

The fire department is sustained at a yearly expenditure of $100,-

ooo. There are eight engines, and other fire apparatus. The chief engineer has a salary of $1,800, and the assistant engineer, $1,400. There is a force of eighty-four men, who receive from $720 to $1,000 each. Connected with the department is an efficient telegraph and telephone service in charge of expert electricians, the superintendent receiving a salary of $1,600.

The white military organizations are the Washington Light Infantry, of four companies, the Infantry Cadets, the National Rifles, the Rifles Cadets, the Washington Light Guard, and the Union Veteran Corps. There are three companies of colored infantry, and the Capital City Guard, consisting of two companies of colored men.

Connecting Washington with the outer world are the Baltimore and

GARFIELD MEMORIAL CHURCH.
(*Christian Disciples.*)

Potomac, and Baltimore and Ohio railroads, extending from New York via the Pennsylvania Railroad, with branches south and west. In the depot of the Baltimore and Potomac Railroad, President Garfield was shot by Charles J. Guiteau on July 2, 1881. On the wall, directly above the spot where Garfield fell, the railroad company has placed a marble tablet as a memorial to the martyred President. There are various steamboat lines on the Potomac River to southern ports. The city has five distinct street railroad companies, whose lines traverse all the principal sections.

The water supply of Washington is obtained from above the Great Falls of the Potomac, and the aqueduct which conveys it to the city has been declared "a triumph of civil engineering." The aqueduct is nearly twelve miles in length, and on its course passes over six bridges and through twelve huge tunnels. The water is received in a reservoir a short distance west of Georgetown, whence it is conveyed in great mains to Washington, crossing Rock Creek by an aqueduct bridge. The water-works were constructed at a cost of about ten million dollars.

CHAPEL AT OAK HILL CEMETERY.

CHAPTER XVIII.

THE environs of Washington have many charming scenes and
interesting objects. From the hills encircling the city one
can obtain extended views of the District and the two neighboring states, spreading out in luxuriant fields and woods;
of the Potomac, curving gracefully to the southward; and of the
beautiful capital itself lying for miles along a wide, irregular valley.
On one of these bold eminences stands Howard University, the well-
known institution for the higher education of the colored race. It
has a conspicuous location north of the Capitol, a short distance
above the boundary line of the city, adjacent to the Seventh Street
road, and is on a plateau comprising thirty-five acres, part of which
is laid out as a park.

The university was established by special act of Congress in 1867,
and named after Gen. Oliver O. Howard, who was its president for
six years. Although more especially designed for colored students,
it is open to all, without distinction of race or sex, and among its instructors and students are white and colored persons of both sexes.
There are four hundred students from all parts of the United States,
and six departments — theological, medical, law, college, normal, and
preparatory, and the courses are from two to four years. The medi-

cal department is largely attended, the classes having the benefit of clinical instruction in the Freedmen's Hospital. There is an able corps of instructors, and tuition is free in its preparatory, normal, and college departments, and very low in the others. The general management is vested in a board of trustees. Congress yearly makes an appropriation for it.

The main building is of brick, is four stories in height, and attractive in design. It has ample accommodations for the lecture and recitation rooms, the chapel, the library, the museum, and offices. The library has 8,000 volumes, and in the museum are valuable collections of minerals and curiosities. On the grounds are two large buildings used as students' dormitories, one known as Miner Hall, and the other as Clark Hall. The buildings and grounds are valued at $600,000.

Columbian University is situated on Meridian Hill, near the northern terminus of Fourteenth Street. A new college building is to be erected in the city on the corner of Fifteenth and H streets northwest, which will be occupied probably in 1888. This institution was established in 1822, and incorporated as a university in 1873. Besides its collegiate departments, it has those of law and medicine. It is under the direction of the Baptists, has many students, and is in a prosperous condition.

Wayland Seminary, which was established in 1865 for the education of colored preachers, is located near Columbian University. It has academic, normal, and theological departments, and is supported by contributions received by the American Baptist Home Mission Society. It occupies a handsome edifice, erected at a cost of $35,000, and has accommodations for two hundred students.

The Columbia Institution for the Deaf and Dumb is situated on Kendall Green, a plot of one hundred acres near the northern terminus of Seventh Street east. It was established in 1857, and is now conducted under government auspices. Here the deaf-mute children of the District of Columbia, and those whose parents are connected with the army and navy, receive free education. Its collegiate branch, known as the National Deaf Mute College (the only one of the kind in the world), was established in 1864. Students are admitted to this college from all parts of the country. It has numerous instructors, and every necessary appliance for the thorough education in the higher branches of the unfortunate class for which it was designed.

ARLINGTON HOUSE.
(Formerly Residence of Gen. Robert E. Lee.)

The central building is of Gothic architecture, and all the buildings are spacious and conveniently arranged.

On high ground on the south side of the Anacostia River, near the point where it mingles its waters with the Potomac, is the Government Hospital for the Insane, which was erected in 1855, at a cost of nearly $1,000,000. It has a commanding site, overlooking the city of Washington, and from its grounds the finest view of the Capitol can be obtained, the majestic edifice showing clearly and fully from this locality, with nothing to diminish its grandeur. The grounds are four hundred and nineteen acres in extent, and the building, with its buttresses and parapet, has been likened to a great feudal castle.

it has a four-storied centre, with long connecting wings, and is seven
hundred and fifty feet in length, and two hundred feet in width, and
has nearly six hundred apartments, with accommodations for one
thousand patients.   It ranks among the prominent institutions for the
insane in the world.   The insane of the army and navy, and of the
District of Columbia, are treated here.

GEORGETOWN, or West Washington, as it is now called, was incorporated as a town in 1789.   It is situated on the western border
of Washington, and is separated from it by Rock Creek, a narrow
stream spanned by three bridges.   It lies as the base and along the
sides of steep hills, and contains many old family mansions, as well
as many modern residences of people doing business in Washington.
It has a number of fine business blocks, and several large churches
and school-houses.   The most important edifice is the Georgetown
College, or College of the Jesuits, which is situated on the crest of a
hill in the western part of the town, its grounds covering an area of
one hundred and seventy acres, comprising heights and valleys of
rare beauty.

The old or original college building was erected in 1792, and
work on the new one — a palatial structure — was begun in 1877.
The new building is one of the largest devoted to college purposes
in the United States, and is of the type — the Rhenish-Romanesque —
which is usually selected by the Jesuits in Europe for their institutions of learning.   The material is gray freestone, finely hewn blue-
stone, and blue gneiss.   It has a high central tower, and several
lesser ones, is many storied, with a bold, deep roof, and stands out
upon the bank supporting it with a grand appearance.

This college is the oldest and most prominent of the Jesuit institutions in the United States, and came into existence through the
efforts of the Rt. Rev. John Carroll, the first Catholic bishop of Baltimore.   It began its work in an humble way, and in 1815 was
raised to the dignity of a university.   It has a large number of
students, mostly from the South, a learned corps of instructors, and
bears a high reputation.   In its extensive library are many ancient
and rare volumes, and sundry relics of great interest and value, one
being the dining-table of Lord Baltimore, around which he and
the council of the Maryland Colony have often sat discussing questions of state over the walnuts and wine.   The table was originally

brought from England, is of solid mahogany, and of enormous weight.

THE Great Falls of the Potomac, some fourteen miles above Washington, possess an indescribable grandeur. The Potomac rises in a spur of the Alleghany Mountains, and several streams are combined with it in its downward course. Forty-seven miles below the gap at Harper's Ferry, where the river bursts through the mountains, are the Great Falls, formed by the waters impetuously forcing a passage through a stupendous ridge of granite which here restrains the current from side to side. The river gradually narrows as it approaches the barrier, until it is only about three hundred feet wide, and then

NATIONAL MILITARY CEMETERY AT ARLINGTON.

with a mighty effort rushes over the granite walls, making a descent
of forty feet into hollow rocks. It then continues its course with
amazing velocity, dropping foot by foot in a series of cascades, until
its " perpendicular pitch " is eighty feet in a distance of about two
miles. On the Virginia shore huge masses of rock stretch upward
for seventy feet, and on the Maryland shore are ledges and boulders,
over which the waters dash in great billows of foam. Ten miles
below the Great Falls are the Little Falls, a succession of rapids with
a total descent of twenty feet. Leaving these rapids, the river glides
calmly toward Washington with nothing to obstruct its passage.
The scenery around the Great Falls and Little Falls is very wild and
picturesque. Cabin John Bridge, a notable example of bridge building, crosses the river between the two series of falls. It conveys the
aqueduct of the Washington Water Works. It is four hundred and
twenty feet long, and has an arch of two hundred and twenty feet,
which is said to be the largest in the world. The bridge is constructed of massive granite blocks, and cost $237,000.

THE Chesapeake and Ohio Canal, by means of which immense
quantities of coal are brought to Georgetown from the mines of West
Virginia and Maryland, and grain and produce from the West, extends to Cumberland, Md., a distance of one hundred and eighty-
four miles. For the first fifty miles from Georgetown, it is sixty feet
in width ; then it has an average width of fifty feet to its terminus,
with a depth of six feet. On its course are seventy-five capacious
locks, eleven aqueducts, and nearly two hundred culverts. Water is
supplied to it from the Potomac by numerous dams. The canal was
first chartered in 1784, and constructed as far as the Great Falls.
In 1828 another charter was obtained from Congress, with the inten-
tion of extending the course to Pittsburg, a total distance of three
hundred and sixty miles. Work upon the extension was continued
until 1841, when Cumberland was reached, and, for various reasons,
it was made the terminus. The construction was exceedingly difficult, and cost $13,000,000. Congress appropriated $1,000,000 for
the great enterprise, and Washington subscribed $1,000,000, Mary-
land, $5,000,000, and Alexandria and Georgetown, $250,000 each.
From Georgetown a considerable part of the coal and produce received by the canal is shipped to Southern cities.

At the Georgetown canal terminus is an aqueduct bridge, 1,446

ALONG THE WHARVES AT GEORGETOWN.

feet long, connecting with the Virginia shore, which carries the Alexandria Canal across the Potomac. The bridge is constructed on huge granite piers of sufficient strength to resist the shock of the masses of ice which come sweeping down the river in the early spring. The canal was incorporated in 1830.

Crossing the aqueduct bridge on to the soil of Virginia, a drive of a mile southerly will bring one to the National Military Cemetery at Arlington — a vast field of the Nation's dead. Here, under the shade of noble oaks, are buried 16,264 soldiers of the Rebellion, their last resting-place graciously cared for by the government they died in defence of. The cemetery covers two hundred acres on Arlington Heights, which rise two hundred feet above the Potomac River, and command a fine prospect. It has an eastern frontage of 3,500 feet on the Alexandria turnpike, and extends westward for nearly one-half mile. A handsome rubble-stone wall encloses the grounds, and near the southern end of the front is the main entrance, over the gateway of which is a large arch formed of marble pillars from the portico of the old War Department Building. The larger portion of the burials are made in the southwest section of the cemetery, which is very nearly a level plateau covered with groves of

18

ancient trees. The graves are arranged in long parallel rows, and each grave of the 11,915 soldiers who were known, bears a small, white marble head-stone inscribed with the name, company, regiment, and date of death. The graves of the 4,349 unknown soldiers who lie here are suitably inscribed. These burial-fields have a calm, mournful beauty; there is no sound save the song of birds and the wind sighing through the lofty trees, and one can imagine the long lines of white head-stones to be a vast, silent encampment — an encampment indeed, waiting the final order of the Great Commander.

The main avenue passes by the side of an extensive garden, and between the avenue and the garden are forty-five graves of Union officers. To the west of the garden is a large vault containing the remains of 2,211 unknown Union soldiers gathered after the war from various battle-fields. Over the vault is a massive granite sarcophagus surrounded by four field-pieces on their carriages, with piles of cannon-balls between them. Here and there on the borders of the burial-fields iron frames are placed, each one bearing a poetic inscription in large letters. The following are some of the inscriptions:

> " No rumor of the foe's advance
> Now sweeps upon the wind,
> No troubled thoughts at midnight haunts
> Of loved ones left behind."

> " The neighing troop, the flashing blade,
> The bugle's stirring blast,
> The charge, the dreadful cannonade,
> The din and shout are past."

> " Rest on, embalmed and sainted dead,
> Dear as the blood ye gave:
> No impious footstep here shall tread
> The herbage of your grave."

> " No vision of the morrow's strife
> The warrior's dream alarms:
> No braying horn, no screaming fife,
> At dawn shall call to arms."

"The muffled drum's sad roll has beat
  The soldier's last tattoo;
No more on life's parade shall meet
  That brave and fallen few."

" Your own proud land's heroic soil
  Must be your fitter grave;
She claims from war his richest spoil,
  The ashes of the brave."

The entire Arlington estate consists of 1,160 acres.   It was originally part of the vast landed possessions of Edmund Scarburgh, who
was surveyor-general of Virginia in the early colonial period.   Later
it came into the possession of John Custis, a wealthy planter, whose
only son, Daniel Parke Custis, married " the beauty and belle of
Williamsburg," Martha Dandridge, and inherited the estate.   Martha

THE COLLEGE OF THE JESUITS, AT GEORGETOWN.

Dandridge Custis, after a few years of happy married life, was left a widow with two children, and in 1759 was wedded to George Washington, then a colonel in the Virginia militia. The widow Custis " was fair to behold, of fascinating manners, and splendidly endowed with worldly benefits." She held the Arlington property for her son, and eventually her grandson, George Washington Parke Custis, became the owner of it. He erected the fine mansion now standing on the eastern portion of the grounds, and lived in it until his death, in 1857. Arlington passed to his daughter, Mrs. Lee, the wife of Gen. Robert E. Lee, for life, and afterward was to descend to her son, George Washington Custis Lee. The Lee family lived on the estate until the beginning of the Rebellion, leaving it forever in April, 1861, when General Lee removed to Richmond.

The United States took possession of the estate soon after the war began, and under the direct tax act of 1862 a tax was assessed against it. As the tax was not paid, a sale was ordered, and President Lincoln directed that the estate should be bid in for the use of the government, which was accordingly done. It was decided to take part of the land for a military cemetery, and the first interments were made in May, 1864. Arlington was subsequently claimed by George Washington Custis Lee, on the ground that the tax sale was defective, as a tender of the tax might have been made but for a rule of the tax commissioners which required that the tender should be made in person. He brought a suit of ejectment against the United States officers in charge of the estate, and judgment was given in his favor. A writ of error was taken to the Supreme Court of the United States, which court affirmed his judgment. He then offered the estate to the government for the sum of $150,000, which offer was accepted by Congress, and Arlington is now in undisputed possession of the Nation.

Arlington House consists of a large centre building with two wings, the whole having a frontage of one hundred and forty feet. It is constructed of brick covered with stucco, resembling freestone. There is a central portico, the pediment of which is supported by eight ponderous columns. The house is occupied by the superintendent of the cemetery, and the lower story can be inspected by visitors.

ABOUT seven miles from Washington, down the Potomac, is the ancient city of Alexandria, which was founded in 1748, and for

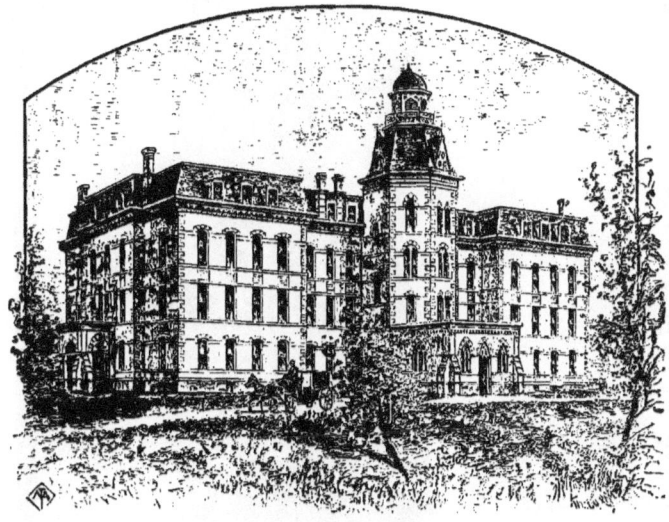

HOWARD UNIVERSITY.

some years was called Bellhaven. In its early days it was a thriving port and had a large foreign trade. The Virginia planters shipped great quantities of tobacco and flour from its wharves, and received supplies for their plantations. Its warehouses, most of which are now empty and dilapidated, were then filled with goods, and for a time it was an important commercial rival of Baltimore. So thrifty and enterprising was the town, so promising seemed its future, that it was even proposed to locate the national capital in it. But the promise of its youth was never fulfilled, and to-day it is chiefly notable for what " might have been."

The city lies on the sides of a range of hills, and is in the centre of a fertile agricultural district. It has nearly fifteen thousand inhabitants, one-third of whom are colored. The city hall is in a fine building used in part as a public market, and there are a number of large business structures. An object of interest is Christ Episcopal Church, erected in 1765, which was attended by General Washington, who was a member of its vestry.

MOUNT VERNON, FROM THE POTOMAC RIVER.

CHAPTER XIX.

WHILE the homes of most of the illustrious men who founded the American Republic have been suffered to decay, and finally to disappear from the earth, the home of George Washington has been fortunately preserved. That home to which he brought his lovely bride in the blithesome days of youth — those days of pleasant company, of country merry-makings, of riding to hounds, and the sports of the field, of sweet domestic bliss ; that home whence he departed to fight the battles for his country's freedom and independence, and to which he returned crowned with more than the laurels of Miltiades ; that home whence again he departed to guide the Ship of State on its untried course, and to which he returned when he had relinquished his great office, never more to depart from until death claimed him — that beautiful Mount Vernon is to-day in almost as substantial a condition as it was when the First President sat under the venerable trees, or walked the broad piazza of the commodious mansion a hundred years ago.

This cherished spot, the home of Washington, is situated on the western bank of the Potomac River, in Fairfax County, Virginia, and is sixteen miles from the city that bears his name. The steamer "W. W. Corcoran," Capt. L. L. Blake, makes daily trips, leaving Seventh Street Wharf at 10 o'clock, A. M., and returning at 3.30 o'clock, P. M., and visitors are permitted to explore all portions of the historic estate, and to wander at will over the mansion. The association in whose charge it is provides a guide, and the various objects of interest are explained in an intelligent manner. Thousands of people from every section of the United States, and even from foreign lands, visit Mount Vernon yearly. In 1876, the centennial year, there were forty-five thousand visitors. As the river steamers approach the hallowed grounds they slacken speed, toll their bells, and go " slowly sailing, slowly sailing, past the tomb of Washington."

The Mount Vernon mansion stands near the brow of a sloping hill which rises one hundred and twenty-four feet above the river, and can be seen from a great distance. A spacious lawn extending to the river, and majestic trees, give it a setting of rare beauty. At this point the Potomac is two miles in width, and its course is westerly until it borders the estate; then it makes a sudden, sweeping bend to the southward, displaying a long stretch of glittering waters. The mansion overlooks the river as it flows south, and the thickly wooded Maryland hills on the opposite bank, for many miles, and the prospect from its piazza and upper windows is most charming and picturesque. The grounds adjacent to the mansion are covered with an extensive variety of shade-trees, most of which were planted by Washington, and many of them have remarkably luxuriant foliage. In one flourishing thicket are hemlocks, lindens, chestnuts, and beeches, all of which Washington planted when a young man, and carefully nourished. The estate in his time comprised eight thousand acres — a princely domain, even in those days of vast landed possessions. More than one-half of it was wood land, and the remainder was divided into five farms tilled by several hundred negroes. Each farm was devoted to special crops, the principal ones being wheat, Indian corn, and tobacco, and was in charge of an overseer who made weekly report to a general superintendent, who in turn reported to Washington. After the death of Washington the lands were sold by his heirs, from time to time, nothing being retained except the homestead or "mansion-house farm," which now consists of two hundred acres.

Around the mansion is a lawn of ten acres, laid out in the olden style of English landscape gardening, and on one side is an orchard of about twenty acres, filled with peach, nectarine, apricot, plum, cherry, and apple trees. Twenty acres are devoted to grains and vegetables, and the remainder are wood and pasture lands. The farm is considered one of the best in that section of Virginia, and is very skillfully managed by its superintendent. Adjacent to it quite

THE MANSION HOUSE AT MOUNT VERNON.

a village has grown up, and a post-office for the residents is located on the Mount Vernon grounds.

The main portion of the wharf at the river-landing was constructed by Washington, but within a few years additions have been made. Here vessels were laden with great quantities of tobacco, and also with flour ground in the Mount Vernon mill, each barrel bearing the widely-known brand, "George Washington, Mount Vernon." The old flour-mill is located about three miles from the landing, but it is now only a heap of ruins. A short distance above the wharf, on the path to the mansion, is the decaying stump of the once magnificent and famous "Washington Oak," in the grateful shade of which the illustrious farmer was accustomed to rest when returning from directing his shipments. The tree was twelve feet in circumference, and was supposed to be more than two hundred years old. It was blown down during a severe storm on the 8th of August, 1882. Pieces of it have been taken as relics to most every part of the world.

The mansion fronts to the northwest, and that portion of it seen from the river is the rear, or, as it may be called, the southeastern front. It is constructed of wood, cut in blocks and painted in imitation of stone, is ninety-six feet in length and thirty feet in width, and has colonnades at its sides. It has two stories and an attic with dormer windows, and on its peaked roof is an octagonal cupola crowned with an ancient weather-cock. On the river front is a piazza extending the entire length of the mansion, and which is fifteen feet wide and twenty-five feet high, with a roof supported by eight pillars and surmounted by an ornamental balustrade. The piazza has a paving of well-worn flag-stones imported from the Isle of Wight. When the weather in winter prevented Washington from taking his habitual horse-back rides over the plantations, he would frequently walk on this piazza for an hour or two at a time. The central portion of the mansion was built by Lawrence Washington, the half-brother of the General, and the first to reside on the " Hunting Creek Estate," as Mount Vernon was then called. When the estate descended to George Washington he re-named it in honor of Admiral Edward Vernon, of the British Navy, in whose fleet Lawrence Washington had performed service in the West Indies. After the Revolutionary War he added north and south extensions to the mansion, thoroughly refitted its rooms, erected out-buildings, and greatly improved the estate.

Extending from the northwestern front of the mansion is a half-mile circular drive-way, which terminates at an arched gate opening into the high road. In 1759, a few weeks after their marriage, Washington brought his wife through this gate to her future home ; and in 1799, forty years afterward, his funeral cortege solemnly passed through it. On the line of the drive-way is a luxuriant flower-garden and a new conservatory, and the ruins of the original brick conservatory, constructed by Washington, which was destroyed by fire on Dec. 16, 1835. There are also the old brick " cook-house," or family kitchen, in which the food for the family was prepared; the butler's house, and servants' quarters. On the south is a barn with a long slanting roof, erected by Lawrence Washington in 1733, of English brick. The mansion and out-buildings appear in a good

state of preservation, and, as great care is taken of them, are likely
to stand for many more years.

A few yards from the mansion, down the sloping southern bank, is
the old family tomb in which the body of Washington was deposited
for nearly thirty-one years, or until the new tomb was constructed.
It has recently been restored, and made to look as it is believed to
have appeared in former years. Here the bodies of Washington
and his wife, and those of other members of the family, rested until
April 19th, 1831, when they were conveyed to the new tomb.
In 1825, when General Lafayette made his last visit to Mount
Vernon, he went into this old vault, and lovingly kissed the coffin of
the hero who had been almost as a father to him in his youth.

THE EASTERN PORTICO,
MOUNT VERNON.

The present tomb of Washington is situated on the road from the river-landing, a short distance south of the mansion.   In his will Washington stated that " the family vault at Mount Vernon requiring repairs, and being improperly situated, I desire that a new one, of brick, and upon a larger scale, may be built at the foot of what is called the Vineyard Inclosure, on the ground which is marked out, in which my remains and those of my deceased relatives (now in the old vault), and such others of my family as may choose to be entombed there, may be deposited."   But his heirs, strangely tardy, allowed more than thirty years to pass away before they erected the new tomb.

The tomb consists of a large vault, extending into a bank in a thickly wooded dell.   It is enclosed by a brick structure with a high, arched entrance, in which is a gate fashioned of iron bars.   Within the enclosure, and plainly to be seen through the gate, is a massive marble sarcophagus, impenetrably sealed, containing the coffin of Washington, and bearing on its top only the coat of arms of the United States upon a draped flag, and the name, "Washington."   At the side of this sarcophagus is another, similar in construction, which contains the coffin of Mrs. Washington, and which is inscribed : " Martha, consort of Washington.   Died May 21st, 1801 ; aged 71 years."   Above the door of the tomb are the words : " Within this enclosure rest the remains of Gen. George Washington."   The sarcophagi are covered with choice flowers, which are continually renewed.

The vault at the rear of the enclosure contains the remains of Judge Bushrod Washington, and other members of the Washington family.   It is closed with a solid iron door, over which is inscribed : " I am the Resurrection and the Life.   He that believeth in Me, though he were dead, yet shall he live."   In front of the tomb are two marble monuments erected in memory of Judge Washington, and John Augustine Washington.

In a small room in the second story of the Mount Vernon mansion which he had used for a bed-chamber for many years, the Father of His Country died on the 14th of December, 1799, between the hours of ten and eleven at night.   After his death the room was closed for a long time.   The bedstead on which he lay in his last hours has been preserved, and the room is now arranged in much the same manner as it was on that sorrowful night.   The bedstead is of mahogany, dark with age, is six feet square, and has four high posts.   It was manufactured in New York in 1789, and was used by Washington during the eight years he served as President. It stands between two long windows opening on to a balcony from which a delightful view of the Potomac can be obtained. The room has a spacious fire-place, in which are the andirons in use on the night of Washington's death. Several small pieces of furniture then in the room also have been preserved. There is a closet containing various articles of the great soldier's campaigns, and placed here and there are other mementoes.

After her husband's death, Martha Washington occupied a room in the attic, from the narrow dormer-window of which she could view the old tomb. The tradition is that she never left this room during the eighteen months of her widowhood, and that she would see no one except her two grandchildren and a favorite serving-woman. This gracious gentlewoman is said to have spent the time in gazing at the tomb containing her husband's body, and in lamenting her loss. For forty years man and wife, loving, tender, and true, the peerless couple were not long separated by death. Mrs. Washington's room now contains but one article of furniture she used—a mahogany wash-stand ; but the bed, the bed-hangings, the carpet, etc., have been carefully reproduced in close imitation of the originals.

The interior of the mansion is constructed in a strong yet elegant manner. It is wainscoted in the style prevailing at that period, and has elaborately carved cornices, and heavy shafts. It is nearly as substantial as it was when occupied by the Washington family, the decaying parts having been thoroughly repaired within a few years. A wide central hall extends from the front door to the rear, and there is a spacious staircase to the story above. On the front door is the huge brass knocker used by the guests of Washington to announce their arrival. A prominent object in the hall is the Key of the Bastile, presented to Washington by Lafayette in 1789, soon after the famous French prison was destroyed. There are six apartments on the ground floor, namely : the banquet-hall, the music-room, the west parlor, the family dining-room, Martha Washington's sitting-room, and the library-room. The Mount Vernon Association has furnished the rooms with ancient pictures, tables and chairs, and other articles, some of which were the property of Washington.

The banquet-hall, or the state-parlor, as it was frequently called, is a fine large apartment in the north extension, which in its day was richly adorned and furnished. It has a high ceiling with designs in stucco, and its walls are painted gray and have a wide frieze. At

THE OLD TOMB AT MOUNT VERNON, BEFORE THE RECENT RESTORATION.

one side is a fire-place, around which is a beautifully carved mantel of
Carrara marble, wrought in Italy, it is supposed by Canova.   It has
three panels in which are scenes of agricultural life.   It was presented
to Washington by an English gentleman, and it is related that the
vessel bringing it to the United States was captured by pirates.   When
they learned that the mantel was intended for Washington they forwarded it to him uninjured.   Extending across the western end of
the apartment is a colossal painting by Rembrandt Peale, entitled
" Washington at Yorktown," which was presented to the Mount Vernon Association in 1873.   In a glass case is a model of the Bastile,
the gift of Lafayette ; and in the apartment is also the celebrated
arm-chair which " came over in the ' Mayflower.'"   In this old slat-
back oaken chair more than 100,000 visitors to Mount Vernon have
sat.   One short sitting is usually enough, as the chair is very hard
and uncomfortable.   Several pieces of antique furniture, portraits,

THE TOMB OF WASHINGTON, MOUNT VERNON.

and the military equipments used by Washington while serving in General Braddock's army, are disposed about the apartment.

In this grand hall Washington gave his state dinners when entertaining the distinguished men and women who visited him; and many a brilliant reception, followed by a ball, also has been held here by Martha Washington. If the old walls could speak, what interesting tales they might tell of the scenes they have enclosed — the entertainment of Lafayette, Rochambeau, and the French officers; of the illustrious American generals of the Revolution; of Franklin, of Jefferson, of Hamilton; of the heroic men and the stately dames of the Old Dominion in those far-off days when the mansion was bright and cheerful with the highest social life.

There still remains in the music-room the harpsichord Washington gave his charming adopted daughter, Eleanor Parke Custis, on her wedding-day. It is a fine instrument, with two banks of one hundred and twenty keys, and cost $1.000. The furnishing of this room is a faithful reproduction.

The library is a square room in the south extension, with windows opening on to the portico. It has a large fire-place with a wide hearth-stone, and on three sides are many small closets, some of them mere panels, in which silver-plate and china, valuable papers, etc., were kept. When it was used by Washington it contained numerous fire-arms, swords, and military accoutrements, and his private collection of books. These books were all stamped with his book-plate, and also bore his autograph. Many of them were purchased in 1849 by the Boston Athenæum. Here Washington was accustomed to sit in the afternoon, attending to his correspondence and business affairs, and often of a winter evening the family gathered around the glowing fire-place. None of the original furniture is now here.

In the second story, and in the attic, are numerous chambers furnished by the Mount Vernon Association with antique articles and revolutionary relics, and mostly named after different states. The one known as "Lafayette's room," at the head of the first landing, was always occupied by the gallant Frenchman whenever he passed a night at Mount Vernon. The only original piece of furniture it now contains is the bureau, but it has been reproduced nearly as it was when he used it. Near this room is the one occupied by Miss Custis, all the furniture of which is a reproduction. One of the rooms has a case of relics of Washington.

The mansion contains little of the original furniture, from the fact that there was a sale by the heirs of the entire household effects, not disposed of by will, soon after the death of Mrs. Washington. The most notable articles were purchased by George Washington Parke Custis, and taken to his mansion at Arlington, but a good part of the ordinary furniture was scattered throughout Virginia and Maryland, and is doubtless now in the possession of old families in those states. Mr. Custis presented a number of relics to the government, some of which are in the National Museum, and those he retained were inherited by his daughter, Mrs. Lee. When the Lee family departed from Arlington at the beginning of the Civil War, they had the valued memorials conveyed to a place of safety. Afterward, members of the Lee and Lewis families contributed the Washington articles at present in the Mount Vernon mansion.

The title to the Mount Vernon estate originated from a patent issued by Lord Culpepper in 1670, to John Washington, the founder of the Washington family in America. He was of English parentage, and had settled in Virginia in 1657. His son, Augustine, married two wives: the first, Jane Butler, bearing two sons, Lawrence and Augustine; and the second, Mary Ball, a member of one of the prominent families of Virginia, bearing five children, of whom George Washington was the oldest. At the death of the father in 1743, Mount Vernon descended to Lawrence Washington, and at his death to his only child, an infant daughter. George Washington was the guardian of this child, and at its death he inherited the estate. He was born Feb. 22, 1732, and when he had barely reached his twenty-first year, became the owner of Mount Vernon, and also of a fine estate on the Rappahannock, and took a position among the opulent landholders of the Old Dominion.

Until 1758, when he closed his service with General Braddock, Washington was constantly engaged in military campaigns, and passed but little time on his plantation. When the young soldier was freed from the toilsome duty of camp and field, he became a member of the Virginia House of Burgesses, and for a number of years performed legislative work. On Jan. 17, 1759, he was married to Martha Dandridge Custis, a widow with two children. She was young, beautiful, and accomplished, and the possessor of $75,000 in her own right, as well as the guardian of a large fortune for her children. Then began a gladsome domestic life at Mount Vernon, extending through sixteen tranquil years — Washington as the lover and attentive husband, as the farmer profitably engaged in crops, as the fox-hunter and fisherman in his hours of leisure, as the gay, liberal host in a social community, his "bruised arms hung up for monuments," as he thought, forever.

But it was not so to be, for in 1775 the war for American Independence began, and Washington was appointed as the Commander-in-Chief of the Continental army. During the war he seldom visited Mount Vernon, but when it was over he resumed his life on the estate, and for five years the mansion was continually full of distinguished guests, who came to pay homage to the patriot and soldier who had achieved the liberty of his country. He became once more the active farmer and the profuse Virginia host. In a letter written to Lafayette in 1784, Washington said: "I am become a private citizen on the banks of the Potomac, and under the shade of my own vine and fig-tree, free from the bustle of a camp and the busy scenes of public

19

WASHINGTON'S BED-CHAMBER.

life, I am solacing myself with those tranquil enjoyments of which the soldier, who is ever in pursuit of fame, the statesman, whose watchful days and sleepless nights are spent in devising schemes to promote the welfare of his own, perhaps the ruin of other countries, can have very little conception. I have not only retired from all public employments, but I am retiring within myself, and shall be able to view the solitary walk and tread the paths of private life, with a heartfelt satisfaction. Envious of none, I am determined to be pleased with all, and this, my dear friend, being the order of my march, I will move gently down the stream of life until I sleep with my fathers."

But again it was not so to be, for on the 14th of April, 1789, a messenger rode up to the door of the Mount Vernon mansion, bearing the official intelligence that Washington had been unanimously elected as the First President of the United States, and that he was requested by Congress to immediately assume the office. Two days later, Washington departed for New York to be inaugurated as President, and on his journey thither he was the recipient of ovations in

MARTHA WASHINGTON'S BED-CHAMBER.

the towns and cities through which he passed, and his entry into the metropolis was made the occasion of a grand jubilee. He took the oath of office on the 30th of April.

Then followed eight years of the honors and duties of the Presidency, relieved now and then by short visits to the Virginia home. A few days before he finished his official career he celebrated his sixty-fifth ·birthday, and on the 4th of March, 1797, he attended the inauguration of John Adams as President, and soon after departed from Philadelphia for Mount Vernon. Throughout his long public life he had been faithful to the trusts confided to him, and no taint of dishonor had ever sullied his character.

During the two years and nine months which passed between his retirement from office and his death, Washington never went twenty miles from home. Occasionally the cream-colored chariot he had used while President would be brought out, six blooded horses attached to it, and, with servants in livery, away would go the hero and his wife to pay ceremonious visits in the neighborhood, or to

Alexandria, or to the new capital city slowly and toilsomely being prepared for the use of the government. But usually, day by day he was busy with his farming operations, with improving his property, and putting his long-neglected affairs in order. He had a host of farm hands, and their little cabins dotted the estate; he had nearly one hundred horses and mules for heavy work, and a stable full of steeds in whose blood and beauty he took considerable pride. He had more than three hundred head of cattle, and great numbers of sheep and swine, and raised bountiful crops of the staples. He relinquished the field-sports of his earlier life, saw less company, and was very methodical in the disposition of his time.

His habits and tastes were simple. It was his custom to rise early, to shave and dress himself unattended, and after a frugal breakfast of Indian cake and tea, to mount his horse for a long ride round his plantations. He would closely inspect the work of his laborers, consult with his managers, and be entirely absorbed in the extensive agricultural operations. Dinner was served at three o'clock, after which he would employ himself in the library with his private secretary for two or three hours. The evenings were devoted to amusements with the family. He was free and kindly in his manner, was always in a cheerful mood, and frequently laughed heartily at the jokes and pleasantries of his adopted children and relatives; and, as his nephew has said, "was so agreeable to all that it was hard to realize that he was the same Washington whose dignity had awed all who approached him." On his cheeks was a clear, healthy flush, and he had retained much of the grace and comeliness of youth. In height he was two inches over six feet, and was slim and straight, and he had remarkable muscular power and endurance.

Thus, in congenial occupation, and by the side of that sweet and affectionate woman who had been his constant companion for two-score years, the last days of the eventful life of this greatest of Virginia planters glided peacefully away.

A circumstantial account of the death of Washington, written by Tobias Lear, who was his private secretary for nearly fifteen years, is preserved. It appears from this account that on the afternoon of the 13th of December, 1799, Washington was engaged in surveying the lawn round the mansion, and marking some trees he wished felled. He had taken a slight cold the day previous while riding in a storm of sleet and snow, and had remained in-doors on the morning of the 13th, but as the sun shone warm in the afternoon, he went about the surveying. That evening he complained of hoarseness, but sat up later than usual, reading the newspapers that had just arrived, frequently reading aloud to the family, in spite of his hoarseness. About two o'clock the next morning he woke his wife, saying that he felt ill, but would not allow her to rise and attend to him for fear she should catch a cold. At daybreak, when the servant came into the chamber to build the fire, she was sent to arouse Mr. Lear, who immediately responded to the call. Horses were saddled and servants dispatched at once to Alexandria and Port Tobacco for physicians, as it was seen that Washington was seriously ill. He was bled, and when the physicians arrived they repeated the bleeding, and used their utmost skill to relieve him, but he lay in pain and distress all day, breathing with great difficulty, and scarcely able to speak at times. Toward night he said to his attendants: "I feel myself going; I thank you for your attentions, but I pray you take no more trouble about me. Let me go off quietly; I cannot last long."

Mr. Lear says: "About ten o'clock he said to me, 'I am fast

THE HALL AT MOUNT VERNON.

going. Have me decently interred, but do not let my body be put into the vault in less than three days after I am dead.' I bowed assent. He then looked at me again and said: ' Do you understand?' I replied, ' Yes.' ' 'Tis well,' said he. About ten minutes before he expired (which was between ten and eleven o'clock) his breathing became easier. He lay quietly; he withdrew his hand from mine and felt his own pulse. I saw his countenance change. I spoke to Dr. Craik, who sat by the fire. He came to the bedside. The General's hand fell from his wrist. I took it in mine and pressed it to my bosom. Dr. Craik put his hands over his eyes, and he expired without a struggle or a sigh."

"While we were fixed in silent grief," continues Mr. Lear, " Mrs. Washington, who was sitting at the foot of the bed, asked with a firm, collected voice, ' Is he gone?' I could not speak, but held up my hand as a signal that he was no more. ' 'Tis well,' said she in the same voice; ' all is over now. I shall soon follow him. I have no more trials to pass through.'"

In this manner passed from earth this pure spirit, this patriot and sage, before he had completed his sixty-eighth year. The cause of his death was acute laryngitis.

Washington never had a child of his own, but at the death of Major John Parke Custis, the eldest son of Mrs. Washington by her first husband, he adopted his two younger children, Eleanor Parke Custis, afterward Mrs. Lawrence Lewis, and George Washington Parke Custis, and they lived at Mount Vernon until after the death of their grandmother. As his wife was amply provided for, having a fortune of her own, and as the Custis children inherited their father's large estate, Washington bequeathed Mount Vernon to his nephew, Judge Bushrod Washington. He also made bequests to all his relatives, and directed that his slaves should be liberated and provided with the means of obtaining their livelihood. Some of the descendants of these slaves still live in that portion of Virginia.

After the death of Judge Washington in 1826, Mount Vernon descended to his nephew, John Augustine Washington. He died in 1832, and his widow, Jane Washington, was the next heir. In 1855 her son, John A. Washington, was the last of the family to hold possession of the estate. He had not the means to keep it in proper order, and in 1860 disposed of it through the State of Virginia to the Mount Vernon Association for the sum of $200,000. This association was incorporated for the sole purpose of acquiring Mount Vernon, and by the terms of its charter the estate can never pass from its

THE STATE PARLOR,
MOUNT VERNON.

possession. Virginia retains a supervision over it, and appoints a board of
visitors whose duty it is to examine the
property annually and report if the charter conditions have been faithfully observed.

The project to purchase Mount Vernon, and preserve the home of
Washington from decay, originated with a Southern woman named
Pamelia Cunningham. When its last proprietor announced his intention of selling the estate, this devoted woman quickly obtained the
refusal of it for a certain time. She first appealed to Congress for
the purchase-money, but without success, and then, under the title of
" The Southern Matron," caused to be circulated a strong appeal to
the women of America for aid in the patriotic work. She secured a
charter from the Virginia Legislature, organized an association, of
which she became the Regent, appointed vice-regents in the various
states, and began to collect the funds. Contributions, large and
small, were received from all parts of the United States. Edward
Everett, by his writings and lectures, contributed over $68,000, the
largest single contribution. In one way and another the full amount
was obtained, and Mount Vernon was saved to the Nation.

CHAPTER XX.

TO become well acquainted with the National Capital, and to thoroughly enjoy its many distinctive features, an extended visit is necessary. It is a spacious city, branching out in all directions, and everywhere within it are numerous objects of interest and beautiful localities which will repay careful and repeated inspection. But as hundreds of visitors are pressed for time, and yet desire to see as much as possible, and the most interesting things, a few hints and suggestions may be of service.

A good way to begin sight-seeing when limited as to time, and perhaps when not limited, is to take a carriage with an intelligent driver, or one of the many hansom cabs, and leisurely ride through the centre of the city — the northwest quarter. A ride like this will enable a stranger to obtain a general view of the prominent localities in a short time, and serve to fix them in the memory. The route should be taken through the central portions of Pennsylvania Avenue, and Seventh, Ninth, and F streets, and afterward through the fashionable West End.

By riding the entire length of Connecticut Avenue from Lafayette Park to Dupont Circle, then by extending the route through Georgetown, up Georgetown Heights, passing Oak Hill Cemetery out on the Tennallytown Road may be seen Oak View, the residence of President Cleveland : by such route, returning by the way of Woodley Lane through Massachusetts Avenue, much of the "palatial section" will be traversed. Again, by continuing the ride on Seventh Street, below Pennsylvania Avenue, the grounds of the Mall can be inspected, with the Smithsonian Institution, the National Museum, the Department of Agriculture Building, the Bureau of Printing and Engraving, and the Washington Monument. In fact, a ride over such a route will enable one to see in rapid succession the White House, the Treasury Building, all the department buildings, and many of the finest churches, mansions, institutions, parks, squares and circles, and business structures. Afterward the ride might be continued to the Capitol and through its grounds, and then down East Capitol Street as far as the statue of Emancipation, returning by way of North Carolina and Pennsylvania avenues. A good view of Capitol Hill can thus be obtained.

The Capitol should be thoroughly inspected, even if other objects of interest are slighted. It is the

THE SENATOR BAYARD MANSION.

grandest edifice in America, and in many particulars in the world No picture can do it justice ; no hasty inspection will reveal its manifold wonders. The time taken to carefully examine its massive and splendid architectural features, and its interesting special departments, will be well spent, and the intimate knowledge gained will be much appreciated afterward. The Halls of Congress should be closely studied, and if an opportunity is afforded to attend a night-session of Congress, it should be improved. By no means fail to ascend the dome of the Capitol, even if it does require rather severe exercise. A guide can be profitably employed in the building, as it is one to easily " get lost" in.

The White House is open to visitors from 10 A. M. to 2 P. M., every week-day. The East Room can be entered at any time during these hours, and at short intervals an attendant escorts visitors through the other state parlors. The President is usually "at home" to those who desire to pay their respects to him, but being a man of many important affairs, he frequently keeps his visitors waiting for an hour or two before he can receive them. While calling on him it would be well to bear in mind the old adage about " short visits."

The department buildings are all open to visitors from 9 A. M. to 4 P. M. The State, War, and Navy Building has innumerable finely furnished apartments, but few objects of special interest. When a visitor has walked through one long corridor, and looked into two or three of the apartments, particularly those occupied by the Department of State, and taken perhaps a glance at some of the ancient historical documents in this department, the building will be " done" well enough for ordinary, hasty sight-seeing. Of course if a visitor has plenty of time an entire day might be spent in this great building, and the luxurious appointments of the three departments carefully inspected. In the Treasury Building the cash-room, the money-vaults, the counting division, and the Secret Service office, are about all the places worth paying much attention to. In the Patent Office the Model Museum, and in the Post-Office Department the Dead-Letter Office, are of interest, but the remainder of these buildings can be very quickly disposed of. The National Museum should be thoroughly examined, as it is a great " world's fair," and full of attractions. The museum in the Department of Agriculture, and the Army Medical Museum are replete with interest. An hour or two may be agreeably spent in the Government Printing-Office, and in the Bureau of Printing and Engraving, where the government currency is printed. Visitors will find the department employés very courteous as a rule, and there need be no hesitation in applying to those stationed in the corridors of the buildings for information, as in most cases it is part of their duty to attend to persons seeking information.

A spot which is of great interest to visitors is the new Garfield Circle, where the Garfield Monument is located, at the intersection of Maryland Avenue and First Street, west of the Capitol, and adjoining the Capitol grounds. It was erected by the members of the Society of the Army of the Cumberland, on May 12th, 1887. It represents Garfield standing, and in the act of delivering his inaugural address as President of the United States. The statue is cast in bronze, and stands upon a circular pedestal of granite. At the base of the pedestal are three bronze figures, each in a reclining position. One of these figures represents a student, one a warrior, and the other a statesman, each being typical of the three important stages in Garfield's life. The granite pedestal is inscribed upon three sides with suitable inscriptions, and the whole monument is one of the most tasteful and pleasing in the city. It cost $65,000.

THE SMITHSONIAN INSTITUTION.

The Navy Yard is open daily from nine to four. Visitors, by applying at the office of the commodore in charge of the yard, can obtain a permit to inspect the naval museum, the monitors and ships of war, and the great work-shops. The cars of the Washington and Georgetown street railroad, and the herdics running on Pennsylvania Avenue, will convey visitors directly to the Navy Yard entrance.

The Marine Barracks and the United States Barracks are open to public inspection every day. The cars of the Seventh Street line go to the entrance to the grounds of the United States Barracks.

In the Smithsonian Institution will be found many curious and interesting objects. The institution is open daily from nine to four, and its collections of natural history can be freely inspected.

Persons are frequently allowed to ascend to the top of the Washington Monument. Application for a permit should be made to the official in charge of the monument. The view from the top is exceedingly beautiful.

The best time to visit the great Center Market is early in the morning, or on Saturday evening. The Northern Liberty Market is also worth a visit.

On Tuesdays, Thursdays, and Saturdays there is no charge for admission to the Corcoran Gallery of Art. On other days tickets of admission are twenty-five cents. The gallery is open from 10 A. M. to 4 P. M.

It will be necessary to take a carriage to the Soldiers' Home, and to the Arlington Military Cemetery, as there are no regular conveyances. They can both be visited in a morning's ride, and ought to be included in the list of things worth seeing. On the way to the Soldiers' Home an inspection can be made of Howard University, and on the way to Arlington the Georgetown College and Oak Hill Cemetery can be inspected.

The Government Hospital for the Insane is open to visitors only on Wednesdays from 2 to 6 P. M. A private conveyance will be necessary.

No one should leave Washington without visiting Mount Vernon. The steamboat leaves the wharf, foot of Seventh Street, every morning at 10 o'clock, and returns to the city at 3.30. The fare is one dollar, which includes admission to the grounds and mansion. Visi-

THE ENGLISH LEGATION BUILDING.

tors have little more than two hours in which to inspect this most famous of America's historic treasures.

The fare in the street cars and the herdics is five cents, or six tickets for twenty-five cents. Cab rates are, by the trip, fifteen blocks or less, each passenger, between 5 A. M. and 12.30 noon, twenty-five cents ; between 12.30 noon and 5 A. M., forty cents.   By the hour, for one or two passengers, between 5 A. M. and 12.30 noon, seventy-five cents; between 12.30 noon and 5 A. M., $1.00 ; and hack rates are nearly the same.   Special rates are made for excursions.

The city post-office is located on Louisiana Avenue, near Pennsylvania Avenue and Seventh Street.   The money-order office is in the second story.

The three regular theatres, Albaugh's Grand Opera House, the New National Theatre, and Harris' Bijou Opera House, furnish ex-

cellent entertainments during the dramatic season. They are conducted in a first-class manner.

There are many hotels in the city, and visitors can easily suit
themselves as to prices, etc. Persons intending to remain for several
weeks can secure pleasant rooms in private families, with or without
board, at reasonable prices. There are many good restaurants
throughout the centre of the city.

Washington is a progressive city, and is continuing to have a
great development, with every promise of still greater prosperity. It
will develop in art, in taste, in business facilities, and in all those
things which make a city really prosperous and delightful. Beautiful
and attractive as it is at present, its beauty and attractions are likely to
be greatly enchanced. No one is jealous of its growth and increasing
prosperity — no one would stay its progress; for it is the Nation's city
and reflects the grandeur and importance of the American people.

THE FRANKLIN SCHOOL BUILDING.

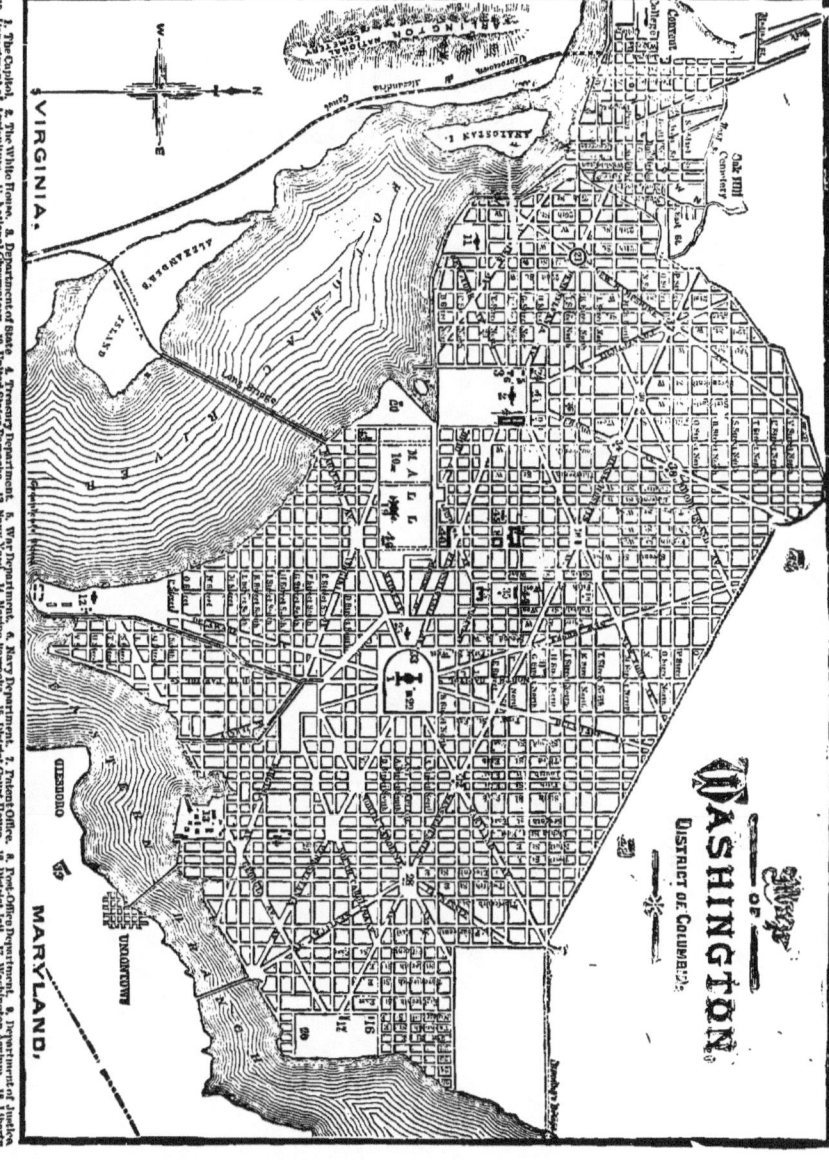

INDEX.

www.ingramcontent.com/pod-product-compliance
Lightning Source LLC
Chambersburg PA
CBHW060553030726

47498CB00005B/1375